Lis Leigh was born in Hampstead, and was educated at the North London Collegiate, and Somerville College, Oxford, where she read French and Italian.

She worked for five years with the BBC, before going freelance as a producer/director. Her writing career began with the *Sunday Times*, where she won an award for a series of articles on food additives.

Lis Leigh lives in West London.

GREED

Lis Leigh

BANTAM BOOKS
TORONTO · NEW YORK · LONDON · SYDNEY · AUCKLAND

GREED
A BANTAM BOOK 0 553 40505 5

Originally published in Great Britain by
Hutchinson, Random Century Group Ltd

PRINTING HISTORY
Hutchinson edition published 1991
Bantam edition published 1992

This book is set in 10/11pt Plantin by
County Typesetters, Margate, Kent

Bantam Books are published by Transworld Publishers Ltd,
61–63 Uxbridge Road, Ealing, London W5 5SA, in Australia
by Transworld Publishers (Australia) Pty Ltd, 15–23 Helles
Avenue, Moorebank, NSW 2170, and in New Zealand by
Transworld Publishers (NZ) Ltd, 3 William Pickering Drive,
Albany, Auckland.

Made and printed in Great Britain by
Cox & Wyman, Reading, Berks.

To Paul and Clancy and the chefs
who can cook

1

Charlie Braithwaite opened the passenger door and dropped his half-smoked cigar into the snow.

'Magnificent! I could stand here all night, just looking,' exclaimed his wife Elaine, gazing at the restored farmhouse belting out cyclamen pink light from every mullioned window, turning the snow into a sea of raspberry ripple. She stretched out her feet, bulging round the rhinestone straps of her stilettoed evening sandals, until they gingerly touched base on the rough grass below the white ground, raised herself upright and sniffed the sharp, clean night air. Then she hitched up the stiff folds of her trailing emerald green satin gown with one hand and drew her fox fur tightly round her neck with the other. They were neither of them bothered by the large soft flakes eddying around them.

'How about that sign?' asked Charlie. 'I wanted it bigger but John said not to. You don't have big signs at a place like this, he tells me. They know it all these youngsters.'

'Moorland Haven.' She sang out the name. 'I knew it was a good name. And the writing's lovely. I do like Gothic, don't you?' A gust of wind slapped and reddened her face. 'Oh, look, Charlie. It's swinging. You'll have to catch the bottom.'

'Right. Didn't think of that. Will do . . .' Charlie gazed at the tortured script. 'Can you read it from over the road?'

'Yes. There's a light, Charlie.'

'Good that landscape. He's painted it just like the photograph. That's the moors looking the other way. Can you tell?'

'Oh, I can, yes. Very good likeness.'

'Hey, can you walk in those shoes?'

''Course, love'

'Then we'll take a look at who's come.'

Charlie put a cashmered arm round Elaine's furry shoulders and walked across the car park, a terrace overlooked by newly positioned, buxom, Grecian-style, plaster-moulded statues now lent grace by a thickening white mantle, spotlights picking out their pert, smudged faces.

'There's the Mayor's Daimler . . . Oh, I know that one. Harry's Porsche . . . And Dave's new Volvo. A good buy. Gerry's Ford. Mean bugger, he should buy better. Who's that then?' He paused and bent down to examine a long, low, powerful machine. 'A Lotus, eh? Must be Tony Banks reaching the male menopause. He'll have trouble starting that thing.' He chuckled and surveyed the row of cars with approval. 'Glad to see we've got the right crowd tonight.'

'I'm hungry,' said Elaine. 'I'm glad I'm off that diet.'

'Well, you'll get no steak and kidney pud tonight. This is what they call French cuisine. One mouthful, and that's a course gone. But I must say it's cost effective.'

'And you don't put on weight, either.'

They walked together up the path and knocked on the studded oak door, lit by a massive coach lamp. It gave way to a smiling face.

'Good evening, Mr Braithwaite. And Mrs Braithwaite. You look ravishing, if I may say so.' A giggle from Elaine. 'May I take your coats?'

'Have we got the best table or has the Mayor got it?' asked Charlie.

'Honestly, Mr Braithwaite. Would I give you anything but?'

'Thank you, George.' Charlie pressed a few coins into his hand, and he and Elaine, divested of their animal glory, strutted over to the bar.

'He's a right poof but a good manager,' whispered

Charlie, then he cleared his gravelly voice and shouted to the barman, 'We'll have pink champagne tonight, Tony.'

From the bar, Charlie could see into the dining room. Elaine had chosen the colour scheme, and it had turned out just like she said. Total transformation from caved-in derelict farmhouse to elegant dwelling in three months. Southern builders couldn't do that.

'How about a few nuts? Come on, Tony, give us that dish.' The barman obliged with a fine china, gold-rimmed segmented bowl. Nuts, olives and twiglets.

'Don't spoil your appetite, love,' cautioned Elaine.

'Have you ever known me with no appetite?' Charlie looked her up and down appreciatively, lingering on the rounded green satin breasts which had suckled three strapping boys, and raised his glass to her.

'Here's to the best in the world.'

The overtone was pink. Pink light picked up by pink detail. Elaine had gone for the warm look, so guests could escape from the leaden skies and scrubby brown moorland outside. That's what a restaurant was, an escape. Multi-paned windows swathed with pink floral curtains frilled in powder blue, ruched pelmet, creamy nets, pink linen on the tables with deep blue glass vases sporting pink silk anemones, sparkling silver, gilded chairs and a top-class deep cerise Wilton carpet . . . couldn't be equalled by any other locale in the North, thought Charlie. The waiter was passing round pink, silver and blue menus as big as the *Northern Gazette*, whose editor was peering round the room waiting for recognition.

'Must say hello to Gerry,' said Charlie. 'I'll be back shortly. Don't chat up the fellers.'

'Would I do that, Charlie?' answered Elaine, with a light titter.

Chairs were being pulled out by attentive waiters. There was going to be a full house, and quite right too. Charlie knew how to create excitement and anticipation. Opening a restaurant, he was quoted as saying in the *Northern*

9

Property Review (which he owned), was like opening a musical in London's West End. Glamour, excitement and theatre. Those who didn't understand that should stay at home, watch TV with a takeaway and good luck to 'em.

'Well, Gerry? What do you think?'

'Hello, Charlie. Come on then, what's it to be? Never could get on with French menus.'

'It may be in French but it's a Yorkshire lad doing it. Why don't you take the set dinner? Good value, that is.'

'All right, I will. Who's cooking then?'

'John Crabtree. Remember that name. Only twenty-three but made of talent. We'll have the best restaurant in the North. See if I'm not right.'

'Makes a change from converting mills into boutiques.'

'Do I get a front page with a photograph then?'

'You expect good news on the front page? Cheeky bugger.'

'Bong appetite, as the Frenchies say.'

Charlie walked away with a wave, manoeuvred his large frame and short legs skilfully around the packed tables and headed for the kitchen. He held the swing doors open and shouted, 'Where's my lad?'

Seven sweaty faces looked up, activity stopped for a frozen second and then frantically continued. John Crabtree wiped his hands on his whites and took Charlie's outstretched hand.

'I could eat the lot,' said Charlie, ogling the bubbling contents of copper pans and breathing in the edible fragrances emerging from the ovens.

'You think they'll like it?' asked John.

'Like it? They'll bloody love it.'

'Have you seen me Mum and Dad?'

'They're here. Take that frown off, son. Did I ever back a loser? In no time you'll be driving a Jag like me. Go on, back to that stove.'

John's doubts were soon submerged in the incessant activity of the kitchen. The first orders were starting to arrive. Sixty people to feed but he was on his way. Walter, the newly appointed head waiter, came through the door and beckoned to John.

'Excuse me, chef, but table six wants the lamb grilled and they want more veg and mint sauce. And some roast potatoes. What do I say?'

'Tell them that *rosti* is roast potatoes. And that it comes with the sauce. Jesus! Chat them up. They'll have to bloody learn. They're not eating pie and peas here.'

'I'll try, chef.'

Walter, trained in the Harrogate customer-is-always-right school of service, clucked as he left the kitchen and nervously pulled down his waistcoat.

'Chef, we can only do four more lamb,' shouted the sous-chef.

'How about cutting it in half?' yelled someone else.

'I'll cut you in half,' retorted John. A waiter swung through the doors with his order. 'Six lamb.'

'Hey.' John stopped him as he turned on his heel to go out. 'We can do four. Persuade them to try the monkfish. Tell them it's the chef's special. Tell them it's Princess Di's favourite. Anything. Use your wits.'

'What's this?' asked Gerry, pointing to an arrangement of leaves encircling a small white mound.

'*Salade de mâche avec crottin de Chavignol,*' replied the carefully briefed waiter, who'd done a stint in a French hotel in Switzerland, 'is a green salad with a warm goat's cheese.'

'I had that once,' said Gerry. 'Give us that with a mixed salad, no onion.'

'I'm sorry, sir,' regretted the waiter, 'the dish comes with *mâche*, a delicious salad leaf. If you have mixed salad, it destroys the flavour.'

'OK. If you say so.'

'Thank you, sir.'

Gerry's wife, in buttercup-yellow wild silk highlighted by gold chain necklaces jangling and glinting in the pink light, started to object.

'If you want a mixed salad, what I say is—'

'It's the first night. They'll learn,' said Gerry. 'Probably got it ready yesterday.'

The *carré d'agneau au Porto avec galettes* was lowered gracefully past Tony Bank's left shoulder.

'Too pink for me.' He prodded the tender flesh with his knife. 'Well done, please. Stick it under the grill for a few minutes. And if you've got some roast potatoes—' The waiter inwardly winced, and removed the perfectly cooked lamb.

The pandemonium calmed and John perched on a stool. Most of the puddings had been prepared the night before and needed only a little last minute preparation: fruit garnishes to be laid on, ice cream to be scooped into tuile baskets. He gently prodded the cheeses which were slowly sweating out their aromas on a bed of straw. All the way from France from his supplier in Bradford. They were top class and he hoped someone would notice. No time to reflect, though. He leaped up and watched the plates springing to life with the design he had scribbled out for the kitchen. Each one must be the same, each one perfect.

'That radicchio leaf is brown. Take it off . . . Do that again, the sauce is a mess.'

Every time the swing doors opened, he heard a louder buzz of intermingling voices. Then laughter. They were having a good time. John wanted to be out there amongst them, invisible, watching his plates wiped clean.

Charlie leaned over Elaine. 'Are you leaving that?'

'I don't like mushrooms.'

'That's not mushrooms, you silly woman, that's truffles. You know what they cost per kilo? More than I paid for your engagement ring. Eat up.'

Elaine scooped up a tiny black fleck and tasted it.

'Well, do you like it?'

'I don't mind it,' she replied, wrinkling her nose.

Charlie paused from stuffing down his *selle de lièvre fourrée au confit d'artichaut*, looked round, waved a couple of times to distant tables then carried on spearing the dark meat. They were well down into their plates. Don Service was eating a hunk of pigeon in his fingers and why not? Lady Chevening, the overawed waiter informed him almost inaudibly, had chosen fish. Monkfish. Delicate eater she was, but liked her food, he could see that. Napkins smeared across mouths, the conversation was muted. Waiters deftly crisscrossed, filling glasses, removing plates at the right moment.

'Taste this,' he said to Elaine. 'Guess what?'

She opened her mouth wide like a fledgling and he pushed a forkful in.

'Potatoes. I've never had them like that.'

'Cooked three times three different ways, so John told me. Isn't that just miraculous?' Charlie now had valuable knowledge of what each table had ordered and was doing quick sums in his head. Oh, there was one he'd forgotten. Charlie beckoned over Walter.

'Yes, sir?'

'What's she eating, her over there?'

'*Suprême de canard fumé aux lentilles.*'

'I bet she's the only one having lentils. I said to John, no hippie food in here but he didn't listen. Still, no accounting for tastes. She's taking a while about it.' Charlie watched her carefully considering each mouthful. 'On her own. That's funny. Not from one of those food guides, is she?'

'She has been writing things on the menu, I noticed,' said Walter.

'Keep filling up her glass. We want her well tipsy before the evening's out. And make sure she gets one of them pink roses we're giving to the ladies as they go out, with my compliments.'

'Yes, sir.'

'Those that can, cook. Those that can't, criticize. Who needs 'em?'

'Who indeed, sir?' answered Walter over his shoulder, as he walked ponderously towards table sixteen.

'Good looking bird, though.'

Pretending to be anonymous. Fat chance. Anyone who ate alone in a suit had to be from a guide. A Londoner. Never dressed properly.

'Who are you looking at?' asked Elaine. 'Anybody famous?'

'No-one I know. I'll find out, don't worry.'

'All this lovely fish and no orders,' grumbled Martin, the sous-chef. 'Bet it would go deep fried in batter.'

'Give them time,' said John. 'Don't worry.'

His staff trusted him; he liked that. They trusted someone who stood by what he did. As long as Charlie realized what was at stake.

'Oh. I really shouldn't,' exclaimed Elaine, ogling the *rondin de chocolat à la glace en cage*.

'Go on,' said Charlie. 'Spoil yourself.' He stuck a spoon into his wife's rich dark chocolate pudding and swirled it round his mouth in ecstasy. 'There's nothing like chocolate.' He scooped again.

'Greedy bugger. Eat your own,' said Elaine, sucking her lips over the sweet confection then crunching on the filigree spun sugar.

Soon the whole dining room was sucking, licking, crunching, savouring, swallowing, wiping lips, remembering, trying to remember, the delectable taste of ingredients before they vanished into the digestive system beyond recall.

Only the woman at table sixteen remained coolly aware. She would remember. Much to Walter's astonishment, she had ordered more than one dish from each course. And only taken a few mouthfuls.

'Would madam perhaps like something which isn't on the menu?' he had ventured.

'No,' she had replied smiling. She wasn't giving anything away, but she looked pleased. Far too beautiful to be eating on her own or to be a guide inspector, Walter thought. Must be on business. Southern accent. Now she was studying the wine list.

Many orders later, John heard the sound of cutlery hammering against glass. Then there was silence. He pushed the doors ajar and listened, breathing fast.

'Ladies and gentlemen, can I have your attention?'

Charlie Braithwaite's confident voice bounced back off the stone walls, the glasses, the gilt-framed pictures, the bronze Cupid set upon a plinth and boomed round the room undaunted by the sound-absorbing thick carpet, the heavy linen cloths and the thickly lined curtains draped stiffly into sculpted folds. 'Our Mayor, Mr Hargreaves, would like to say a few words.'

The Mayor rose and stood by the jovial Cupid poised on his plinth. 'It gives me enormous pleasure to be here tonight, and after what I've just had I can confidently say that I can't wait to come back.' ('Hear, hear.') 'Don't think me fanciful, but I see this place becoming a temple of the gastronomic art.'

Phrases of approval resounded round the packed tables. John continued to hold the door ajar. The whole kitchen was on red alert, straining to catch every word.

'And don't get me wrong. A top class restaurant such as this not only means employment for our talented youngsters, but provides a showcase for excellence. It makes me proud . . .'

The mayoral praises gathered momentum. Charlie Braithwaite was thanked for this, his latest venture, and all he had done for Yorkshire. The guests were thanked for coming. The waiters were thanked for doing such a grand job.

'And finally I would like to introduce you to the man who has made all this possible. Chef John Crabtree.'

Charlie opened the swing doors and led John forward. The two stood together, John towering over Charlie. Thunderous clapping from every table. Some stamped their feet.

'Say something,' whispered Charlie into his ear.

'What type of thing?'

'Oh, thank them, you know. In your words, lad.'

John wiped his brow and looked at the faces smiling at him. 'I hope you've had a good evening. And I hope to see you again when the food will be even better.' (Clapping.) 'Thank you, everybody. And thank you, Charlie, for your help and encouragement. It's meant a lot to all of us. And last but not lest, I'd like to thank me Mum and Dad for being the greatest.' (Louder clapping, especially from the wives.) 'And now I'd like to ask the boys and girls to say hello.'

The kitchen brigade trooped forward and stood in a shy line to thunderous applause. Charlie then beckoned to Walter and a few seconds later he reappeared with a jeroboam of champagne. 'On the house!' he shouted.

Friends and acquaintances swopped tables; they would stay for an hour or two yet. Cigar smoke filled the room. Unleashed by good wine, loud northern voices, accustomed over several generations to rising over winds and clattering machinery, relayed greetings and embroidered well-worn tales. Times were always being remembered. The time when Jack was stuck in a drift . . . the time when Bob bought his own pig by mistake . . . the time when George lit a barbecue and set fire to his house. The time when . . .

Outside the snow had stopped falling and a northerly wind was brushing the thin overlay from the bushes and exposing a few shrivelled leaves. A month later it would be thick and everyone would have left by now, but the first October snow was nothing to reckon with. Only southerners minded that.

The solitary occupant of table sixteen was looking anxiously out of the window, parting the swathed net curtains and trying to see beyond the blackness. As Walter started to fill her glass, having surreptitiously replaced the empty bottle with another, he noticed that she had kept the menu. It was covered in spidery writing.

'Just a little. I'm driving.'

So was everyone else, of course. But then so was the Chief Inspector who found himself a popular member of local gatherings. No point in booking your fellow guests,

16

and if one of them knocked down a wandering sheep in the dark they quietly paid up. No-one walked these desolate moorland roads at night except in the lambing season.

'There'll be no more snow,' he said comfortingly. 'Have you got far to go?'

'Is Halifax far?' she asked.

'Oh no, madam.' Nowhere was ever far for a southerner.

A junior reporter, notebook in hand, went up to John as he sat at his parents' table. Could he ask him a few questions? Fire away. A photographer hovered, waiting for John to lean back so he could get a shot with Mum and Dad on either side. Yes, Heckmondwyke Catering College. He'd spell that. And he'd worked in the Majestic in Harrogate, and the Queen's in Leeds and a place in Ilkley. How old was he? Getting on. Twenty-three. Yes, Mum was a wonderful cook. The best. He couldn't bake a cake like she did. Mum smiled. Give over. They'd had rough times, with Dad out of work, but she always came up with something. What was the first thing he cooked? Fried egg. He was five and the yolks didn't break. Always good with his hands. Steady. What was his secret? Never being satisfied. You could always do better. Yes, it felt great. He never thought he'd have his own place. At college, you dream about it, and you still dream about it when you're sweating in a hotel kitchen. He knew he was lucky. (At last, John leaned back, allowing the photographer to press a volley of flashes.) No, not lucky, Dad contradicted. He gets what he wants, this one. But he's good with it. Good to us. Where did he get his ideas from? Who? French chefs. They all write books. What do you do in your spare time? He thinks up recipes. He cooks. He always cooks. Come off it. I go down the pub with the lads. Play pool.

'Well, what's it like to be famous? I hope Gerry's lad has got your good side,' said Charlie, coming over and ruffling John's hair.

'Fantastic. Really fantastic.'

'You seen who's here?'

17

'I wouldn't know.'

'Everybody of consequence, lad. All bar royalty, and we'll get them soon, you wait. Lady Chevening's here. Big mansion near York, she has. Breeds horses. Must have a word. I've got a luxury development planned for around there. Can't have milady objecting . . .'

Charlie rose and started roaming again, his agile small feet bearing that big body away. He moved constantly. Kept the ideas flowing, he said. If he stayed still he froze his bank account.

Ronnie Crabtree, father of John, was growing mellower and less irritable.

'You know it's a funny thing,' he said. 'In my day they didn't call them chefs. Cooks, that's what they were, and no-one knew their names. How things have changed.'

'It's much better now,' said Elaine, edging into the Crabtree circle. 'Who would have thought you could eat like this? That chocolate! If I was at home, I would have licked the plate.'

'Dad, this is Mrs Braithwaite.'

'Oh, how d'ya do.'

'Don't look now,' said Elaine into John's ear. 'There's a lass over there. She's had nearly everything on the menu. Charlie thinks she's a spy from a restaurant guide. I don't know though. She could be famous. So many famous people nowadays I can't keep track.'

John gave a quick glance and saw a young woman on her own, finely modelled face, blonde hair tinged pink from the frilled shade on her table light. He wasn't sure about those lights but he didn't give a damn if she was from a guide. This was as good as you'd get anywhere in the country, he was sure of that.

Mum and Dad were quiet. Dad sucked at his pipe and told John he was having a good time, although John knew he would have preferred chatting to his friends in the Working Men's Club over a pint. They were polite, like they were at the weddings of people they scarcely knew. Mum said the meal was a bit fancy for her but very nice, very nice indeed. Dad also said it was very nice, but those prices! Like eating money. If folks made it, he supposed, they could spend it. Didn't Charlie Braithwaite burn a five pound note once to light his cigar? And that was in the days when he paid outworkers twenty pound a week for a bundle of shirts. Not so long ago either . . .

It was strange, John thought to himself, cooking the stuff he never ate at home for strangers. Tomorrow he would have Sunday dinner at home. Roast pork and apple sauce. He felt hungry thinking about it for the first time that day. You never felt hungry in a restaurant kitchen. Mum was tired. She had to wash the curtains in the morning, been putting it off for days; wanted to dry them outside before it got too cold and the frost made them stiff as boards. John accompanied his parents to the door, over to Dad's ancient car, then cleared its windows of snow.

'Go inside. You'll catch cold,' shouted Mum, huddled in the front seat. The car spluttered, hiccupped and bumped jerkily along the driveway.

Others were starting to leave. The dark sky was clear of clouds and there was a moon bright enough to illuminate the tufted hillocks of the surrounding moor and the jagged black contours of a neighbouring derelict stone farm-house. John took a deep breath of the sharp air, smelling the tumbling water in the rocky streams and the dank grass. Reluctantly he headed back towards the restaurant, the kitchen. Soon he would return to his warm terraced cottage and flake out until the morning cockerel blasted him out of sleep. He went into the dining room, where only Gerry and Charlie were locked in conversation, and decided that the tables would be cleared the next day. George, the restaurant manager, came over, having finished up the leftovers of the better wines, swaying slightly and glorying sibilantly in the Bradford camp he reined in for customers.

'Well, John, you're a big star, dear boy. They loved it. By the way, there's a lady wants to see you. She's wearing a lovely outfit. Didn't come from Rackham's. Knights-bridge, if you ask me. I had a good look. Charlie thinks she's a guide inspector but I said, sweetie, they don't make that kind of money.'

'Where is she?'

'In the bar. Bound to be drinking *eau minérale*. The cool type, I'd say. Not my style.'

'She can wait. Let's have a brandy.'

'I shouldn't really. I'm getting as pissed as a fart. Still, Lady Farnes Barnes has gone. A cab back to York? I'll drive you myself, dear, I said. Well, no I didn't actually. I got a mate of mine to do it and I'm on a cut. On me, dear boy.'

'On Charlie, this is,' said John, pouring liberally from the 1954 Hine.

George had a matchless reputation as the local arbiter of taste. No-one in the area could match the authority with which George pronounced on the seemingly illogical dictats of fashion. Every top restaurant nowadays was using truffles, he informed Charlie, who was damned if he'd spend that much on a fungus, and if John wanted lentils, well, even André Bouchon at Aphrodite's in London used them as a garnish, and he cooked regularly at Buckingham Palace. Charlie decided lentils could stay on the menu, having been persuaded that their visual resemblance to caviar was remarkable, and therefore remarkably cost effective, and that the exorbitant purchase of a handful of truffles was a measure of the lofty standards of the Moorland Haven which would bring it to the attention of the Michelin inspectors. A Michelin star, George explained, was like getting an Oscar. Full houses every night. Charlie was convinced, and he grudgingly extended the budget to allow for a handful of truffles. For the opening week, anyhow.

John reluctantly left George, who had embarked on a wickedly accurate impersonation of Elaine Braithwaite talking to Barbie, her giant poodle, and walked towards the bar. He wouldn't hurry for a woman, having adopted from an early age the studied pride of the Yorkshire male. The woman who had summoned him slid down from the high stool and her pearly grey wrapped skirt parted over elegant legs.

'Congratulations.' Her voice was confident, soft. 'I'm Laura Douglas.'

John extended his hand. 'Pleased to meet you. Is it true you're from one of those restaurant guides, or aren't you going to let on?'

'They couldn't afford me! You can really cook.'

'What did you have?'

'As much of everything as I could manage,' she said. 'Where did you work before?'

'This sounds like a job interview,' remarked John. 'Are you about to make me a fantastic offer? Because I'm not ready yet.'

She smiled, and he noticed the smile. It happened slowly. Wide mouth. She didn't laugh, talked almost in a monotone, blue-grey eyes. So palely beautiful, unreal, it made him uncomfortable but he couldn't stop looking at her. She must live indoors. Couldn't tell what age she was, difficult with southern women. It didn't show. Older than him. Thirty, maybe.

She handed him a card, extracted from an enamelled holder.

'"Laura Douglas Associates". Could be anything, that. What you up here for?'

'I'm in the restaurant business, like you.'

'This place isn't mine. It's Charlie Braithwaite's. I'm just the cook. Do you want to speak to him, if he's still about?'

'No, no. Let me explain. Suppose you open a restaurant. It's good. Everyone talks about it. For a week maybe. Then what happens?'

'Customers come again. They tell their friends.'

'You do lunch and dinner?'

'Yes.'

'You think you'll have full tables twice a day?'

21

'Oh, yes. Charlie's got it all worked out.'

'Has Charlie run restaurants before then?'

'No. But he doesn't make mistakes.'

Laura leaned forward. 'Don't misunderstand me. I think you've enormous talent, but you'll be here for a year at most.'

'Rubbish.'

'Can people stay? Have you got accommodation?'

'It's a restaurant, not a hotel. Come on. Why do you want to know?'

'I'm in business to make sure you're in business. I promote restaurants and chefs, keep people talking about them, make them successful.'

'Oh.'

'I call it personal management.'

'Public relations. We have them up here too, you know. We had someone ring up. Get you in the paper, he says. Heard of the *Northern Gazette*? I said. The editor is a close mate of Charlie Braithwaite's, I told him, and Charlie owns a paper as well. We don't need it. We're having half a page in the *Gazette*, and they took my picture.'

'Do you mind if I tell you what I think?'

'Go ahead.'

'The menu isn't quite right, yet.'

'I know that. I'll be changing quite a few things. There's too much the kitchen finds difficult to handle. I suppose we all want to show off at the beginning.'

'Of course you do. But I think you need to change the direction of the menu.'

'Oh? How's that?'

'If you look at what's going on in top restaurants here and in France . . . Well, it seems a little dated, a little over-elaborate, too rooted in what they used to call Nouvelle Cuisine. Even Paul Bocuse . . . I don't mean to criticize.'

John stared at her. 'It's different up here. No-one's heard of Bocuse, or the Troisgrois, or Girardet. They don't care where it's come from, but they know what's good.'

'No,' interrupted Laura. 'You're different. I don't see

22

you really fitting in in a place like this.' She gestured dismissively towards the dining room. 'Surely you didn't want that?'

'We had a crowd in here tonight you wouldn't find anywhere else in Yorkshire. From Leeds, Manchester, Harrogate. He even had a couple up from London. They loved it . . . Well, nice to meet you. I'm shagged out. Must go home.'

'Just a minute. I want to help.'

'Go on.'

'You'll never do what you're capable of here. Feeding northern businessmen who would rather be eating steak and chips and Black Forest gâteau. They'll gulp down your "foreign food" for a while, then go back to what they know. Do you think they'll appreciate how daring you've been with tastes, flavours and presentation? Stay here, and you'll end up cooking rubbish.'

'We're used to it, you know. People coming up here and telling us what to do. We don't mind. We listen. But it's water off a duck's back. I've lived here all my life and I know the folk roundabouts. They know what they like, but in the end they'll try what they don't know out of curiosity. They may not make a song and dance about it, or say clever things, but they like their food. That's all that matters to me. Do you see? If they want fish and chips, it'll be the best bloody fish and chips they've ever had. Isn't that what a chef is for?'

'Then why aren't you running a fish and chip shop?'

'I didn't spend three years at college to wrap up cod in newspaper.'

'Exactly. That's what I'm talking about. Look, I know you're tired. Go home and think about what I said. Call me in London if you feel like it. I'd like to know how you're getting on. I might be able to help you.'

Women didn't tell him what to do, certainly not this southern stranger. What did women know about restaurants, real restaurants? They were good at doing cream teas and making bacon butties.

'What exams did you pass to do your job, Laura?'

'I used to be a designer. Worked as a waitress in the early days.' She smiled again as though confessing a secret. 'I've always been around restaurants. In the family, you might say. And food and design are closely related, I find.'

'Oh, yes.' John spoke in a flat voice and smiled back to mask the hostility which was rising up through his blanket of fatigue. 'Shall I get your coat?'

'Thank you.'

Laura walked ahead of him towards the cloakroom, and John observed the straight back, the fine hair hanging in a well-cut mass to the shoulders, the faint aroma of an unfamiliar perfume.

'I hope we'll see you again here.'

'I'll certainly come if I'm up this way.'

Always be polite to customers. After all, that's what she was. A customer.

John watched her through the window as she crossed the terrace and got into a car he didn't recognize. The engine roared like a bull on the loose, strong beams made a tunnel of daylight in the blackness and she was away. He turned back into the entrance hall, and smelt with pleasure the residual mixture of cigar smoke, brandy, fish, garlic, cheese and fruit which had given over sixty people an evening to remember.

2

The daffodil trumpets were already browning round the edges in London parks, but two hundred miles further north where spring was more slothful a hint of yellow was just starting to emerge from tight furled buds bobbing and bending in the sharp breeze. Winter-bare trees showed a hint of green and the streams were noisier, now that the snow and the icicle chunks had melted, filling up the narrow banks with swirling water. People were saying how warm it was. Labourers were repairing the pitted roads, stripped to their vests. The spring sun lit up the stone walls and the yellow eyes of the black-faced, matted sheep, but still, in the early morning, breath was transformed into furling eddies and the grass was stiff with frost. This was early April, the beginning of the going-out season when you walked only as far as the nearest pub for sustenance, dreamed of hot, white deserted Spanish beaches promised in the mendacious images of the travel brochures, and saw none but the nearest neighbours.

Spring was also a time of reckoning. The end of the financial year was nigh.

Charlie Braithwaite rolled up his sleeves and sat ready and waiting at the long mahogany table in the conference room of Braithwaite Holdings PLC. Two places were laid with the customary clipboard, jotter pad, pen and calculator. The Braithwaites' glorious past was depicted in the grainy blown-up photograph of a mill with early morning workers streaming through the gates. The company accountant was five minutes late. Charlie pressed the button of the phone by his side. He hated people being late, would not listen to excuses. Better to be half an hour early.

Albert Gorse, the accountant in question, was standing in reception pondering whether he had time to disappear into the men's toilet, pee and brush his teeth or whether he should arrive one minute early with smelly breath and slip away after the first coffee to answer the desperate call of nature. There had been a hold-up on the Bradford to Leeds motorway. Not his fault: he'd started early enough without completing either breakfast or his morning ablutions. He made a slow decision as the receptionist gestured him to the lift whilst deftly flicking buttons and juggling with a multitude of callers pressing for the attention of one of the Braithwaite Holdings' employees.

'Mr Braithwaite's ready for you now, Mr Gorse.'

Albert shook his head and furtively headed for the trousered sign down the corridor.

'Well, Albert, now we've lost five minutes we'd best get on.'

Albert might be slow but he knew every secret, every twist and tax-avoiding turn of Braithwaite Holdings PLC and Braithwaite and Sons before that. Men like him didn't get fired.

'Give us the figures, then.'

Albert delved into his swollen, battered, ink-stained briefcase, brought out a well thumbed file and extracted the relevant sheets.

'You won't need to see all this.'

'Oh yes I will,' said Charlie, grabbing a handful of receipts in his large, hairy hand, still dark brown from a late holiday in the Bahamas. He put on a pair of thick-lensed glasses, told his secretary not to put any calls through and said not a word for a good half hour. To judge from his rapt expression, he could have been opening himself to the mysteries of Divine Revelation.

It was Sunday, the only time that John Crabtree allowed himself to wallow in sleep, for lunch would be taken care of by the sous-chef. Struggling out of warm oblivion, he blinked, sniffed, sat up and looked across his bed. Socks, underpants, a shirt, a flimsy bra and inside-out tights. She had come knocking on the door of his little terraced house at one in the morning. Knew he got back late. Cathy had been visiting for a few months, but he had told her he wasn't going steady yet. This she accepted, as courtship around here was a protracted business. Everyone knew you had to wait until the weekly money deposited in the Halifax Building Society had grown substantial enough to start thinking of a three-piece suite, a large double bed and a house of your own. Cathy wouldn't expect to take over John's house. They would find another, bigger one, space for you know what . . . maybe a bungalow. She fancied that.

Cathy's girlfriends already knew which curtains she liked, which oven, which sheets, which rugs, which china, and accompanied her on female forays to Leeds where they reviewed every household item in Lewis's in order to earmark the desirable ones for the Bride's List. She had already told them that life wouldn't change much after marriage, they'd still be seeing her on girls' outings. It was rather like being married to a long-distance lorry driver, being married to a chef. You didn't get to see him much, but when you did it was really fabulous. Cathy was trying out a few things from one of those TV cookery programmes so John would get a nice surprise when he came home tired and didn't want to cook. For the moment she was saying nothing, though. Marriage should be a surprise, shouldn't it? No, they hadn't fixed a date. Actually the subject had not been mentioned, but that was nothing unusual. Men always pretended they didn't want to get married, everyone knew that.

'Give us a cup of tea, love.' John lay back on the crumpled sheet, half covered by a duvet. He could see the clouds out of the window and the tips of the trees along the canal bank. Last night there had been a drunken party of twenty in the restaurant. They couldn't turn them away because they were mates of Charlie's in the building trade. He hated Saturday nights. Just because it was someone's birthday, they had started singing, upsetting drinks and someone had been sick on the floor in the men's lavatory. The kitchen had run out of beef so they were served unfrozen venison instead, but no-one noticed the difference. Could have been eating horsemeat.

John conjured up different fruits, vegetables, sauces in his mind and then reached for a cookery book by his bedside. Cathy slipped out of bed, tripped in high-heeled mules and housecoat (always brought an overnight bag) down to the kitchen, placed a paper doily on a tray, found some biscuits in a tin and plucked a daffodil from the back yard for decoration.

'Ta, love.'

'You were wonderful last night.'

'Was I?'

He flicked over a page and remembered. He hadn't been making love to Cathy. He had kept his eyes tight shut and seen fine blonde hair spread over the pillow and imagined long, slender, supple thighs quivering under his.

'What d'ya fancy doin' today, John?'

'Dunno yet.'

He knew exactly what he was going to do. What he always did on a Sunday.

The wind howled round the low stone building, meeting little resistance. No-one bothered to plant trees, for their roots could not penetrate the rocky ground below the bristling primeval grass, nor would they find sustenance there. Only pylons could reach high into the sky, or the occasional wild duck on its passage from one remote reservoir to another.

John pushed open the thick door, elbowed his way forward into the crowded Packhorse pub and ordered six pints, shouting over the heads of customers pressed three deep clamouring for the attention of the two barmen.

'And a shandy, please. And a packet of nuts,' Cathy reminded him, wriggling through a barrage of quilted jackets, coarse oiled wool and nylon fur. They were all there, at the usual table next to the fire which was piled dangerously high with enough logs to last out a hard afternoon's drinking. Only the trippers left at two for their Sunday dinner, trailing their young.

John knew what they had done during the week, Pete, Bob, Martin, Steve and Duncan. He had been at school with them, except Steve. He was the only one with any ambition, having studied computer programming, and he was now in full time employment. They always had a laugh, but he couldn't remember exactly what they laughed at. Usually a misadventure, the minor irritants of the week which were aired and dismissed with bravado. What Bob said to the bank manager. ('What d'ya do then? Take him over to John's place for lunch?' 'Don't be daft. I only asked for a five hundred pound overdraft.') Then the topic changed to Steve's pride and joy, polished twice a week so the wife used it as a mirror, this Japanese four-wheel drive job, made for midgets like him. ('Have you got it out of the first gear yet, Steve?' 'Bert's got one of them. He got done for speeding. Thirty-two miles an hour in a built-up area.' 'Give over. It's got pulling power, I tell you.' 'How many birds you pulled then, Steve?')

Cathy hitched up her skirt, crossed her legs, uncrossed them, crossed them again, sipped at her shandy, stuffed down a few nuts and remembered she'd forgotten to put on any mascara.

'You buying then?' asked Martin, as she extricated herself from the fixed wooden seat which always snagged her tights.

'I might,' she replied putting her head on one side coquettishly as though he had invited her to bed, then veering off, hips swaying, high heels clacking on the stone floor until, by pushing her way through the dense bodies, she reached the door marked 'Senoritas'.

No-one noticed her join a group of girls at a nearby table, for it was taken for granted that she wouldn't be staying with the men for long. Strangers mistook this

29

separation of the sexes for hostility, but John's friends would have thought it strange to sit in mixed company for more than half an hour in the Packhorse. For a few hours here, seated on wooden benches, feet on the stone floor, hands firmly embracing tall glasses filled, then half filled, then emptied of the local brew, faces heated by the fire, they were confirming their masculine existence away from the belittling world of bosses, forms to fill in, women nagging, carpets to lay, machinery to mend, relatives to visit, children to discipline, instalments to pay on this and that, grass to cut . . .

As yet another round was lined up on the table, John fell silent. Today he felt uneasy, as though the earth was giving a slight shudder beneath the stone floor.

'What's up, John?'

'Nothing, I'm fine.'

'Charlie Braithwaite treating you right?'

'Oh, aye.'

They understood when he went to college; they understood you have to study so as then you might get a job. They had all come along to the Christmas do at the Packhorse when he cooked ten turkeys and five hundred mincemeat tarts (they thought he spent his time cooking turkeys; surely the rich ate turkey whenever they wanted), but that was as far as it went. They never went past the Moorland Haven Restaurant, no cause to, no pubs they went to round there and if they ate 'out' it was 'going down the Indian for a blast-out' in Halifax, korma for the girls, madras for the men, huge bowl of rice, tray of chutney, a plate full of poppadoms and they'd persuaded Mr Patel to stock Theakston's. You couldn't have Indian without a decent beer.

'My boss went up your place,' said Steve.

'What did he have? Packet of crisps?' asked Bob. 'Or did he take a packed lunch?'

Steve's boss, who had taken advantage of European money available for depressed areas, was one of the 'outcomers' heralded in the *Northern Gazette* as 'ending the downturn in semi-rural localities and spearheading the Silicon Valley revolution in Yorkshire'. They had seen him on television in the pub and shouted their derision. 'Look at him. Silly cunt.' He'd probably go into politics and join the other wankers. It went without saying he was mean. All southerners were mean. Didn't mix with the workforce.

'Funny, i'nt it,' declared Martin, 'how he's got on, that chap? Can't see it myself.'

'Friend of Charlie's,' added John.

'There you go. Though I can't understand the attraction.'

'Cash,' said Steve. 'Folks with cash don't pay. Funny that. I s'pose he got a free dinner at Moorland then?'

'Don't know,' said John.

'Oh, he wouldda done.' Duncan puffed at his pipe knowingly.

'Next time he comes, I'll give you some of that stuff which cleared my barn of rats,' volunteered Bob. 'It would taste lovely in a meat pie.'

'Meat pie?' repeated Duncan. 'Our John don't cook that. It's all that noo-vell-coo-zeen down there. You know, nowt on't plate and call in at the chippie on the way home.'

'So when did you go, mate?' enquired Bob. 'Don't tell me you remembered the wife's anniversary.'

'Me Mum's cousin went.'

'Her in Ilkley that's been married twice and got five kids?'

'Right.'

'Did she tell you about the food?' asked John.

'She said it was all pink in there, very romantic she says and they've got perfume in the ladies' toilet. And like I said, she had French stuff.'

It was John's round but he stayed standing after removing six more pints from the tin tray and downed his final glass.

'You're not off, are you?'

'Must call in at the restaurant. Big day tomorrow.'

'Bloody heathens. Working on a Sunday. You get Monday off, then?'

'Depends.' Meaning never, but they would interpret that as a call for pity.

'Notching up the overtime, you crafty bugger.' Bob, who hired his labour when the beer money dried up, was an expert at that.

'Or saving for Cathy's bottom drawer,' said Duncan, whose sister had talked of nothing but her impending marriage (eight months away) for at least a year.

'I'm too young,' John laughed, for he was the eldest of the group, most of whom were already married.

'Good on you, John. Keep her danglin'.'

'Might see you tomorrow, then?'

'Maybe.'

John raised a hand in farewell and strode over to the other side of the room. All that remained of the Sunday crowd was a thick pall of smoke, ashtrays with mounds spilling over on to the tables, empty crisp packets, glasses with milky residues rim to rim and mud on the floor.

Cathy was leaning confidentially towards a girlfriend, who had a new car and sold body lotions door to door in Barnsley.

'Oh. Hello John. This is Sal.'

John nodded. 'I've got to be off. Told Charlie I'd look in.'

Cathy's face dropped. 'Will you be having some tea then? I got sommat to eat.'

John said yes. It was easier to say yes, he'd have a bite. He would take Cathy home first, but if he was going up to the Moorland, she could drop in on her Auntie May later, couldn't she? Didn't know when he'd be back.

Cathy sat quietly making plans on the winding drive homewards. They sank lower and lower towards the valley, having passed by the sheep clustered at the moorland's edge which occasionally broke ranks to wander calmly across the stony road, testing the braking power of unwary motorists. Then they coasted down to the level of holly and thorn bushes, down further where oaks, beeches, chestnuts and rhododendron bushes shrouded the bare contours, and picture-windowed bungalows with ruched blinds, christened with names like Edelweiss and Casa del Sol carved in thick Tudor-style writing on wavy varnished boards posed smugly below the hills, their tips frosted by a thin blanket of unseasonal snow which had spread from the Pennines and flurried in April.

'Will you be working Wakes Week? Only I thought maybe we could go somewhere. Friend of mine said you can go to Greece for the same as a week in Blackpool. I've always fancied Greece.'

Cathy saw herself in the blue satin bikini she hadn't worn yet, turning dark luscious brown, hair bleaching blonder still in the sun, lying alongside John's long-limbed, firm body. Everyone would look at them, handsome couple. Blue sky, all that blue sky. She was sick of grey, grey stone, grey roads, autumn grey, winter grey, spring mostly grey, touch of green, then summer brown and grey.

'You'll need some sun. Working in that kitchen day and night. Shall I arrange it?'

'I can't take time off. Not yet.'

'Surely Charlie will close in Wakes Week? Everyone goes away then.'

He didn't want to explain that his clientele would never have heard of Wakes Week, brought into being so that the machinery in the mills could rest for an overhaul after months of grinding operation and the workers could head for a good time in Morecambe, Blackpool or Skegness.

'I'm not much good for you, Cathy, am I?'

'I understand. Really I do.' Cathy studied her nails and flexed her fingers. 'You can't be famous and act like everyone else. Not doing your job. Maybe we could go for a weekend, then.'

John laughed.

'What's funny?'

'Me famous? I'm not that. I'm a cook, that's all.'

'You've been in the papers. And everyone knows you. That's what I call famous.'

'You sound like my Mum.'

'It's no good being so modest. I'd brag a bit if it were me.'

In the fading light, the interior of the Moorland Haven looked like last year's well-worn dress sagging on a coat hanger. The frills on the curtains no longer stood out proud and some of the stitching had come adrift. John switched on the gilded wall lights with pink glass shades. He noticed greasy blotches on the pink walls, stains on the skirting boards, a couple of burn marks on the cerise Wilton and the upholstery on the chairs had lost its bloom. Six months of lunches and dinners, lunches and dinners, messy eaters, careless eaters, aggressive eaters, made marks. The decor might last another six months if he turned down the lights to half power and put some thicker nets on the windows to soften the brilliance. There were dirty cloths still on the tables, well, they'd had a lot of mess to clear up Saturday. That pungent smell of leftover wine in glasses and cigars, it did linger . . . Might be an idea to ask customers to have coffee and cigars in the bar area.

John pulled off the tablecloths, piled them up on the carpet, went into the kitchen, surveyed the well-cleaned surfaces, the copper pans hanging in rows, and walked into the capacious fridge. Tomorrow was the beginning of the new menu. He would start the stock, play around with different stuffings. It was good working alone once in a while, to allow ideas to follow their course without having to watch the brigade every minute. Distant bells reminded him of Sunday. The phone rang in the vestibule. Sorry, Dad, I'm not free Sundays for a while. See you soon. He wanted to slough off his friends, his family, Cathy, to be alone. For a while anyway.

Early next morning John set his brigade on course for the new menu, then sat with George, as he always did at that time, going through the bookings. Strangely for a Monday, a line was drawn right through the page, and ASGAM written across it. John grunted. He disliked block bookings.

'Full house for lunch, I see.'

'Isn't that super?' said George, ever encouraging.

'If it's another load of builders, I'll give 'em steak and have done with it. Do we know who they are?'

'There's been a conference at Haslam Hall this weekend. Lunch at the Moorland Haven as the grand finale. We've done them a special rate. At least they'll be wearing ties, and no arguing about the bill neither. I can't stand that.'

'Find out who they are,' John said. 'Best to know.'

'Leave it to me. Just get back to that kitchen.'

The phone was ringing. George ran over. 'Moorland Haven.' He'd practised how to answer, giving the last word a sunny upward inflection. 'Ah. Mr Braithwaite . . . A little difficult this lunchtime . . . Block booking you see.' Mr Braithwaite didn't believe in difficulties, especially when his guest was an executive of the Yorkshire Bank. Yes, George supposed he might push up a couple of tables, put a separate one in the corner. Rather tight, but they would manage.

The phone in Charlie's car crackled.

'Can't hear too well,' said George, then he distanced the earpiece as Charlie's voice boomed full force.

'That's what I like to hear, George. No harm in having visible turnover around. Good for business. And I'll have a word with John.'

'He's in the kitchen, Mr Braithwaite.'

'Well, get him out.'

Cursing, John went to the phone and when he had replaced the receiver he started cursing again. Bloody man. Half a day lost going to Charlie's office in Leeds. Bound to be a waste of time. Why did he have to interfere?

At twelve forty-five precisely, a coach lumbered up the

drive and disgorged its cargo of sixty dark-suited occupants whose name tags, sprouting on every lapel, proclaimed them as representatives of the Association of Sucrose, Glucose and Allied Manufacturers. They stood for a minute, looking around them and sniffing the first breath of unconditioned air in three days, then one detached himself, made for the entrance of the Moorland Haven and the others followed.

George lifted a corner of the net curtain in the lobby and looked out. A big car had arrived and a chauffeur was handing someone a briefcase. Looked like someone important. He must tell Charlie.

Sir Howard Riley was ushered to the best table (the Mayor's favourite) with a little too much ceremony. No, thank you, he would keep his briefcase; yes, thank you, he was being looked after; no, thank you, he wouldn't take a drink in the bar. The Sugar Men had saved him until last. The most distinguished speaker always came at the end. The chairman of Illustra Foods had paid them the extraordinary honour of addressing their annual conference, had taken time off from advising Government ministers, discussing EEC food policy and running a huge conglomerate whose turnover made everyone present, even those resentful of the 'monopoly situation', immediately adopt a respectful tone when mentioning his name.

He yawned discreetly behind his hand. Sir Howard Riley had forsaken conferences long ago. Even regular conference-goers, he had observed, never admitted to learning anything new, but what a marvellous opportunity, so they reasoned, to consolidate policy formulation. Lunch might be passable. There had been one speaker who had shaken off that peculiar somnolence reigning at conferences. Quite a good argument. What was his name? No matter. He was from a leading advertising agency. Clever the way he had sweepingly characterized the whole of the British nation and divided them up into target categories with telling nomenclature and witty projected cartoons. Delegates were reminded six times

(Message Reinforcement) that the category which demanded concerted attack (That Means Action) was the Ditherers' Category, the mysterious Don't Knows of more conventional polling systems. The Ditherers were confused by the Didacts, and the Didacts were the Know-Alls, the self-proclaimed Leaders of Opinion. They called themselves journalists (sniggers) and grabbed air-time, magazine space and newspaper columns . . .

Charlie sat cramped in a corner, using his knife and fork like a conductor recreating an unfamiliar musical score for an orchestra, outlining his five-year plan to the admiring man from the bank who was nervously trying to stop his knees from touching Charlie's under the small table. He was not to know, and would not be told, that turnover wasn't all it might be. Charlie would give the place one more chance, one more financial boost administered via a bank loan, then if it didn't work out he would put it up for grabs. The investment to profit ratio, well, Albert had to agree, was way below the norm for Braithwaite Holdings PLC.

At regular intervals Charlie rammed a chunk of *jambon farci à la mode de Nice* into his mouth, chewed vigorously and fast, and swallowed to release another flow of words unimpeded by edible obstacles. The increase in projected turnover now defied realistic prediction and rose in an ineluctible upward curve traced by Charlie's knife which was pointing at the pink chandelier in the centre of the room.

'Sorry,' said Charlie as a gobbet of half chewed ham hit the table, 'Got a bit carried away there. Anyway, as I was saying . . .'

His dining companion just had time to sample the *symphonie pastorale de fruits avec glace en cage à la sauce de myrtille's* ('Fruit with ice cream,' explained Charlie), then he really did have to be getting back to Leeds.

'Did you enjoy your meal, sir?' George came over, using that hint of obsequiousness appropriate for the banking fraternity.

'Very good. Very good indeed.' He glanced round the dining room. 'Are you as crowded as this every day?'

'We're turning people away,' George replied instantly, summoning up one of the standard fibs in the restaurant manager's repertoire. 'We hate doing it, but if there's no room what can you do?'

Good man, George. As long as he wasn't pissed, he came out with exactly what you wanted to hear.

'I'll be back for cheese, George. Get me a nice piece of Stilton.' Charlie rose to escort his guest to his car. 'Two stone I've put on since I opened this place,' he remarked. 'Still, think big, act big, eat big. That's me.'

As George's ever-shifting professional gaze swept round the room, he noticed the man on the Mayor's table rising to his feet and looking round. He rushed over.

'Is there a telephone I could use?' asked Sir Howard.

'But of course, sir,' said George, noting the expensive cut of his suit. A different class of man altogether. 'This way.'

The phone was in the lobby. Sir Howard turned his back and spoke softly into the mouthpiece.

'I'm at the Moorland Haven . . . can't talk now. I'm sorry you couldn't come, darling. Another time. We must synchronize our diaries . . . You were right. The food has great style. If I get back in time, I'll come round for a drink. Will you be at home later? . . . Must go now. I'm on this afternoon. Oh, you know, usual bunch of dreary people, but one has to show willing occasionally . . . Goodbye.'

Charlie judged the moment ripe to introduce himself to his guests and exchange business cards. By the end of an hour he had amassed enough knowledge about the wavering sugar industry to set up a meeting to discuss mutual developments. Oh yes, he was sure he could help. Anything which brought employment to the North would open every door, none of that sissy Southern mentality where they'd rather accept hand-outs and accumulate debts than do an honest day's work.

'I take three sugars in my tea and no-one can tell me different,' concluded Charlie, clearing the plate of petit fours. 'And I've never met a dentist who does more than operate a drill, stuff a hole and send out bills. What do they know? Bugger all.'

There could be a property deal in this chance meeting. Could maybe get this chap interested in the industrial development he was putting together near the station. Good place for a sugar refinery.

Sixty lunches out of the way. At least dinner would be quieter. Ten bookings, not bad for a Monday. Christ, John was tired. That was the trouble with resting on Sunday; it soothed the body into warm numbness then you had to gear up again, start the blood racing, the fingers working. He'd shouted at Gerard, screamed at his favourite supplier that morning, and now the rage and physical effort were over he was wiped out like he remembered his Dad, coming home when he'd finished his shift in the days when he had a shift to finish, sagging, bloodshot eyes vacant, hands limp on his knees.

John went out of the kitchen and sat at the bar with George.

'Charlie wants to see me tomorrow. Can't think why. We're doing all right.'

'Course we are. Picking up nicely. You know something?'

'What?'

'I know about chefs. There's hard-working ones and lazy ones and arrogant ones and arse-breakers and ones that should be grinding up pig-swill. But you're different.'

'That's right. I'm the genius.'

'Is that what the fiancée says, Marlene or whatever her name is?'

'We're not engaged, me and Cathy.'

'What a relief. I won't have to visit the bungalow and take my muddy shoes off. Thank God for that.'

'Why do you think I'm different?'

'Consistency, dear boy. You've never cooked something I'd throw in your face. And I have done that, you know. At the Metropole, no less. It was a legendary occasion. I won't say who it was, but he had lobster bisque forced down his throat till he sicked it up all over the floor. And I made him clean up on his hands and knees.'

The nerve centre of Charlie Braithwaite's corporate strategy was to be found in a black glass building which stood out so incongruously from the surrounding nineteenth-century monuments to trade that it had become a meeting place for anyone unfamiliar with the streets of central Leeds. How he obtained planning permission to erect such a brash intruder in that solemn Victorian street was a mystery. A university newspaper had tried to dig out evidence of the overruling of planning regulations, quoting officials in local government who had gone to stay in luxury villa complexes in Spain and the Bahamas ('Another Step in the Right Direction from Braithwaite Holdings PLC') helpfully documented in the *Northern Gazette* as an example of Charlie's generosity. ('I'm giving back to Leeds what Leeds has given to me.') But, as Charlie had also supplied substantial funding and assistance with post-graduate courses in computing science, engineering and business management, six months of research by diligent students sacrificing lectures and tutorials in the quest for truth had come to nought.

So the Braithwaite black glass folly (follies were, after all, an accepted part of the Yorkshire landscape) stood its ground, and, five years after its completion, was still greeted with all the vitriol reserved for those who abused children, hunted foxes or experimented on rats, notwithstanding the eulogistic reappraisal in the *Architectural Review*. There was usually a cluster of men and women looking and loitering outside, however cold, wet or windy it may have been, as though some member of minor royalty was about to emerge. They might occasionally have seen Charlie Braithwaite running up the steps in order to lose that extra pound and to promote the impression of constantly being on the move, which he was.

It was only the second time in six months that John Crabtree had been admitted to Braithwaite House. A secretary in a tight, dark suit ushered him into the board room and asked him if he cared for tea or coffee. He cared for neither, thank you, and wondered how many hundreds, thousands, of slightly anxious occupants of this overwhelmingly spacious room had refused, accepted or been bold enough to ask for something else. Suppose he just broke in, omitting please or thank you, and said, I'll have champagne and fresh pressed orange juice? This was Charlie's bevvy of a morning. What they drank down South, he'd told him, freshened up the mouth a treat.

The door suddenly opened and an invisible hand quietly clicked it shut as the man he had come to see moved towards him like a chair on castors across a polished parquet floor. Charlie threw a folder on to the table and pulled out a heavy mahogany chair.

'Hello, John lad. Sit down, sit down. The Japanese, don't half make you sweat. Mister Charry Braithrate, that's what I am in Tokyo. But if this deal comes through I won't give a bugger how they pronounce my name. Coffee, tea?'

John shook his head. Charlie sat back, put on his glasses and pulled the folder towards him. The phone on the wall rang.

'Show him up. I've asked someone along to talk about the Moorland. You and me, we're both new to this game and I want to see we do it right. Don't you agree?'

'I thought that was the general idea, Charlie.'

'This chap writes to me. Says he's been to the Moorland. Remember that interview with me in the *Yorkshire Post*? He saw that. The bit where I say I never stand still, just opened my first restaurant, be the best in the North. Et cetera, et cetera. Remember?'

'I showed it to you when it came out, Charlie.'

'So you did, so you did. Good article, in spite of my

being misquoted. Anyway. Judge for yourself. I won't say nowt. He can do the talkin' to start with. I'll see what he's made of.'

There was a knock on the door.

'Jack Leone, Mr Braithwaite.'

'So in comes this prat, some American. Moment I saw him, I thought, Charlie Braithwaite's going to do you over, mate. Was waiting for his face to crack, grinning all the time.'

'What was he wearing? What did he look like? My type or yours?'

'If you'd have seen him down the Packhorse you'd have bought him a Babycham.'

'More. Did he have a suit on or was it that Ivy League buttoned-down collar look?'

'I've told you, he was American.'

'I like Americans. They buy you drinks.'

'This one isn't from an air base, George. He's heavy. Goes through the figures, asks for a flow chart, projections and God knows what else. Tells Charlie sixty per cent occupancy is due to low profile in the area, that he can up it thirty per cent with, as he puts it, certain adjustments backed by "substantial media promotion". Says he's done eight turnarounds in the last eighteen months.'

'Oh, turnarounds. That does sound interesting. I think I'd like him.'

'Brings out a load of portfolios. Tells Charlie how well all these places are doing, signed accounts. Turnaround, George, has nothing to do with sex up the arse, though as far as I'm concerned it's the same bloody thing. It means turning a decent place into a shithouse for the Torremolinos crowd. This git thinks he knows about restaurants and Charlie believes him. Show him a healthy cash flow and he's anybody's. "I hear what you're saying, Mr Leone, and I like it." I swear the fucking idiot starts putting on the American twang.'

'John, you're being over-emotional. Calm down.'

'OK. Want to know the plan? Waitresses in short skirts. Larger menu, new graphics. Speciality nights. You know: Chinese night, Spanish night with guitarist, Italian night with some clapped-out slag from a working men's club belting out "Sole Mio". Ladies' night where they get a bottle of cheap perfume and a wilting rose. Hold on, I say. You don't need a chef like me. You're so wrong, says the Yank. What we gonna do is graft quality on to the pleasure principle. We are aiming for a holistic dining experience, he says. Charlie was taking it all in like he was watching the Queen giving the fucking Christmas message. Then we get down to basics. Food costs are far too high, he says. Suppliers ripping us off. Too much fish on the menu. Asks about portion control. I couldn't take it, I just couldn't.'

'What did you do then?'

'Walked out. Said I had to get back to the kitchen, which I did. I thought Charlie liked what we were doing. All that enthusiasm. Yes lad this and yes lad that, you're here because you cook like a dream and don't worry, lad, they'll soon be beating a path to your door . . . And then he goes and listens to some American dick-head.'

'Don't take it personally, John. You know Charlie. He gets these ideas about people and then changes his mind next day.'

'I'm going to start looking elsewhere, I tell you that.'

George sipped at a glass of wine as though someone had recently slapped him on the face, hurled abuse at him, kicked his arse and sent him flying face down on the pavement, which had happened more than once. Then he rallied.

'You're tired. It can't be that bad. Sleep on it, don't act rash. I'll have a word in Charlie's ear. The trouble with success is everyone wants a piece of the action. And Charlie wouldn't let that happen, any more than he'd let Leone, or whatever his name is, screw his wife.'

John pondered.

'If you did happen to go . . .' continued George.

'Yeah?'

'You know I wouldn't stay.'

'Don't blame you.'

'I am used to quality clientele. Why should I prostitute myself for the cha-cha-cha punters? I'd rather be a swimming pool attendant and look at bums.' George straightened his back, catching sight of his drooped shoulders in the bar mirror. 'If you go somewhere else, could I ask you something?'

'Sure.'

'Would you put my name forward for manager? Or even assistant manager? I'm not proud if it's the right place.'

John grinned and put his arm on George's shoulder. 'You don't have to even ask. Silly bugger. You and I, we're a team and if Charlie wants to screw it all up he can go—'

'Fuck himself,' said George, jumping down from the bar stool with a balletic leap.

Four weeks later Charlie Braithwaite had two letters of resignation on his desk. The Moorland Haven was closed for refurbishment and there was speedy planning permission for an extension. Well before Wakes Week, Charlie's Brasserie blasted out in red neon lights at the night sky, unmissable and consequently a boon for night navigators on the sparsely populated, unsigned roads and the carefully painted wooden sign advertising the Moorland Haven had become one side of a new kennel for Barbie, Mrs Charlie Braithwaite's giant poodle.

3

The curtains were drawn in the tiny cubicle and the smell of burnt honey lingered in the carpeted corridor outside. The patient lay still on the padded table, alone, covered in a sheet, eyes shut waiting for the operation to begin. It would be painful – it always was – but then followed the longed-for moment of ecstasy when the torment would have completed its cycle. That peculiar elation caused by the absence of pain with the experience of pain still keening the senses was intoxicating. The body would emerge as smooth and fresh as a kernel newly removed from a nut, as free from blemish as the airbrushed perfection masking an imperfect face. One would never confess to a soul the suffering caused by that particular sharp searing agony, any more than one would confess the racked pain of childbirth, for it was a secret between the patient and the efficient white-coated administrator of this intimate torture.

The strips of hot wax crept inexorably up her legs, past the knees, up, all the way, sealing inch after inch of flesh reaching almost to the torso. She flinched as stray pubic hairs spoiling the perfect line of thigh were enveloped in a hot glutinous mass the colour of pine resin. Then she was left alone once more, until the liquid mass had crystallized into a mummy-like casing. Unlike other types of pain, this one had a sequence, a predictability. She relaxed her body. She could do this once she had found the secret of control. Whatever happened now, she was going to be in control of herself. In order to control others.

The savage clean rip from the ankle surprised her the first time, and she had gasped but not screamed as some

45

did. This, she now knew, was only the first degree of pain. Hairs torn from the roots on the part of the leg toughened and weathered by sun, wind, rain and the polluted city air needed no intake of breath, but once the ripping had reached the tender innermost thigh, accustomed to a soft covering of silk, her mastery was put to the test. Today she gave a slight shudder. Next time she would have to learn to lie still, to open her eyes. Cool hands soothed the stinging flesh with sweet-scented balm and it was over. She slowly sat up, felt the long line of velvety flesh and reached for her silk stockings, the lacy suspenders and the wispy covering for the small thatch now remaining, for as yet she could not contemplate removing the last blot of wiry hair from her body but she soon would. It had never entered her head that there was no need for this ordeal, that the fine blonde hairs covering her body were almost imperceptible, nor had it come into being from the demands, imagined or otherwise, of a lover. She did it for herself alone.

The office staff looked up expectantly, ignoring their screens and putting calls on hold, waiting for instructions. The air was charged as soon as Laura Douglas walked in.

'Did you have a good lunch, Miss Douglas?'

This was the latest recruit who had not learned the Laura Douglas code. If she had been to a lunch worth talking about, she would tell them.

'Any calls?' she said. Without looking at any of them, she walked without pause through the room, spreading across the entire floor of a newly constructed block, which she had arranged with the obsessive care of an artist opening her studio to public gaze. The walls were of palest grey, with slate blue mouldings, and were interspaced with fine-lined drawings of sharply angled abstract forms framed in black. The open working space was divided by glass cases holding luminous alabaster pots and small steel objects tortured into strange shapes. By the time she had pushed the sliding glass door of her private domain, known as the Sanctum, where she could observe and be observed, she had been caught up by a hurrying grey-suited minion clutching his notebook in which were catalogued the telephone calls logged during her two hours' absence. He stood by her large grey-grained desk relaying every detail whilst Laura appeared to be busy attending to other matters, opening the window, riffling through a report, replacing papers from one pile to another, scanning newly arrived magazines. She acknowledged neither his presence, nor his information.

'. . . and then a Jack somebody, couldn't catch the last name.'

'Leone?' Laura asked, a little too quickly, turning to confront him at last. 'What did he want?'

'He didn't say. Should I get him for you?'

'Don't bother, he can wait. Who's coming to the launch tonight?'

'Didi Kowalski and Stephen Boyce have said yes.'

'Fine. We needn't bother about anyone else. They'll all come. And those that don't will wish they had.'

The minion left. In common with the other occupants of the Studio (office was far too pedestrian a name) he was a pristine young man chosen for his upper-class lineage, his connections and his unerring dress sense. Laura taught them to be efficient, for anyone could be efficient given the right training, and if they were too incompetent or lacking the necessary handsome profile she fired them.

She had, at the beginning of the learning curve, employed girls but now she had no time for female gossip, premenstrual tension, boyfriend troubles and the attendant emotions. Apart from these, they usually ended up being jealous and resenting a boss whom they could neither marry nor have as a part-time lover – the common aim of the majority of secretaries, Laura found. She did not have secretaries any more, she had assistants. At present there were six seated at their workstations, known collectively in memos as the Team.

It took a little time to learn how to keep the Team together, how to inject the right degree of anxiety and insecurity with the occasional reward of praise and encouragement, how to avoid unruly emotions by encasing them in a veneer of wit, irony and humour, how to resist being over-solicitous when personal woes occasionally intruded into the daily routine of work. But, above all, it took time to believe that she was always right and to rationalize and conceal mistakes as an irrelevant stumble along the long straight road of successful endeavour. Nobody liked the boss to make a gaffe, especially the longer serving minions who were beginning to appreciate the competitive strategy of LDA, Laura Douglas Associates, and to admire the determination with which she translated ideas into hard-headed practice. Laura Douglas, although constantly seeking advice (good for TM, Team Morale) was never in the wrong. Never.

Lesser women were prone to take the model of the family and apply it to business. A fatal mistake. The will to oust all comers, to compete whatever the circumstance and to sacrifice everything to the attainment of a successful goal was not nurtured round the kitchen table. In the rare moments of reflection when she was not dashing from one restaurant to another, one meeting to another, presenting plans, creating press releases, dictating, arguing, formulating and reprimanding, Laura wondered why she had been satisfied with her former life for so long.

Mrs Laura Leone had given up a promising career as a designer at the age of twenty-four, had supported her husband in every move he made, wooed clients for him, administered two residences – the flat in Kensington and the country house in Oxfordshire which she had reconstructed from a ruin – bred miniature ponies, kept bees, organized holidays abroad, tolerated 'meaningless flings' with secretaries and listened to her husband's often repeated jokes while she served up *salmon en croute, carré d'agneau* or rib of beef for twenty guests. For ten years she had done this and cultivated a mask of serenity so that she always looked elegant, unruffled and pleased with life, a tribute to the business acumen of Jack Leone.

'Hi, babe. How you doing?'

He had come through on her private line. Laura swung round in her chair, which was custom crafted and ergonomically designed for the female form, and sat with her back to the Studio.

'I thought you were in LA.'

'Only for a day. Checking out. Food's still B grade. Wine's improving, though. Refined rather than complex, but reliable. Exports building up nicely. I've been talking to a few small growers. Brought back some bottles. You should give it a try.'

'I will, when I've got a moment.'

She wrinkled her brow a fraction. His arrogance still irked her, like grit in mussels. After all this time she should have become immune to it.

'Have you been to the Raw-Raw Bar yet? Opened in downtown LA two weeks ago. Quite a hot place.'

This was easier. She knew that tactic.

'With a new designer it might do OK.' Luckily she had seen it featured in an American glossy.

'I was calling to see if you could make lunch. Be good to talk.'

She winced, wondering what he wanted from her this time.

'How about next Friday?' she said.

Laura knew he always took his lady of the moment to lunch on Friday, the day when serious business ended at noon as executives started to think of heading back for the family home in the country, and nothing important would be missed by lingering over the brandies or groping in the back of a cab whilst they waited for the traffic to clear on the jam-blocked routes to the high-value property areas.

'Er . . .'

'It's the only time I can do.'

'Friday it is, babe.' He made it sound as though he had given a million to charity. 'Have a good week. Look forward.'

They both put down the phone at the same time in a parody of marital harmony.

'What the hell are you doing still here?' Laura shouted in the direction of Leo, senior minion. 'The press will be arriving at any minute. I want you ready and waiting, not late and sweating.'

'I've got to finish this report. For that client meeting tomorrow.'

'What'll it take? Couple of hours? Finish it in the morning before they come.' Leo looked down at his tenth rewrite that day. Laura liked snappy copy and this sounded as exciting as an estate agent selling a semi. Another dawn start.

'If you don't get down there now, it will be a no-go place. Number one rule: everyone cocks up except us.' She moved to another desk. 'Oh, Julian, book a car for Leo. If it's longer than five minutes, I'm moving the account.'

Antony, the new recruit, rose from his position at the other side of the Studio and followed Laura as she started to make the trajectory back to the Sanctum.

'I say, Miss Douglas . . .'

'Yes?'

He stood awkwardly, folder in hand, not knowing whether to wait for her to change course or whether to walk boldly into the Sanctum.

'I've got some stuff for you, Miss Douglas.'

'Bring it in,' she said, solving his dilemma. She looked at him and smiled her melting smile, leaning back in her chair and stretching out her long, smooth legs.

'Laura's my name. Miss Douglas is reserved for clients who take taxis rather than cabs, wear chainstore suits and think champagne is something you drink at weddings. You wanted to show me something?'

'I've got John Crabtree's CV. The chap who's coming to

see you at five. I had rather a job. The restaurant he was at changed its name. He isn't there any more.'

'What? The Moorland Haven? That was quick. It only opened last October.'

'The staff is new. They wouldn't tell me where John was, so I got on to the local paper, the *Northern Gazette*. Here's a cutting.'

'Well done, Antony. That's really helpful.' She smiled again as she took the cutting from him. 'Why don't you come to the meeting too? I'd like to see how John Crabtree strikes you.'

'Oh. Yes. Yes. I've never met a chef before.'

'Most of them are absolutely yawn-making. That's why they need us. But this one's . . . well, you'll see.'

Antony looked promising. He might stay for a while, as long as his initiative was merely a mark of the desire to please.

There is nothing like a sleazy hotel in Paddington for giving the impression that God never existed. J. Crabtree, accustoming himself to anonymity, shoved the dusty bedside Bible into a drawer and opened his case. Cathy's ironing had come to grief, and his best shirt was now irrevocably lined with creases and resembled the map of a many-tributaried river. This was partly due to the method of transportation he had been forced to adopt, the Rapide coach from Halifax which, as it cost a fraction of the train fare, was all he could afford. Cases were thrown into the hold like sacks of coal, which meant that everyone would be guaranteed the insignia of the tripper; crumpled clothes.

John had worked out a month's notice at the Moorland Haven which culminated in a screaming match with Charlie Braithwaite in front of the whole kitchen. Charlie had told him he'd come to no good, his talent wasted; think of the grief to his parents, all he'd done for him, could have had a great future; he was thinking of giving him a share of the action if everything went well . . . A fill-in job in Leeds in a large hotel where everyone knew him as Jack had kept him from the local dole queue until he could stand it no longer and knew he had to uproot himself from everything he had known for the past twenty-four years. George, who knew a little more of the world (he had once worked in a posh hotel in the West End), said London was the only place to go. If you worked there you could get discovered, be a star like Anton Mosimann who, pointed out George, had been photographed in a dinner jacket, not chef's whites, at parties given by the rich and titled.

John listened to George's second-hand exposition of London rather as he had listened to his geography teacher, who had never been further afield than Sardinia, describing remote mountain ranges in China. When George relayed detailed descriptions of restaurants, chefs, menus, design and clientele it bore little relationship to John's experience in the kitchen. Who were they, these chefs whose activities in the kitchen elicited such volumes of prose? What did they cook, where did they train, where did they come from?

John was staring at himself in a pockmarked mirror balanced against the wall on a rickety chest of drawers. He needed a shave. He ran the water, which hiccuped out of a tap with a loose washer and came out tepid. The shaving foam hung in greyish-white globules on top of the water in the basin, like a polluted stream at sheep-dip time. The room smelt of airfreshener, dust, stale nylon sheets and bygone Chinese takeaways consumed in solitude, the mingled odours held captive by a window which had long since ceased to open. Only the sound of a throaty Hoover trundling over a thin, threadbare carpet, the gargling of outworn pipes and the constant flushing of lavatories betrayed the existence of human life in this museum of misery which someone had deemed fit to call a hotel. Then suddenly these sounds were drowned by gusts of shrieking, manic laughter, distorted as though through a drainpipe, vibrating through the chipboard partition. At least the television next door was working, if nothing else was. Definitely time for a drink, whatever time in the morning it was. In a strange place, it didn't matter.

The jacket of John's interview suit covered most of the telltale shirt. He would wear his tie, chosen by George, nearer the time. As he walked down Sussex Gardens the hot July sun scorched the man-made fabric on his back, but he was determined to keep his jacket on to get used to the rare sensation of formal dress. As he rounded a street corner, he saw a crowd of people standing on the pavement in the distance. Nearer, and he could distinguish arms crooked, glasses held. No-one looked at him and several jostled him without animosity as he pushed his way through the open door to the dark bar inside. A pint of beer was shunted towards him, and he struggled outside into the sunlight.

In his pocket he had a map of London. He set down his glass on a dusty sill, unfolded the large sheet and tried to find the names of streets he recognized. George had scribbled circles showing the location of the restaurants people talked about. He couldn't even afford a starter, but he would see what they looked like, observe who went in, and there might even be a menu outside. Later, if he could survive that long, he would ask to see one of those famous chefs. They might need a spare hand in the kitchen. You learned at the bottom. He would learn. For a few months. George had given him a couple of names, men who had catapulted up the kitchen hierarchy whom he had known when they were chopping the veg. At least here no-one knew him and he could do as he liked. After his second pint, the prospect of London, which he had seen only as a collection of landmarks glimpsed briefly on day trips organized by his school, started to become less daunting.

He hoped he'd done right in telephoning Laura Douglas, even though George had shrugged his shoulders dismissively at the mention of her name. 'One of the parasites, dear boy. If you must, meet her away from her office and make her buy you an expensive lunch. Women are used to paying down South, gives them a kick.' John had kept her visiting card, the only one he'd ever had from a woman. He vaguely remembered their conversation, distinctly remembered the cool, fine-boned face, the hanging mass of hair the colour of straw after a long hot summer, the way she tilted her head back when giving her opinion, her long white fingers . . . Grey eyes?

She seemed to remember more than he did. Was quite happy to see him, at any rate. John worked out how to get from Soho, where he had a couple of restaurants to look at, to Mortimer Street. He hadn't time to take in the places in Chelsea and Mayfair. That would be the plan for tomorrow. Then, the next day, Nine Elms Market, Smithfield. He'd ask the suppliers which chefs bought the best produce. They always knew in markets. As he headed towards Marble Arch, he barely noticed the massive buildings on one side, the summery park a world away on the other.

Laura was on the phone, writing some notes with her free hand. What she was writing had nothing to do with the conversation in progress, for she was becoming expert at accomplishing two tasks simultaneously. It was relaxing to be confronted with information rather than hysterics.

'I see . . . Yes . . . Of course. Absolutely the right thing. Very wise.'

Her voice, cued to the automatic response, soothed and reassured one of her first clients, a chef who was now sufficiently established to need little effort on her part.

'Laura?'

'Yes?' Laura pressed the silent button on her telephone and continued to listen and nod her head. Julian slid the door back a fraction.

'Are we having the update session today?'

'Later.'

'I've got to go.'

'Tomorrow, then.'

Leo returned to the Studio and informed the other minions that the update session had been postponed until tomorrow. They duly recorded the change in their diaries.

'I say, what does one do in the update session?' asked Antony, who had not yet been tested enough to attend.

'One gets hold of information which could bag us another client,' replied Julian. 'And one gives the dailies.'

'Dailies?'

'Achievements for each day. And then, of course, next week's objective. Just positive time management, really. Pretty basic stuff. Haven't you come across it before?'

'Not really.'

'I'll ask Laura if you can sit in. I'm sure she won't mind.'

Much of Laura's marital life had pivoted around the update, which, Jack had explained, was the key to successful business enterprise. He wanted her to be part of his world. She was the only person he could really talk to. Some husbands never talked about what went on at work, but he wanted Laura to share everything. (She must have become weary of hearing his endless business homilies. One way of reminding her how wonderful he was, although, of course, she didn't see it like that at the time.)

Information flow, babe. You gotta know what the competitors don't so you can do what they can't. If the phone rings, you goddamn answer. Every time. Jack's mobile interactive multifunction phone had intruded into every intimate occasion, following him into the lavatory, the shower, the dining room and even the bedroom. Faced with this instrument of constant reminder, she had decided to take it in her stride. Talking into it as she walked round the house checking that none of the tropical plants in the indoor atrium were wilting, for Jack took it personally if anything drooped, had helped relieve the periods of tedium and the lack of adult conversation. The telephone became ally, confidante and constant companion as Laura became more and more trapped (how could she not have felt trapped?) in this large atmosphere-controlled, centrally-heated, double-glazed, ring-mained, support-systemed (Calor gas plus generator for emergencies), Grade Two Listed authentically restored Jacobean farmhouse and auxiliary outbuildings comprising indoor and outdoor pool, billiards room, tennis court, croquet lawn, mini-gym and communications room (closed-circuit TV, multiscreen, Inter-State satellite on the roof) triple-backed security systems and external floodlighting. Laura was as familiar with touch control, bleeps and blips, modems and malfunctions as her country neighbours were with foot-rot and warble fly.

'Laura, John Crabtree's here. Downstairs in reception.'

Antony advanced a couple of steps through the open door.

'Bring him up. Be with you in a minute.' She concluded her telephone conversation. 'Must rush. We'll talk later. Will I see you at Petrushka's this evening? . . . Lovely. Goodbye.'

She left the Sanctum, disappearing to her private bathroom in order to give her face a few deft strokes of powder and to emphasise the grey-blue eyes with a hint of darker-toned shadow. Above her cheek bones, she observed a couple of scarcely traced lines. Still, no-one would guess that she was thirty-four. By the time they were truly visible, she was determined to have become powerful enough not to care.

'John, why don't you sit over there while I find a bottle of something?'

Sinking back into a settee covered in pale blue silk, John watched Laura through the glass as she opened the door of a stainless steel cabinet which, surprisingly, revealed itself as a fridge.

'Shall I open that?' he asked when Laura re-entered with some Bollinger.

'It's my exercise for the day.' Laura gave him a quick glance, taking in the crumpled white shirt, the off-centre maroon tie, the dowdy cut of his suit and his heavy shoes.

'Antony, the glasses are behind you, in the cabinet.'

She smiled at John, that welcoming smile he remembered, as she nonchalantly twisted the bottle and decanted

the minutely bubbling vintage liquid into three champagne glasses.

'Thanks very much,' said John, unsure if he should
initiate the conversation. He was about to say 'Cheers' as
Laura raised her glass to her lips, but when she drank
immediately and said nothing, and neither did Antony
who was sitting bolt upright on a steel chair, he checked
his impulse.

'So you took my advice and walked out on Charlie
Braithwaite?'

'I did.'

'That was brave. He's a tough cookie.'

'Oh. Have you met?'

'No, but I have my spies in the City.'

'You wouldn't recognize the Moorland Haven. It's all
changed. Top to bottom.'

'Really? Did he sell out then?'

'I don't rightly know. Some chap walked in with fancy
chat and told him he could triple his money. It's Charlie's
Brasserie now. Wooden bars, shells on nets hanging round
the walls and dripping candles on the tables. They serve
fish and chips and scampi in a basket. I wasn't going to
stay as a chippie.'

'Not even if you'd served the best fish and chips in
Yorkshire?' For the first time John looked straight at
Laura, then looked away, feeling himself flush.

'What have you been doing since you left the Moorland?'

He thought she might ask that and had rehearsed a
plausible answer.

'I can't imagine jobs for chefs like you are falling off
trees,' Laura said. 'Have you had any offers?'

'Well, one or two.' He hoped she would change the
subject.

'And?'

'I haven't made my mind up yet. I thought I might look
around London.' John paused, allowing his glass to be
filled again. 'I mean . . . I thought you might know of a

57

place, a good place mind, that's looking for a chef.'

He dared not mention that he had been scouring the *Hotel and Caterer* for two months, that he had written job applications and torn them up, that he couldn't bring himself to apply for a junior position which was all they offered.

'Antony, could you fish out an LDA brochure?' Antony hurriedly went to his desk, hoping he would soon have a chance to enrich the dialogue with a *bon mot* of his own.

'We must have a strategy,' said Laura. 'Unfortunately, it's not good enough just to be able to cook, particularly when you haven't the advantage of having worked with a Michelin category abroad or having run a successful restaurant before. Am I right?'

'Is it that obvious?' replied John. 'No, I've not been Frenchified yet.'

They both laughed.

'I've done my homework, but I think you should know a little about my company. If we go any further, I'd like to see if you would endorse my approach.'

Strategy and approach. She was beginning to sound like Charlie Braithwaite.

'You look doubtful. I'm only trying to find out if I can help you.'

Laura was wondering if she had time to put in the effort required to change this prickly young man into an asset. No-one else in the organization, not even Leo, could pick him up and guarantee success. She might even have to invest some money, send him to France. With so many new accounts coming in, which entailed a high initial spend, she was having to watch the cash flow. On the other hand, he conveyed a tough, quiet persistence.

As John made his way through the brochure, pondering the Douglas prose, Laura called Leo at Petrushka's, giving him a stream of instructions and questions. Had this been done, had that been done? . . . She put the phone down.

'Sorry about that. I've got a launch on tonight. Hopeless owners, they think everything happens by magic.'

'Can I do anything to help?' said Antony, timidly reminding Laura of his presence.

'If you've nothing on tonight, why not come along with me?' Laura said.

'I'd love to.'

'Why don't you book a car for six fifteen?' Antony bounded enthusiastically into the Studio, like a kennel-bound dog released from his chain.

John folded the brochure, drank some more champagne and caught the time on his watch. Nearly six o'clock and everyone around, phones ringing . . .

'By the way,' said Laura, 'who was it persuaded Charlie Braithwaite to change direction? Maybe I know him.'

'I don't think you'd want to,' John said. 'A right . . .' He stopped himself.

'Bastard?' suggested Laura.

'I was going to say wanker.'

'Oh, you'll find lots of those down here, I'm afraid.'

'He had some foreign name. Let me think. Limone. Something like that.'

'Was he American?' Laura asked, her skin prickling. She slowly got up and went over to her desk, pretending to look for something. 'Leone? Jack Leone?'

'That's it. I knew it began with an L. I hope he's not a friend of yours.' Laura did not reply. 'Well, do you know him?'

'Vaguely. I don't like his kind of business.'

'I wouldn't be sitting here talking if you did, I tell you that.'

The ice had broken and Laura was plunging into a pool of possibilities. He was as she remembered him; she should trust her instant assessments. Passion, persistence and talent. And northern toughness. Her decision was made. John Crabtree would become the star of the Laura Douglas stable and she would make him into the most bankable chef in the country. She did not think of it as a revenge for years of humiliation. Just proving herself.

'I think you and I will work very well together,' she

59

said. 'All I want is for you to do what you're best at. You can leave the fighting to me. You're probably not used to that, are you? Not quite the northern approach?'

Laura had flowingly outlined a plan of campaign. It sounded plausible and possible to John, the right mixture of forward planning and flexibility.

'I could get used to it. You never know.'

He was unafraid to look at her now, lingering long enough to take in her long neck, slightly flushed cheeks highlighting her ivory skin, delicate ears offset by striking jewellery, deep blue-grey eyes which looked unflinchingly into his, hair which she tossed back when it curtained her face. He noticed the way she rested two fingers on her lips when she was thinking, like a child making up an excuse.

'I s'pose we'd better talk money,' said John.

'Of course. We have a standard agency rate of fifteen per cent for the first year – that's the period of maximum expenditure – then it goes down to ten per cent.'

'So there's nothing up-front?'

'Oh, no.' Laura smiled. 'We carry administration costs, print costs, that kind of thing.'

'Sounds OK.'

Antony came into the room, agitated. 'Laura, the car's been waiting half an hour.'

'That's all right, Antony. Tell him we'll be five minutes.'

He ran down to the entrance, marvelling at working for a boss who could pay with such insouciance for a driver just to sit waiting.

'Miss Douglas will be down in about five minutes,' he announced imperiously.

'I do appreciate you taking this trouble.'

That accent. It could be irresistible. Tekkin' trouble. Laura started to hear his voice in her head when he was silent, and she was beginning to detect the times when he hinted at emotion through the subdued delivery, betrayed in a slightly more forceful pronunciation of the consonants.

'Shouldn't you be going off now, Miss Douglas?'

'Would you like to come with me? We're launching a new place. Petrushka's. I could introduce you to a few people.'

John looked at Antony hovering outside by the glass, an elegant outline in Laura Douglas grey. 'I've got no other clothes. I'm not what you'd call right smart.'

'You look great. I like men in suits. Shall we go then?'

Already, Laura was working out where she would take him, how to bring out his well-proportioned solid features, which colours, which fabrics. Neither Jean-Paul Gautier nor Savile Row, but classically inspired with a comfortable, relaxed feel. He could take dark, rich colours with that height, grow his hair a bit longer . . . You noticed him anyway when he walked in, even in that awful Yorkshire version of a suit.

When they entered the discreet doorway of Petrushka's, a champagne and caviar bar which Laura Douglas had metamorphosed from an old-fashioned family butcher's shop into a chic watering hole for those with abundant credit cards and expensive tastes but little time, half the occupants looked up and turned their heads. Chatter was put on hold for a second. Those pausing for an intake of breath knew the name and growing reputation of Laura Douglas, and through the gossip chain had avidly followed every step in her swift progress from back-room office off Charlotte Street to the elegant suite in Mortimer Street. She was only a blank figure to the gate-crashers or friends of friends of the owner, the rent-a-crowd on such occasions whose shadowy presence helped to fill up empty spaces.

'I say, Laura Douglas with a minder? What's she been up to then?' Stephen Boyce dipped a spoon deep into a bowl of passing caviar.

'I could go for him,' said his companion in gluttony, ogling the tall, well-built newcomer. He then stretched out his spoon-wielding hand. Too late: the tray of caviar had passed beyond reach.

'Which do you prefer? I think the Iranian Oscietre has a

lot going for it. If one is going for cut-price caviar, it's not bad at all. Quite good, really.'

The wine writer, not to be outdone, summoned up his scanty knowledge.

'The Russian Sevruga was excellent, I thought.'

'Did you?' was the reply, gently delivered with exactly the right upward inflection to cut this upstart down to size. 'Must say hello to Laura. Excuse me.'

'Darling!'

'Stephen!'

He gave her a smacking kiss. On the lips, John observed with surprise, expecting greater decorum from this pleasant-featured, solidly built man dressed in a bank-manager suit.

'Let me introduce you to John Crabtree. He cooks divinely. This is Stephen Boyce, my favourite writer. He has a weekly column in the *Daily Reporter*. One of the few that actually knows anything about food.'

'A mere gluttonous hack,' said Stephen modestly. 'But I try.'

'What do you think?' asked Laura.

Stephen surveyed the room, sweeping past the low cream ceiling with aubergine abstract motifs, the stark chrome lights, the black bar.

'I like the buzz. A good feel. There must be quite a good lunchtime crowd around here who are bored with smoked salmon sandwiches. Nice size. Good for overhearing gossip, I'd have thought. Should be a winner.'

'Do you think straight caviar with a garnish is going to work, or should we have some ethnic Russian dishes? I can't make up my mind.'

'If it were me, I'd keep it like this. At least for a while. No need to gild the lily. And, after all, one doesn't want to be reminded of dreary old Moscow.'

'Stephen has just come back from a weekend in Russia,' interjected Laura.

'Just the weekend?' said John, thinking he had mis-heard.

'Press trips,' said Stephen. 'Borscht, Bolshoi and bureaucrats. I've been sweating my guts out trying to write a positive piece. Couldn't persuade them that I wasn't excited by queues outside McDonalds in Leningrad.' He sighed. The plate of caviar halted in front of Laura.

'Have you had some?' she asked.

'Yes, but I could do with a second sample.' Once again, Stephen bored his flat spoon deep into the shiny black mass of eggs.

Laura dug her spoon in, and passed it to John. 'Have some. See what you think of the quality.'

John tasted it slowly, delicately. 'Fantastic,' he said, eyeing the bowl. A month's supply back at the Moorland Haven.

Laura gestured with a gracefully pointing finger and the waiter hastened to refill their glasses with champagne. His fifth glass that day, John worked out, the occasion being rare enough for him to count each one.

'Want to hear a caviar joke?' asked Stephen, stuffing another heaped spoonful into his mouth.

'Go on,' urged Laura.

'There's this rich American widow going down the Nile on a luxury cruise ship. She's sitting at the captain's table looking at the menu and calls over the waiter, "Say, what's this here? Cav-i-ar? What's that?"

"Fish eggs, madam," replies the waiter. She thinks for a moment. "Oh, in that case, waiter, I'll have mine poached."'

Laura laughed with Stephen, who giggled endearingly, and John grinned. Then Stephen turned to John, suddenly intent and serious.

'I'm sorry, John, I should know but I don't. Which restaurant are you from?'

'He's been up in Yorkshire,' Laura interpolated quickly. 'But he's going to open up in London.'

'Where in Yorkshire?'

'You'll not have heard of it. A restaurant called the Moorland Haven.'

'Ah yes. Taken over by Jaws Leone.' Stephen glanced at Laura. 'What is it now? A pancake factory or a pizza palace?'

'Calls itself a brasserie,' John replied.

'My, he's going upmarket. What'll it be? I wonder. Leone's New American Fun Cuisine – char-grilled alligator with a salsa sauce and chips? Barbecued duck with cornmeal pancakes and cranberry sauce? I can't wait.'

John was bewildered. Everyone was talking, talking, talking, but their lips seemed hardly to move. Gobble, sip, chat, gobble, sip, chat. Antony hovered in the background, chuckling at appropriate moments, occasionally crossing the room and returning to Laura, unable yet to identify the people one talked to and those one ignored.

'Are you getting bored?' Laura asked, as Stephen moved away to winkle some column information from the owner of Petrushka's, who was standing on his own gazing at the gathering.

'Oh, no. It's new to me, this. I'll get used to it.'

'There are some people I must talk to. Be back in a minute.'

Laura left him and insinuated her way through the bodies crammed together in the small, hot space. For a moment he missed her warmth, which had brought out the peculiarly evocative scent of the expensively dressed woman. Traces of classic perfume mingled with the sweetness of her body clung in an indeterminate aura of luxury, remaining a few seconds after she had moved away.

'Should I know you, dear?'

A small, rotund figure propelled herself into John's few square feet of floor space. She was carrying a motorcyle helmet and wearing waterproof trousers topped incongruously by a sequined cocktail blouse which sparkled in the spotlights.

'So many people here one doesn't know. And they all know my name. Isn't that extraordinary?'

'I'm John Crabtree. How do you do?'

'Caliope Fortescue. That's my nom de plume. Generally known as Cal. Do you cook, do you write, or are you one of those dreadful people in the restaurant trade?'

'I'm a chef.'

'Oh!' she gasped. 'I simply adore chefs. You're such good people, don't you agree?'

'As long as we're not cooking fish and chips.'

Caliope Fortescue doubled up with laughter. 'Oh, you darling man. A chef with a sense of humour. Even better. I shall pen a few words. I do have to say that I write for a frightfully literary publication. They think I'm *très* snob. Which I suppose I am. Have you a visiting card, dear?'

John shook his head.

'Then I shall have to write down your name. Just a moment.' The redoubtable lady put down her helmet on the floor, groped in the pocket of her capacious trousers and produced a lined exercise book. 'You try riding a Motoguzzi in a skirt. Impossible. Do you realize, I am the only woman allowed into the Ritz cocktail bar in rainproof trousers?' The small round figure rattled with hilarity, quaking as she bent over to write 'John Crabtree. Chef. Petrushka's' with a blunt pencil but in a stylish hand. 'Crabtree. That's a fine Yorkshire name. I once knew a Lady Cynthia Crabtree from Darlington. She sang madrigals beautifully. Charming woman. Are you by any chance related?'

'Not that I know of.'

She stared at him, sizing him up blatantly from head to toe, then said lugubriously, 'Probably the wrong side of the sheets.'

Laura quickly joined Stephen, whom she had noticed talking to her client, not someone known for his originality of expression. He would need a little assistance to give Stephen enough for a sparkle item in his column.

'And for the first month, we're holding a low price on champagne as a loss leader.'

'Good thinking.'

'How did it strike you?' Laura asked.

'Yes. Quite good.'

'I'll bike round a few samples, together with some caviar so you can try it at home. It's so difficult to judge anything at a launch.'

'Thanks a lot, Laura.' Stephen said this as though it was his due, which it was. Petrushka's opening could run to a hundred and fifty words, not the lead item but frivolous fun. Maybe an end piece.

'Oh,' exclaimed Laura, noticing a white-haired, trim-bearded man peering round. 'You haven't met Count Alexei Zamoiski. He's supplying the caviar. Great character. Can I introduce you? Might help with your Russian piece.'

'Super. Let's go.'

Stephen crossed the room again, reading over his inadequate shorthand as he went to see if Laura's client had said anything interesting, which he doubted.

The Russian count was from the ancient regime, fluent in French, Russian and English, thank God. He and Stephen were soon roaring with laughter. Now Laura could leave them to it and return to John. He really did need looking after.

'Laura, dear. Who is this delectable young man? I could eat him up.'

Caliope Fortescue was on the B Press List, fun at openings but classified in Laura's Blue Book (the Team bible) as LCLV (low circulation, low volume) since she wrote sporadically for a journal with less that fifty thousand circulation. Office instructions for the B Press List were: minimal telephone time, keep informed by post, generalized releases only, no personal notes.

'Must dash now, Cal. I'll give you a call tomorrow. Time we had a talk anyway. John, can you find your way back? I've got to have dinner with a client. We'll talk tomorrow. Call me around eleven.'

Taking advantage of Laura's exit, John followed her and stood near the open entrance, breathing a little of the cool evening air, watching the security guard posed belligerently on the pavement, giving himself a few more minutes before he headed back to his lumpy bed in Sussex Gardens. Laura swept out of the door, blowing him a kiss, and into a waiting car. Stephen Boyce followed a minute later with his arm round an impossibly desirable creature who flashed a provocative glance at John, drew her peacock-patterned silk shawl around her and tossed her cascading black curls like a horse in the ring. When she had reached the steps outside, she removed a pair of skyscraper heels and ran down the street on tiny stockinged feet followed by Stephen who was puffing, panting and between times shouting, 'Didi! Didi! Stop! Stop! Why are you doing this to me?'

Like some inconvenient roadwork grudgingly circum-navigated by a stream of impatient drivers John was surrounded by people battling for the odd taxi which deigned to stop. They were still gossiping, asking one another where they were going to next, scribbling down phone numbers. Where was John's car, where was his fancy companion who would run down the street with everybody admiring her and envying him? Why hadn't some beautiful female sidled up waiting for him to ask if she was free for the evening?

He started his lonely walk back. The pubs were open, but he didn't fancy propping up the bar drinking beer. Minimally clothed, bare-legged girls passed him, unseeing, followed by swaggering youths. He passed through swathes of litter, stepped aside to avoid sleeping figures sprawled over basement air vents, was jostled, then accosted by a gang of girls who shouted obscenities as they passed. He quickened his pace. Something was banging against his body. He put his hand in his jacket and felt the hard edge of a tin. Oh yes, a present from the nice fat lady who rode a motorbike. Well, not exactly a present. She had demanded a sample of caviar from one of the young men dressed in grey. And given it to him. She didn't have to do that.

He was hungry, yearning for a hunky steak sandwich with onions, but he decided to resist. His daily allowance was already spent. There was still some evening left. He passed a late-night shop, then retraced his steps. What the hell? The Asian behind the counter smiled at him as he stood undecided in the doorway. He bought a dried-up onion bhaji, a can of beer and wandered over to a stand of newspapers and magazines. There were a couple he recognized, George's regular reading. Glancing up at the shopkeeper, who was bagging up change, he picked one up and turned the pages quickly one after another.

A headline caught his eye. 'Food Fit for the Gods.' Underneath it was a blurred picture of a wild-eyed chef with a spoon in his mouth. John turned the page. Another picture. What kind of a prat was this? Here he was again, a full-length lean figure with a naked torso, tight jeans, laurel leaves round his head, holding a peacock feather, leaning against a fluted, ivy-covered column with a dreamy expression on his ethereal face. They must be bloody joking.

'Tadeus Freeman has all the energy of a piranha demolishing a whale. "I don't talk to fucking idiots," he answered, when I asked to interview him. "Neither do I," I replied.'

John read on and his jaw dropped. Here was the talking chef.

'I think it was Bocuse who said "*un chef qui fait la cuisine mais qui ne fait pas l'amour n'est rien qu'un homme de technique.*" Which, translated for your dumb-bell readers, means, if you cook but you don't fuck, forget it. I do both. When I'm in the kitchen I'm thinking of fucking. When I'm fucking I'm thinking of food. That do you for a quote? Now I'm going to make something for the stupid arseholes who'll pay my ridiculous prices to stuff their faces and turn their money into shit.'

I watched Tadeus dancing round his brigade in a mad tarantella of frenzy, like some demonic chef destined to stir and taste for eternity in a fiery circle of Dante's Hell.

Who wrote this kind of stuff? John turned back to the beginning of the article. Stephen Boyce. The one he'd been talking to? Was this what food writers wrote about? Was this what a chef was supposed to look like? He replaced the magazine, heard 'Have a nice evening, sir' over the rattle of coins and went out of the shop. If Tadeus Freeman was a piranha, what was Charlie Braithwaite? They didn't tell you in catering college that you had to take your clothes off and insult your customers in order to be a chef.

A 'No Vacancies' sign was hanging in the front window of John's hotel by the time he returned, and the door was locked. After he had pressed the bell intermittently for five minutes, it was slowly opened by a surly man who appeared to have been asleep. The place reeked of disinfectant.

'We had a man vomit over the carpet,' he informed John. 'That carpet was new two years ago. You'd never guess. Having breakfast, are you?'

Politely, John declined. Tomorrow he would be up early. If he could cook what he wanted, he wouldn't mind taking his clothes off. Preferably in Laura's office . . . Tadeus Freeman, was it? Lucky bugger. Only three years older than him and he said he'd retire at forty. And over one million pounds. From just one restaurant. From cooking.

4

'Sorry, babe. But I've been stuck here for an hour. Missed two meetings already.'

Jack Leone switched off the ignition of his Ferrari with one hand, put the phone close to his ear with the other and watched a large refuse disposal truck slowly grinding and crunching several weeks' detritus to a stinking pulp. Two men in the new Clean-Up London uniforms were shouting at a driver who had challenged their right to block the road.

'And you can fuck off, too.'

'I'll report you.'

'Go ahead, mate.'

'I've got a job to do.'

'What do you think I'm doin' then? Playing cowboys and Indians?'

'There's no need to be insolent.'

Jack listened, grinning at the quaint way the British complained. Back home they'd have been slugging it out or fingering the gun in the glove compartment.

'Can't hear you, Jack. You in the office? What's going on?'

Jack wound up his window and repeated his opening sentence.

'Oh, honestly,' crackled twenty-year-old Miss Friday Lunchdate (agency statistics, a data-banked 5'11" 36–22–35). 'It's not fair. Letting me know at the last minute. And what's more, I cancelled a photographic session.'

'How much are they paying you?'

'What?'

'Your fee. Tell me and I'll pay.'

Miss Friday made a quick calculation and doubled it.

'That much? You're getting to be a pricey dame.'

'It was a cover pic.'

'OK, OK. I'll give you a cheque next Friday.'

'You won't cancel again, will you? It's not nice . . .'

'Listen, I could drop in Tuesday night. I'll be round your way.'

'Promise?'

'Course, babe.'

Tuesday's date would have to be content with a shortened session. Going from one bed to another in an evening was quite a turn-on, good for the performance. Jack was used to having dinner at two restaurants, starters and fish course at one, main course and pudding at another and he was merely applying the same principle to sex. Two restaurants and two women in a night might be pushing it, though. He'd eat light on Tuesday and do extra work-outs at the health club.

The car in front of him inched forward, but there seemed little chance of serious movement. Time to dictate a few letters. The car behind hooted and Jack waved a hand in the air dismissively, fast-talking into his pocket recorder.

In rural Oxfordshire, it was still possible to hear the high trills of birdsong against the distant roar of the motorway. Jack was contributing to the roar, briefly touching a hundred and twenty as he flashed his headlights to make a clearway through the dawdling traffic, not because he was aware of being in a hurry, but in order to give the frustrated six-litre engine some exercise. Go, baby, go, he urged in the fast lane.

Laura was projecting herself through time. He would arrive and find her sitting regally outside, looking through some papers. No, I haven't been here long. I was late myself. The drink before lunch. He would talk, talk, talk. Of his phenomenal success. How stupid everyone else was. She must listen, smile, agree. Listen, smile, agree.

71

She was used to doing that. Imagine he was a client. That was the key to composure. Give no hint of the sour pain of apprehension cramping the gut. Reveal nothing. She must pretend to be hungry. Drink little, sip slowly. Listen, smile, agree. Be immune to those reminders of the past. Don't talk fast as women do when they're agitated. Reveal nothing. You know why you're here.

She strolled round the rigidly landscaped garden of this stone-built, perfectly restored, perfectly accoutred former manor house now turned gourmet staging post for the wealthy rolling up in their perambulating offices. Eventually she tired of the garden, the roses, the honeysuckle, the lupins and delphiniums, the rolled-out lawn, the topiaried bushes, the tinkling fountain spraying over into the pond stocked with fantailed, colour-splattered fish of rare origin.

She came to rest on the terrace and within seconds a white-gloved hand placed a chilled, frosted glass gently fizzing with an indeterminate fruit-scented cocktail on the white wrought-iron table in front of her. Arranging the silk pleats of her cream skirt in their correct folds, Laura sat waiting but pretending not to wait and bent down to open her briefcase.

She had not spotted Jack running across the lawn. There he was, his lips on hers. She withdrew for a fraction of a second, but her brief moment of revulsion was unobserved. Pink Heaven on his lips.

'Hi, Laura. You look great.'

She wiped her clownlike imprint from his mouth.

'Really. Fantastic.' He eyed her up and down as though sizing up a property ripe for development. 'What's with the legs?'

Laura raised an eyebrow quizzically.

'Long skirt. What's this?'

She gave a dismissive half turn of her head, watching the waiter approach with a menu the size of the Domesday Book.

'I mean, you've got great legs. I like to see them.'

'You looked at them for ten years, Jack. I didn't think you needed reminding.'

For a few seconds he scanned the heavy parchment pages. 'Have whatever you like. Forget the diet.'

'I never needed to go on a diet, remember?'

'Come on. You were always on to some crack-pot system. Always following some goddamn quack. Used to drive me crazy.'

Laura checked herself, but even so her cheeks flushed with irritation. That 'always' hurt. 'Always' preceded the lies created in retrospect. You always did this, you always did that. 'Always' gave trivial happenings the status of judicial evidence, justifying the condemnation of a marriage. Did he remember anything as it was? Were all women the same to Jack? Was there one female cardboard cut-out stand-up model with the same face but different names . . . did any of them matter? Jack leaned towards her and cupped her face with his hands.

'Enjoy. I've cancelled everything. Just for you. We're gonna have a great time. Right?'

Laura smiled. It was time to smile.

'Look at that sun. That greensward. That's real long-term cultivation. What a place. Put this in the Hamptons, and you'd be talking big bucks.'

Once Laura had regarded his enthusiasm as love of life, love of her. He never said, 'Could you possibly? . . . Would you mind awfully?' like the wilting young men who had handed her out of taxis and petitioned for a goodnight kiss. Today the energy of his phrases seemed as false as the pumped-up cheerfulness of a broker selling a life policy.

Two smartly suited, prematurely fleshy young men passed them by on their way to eat. One looked at Laura and gave Jack that particular man-to-man glance of knowingness. You've done all right. Wouldn't mind being in your shoes. And it was Friday. Jack returned the look with a complacent grin.

'I could eat the whole menu right now. What's happened to the service around here? Hey!' Jack caught the watchful eye of the manager and shouted, 'We haven't got all day.'

The manager instantly beckoned them into the dining room and sat them at a prominent table as though preparing for the levée of Louis XIV, whipping out chairs, pushing in chairs, unfolding napkins, nudging a misplaced spoon an inch further from the battery of mirror-polished cutlery, adjusting the position of the vase of flowers on the table, moving Jack's briefcase out of sight, each gesture knowingly and elaborately accomplished. The softly lit room was populated by corpulent men whose sagging stomachs, briefcases and gleaming, barely worn shoes were concealed by the pale almond napery. They leaned back, breathing in the expense-account aura of their exclusive temple, salivating as a large silver rotunda was lifted up high by a waiter with the solemnity of a priest giving a blessing. There were gasps at the outcome, a beautifully modelled and glazed pastry duck sitting on a bed of deep green sea asparagus. And there were further gasps as a waiter came forward with a knife, slipped the blade round the circumference of the duck's body and neatly separated the top half from the lower. From the nether regions of the sacrificial bird arose plumes of steam and as they cleared those nearby were able to see four quails, in immaculately garnished splendour, offset by roundels of foie gras. The first act was over and accompanied by clapping from around the room. Then there was a pause as the gamey aroma pervaded the dining room, and even jaded appetites were coaxed into expectation. With perfect timing, another knife-wielding acolyte appeared and proceeded to dissect the tiny carcases into bite-size pieces fit for mouths shored up by Harley Street dentists.

'What a show,' said Jack. 'Clever, these guys. Must have practised that little number. I like to see a well-run establishment. I always tell my boys if you're doing a hamburger, if you're doing a T-bone, even if you're doing French fries, do it like it's the last meal on Death Row. Do it right. That's what the Brits don't understand. OK, so this place is in a different league, but the principle's the same.'

'I think I'll have the langoustines followed by turbot,' Laura announced, as two waiters arrived to take up the right position at the correct distance from the table.

'And for me, double portion of quail, and I mean two birds. I'll have the wild salmon tartare to start. And it'd better be wild, none of that stuff swimming around in a tank.'

The waiter inclined his head, interpreting the order back into the elaborate French of the menu.

The second-waiter moved forward as the first retreated.

'A Puligny Montrachet for my wife – that do you? And a bottle of Chateau Latour.'

Laura winced.

'What's up?'

'We divorced, remember?'

Jack wagged his finger. 'Correction. You divorced. Look, let's not get into a dispute. We're friends now. I want to keep it that way.'

'Not wife.'

'Oh. Habit, babe. Anyhow, what do I say? Meet my ex? Do me a favour.'

'You could call me Laura.'

'Yeah. I could.'

Jack sucked in the salmon which had travelled from Scotland on the overnight train, been prepared by one hand, then another, perfected by a third and supervised by the *chef de cuisine*, and consumed it within one and a half minutes, wiping his face as a trace of sauce started to dribble down his chin. Then, with a clatter, he stuck his knife and fork face down, apart, American style, on the plate.

'I see Leone shares are still on the up. Everything else goes down. How do you manage it?'

'I see what these guys around here don't see.' Jack gestured round the room. 'Potential. I grab the cookies when they're still in the oven. And that's what you've

75

gotta learn. Act small and think big till the moment's right.'

'I don't quite understand,' she continued, slowly edging a morsel of langoustine into her mouth.

'Look,' explained Jack. 'I read about some guy, a property dealer in the north of England, who opened up a pricey eating place in the sticks. That doesn't add up, I think to myself. Anyway, this guy gets himself a big spread on the business pages. Why? A, because he's made the connection between owning property and running restaurants. B, because he's charging twice as much as anyone else and getting away with it. C, he's already talking of expansion. And the big D, he's got a marketing policy. That's sharp. Even though I knew he'd fail with this one, I liked the sound of Charlie Braithwaite.'

'Charlie who?'

'Braithwaite. So I go up there, see the potential and buy in. With my catering experience and his owning chunks of Bradford, Leeds and Manchester, I couldn't lose. Next year there'll be a Charlie's Brasserie in all three. I found he'd got the wrong idea, understandable when you start. Too upmarket. They don't understand it there. Give 'em what they want. Basics, no frills, friendly service, snappy uniforms, happy hour cocktails. I understand these northern guys. They're like Texans. Warm, friendly people. But you don't give caviar to the cat. Braithwaite understood, once I'd analyzed the figures. Now we're talking about a theme park in the Dales. The working man down the ages kind of stuff where the kids can work a shuttle and loom, dig out coal.'

'Do we get the working woman, too?'

'Oh yeah. Trust you! The girls can bake their own bread in a genuine farmhouse kitchen. It's all worked out.'

'The girls worked down the mines. Pulling trucks.'

'If you say so. Anyhow, we found a great site and I'm getting a consortium together. There's big money up North but they keep it quiet so the southerners won't be after it, that's what Braithwaite told me. He's a real character. Built like a ton of bricks but moves nearly as fast as I do.'

'I thought the Dales were a conservation area?'

'What d'ya mean? This is conservation. Preserving the past. That's what *we're* doing, and if it keeps the kids of the unemployed from beating the hell out of old ladies, they'll buy it. And, like Braithwaite said, a theme park is environmentally sound. Not like coal mines or chemical factories. Nowadays, you've gotta paint your arse green to make the sun shine out.'

Jack noticed that Laura had put down her knife and fork, her dish only half completed.

'Anything wrong? You feeling OK? Not time of the month? Still having trouble?'

'No, no, I'm fine.'

Forced exposure. Female secrets no longer secret. Stained sheets, doubled-up with cramps, the painkillers, dreading long journeys, the looks of pity. You just rest. Know something? I really like it now, shame you don't, there's no shame. What's bugging you? English boarding school, junior concentration camp, that's what's bugging you. Why shouldn't I know? I'm your husband, relax babe . . . Leave me alone. Leave me alone . . .'

'I eat slowly. Remember?'

'Yeah, yeah. Hurry up. My quails'll be getting over-cooked. I like 'em rare. Always like some blood with game. Like they do in France.'

'Jack.'

'I'm listening, babe.' He was stretching up in his seat, watching for the waiter's eye, his head turned away.

'Don't worry. He hasn't forgotten.'

'I don't want those quails heated in the micro.'

'Not here.'

'Wanna bet?'

Laura watched Jack, anxiety level rising and decided to postpone her contribution to the conversation.

'Everything OK?'

'Fine. Really good. Lovely sauce.'

'Workwise?'

'Workwise? Fine too.'

Laura put down her knife and fork for the last time and Jack sighed with relief. 'Everyone says I eat too fast. What do you reckon?'

By the time Jack had consumed four courses and, after telling the waiter which were best, had selected six portions from a trolley of cheeses from the choicest regions of France, Italy and even Britain, he paused from devouring and put his hand on Laura's arm.

'Tell me. How's your little company going? You busy?'

'Quite good really.'

'You were silly to move, babe. If you wanted more space, I could have got you one hell of an office suite, landscaped gardens, twenty-four-hour security, de luxe entrance . . .'

'Oh. Where?'

'Aylesbury, Bucks. I'm opening another Pizza Palace down there in a new precinct.'

'Bit far out, Jack. My clients walk to appointments, occasionally take a cab. Otherwise they won't come.'

'Have it your own way, Laura. But it's not business sense. Not with your overheads.'

'I got a good deal, and I designed it myself so it didn't cost that much.'

'I know what "not much" means to you. How much rent you paying? How much the staff cost you?'

Laura told him, a little more than the truth. His reaction was the same as a doctor listening to an overweight patient confessing to his weekly diet.

'Jesus! You wanna have permanent cash-flow problems?'

'What do you mean?'

'You must be screwing the bank manager. You're crazy. Do you think running a company is like going shopping down Sloane Avenue?'

'Of course I don't.'

'Sorry, Laura, but you really don't have a clue. Not. A.

Clue. And how do you think I feel watching you heading for one hell of a mess?'

'Please understand, Jack,' said Laura, putting her head to one side and gazing into his eyes. 'This is the first thing I've done by myself. I'm not like you. I'm not in business to be biggest and best. I just want to create something that's mine. When I go into my office I feel ten feet tall, I feel at home. Do you understand?'

'Well . . . Kinda. But I don't see you in business.'

'I'm on my own, Jack. I have to make the decisions myself and don't have an experienced team around me like you do, so it's very likely I'm making some mistakes.'

Jack lit a cigar and pondered. 'There's mistakes and mistakes.' He leant back, wreathed in smoke and his mouth twitched. 'What you need is a long-term plan. You gotta know where you see yourself in ten years' time. Twenty years' time. That's what it's all about. When I started serving burgers, I knew that was only the start. Leone Leisure was already a concept. I was heading up main street, not getting caught in some goddamn side alley. Where are you heading? Come on. Think.'

'I know what I want.'

'That's a start, babe. What—'

'Let me finish.'

'Sure, sure.'

'What I really want is to open my own restaurant. And I want it to be the best in the country. A three-star Michelin place with a British chef.'

'Huh! What? You joking!'

'No. I've thought about it for a long time. I think I know what it takes. As long as I can do it the way I want it. When I've made enough money from my business, I'll do it.'

'Now I know you're really crazy. Number one crazy is you can't run a top-class place with a British chef. Number two crazy, no-one makes money with a one-off. Number three crazy, you know what investment you're into with that kind of a place?'

'A lot.'

'Two mill for a start, let alone extra injection capital when the dining room's empty due to economic downturn. You got that kind of money?'

'You know I haven't. But with the right person and the right place, I could raise it.'

'OK. Honey, here's my cheque book. Two mill and you open. Whose gonna call the tune? Who owns the goddamn place? Jack Leone. OK, so you do your thing and I'm not getting my return. Three-star Michelin, forget it. Percentage we're talking. I'm gonna make sure there's a turnaround to give me my profit, 'cause even for you Laura, I don't give handouts. If money doesn't make money, you shouldn't be in business. Any business. Restaurants, like everything else, are a pure case of economics.'

'If that was so, there wouldn't be any good restaurants anywhere.'

'You may not call my places good restaurants, but everyone else does. They're packed. That's what I call a good restaurant.'

'This is a good restaurant.'

'Sure. Know who owns it? Meadowside Hotel Group. They bought in last month. Place was on the rocks. Needed somewhere to entertain potential big earners, looks good in the company report, flagship enterprise. If they've any sense, they'll build a small hotel in the grounds. Forty-bedder would do it. Conference facilities. Health centre. Then you're talking. You get the idea?' He placed his smouldering cigar on the ash tray. 'I'm going to the bathroom.'

'When he returned, Laura was slowly sipping her coffee, her head bowed.

'You OK?'

Laura looked up. 'I'm thinking.'

'Is that really what you wanna do? Open up a restaurant?'

'Yes.'

'Why didn't you ever say?'

'Perhaps you never asked me.'

'Hey. You don't go asking what your wife wants if she's happy.' Jack saw Laura turn away. 'OK, OK. I know . . . Tell you what. How about this for a deal? The Aylesbury development. Well, we're planning a restaurant. Good location. Smart neighbourhood. How about you set the whole thing up? Design, chef, menu. I'll give you a couple of years. Couple of years to learn the business. My finance director's great on that kind of stuff. Two-year option. That's what I'm giving you. How about that?'

'Jack, I couldn't. I just couldn't.'

'I'd give you anything. Didn't I always? When did I say no? I'm giving you a chance to do it your way. No strings. For two years.'

'It's . . . it's not where I want it to be. I do appreciate it but—'

'Like you appreciated everything else I gave you? What's wrong? What do I do wrong all the time?'

'We've been over that, Jack. Please.'

'I still don't see. You knew what kind of guy I was. Am. The girls mean nothing. Never did.' He leaned forward. 'I thought you loved me. In your way.'

Laura looked into his strong, well-proportioned face, the long, fine dark hair and was unable to reply for a while.

'Perhaps – I don't know,' she began. 'Perhaps living with you was too safe. Perhaps I want to take my own risks.'

Jack reached for another cigar, lit it and puffed volumes. 'There's a big difference. I was raised to take risks. When I was seven I had my own gang. Never knew who was round the corner. All Pop wanted was for me to be good at sums. I quickly figured out that some things make money and some things don't, and that's what he meant by being good at sums. And if you make money other guys want to take it off you, so you have to fight. That's why I am where I am. I ever tell you I had my own business at ten, cooking popcorn in Ma's kitchen?'

'I think you did, Jack.'

'Well, when I was doing that think what you were doing. Reading about the time Christopher Robin went down to Buck-ing-ham Palace. I tell you one thing, Christopher Robin may have done his sums like a good boy but he sure didn't understand about profit.'

The dining room had become quiet, the waiters wondering if they might soon be able to give the signal to clear. One was bold enough to approach. 'Would you care to take liqueurs in the Blue Room, sir?'

'Yeah. Why not? I don't need to get back into town for a while.'

Laura glanced at her watch and gave herself half an hour.

'Reminds me of home,' remarked Jack, gazing round at the prints of English country flora, the Regency striped wallpaper, the chintz-covered heavy frilled settees and matching armchairs lavishly positioned around the room, the towering arrangements of flowers arising from ceramic trunks reflected in Venetian mirrors, the sporting water-colours and pallid prints of bygone varieties of roses arranged like a military parade across the blue striped wallpaper.

'You used to do stuff like this, didn't you?'

'Only when I had to. It was never exactly my style.'

'You know, our place still looks good. I haven't changed a thing. People come, they still admire. Ask the name of the designer. I've had several offers. No, I say. No way.'

'I wouldn't do it like that now.'

'I've got to say, Laura, you had a real talent going there. Look at that woman with the same name as you, Laura . . . Ashford? Ashton?'

'Ashley.'

'That's who. Yeah. She did OK.' Jack leaned over and stroked Laura's knee through the silk pleats. 'You OK?'

'Yes. Yes. I'm fine.'

He moved his hand upwards and stroked between her legs.

82

'Don't do that,' said Laura icily.

'You still turn me on. I feel randy as hell. There's no-one looking.' Jack turned round, observing a couple sound asleep, snoring gently in the corner in front of two empty glasses.

'Is this your way of presenting me with the bill for lunch?' Laura said, moving to the other end of the settee.

'Ah hah! I knew you were hiding something from me.'

'Hiding what?'

'There's another guy. I knew there was. One of the cheerleaders in the Team is it?'

Laura rose to her feet and stared down coldly at him. 'There isn't anyone. And I don't want anyone. Not even you.'

'From anyone else that would be a slap in the face, but from you . . . I guess some girls simply aren't turned on by sex.'

'If that's what you want to think.'

'You never were that keen.'

'Perhaps I had other things on my mind.'

Jack laughed. 'Sometimes you're like a kid. Maybe you should have screamed at me once in a while.'

'Any minute now.'

She started walking out of the room, and Jack followed close behind. 'I've signed the bill,' he said as he passed reception. They both blinked when confronted with the searing light outside, for the late-afternoon sun was still strong, but neither spoke.

In the car park, Jack stopped in his tracks. 'You can always call me. Any time. Keep in touch, Laura.'

She watched him fling himself into his Ferrari, slip on the black-screened, gold-edged sunglasses, turn up the quadraphonic stereo to full-blasting thudding cacophony and waited until the racing tyres raised a tornado of gravel. For an instant she admired him, the man who had made himself impervious and crashed into her life, then she shuddered and wondered what had brought her to marry this man who would clear a jungle if it stood in his way.

The air conditioning was turned up high, the cream blinds closed when she returned to the cool order of the Studio. Everything was neatly ranged for her attention, letters ready to sign, a copy of faxes logged in and out, copies of briefings, all the cuttings laid out in sequence on her desk. Leo had stayed late. As she removed her creased silk jacket, thinking she would never wear this suit again – it would conjure up that place, his hands, his voice – there was a moment when the strain showed.

'Tough lunch?' Leo asked.

'Not really, but I don't think anything will come of it. The food was good, though. The place was packed.'

One of the telephones in the outer office rang and Laura jumped. 'I'm not in.'

Leo left to answer it, then went quickly downstairs. Laura looked towards the Studio from behind her desk, and in spite of the cool air purring round the room she felt clammy with apprehension. Who could be at reception? She wasn't expecting anyone at this late hour on a Friday evening. Howard? He would have rung, surely?

The apprehension lasted only for a moment. She had to work out a plan for John Crabtree. He must be getting desperate. Suppose he had gone back to Yorkshire without telling her?

Leo walked through into the Sanctum, smiling and cradling in his arms an enormous bouquet, garlanded with streamers of red ribbon. 'Another tribute from a grateful client.'

'I hope it's anonymous then we can both guess.' Laura peeled back the cellophane and smelt the rich scents of summer profusion. 'How lovely.' Dear Howard. Flowers to remind her of him. Every time he went abroad and had been forced by family pressures to go straight home from the airport instead of following his impulse to knock on her door, he sent her a floral apology for his silence. She kept his vivid flowers until the petals shrivelled.

'Look, you've missed it.' A tiny envelope lay at her feet. Leo bent down, handed it to her and she ripped it open.

There was a small, gilt-edged card inside covered in the round loopy writing of handwritten menus chalked on blackboards. The unfamiliar lettering prevented Laura from instantly recognizing the familiar phrases. For a second. Then she tore up the card and tossed it in the basket.

'Why do the wrong people always send flowers? Here. You take them.'

'Do you want me to come in tomorrow?' asked Leo.

'That's sweet of you, but I don't think I'll need you this Saturday.'

'Goodbye then.'

Leo kissed Laura on the cheek, gathered up his briefcase and hoped there wouldn't be a crush on the tube. He liked the flowers. All those colours were rather jolly, even though he didn't have a place to put them in his tiny bed-sit. In a few months' time he would start looking for a flat . . .

'To remind you of good times. Love you always. Jack.' Courtesy of the nearest Interflora. On his account. She imagined the call. No, you choose. No price limit.

'Did he ever buy you presents, Mrs Leone?'

Oh yes, lots of presents. Fur coats. He knew I hated fur. Huge rings I couldn't wear. Endless voluminous silk negligees as though he cared what was inside them. Large bottles of Joy which I gave to the daily, but he didn't notice. Oh, yes, and a camouflage-painted Isuzo four-wheel-drive truck with a cattle grid at the front equally at home in a jungle or desert, but laughable on the Oxford ring road. Everything he gave me was oversized, expensive, stocked by Harrods and chosen by his secretary.

The divorce laywer spent many costly hours trying to find out why she had rejected Jack. Would you say you were unable to accept gifts, Mrs Leone? No, I've just told you, he never bought me anything I wanted. Perhaps your husband may not have had the best taste, but from what you have told me so far he had a loving disposition. Did he ever inflict physical violence? He slapped me once when he was drunk. Did you report this? Good heavens, no! Did he, how shall I say, indulge in unusual and unacceptable sexual practices? To me, yes. But were they unusual and unacceptable? I don't know what you mean. But you were unhappy. Unhappy? Yes. Yes I was. Looking back on it, I was desperately unhappy. This is hardly grounds for divorce, Mrs Leone. He wanted to keep me on a chain. Literally? No, not literally. Mrs Leone, did you love your husband when you were first married? Love him? I suppose I did. I admired him. Then. Ah, I see.

Let us move to the financial arrangements. Were these satisfactory? Oh yes. Jack never queried anything. He liked me to spend money. And did you do so? Only on what I thought he would like. Such as? Improvements for the house. Dinner parties. Mrs Leone, this is really a most difficult case, but we have to ensure that Mr Leone is unable to counter-claim on the grounds of desertion. Are you absolutely sure, in every respect, that you left the marital home freely and of your own volition? Yes, I did. No mitigating circumstances whatsoever? I just wanted to. I'd had enough. I see.

This may be painful for you. Were there any other women? Oh yes. Always. Always? You mean there were several? Yes, several. But he never took them seriously. And did you? How could I? I had everything. They had nothing. Jack kept his love for me. Mrs Leone, what we have here is a history of sexual misdemeanours. This is not a characteristic of marriage. I think we have a sustainable case of cruelty here, but I'm afraid you will have to furnish us with evidence of consistent adultery for that is what we are talking of, is it not? The courts will not accept the wife's suspicions on this point. Am I right in thinking that the reason for your leaving the matrimonial home was because you were in a serious state of unbalance due to your husband's promiscuous behaviour? No, not really. Think again, Mrs Leone.

She did think again. Back to her childhood. Genteel poverty. Hiding from her schoolfriends that her education was paid for by a trust, that her parents lived in penury, that they didn't go off skiing in the winter, sailing in the summer, house parties in between. Timid well-spoken Laura Douglas had nightmares of living in a council flat on the new estate where the rough kids lived . . . The private detective spent two months following Mr Leone's Ferrari, with the help of a powerful motorbike and a messenger's uniform. He also became familiar with the streets where it might be found parked on certain nights of the week. Mrs Leone obtained her divorce.

Laura Douglas filled up her glass, kicked off her shoes and prepared to attack the evening's workload in welcome solitude. There were glowing reports of Petrushka's, but this did not surprise her. Even 'the rads', those writing mildly left of centre, had enjoyed themselves and they liked to show their appreciation, occasionally, of the delights available to the moneyed classes. 'Champagne socialism' had long since ceased to be a term of abuse and now implied the democratisation of wealth. Anyone could walk in, explained Laura, sit down in Petrushka's, have a glass of champagne and some toast and caviar for the same price as some ghastly microwaved steak and kidney pudding, a limp salad, a reconstituted apple pie and a glass of no-alcohol wine of disgraceful parentage served in the pub down the road. Five times as many calories, she had calculated, not to mention the appalling additives, the sugar and salt, needed to make this atrocious apology for a meal palatable.

Laura had insisted that, at least for the opening, the caviar was fit for a connoisseur, challenging guests to give considered opinions as to which was superior, the potent Beluga or the assertive Sevruga and to ponder the virtues of the lesser Osietre. Once Petrushka's reputation had reached its publicity peak, with inevitable mentions in the high-style monthlies and business magazines, the quality, she reassured the anxious owners, could go down a notch or two and they would start making a profit. She would introduce the cheaper pressed caviar, the portions would be smaller and there would be sparkling wine as an option to the champagne. A selection of euphoric reviews would be reproduced with a touch of Russian graphics and placed in a mirror-frame to hang in the window, perhaps held up by a mocking gilded Cupid – why not – against a draped red velvet hanging. Very tongue-in-cheek. A little task for Antony.

She picked up the phone and rang Stephen Boyce. He was just going off for dinner, having finished lunch a mere two hours ago but he was prepared to make himself late for Laura.

'I'm ringing to say I liked your piece,' she began.

'It's a good place. And, on reflection, the caviar is very, very good. I had some with scrambled eggs. Very more-ish I must say. I've left a tiny bit for breakfast.'

'You know you can drop in whenever you want to. Be my guest.'

'You're a darling. Is it packing the crowds yet?'

'They're starting to come . . . By the way, we're going to change the colour of the walls. I think you were right to mention that.'

'One is getting a little chilled by the cool look. A touch of warmth, I thought.'

'Oh, by the way, the French trip. I thought you might like to take in a decent restaurant so I've booked a table at Antoine's – just you and Didi. So you can disappear discreetly.'

'What a treat! I tasted Bernard's cooking when he guested at the Inn on the Park. If he's as good in France as he is out of it—'

'They say he's about to get his third star.'

'Fantastic! Must rush. I'm going to see if Courtney's new chef is any good.'

'If he is, let me know. Is anyone representing him, do you know?'

'I'll find out.'

'Don't forget. Heathrow at eight a.m.'

'Bye.' Stephen made kissing noises down the phone and hung up.

Twelve excessive hours later, Stephen gave a loud burp as the doors of the departure lounge slid open. Heathrow again. Which desk? He rummaged in his shoulder bag and found a grubby piece of paper. The wrong grubby piece of paper. That was last week. The garlic heaved up his throat and he felt as steeped in alcohol as an oak wine vat which had been used for generations of vintages. Oh well, occupational hazard. Not having a clue as to where he was going gave today a certain piquancy. He had packed in five minutes. His mother took a week to prepare for the train journey from Bournemouth to London. August the fourth. Mother. Bournemouth. He must remember that.

A tall young man dressed in grey approached, stopped, stared and broke into a studied smile. Stephen could spot Public Relations even in a packed airport lounge. It was the tie, always clamouring for attention and that just-shaved, sun-bed tan look. If he ever got going on his modern *Inferno*, he'd have one of these despicables suspended up to the neck in a tank of boiling Bailey's Cream Liqueur. Laura, of course, was different, being possessed of Intelligence and Wit. She might not make Paradise, but he'd make sure she was comfortable in Purgatory.

'Hello. I'm Mark.'

'I do remember.'

'Good to see you, Stephen. Last time was the wild boar trip. That was such fun.' Mark smiled again. Stephen didn't. He wasn't selling anything.

'We're all set. Everyone's here. A super crowd. Let me check in your bag.'

Mark had the good sense not to tell him off for arriving ten minutes before take-off. Apparently they were heading for Tours, France. With a swift movement, he took out Stephen's ticket from his wooden slimline case (matt black rubber was awfully passé now), gave it to the sour man at the desk and looked infuriatingly affable, unforgivable at this early hour. Stephen followed Mark and strolled on to the plane. Inside, everyone was also smiling. Well, fancy. Darling Didi. He raised a hand in greeting, sat down and pondered his column, hiding himself behind the *New York Review of Books*. Anyone reading a literate journal on a plane journey was unlikely to be interrupted.

Petrushka's was filed away in Stephen's data system. Was it last Tuesday? He couldn't remember, but by now he had become used to not remembering once his copy had gone to bed. It was a day in the life of his cuttings file. Last night had ended with a finale of at least ten brandies. He should have refused, but the chef was so charming and so eager and one did need to sample the whole menu to get the feel of what he was aiming at. Was it a new interpretation of *cuisine du terroir*, a return to *cuisine bourgeoise* or an individual plundering of both? He would decide later.

What on earth was he going to fill his column with this week? Next week was agreed. France. Bread piece. Serious. (Laura's client, Bon Arôme bread, had coughed up for this trip, after all.) Will it, won't it, will it get the three-star Michelin? Antoine's was good for a lofty restaurant piece, serious assessment of the *joli* Bernard. Freeman starts Sunday Funday for Foodie Kids. Joke piece, good-quote piece. 'If they want to throw food at the wall, that's fine by me.' Get in a load of ten-year-olds and let them loose with a photographer. This week, though, was a pain and his brain was singularly lacking in effervescence.

'Would you kindly fasten your seat belt, sir?'

The air hostess had peered beneath his paper, having spotted a rebel.

'I thought there was a delay,' said Stephen, without looking up. As there was always a delay on aeroplanes, with either something to fix or something clogging up the pathway to the sky, this was a safe excuse.

'We do ask passengers to keep their seat belts fastened

prior to take-off,' intoned the automated keeper of order and demonstrator of oxygen masks.

Stephen sighed and gave in, saving his energy for more worthwhile, cerebral activities, and extended his belt so that it did not remind him of his bulging stomach.

It had been suggested by his editor that the following subject would be most welcome: strawberries. The new Euro-strawberry, developed by biotechnologists in France and now flooding the market (bigger, better, longer-lasting, hated by birds, loved by supermarkets) versus organic versions (smaller, better, lasted a day once picked, loved by birds, hated by supermarkets). Yes, of course, very interesting. (Why couldn't the bloody farming correspondent do it?) Oh well, so be it. She who gaveth contracts, took away contracts, and raised up expiring contracts from the deathbed of oblivion, had spoken. One needed a new, provocative approach to the strawberry, avoiding the hackneyed paths of more pedestrian writers on rival food pages. Suppose one started with the Perfect Strawberry. How did one define it? What was the essence of strawberry-ness? Stephen strayed from the limitations of terrestrial fact and press briefings from government-aided agencies to embrace his poetic muse in a Strawberry Rhapsody.

Or, more precisely, a panegyrical meditation on the shape of this inspired fruit. Female, certainly. A breast? A small adolescent breast, perhaps. Just the right degree of roundness, fullness with the hint of angularity at the tip. Like the crimson of a setting sun over springtime Tuscan hills. Pitted like the beauty spots on a courtesan, signalling perfection by imperfection. And now, whence this strawberry? Plucked or eaten? Stephen glanced over his paper at Didi, leaning out into the aisle, sucking round the contours of a chocolate truffle. This poem would be for her. Her parted lips would caress the fruit, her white teeth would sink slowly through the succulent deeper red of yielding flesh to the hard white core, spurting scarlet honey juice on silken sheets . . . Alas. The hallowed season of the strawberry was long in coming, short in ripe fruition. Taunting nature, cruel mistress of the appetite . . . Stephen fumbled for his battered notebook which he kept in the inside pocket of his jacket and wrote '"Ode to a Strawberry" by Stephen Boyce'.

Interrupting the languid flow of his poetic imagination, his stomach once more imposed its presence, regurgitating the warm, acrid taste of garlic and barely blanched, minimally cooked, minimally digestible green vegetables which eddied up through the oesophagus and exploded into his mouth.

The plane took off and as soon as the floor tilted back to the level, Stephen pressed the button over his head. His palate demanded champagne, even though it would have to be a half of semi-tepid Moët. Where was that itinerary? Stuffed in the duty-free bag. For hour upon endless hour, he would have to endure every hygienic inch of the bread factory. But then, after all, it was only twenty-four hours out of his life, twenty-four hours when he didn't have to make a decision about whether to stay in and wash his piled-up underwear, catch Didi's *Table for One* on TV or write a few more paragraphs of the Novel, resist the temptation of an eminently describable, delicious and memorable five-course dinner, paid for by somebody else . . .

Didi came running down the aisle. She had put on weight again. He hadn't noticed in the crush at Petrushka's. Abundance suited her.

'Stephen, darling, have a truffle. Absolutely the best I've ever tasted.' He gave her the obligatory kiss, and she placed a melting chocolate on his raddled tongue. 'Tourist class. Not on. And you should see who's here. My dear! Hacks' coach party. I'm not going back with them.'

Didi's perfumed breath activated her voice box, producing husky sounds which dropped an octave and swept past his ear.

'I think I'm going to be naughty.'

'With whom, may I ask?' enquired Stephen.

Didi looked hurt. 'I'll think of someone.'

That first evening in France (there would only be one evening this time) they were spirited away on a fifty-kilometre journey (car and driver provided by Bon Arôme) alone together, salivating at the thought of the awe-inspiring gastronomic pleasure which lay ahead (courtesy of Bon Arôme) instead of drinking *vin ordinaire* and listening to folk music in a local *hostellerie* with the others. Didi put her head on Stephen's shoulder, deliriously happy.

'Which would you rather? Anticipate with desire or look back in satisfaction?' Stephen asked.

'Oh, I'll have the desire. It lasts longer. Satisfaction is boring, don't you think?'

'I can't say it's one of life's major experiences.'

'Mind you . . .' Didi nibbled his ear. 'We've never tried it.'

Dinner at Antoine's, Didi and Stephen agreed later, had its good points, but the place lacked *l'esprit de gastronomie*, the visible and aural evidence of appreciation. The other diners were '*très sérieux*', which Didi attributed to the women they were with – 'Must be wives' night' – and the mud-coloured wallpaper. Stephen's wit was becoming more and more devastating, Didi's shrieks of laughter more unrestrained, but they ignored the occasional mutterings of '*les Anglais, ça se voit*'. They were being rather bad, Stephen decided.

'Sh.'

'Am I being loud?'

'A weeny bit. I suppose I'd better interview the chef,' said Stephen, cramming the last *petit fondant* into his mouth at the conclusion of the meal.

'Aren't you going to write about it?'

'Can't make up my mind. I mean, the food was competent—'

'But not inspired. Won't Laura be expecting . . . ?'

'No need to be crude. All right. I'll do a quickie.'

'And then?' said Didi expectantly, nuzzling his neck.
'Early to rise.'
Didi lowered her eyelashes and raised them fluttering.
'Work, my gorgeous.'
'Oh dear. I've eaten too much again,' she sighed.

Mark had done his job efficiently, knowing that one slip-up would invoke the combined ire of Stephen and Didi and banishment from the Team. A decent lunch with the local Chambre de Commerce had followed the informative tour of batch production. The white-hatted, white-booted, white uniformed bakers, they were told by the marketing manager, possessed all the skills and training of the traditional artisan allied to the benefits of microprocessor-controlled technology. Didi, who was not listening, swore that she saw them pick up some dough from the floor and throw it back into the mixer. 'He's for the guillotine,' whispered Stephen. 'Honestly?' shrieked Didi, through her visitors' mask of hygiene. 'Sh,' the boss, Monsieur Bon Arôme himself said. 'Please to follow me. Forgive my English. *Excusez-moi*, if I explain you some technical aspects.'

Food factory tour completed, questions answered, notes taken, samples given, statistics in a plastic folder, half an hour for shopping. Didi and Stephen escaped together and drooled over *confits d'oie, pâtés, tartes aux cerises, pâtisserie,* candied fruits, *fruits à la liqueur, bonbons* . . . They had each bought a large reinforced Prisunic bag conveniently provided with wheels to accommodate the few little things one had to take back.

The plane was due to leave for London at five. The coach was ready. Mark was ready. Everybody was ready. And Caliope Fortescue, still sporting her weatherproof trousers and carrying aloft a gigantic earthenware pot of Etruscan pattern in which, she informed everybody, she intended to grow a vine on her patio, was ready.
'Two are missing, dear,' she informed Mark. 'Stephen

94

and Didi, if I'm not mistaken. Do we go without them or are we called upon to make the supreme sacrifice and have another meal in France?'

'They're following up a story,' he explained. 'So they'll be getting a later plane.'

'I wonder if Bon Arôme has a budget for hanky-panky?' she retorted acidly, wishing for a moment that her magazine had a more impressive circulation so as to merit greater flexibility of travel. No doubt they would be flying first class. Caliope stumped towards the coach and announced to Mark in particular and the group in general, 'I have to be in town for eight as Lord and Lady Knowles have kindly invited me to dinner. Tell Air France to pull out the throttle, or whatever their chaps do to go faster.'

Stephen returned to his poky hotel room as the rest of the group were attacking the in-flight 'dinner' and itemized the drawbacks in case he ever met a director of the chain who owned it. There was no video channel; the bed was punitive enough for a monk; the bathroom was lacking in free body lotions, shampoo, bubble bath, bathrobes and other creature comforts he had learned to expect, and there was a packet of instant coffee standing next to the kettle. Ugh. Nothing worth taking.

Nothing worth taking from the bread factory, either. That dreadful marketing man! He was destined for another circle in Stephen's *Inferno*, the Circle of Hypocrites. (The Gourmets had a place in Paradise.) The *croissants* were stale, the *baguettes* over-baked, the loaves pappy and the factory turned out not even to be French but was owned by a familiar British conglomerate, part of their European initiative, he discovered, skimming through the Bon Arôme portfolio . . . Just a moment. Could this somewhat routine visit to Tours form the basis for his very own specially tailored (all expenses paid), chauffeured limo, best-hotel-suite, three-star Michelin-restaurant-reconnoître trip? Would his editor buy it? Yes, as long as the angle was serious.

Something about the impact of hypermarket food on rural France. Périgord, Alsace, the real food producers. Quality versus convenience. 'The French Resistance Lives Again' . . . 'Last time it was the Germans, now the brown-bagging Americans flooding the market with *le fast-food* are destroying the very essence of La France Gastronomique.' An idea was taking shape. He would talk to Laura about it.

Didi was in a bad mood because the long-awaited night of sensual passion with the man she loved had been sacrificed yet again to the demands of her belly. If she had stopped at the third course, if only, and had persuaded Stephen to do likewise, he might have been swept along on the airy waves of desire and then transported her. No, perhaps not, led her, yes, led her into his bedroom and revealed his manhood in all its glory whilst she slipped the Valentino blouse slowly off her shoulders and the crickets sang outside on the balcony . . . She knew that they were meant for one another, which she judged from similar fated relationships depicted in the romantic novels hidden under her frilly pillows which she devoured along with chocolate truffles before sinking into chaste sleep. Eating, she was forced to realize, was not the stuff of romance, although the occasional grape was allowed. How sad. But she understood. Any man's sexual fervour would come to grief following a six-course meal. And how could a man be heroic at the dinner table confronted with a plate of foie gras? Her life was destined to be tragic, she decided. She and Stephen would have a love as doomed as Byron and his sister Augusta. She sighed and touched Stephen's arm.

'Stephen, what are you thinking about?'

'Strawberries,' he replied. 'And you?'

'Really?' Maybe her destiny would change.

Bon Arôme, yuck. She was determined to cut out bread (thighs problem) even though the diet experts said you shouldn't. The journey back was as tedious as the journey out, even though she could stretch her legs in the extra first-class footage. How on EARTH was she going to be her usual WITTY, PROVOCATIVE self with a ten-minute slot devoted to BREAD?!

Hold on. Maybe there was a scare in it somewhere. Didn't bread contain gluten? And weren't some people allergic? Oh, yes. She could fix up a meeting with that incredibly sexy doctor who ran an allergy clinic. (Always good for the ratings.) Then she'd have a two-minute interview in which he'd say, 'Bread should be given a Government health warning.' Yes, she'd get him to say that, easy peasy. And they could have lunch beforehand, maybe even dinner afterwards. Where should she take him? . . . This week's programme would be provocative rather than witty. No harm in that. Her producer (gay, unfortunately, but a sweetie) liked heavy items occasionally, as long as they were brief.

As Didi scribbled notes beside him, Stephen counted the plusses. One carrier bag of different breads (over six hours old, no good). One half hour of tape about how you overcame the problems of continuous batch production when the Canadians had hoiked up the price of wheat, and how the French housewife was delirious about the pre-packed multi-grain loaf. And one hefty bottle of Macallan whisky from the duty free. Didi put aside her notebook and started to sniff her wrists, which she then held up under Stephen's nose.

'Smell me.'

'Do I have to?'

'I had to buy it. I thought it was very me. Do you find it sexy?'

'Overpowering.'

'Do you think it would put a man off?'

'Your fishmonger will love it.'

Didi turned to the window and sulked. Now Stephen was being impossible. He hoped her mood would last until they landed so he could jot down a thing or two in silence.

The flat in Notting Hill looked no different from when he had left. Food packages, books, papers, underwear still in the same place. Plants not watered, more yellowed leaves on the floor. Mary hadn't been again. Must be the arthritis. The mail could wait. Straight to the answerphone. Fifteen messages. Stephen opened the Macallan, lay on his bed and started the machine. Why couldn't people say what they wanted in a sentence? And what wimpish suburban voice was that? 'Hi Steve.' Hi Steve, indeed! Obviously someone from the Lower Circle, no-one he knew. Ah, good. A call from Laura. Where was his diary? Damn, he'd be in Rome that day.

5

Dear George. Having a great time, just looking around. Fantastic markets, and shops with food halls big as Leeds Town Hall. Beer lousy, hotel stinks, but you can't expect everything altho' I do. Am seeing Laura Douglas (not what you think) and smart people. I'm finding a job for both of us, don't worry. Write. John.'

John turned the postcard over. George would like it. Marlene Dietrich in a black dress sitting on her haunches, resting her chin on those fabled legs. Mum and Dad would get the Queen with corgis.

'One sausage, bacon, egg and chips,' called out the Italian behind the counter. The British breakfast, chalked up on a board in all its infinite variety: sausage egg bacon, sausage egg mushroom, sausage bacon tomato egg, bacon tomato egg, bacon mushroom . . . Those who said it was bad for you had never been hard up. Try lasting the day on a few spoonfuls of muesli and a glass of orange juice. Here they handed out the full greasy Monty, burnt-striped sausages fit to burst, eggs slithering about the thick white plate, chunks of pale pink fatty bacon curled up round the mound of thumb-sized chips, half a large watery wrinkly skinned tomato spilling its seeds, and a mug of tea, milky, sweet and lukewarm.

This was London's other world, almost extinct, an early-opening family café which had remained a café with chairs that could be moved and stacked, and peeling posters on the walls of the Leaning Tower of Pisa and Michelangelo's David to remind the owners of La Bella Italia and 'Sole Mio' of the land of olive oil. Mamma wiped over the Formica tables, still Formica, whilst Papa and his son manned the blackened frying pan and the till. They had hoped to return to Italy years ago, but, *ma che!*, everything expensive, not make enough money. John wanted to talk, sick of silence and his thoughts, but La Signora hurried away to clear, to wipe, to dry the mugs. The air was thick with the smell of smoking lard and high tar cigarettes burned to the stub. The men surrounding John were barricaded behind newspapers, flicking past the lascivious airbrushed girls with hobbies to pore over the sports results. These men without women wore short-sleeved sweat shirts, black-lettered slogans over the chest, bulging arms tattoo-covered with inky blue and purple red dragon curls and flower flourishes. When one of them rose to go, it was with slow reluctance, meeting no-one's gaze. No need to, nothing to say. No-one could tell them to get a move on, to shin up the scaffolding of a building site, to hasten the delivery of letters, to scoop up the cartons, cans, obsolete cookers, unwanted carpets, rotting fruit and vegetables heaped up on the pavement, to lose five minutes from their allotted break. They had chosen to work, that's right mate, and who would do their jobs?

Had he been stronger, had his health not failed, John's father could have been one of them, propelled into redeployment, fitness-fodder to keep the cities on their feet. And John, too, except that by some strange accident he possessed a skill which the rich would pay for. Over a million a year from cooking. If that's what you could get, he was going to get some of it. Not that he was greedy, mind, but it was his due. No gorging champagne-and-caviar bastard was going to make him live on a pittance and have breakfast as the main meal of the day. And why should he hole up in that filthy hotel? Cathy wouldn't even walk through the door. Heck, he hadn't sent her a card. On the other hand . . . No. She might decide to catch the coach. Laura Douglas would not appreciate that, a girl from Elland saying no, she'd rather have a Babycham.

There was no evidence of a post box. Perhaps there was

a system he knew nothing about, perhaps there was a different place for putting letters. In the bank, maybe, or the building societies he was constantly passing, where they would be safe from vandals and football hooligans gathering for a tribal ritual. He passed through the open wire-meshed door of Hassan's Mini Market and asked where he could post a letter. Here. Where? Give it to me. The store-keeper took his cards and John followed him down to the end of the shop, past the shelves crammed with perfumed dustbin bags, toilet rolls, lavatory cleansing fluids, dish-washer sweeteners, laundry deodorisers, carpet deodorisers, shoe deodorisers, air fresheners, room sprays, jumbo sizes of eco friendly and biological washing powder, garden-scented biodegradable cat litter and Doggie Pooper-Scoopers with disposable Fit-In-A-Trice bags of different sizes. Taking a key which was hanging round his neck, the shopkeeper opened a thick metal grille guarding a tiny no-man's-land of floor space, locked himself in, and put John's card in a sack.

'That will go first class, maybe arrive in two days,' he remarked as he reversed the procedure and went to his counter. As he seemed helpful, John asked him where to find an Underground station.

'Underground? Oh, tube train. You want tube?'

'I have to go to Goodge Street.'

The man went just outside the shop to point the way, and as he crossed the threshold with John there was a guttural, oscillating growl from inside. A black-faced Alsatian dog with a wide, spiked collar had sprung up and was standing on his hind legs with two paws on the counter. Without pausing to hear the end of his detailed instructions, John hurried away.

He found the Underground sign scrawled over a temporary board. An arrow pointed down some filthy steps, and as John started to descend he wondered why he was alone but continued until he found himself in an entrance hall. The ticket office was closed and next to the lift sign was a hand-scrawled notice: 'Out of Order. Sorry.' He heard the distant vibration of a train. Down another dimly lit stone staircase, and he quickened his rhythm, turning corner after acutely twisting corner and there was the platform. A large video monitor hung overhead showing sweaty close-ups of someone singing, but the few people waiting ignored it. Tourists probably, John thought, as some were looking at maps, carrying rucksacks or looking unbelievingly at the empty track. John went over to the graffiti-covered map on the wall, worked out where he would have to change and started sweating. He couldn't smoke, though he'd heard they had fires all the same. He fingered the cigarette packet in his pocket, and walked down the silent platform. A train rumbled in and squeaked to a halt at the platform on the other side and rumbled out. There was no phone, and if he walked up all those stairs he might miss the train. What a dolt he would seem. Sorry I'm late but . . . He imagined the remarks in the office. Can't even turn up on time. If he thinks we're going to hang around . . .

John sat down on a minimal plastic seat which barely supported his buttocks and leaned back against the tiled wall. He mustn't let London drag him down. He thought of his kitchen when it was going well, one dish after another coming out just right, everyone pleased. Maybe he should have tried harder, tried to talk Charlie into hanging on longer. Could have been a mistake, that. No. Mustn't look back. If today went wrong, there would be tomorrow. If André Bouchon, the legendary, the unbeatable, wouldn't see him today, he would make sure he saw him another day. George said he was a hard man, made even the strongest tremble. Man of the old school, dear boy, you know the type. Perhaps this was a test. Be persistent lad, said his father. Don't take no for an answer. Look on the bright side. Cheer up it may never happen. You'll be all right, son. You've got what it takes, let no-one say otherwise. He never took his own advice, of course, probably knew it was too late.

The track started to vibrate. John leaned out from the

platform and saw two distant spots of light. A train lurched into the station, every door black with crushed travellers attempting to look away from one another, to ignore the bodily contact by imagining a space of their own. The doors opened, but nobody moved, as though welded into a city monument depicting the miseries of war. John saw two people struggling to emerge farther down the platform, ran and hurled himself into the jam. If two had come out, one could go in, or so he reasoned. The door closed an inch from his face and the mass of people started to wriggle, sifting down, pressing in on the straphangers. 'Mind the doors,' crackled the loud-speaker, and the train slowly gathered speed. But after a couple of minutes, like a sprinter's all-out effort collapsing into seizure, the wheels stopped turning and the carriage was jolted into immobility. No-one moved. 'Open a window' demanded a voice. 'They're open,' said another as the temperature appeared to approach that of a bread oven. Then, silence again. A newspaper rustled. Hardened travellers gazed in front of them, suspended in time and space.

John, towering above most of the occupants, breathed in the hotter and hotter air rising to the top of the carriage, his damp shirt clinging against the prickling static from his one and only suit. The heat of the kitchen at full pressure was nothing like this dusty, muscle-sapping, brain-fatiguing heat. If this was London, he'd head straight back, straight into the cool, sheeting summer rain, the moors stretching into empty horizons, the streams forcing their way over rocks, the eerie sound of snipe diving into the empty sky, the bleating of sheep wandering unhindered over miles and miles of bleakness . . .

The train lurched, stopped, lurched and stopped again, and finally decided to inch forwards. How could anybody do a day's work after this? Maybe they didn't. 'Folks don't know what work is down South, and what's more they can't spell it.' One of the Braithwaite sayings repeated over the brandies in the Moorland Haven. John loosened his shirt. A few laborious stations later, the carriage had cleared enough for him to read the map opposite. Four more stations and then a change. What was Laura Douglas doing now? Was her car waiting below? Or was she sipping champagne with the grey men? Had she even thought about him? An appointment missed, that's all he might be.

An hour later than his appointment time, John ran down Mortimer Street, clipping the bodies of the slow-motioned visitors gazing at the jumbled objects outside shops which still sold some of life's necessities, past scruffy restaurants not handled by Laura Douglas, and arrived breathless outside the glass-fronted building of functional design.

He announced himself, the buzzer sounded and the door opened a fraction, admitting him into the foyer. Sitting behind a raised, shielded podium was a diminutive figure, the receptionist.

'Is Laura Douglas still here? I'm late. Got held up.'

The exquisite figurine at reception looked down at John and pressed a button. 'Mr Crabtree to see Laura Douglas. Do take a seat.'

'Will I be able to see her?'

'Why not? She's up there.'

'She hasn't left then?'

'No. Like I said, she's there. Go up if you like. Third floor. She won't mind.'

She looked like a model and John couldn't imagine her packed into a carriage deep below the streets.

'The lift's come,' she said.

'Hey,' said John. 'Are you from up North?'

'Can you tell? I left ages ago. Well, two years actually.'

'I'm Yorkshire myself.'

'Give over!' The tiny girl then dropped back to her almost perfect, over-articulated adopted accent. 'I tell you I wouldn't go back, not if you paid me. London's super.'

'We'll see,' John said, walking over to the lift and wondering if she would say yes.

Leo came strolling over, creaseless and noiseless. 'I'll be with you in a moment.' And then John saw him close the glass door of the Sanctum. Laura was standing up, pacing, tossing her hair, seemingly haranguing the young men standing to attention round the room. One would lean forward, lips moving, eyebrows raised, but John could hear nothing.

Then she gave a quick glance, as though she'd seen him down the far end of the Studio, parted the sliding door and called out, 'John, do forgive me. I'll be with you in a moment.'

Antony looked up from his screen. 'Sit down. Have Leo's chair, and help yourself to a drink. Over there, in the fridge. Laura will be with you in a moment.'

Everyone, it seemed, would be with him. In a moment.

'Sorry to keep you waiting,' added Antony. 'There's been a little crisis.'

'What sort of a crisis?' asked John.

'Oh the usual,' replied Antony, typing away.

Laura came out first, the Team followed, their faces serious.

'I simply don't expect people of your intelligence to act like idiots,' Laura said, and one by one they sloped off to their allotted space. 'Let's go,' she said to John. On the way down in the lift, she told him what a trial it was, no-one remembered the simplest things. London was impossible. Everyone was impossible. Nothing worked. No phones for a day and then the fax machine goes down. 'Sometimes I wonder why I bother.'

For a while, Laura said nothing, as the car wove in and out of traffic, hooting and flashing, as though on a mission of mercy.

'Did you get my message?'

'No.'

'I rang your hotel to say come later.'

'Oh. It took me an hour and a half to get here.'

'Really?' She didn't register.

'We are going to see André Bouchon, aren't we?'

105

'That's the idea.'

'Have you asked him if he wants someone?'

'You don't ask André. He does the asking, I do the suggesting.'

'I can't afford to muck about,' John said. 'I worry I might forget how to do things. You don't just stop and start, you know.'

'I know that.'

'Well, put it this way. I'm nervous, I'm hot and bothered, I'm out of cash and sick to bloody death of wearing this suit. Makes me look like a commis.'

At last, Laura turned to face him, instead of staring angrily out of the window. 'If you judged a chef by his suit, most of them would be out of work. But you look good to me.'

'Thanks. I could say the same.'

Laura picked a stray hair from his jacket, and smiled as she observed his face, as though daring him to come closer, but before he could decide, the car came to a halt.

Here it was, the fabled Aphrodite's. Laura swept in, past the gilded desk at reception and up the lushly carpeted cream stairs. John just had time to peer briefly through the etched glass doors leading to the dining room, and wonder at the opulence – oil paintings, dark wooden panelling, chandeliers, tapestry and widely spaced white-robed tables singled out in pools of light.

'John. Up here. The chef's office.'

He rushed up the stairs, to find Laura waiting outside a large panelled door. She knocked and they both entered. Chef's office? It was usually a term of abuse, describing a rickety desk hidden in the bowels of a restaurant with a phone which sometimes worked and a scrawled sheet announcing what was being cooked, and by whom. This was a right royal chef, entitled to space and upholstery. Sitting composed on an ivory velvet settee reading a menu with the aid of a gold lorgnette, was a thick-set, powerfully built man in chef's whites. He looked up for a moment and motioned for them to sit down. André Bouchon, *the* André

Bouchon, television personality André Bouchon, the (almost) one and only three-star Michelin André Bouchon, senior representative of the Académie Culinaire de France, Filiale de Grande Bretagne. André Bouchon, Légion d'Honneur, but having no honour in his adopted country, repository in Britain of the hallowed tradition of French cuisine handed down through generations of cooks trained according to the diktats of the great and good, chef of the kings and king of chefs, Auguste Escoffier.

John could not take his eyes from his glossy walnut brown complexion, the black bushy eyebrows, the heavy, lined jowls. Neither he nor Laura stirred, for this man's concentration froze every movement like a great Shakespearean actor who stands in silence for two minutes, fixing his gaze on the audience in preparation for the speech that everyone knows by heart and awaits with bated breath. He put down the lorgnette, placed the menu beside him, gave a measured smile, uncrossed his legs and leaned back.

'So. Everything is good, Miss Douglas?'

'Very good, thank you, Monsieur Bouchon.'

'And this is the young man who come from . . .' He paused, to enunciate what were for him, after twenty years in England, formidably difficult sounds. 'York-sheer.'

'John Crabtree.' John shook hands. André's grip could have crushed a dozen eggs in a second.

'My pleasure,' said Monsieur Bouchon. 'First, Miss Douglas and I will talk. Then we will see about you. *Ça va?*' Laura nodded.

'*Il a le style séducteur, ce garçon,*' he remarked to Laura.

'Now. First I have to say something. I am not pleased by what Monsieur Boyce is writing recently. You have seen his article of last week?'

'Yes,' replied Laura. 'An excellent write-up.'

'You think so? A moment. I read.' Monsieur Bouchon went over to his desk, and immediately laid his hand on a cutting. '*Par exemple.* "The design of the plates would have suited my Aunt Mildred's china cabinet, but hardly what one expects from a restaurant where the menu has the authority of the *Oxford English Dictionary*." So? You think it is right to make criticism about my plates?'

'But he raves about the food.'

'Of course. But is he a connoisseur of plates?'

'Well, not exactly.'

'So he should write about what he knows. And I tell you something. My plates were designed specially. You know by whom? I tell you. By Wedge-wood. Yes. Tell that to Monsieur Boyce.' The phone rang. 'I take no calls,' he barked into it. 'Now, as I was saying. You will please invite Monsieur Boyce to lunch and we will discuss this matter. I also have other things to discuss with him.'

'I'll see when he's free and let you know,' Laura said.

The chef reached for his diary. 'He can come next Wednesday.'

'I'm afraid he'll be in Rome.'

'Oh, yes? What is there to write about in Rome? The Italians are good for pasta and ice cream. Which the French, including myself, I must say, make much better.'

'Chef, you're incorrigible.'

He laughed. 'OK. The Wednesday after I see Monsieur Boyce.' He looked at John. 'You think I am arrogant, like they say?'

John glanced at Laura.

'Come. I like people who say what they think. Very difficult for the English. Well? Is it true I am arrogant?'

'Perhaps. I suppose some people might say so, but if I could cook like you I'd be arrogant, Monsieur Bouchon.'

'Good. Good. Very good. Laura tells me you already know a few things. Sometimes I trust her. She says nice things about you.'

'That's for you to judge, I think,' John said.

'So. Let us now call a spade a spade, *comme on dit en anglais*. You speak French?'

'Menu French.'

'OK, we make a little test. You come to my kitchen, and you cook me something for my lunch, something you think I will like. Then we see. Tomorrow, perhaps? You come at eleven o'clock?'

'Oh yes. I mean, thank you so much. It's an honour, Monsieur Bouchon.'

'Good. One thing more, Laura. In two months' time, as you will remember, my next book is published. Do you think Miss Kowalski will like to make a little programme about it?'

'We're having lunch together soon. I'll mention it.'

'You tell her I am cooking for the French ambassador a very grand dinner, *très classique*. I can ask him if he will permit a brigade of television.'

'Excellent idea.'

'He is a friend. Very nice man. He like my cooking and he understand what I do. But is not as good looking as me!' Monsieur Bouchon winked. 'Now I get some champagne.'

John was in turmoil, momentarily off-guard. André Bouchon had not been a disappointment, but floating in London's muddy waters away from the kitchen his chef's mind was a grey blank.

'Laura, are you busy tonight?'

''fraid so.'

'Can you cancel your appointment? I've got to eat in André Bouchon's restaurant and you've got to take me. I must see the menu, see what he's about. I mean, his book's fantastic, but it's not the same. I must know his mind, what he's doing. Else I might do something which is wrong, and I'm not going to do that. I'm asking you because right now I haven't the cash.'

'Well—'

'Do it for me, Laura. Just tonight. See whoever it is after. Or before.'

'It's a bit difficult.'

'Please.' He stared at her and she saw how he would command a large brigade in the kitchen. 'I don't normally say please.'

The door clicked, opened, and André Bouchon re-appeared carrying a silver tray laden with sparkling, elegant champagne glasses, an opened bottle and a plate of *amuse-gueules*, little pastry cases with quails' eggs, caviar, smoked salmon and asparagus tips and another plate of finely sculpted peeled white vegetables accompanied by pale yellow pats of butter sitting in a bowl of ice. He set the tray down on a low table and poured out the champagne with a single, flowing gesture.

'You know something? My favourite one is this.' He handed John a morsel of the white vegetable. 'Eat it like I do.' In his thick fingers, he delicately took a portion for himself, spread it with butter and poured salt liberally over it. 'The French peasant, this is how he eats it. What is more delicious? Who needs those potato crisps the English like?' He looked towards John. 'You know what is this?'

John did as was suggested, and savoured the sharp refreshing tang. 'I've not had it before, but it's a bit like a radish.'

'*Exactement. Radis noir.* Take more. I tell you something: we chefs who come from the earth, like this *radis*, we are the powerful ones. When those people who call themselves journalists – huh! – are doing whatever they do in college, what are we doing at this age? I tell you. We are working in the best kitchens in the world. We are working eighteen hours a day. We are sweating, swearing, learning, being on guard all the time. You think I care about Mr Boyce? He knows nothing, and he criticise my plates.'

Laura and John shared the miniature meal and drank the drink of chefs. When every delicacy had disappeared, André Bouchon stood and accompanied Laura and John to the door.

'So, John. I see you tomorrow.'

'I think you made an impression,' said Laura in the car. 'He can be very difficult. The British aren't used to treating a chef like an artist, and he can't understand that.'

'You get on with him though?'

'I'd do anything I could for him. And now, I suppose, I'm taking you to dinner and putting off my appointment.'

John grinned and kissed Laura lightly on the cheek. 'That's right.'

She moved her head away a fraction.

Next morning, John awoke when the first light shone through the thin, threadbare curtains. He was hardly aware of the uneven lumps in his bed or the droning fly. On the chipped table next to him lay the treasure he had come away with on the previous night, the menu from Aphrodite's. He studied it closely, conjuring up how each dish might have been put together. Most of them were the classics – consommé, vichyssoise, even a *soupe à l'oignon*, lobster Thermidor, *carré d'agneau, salmis de canard, millefeuilles*, soufflés. Escoffier would have recognized nearly every dish. And that was why, Laura explained, Stephen Boyce had written about the plates. His readers would not be interested in hearing about a perfect lobster Thermidor when the young lads starting up in their own places were provoking diners with unheard of combinations, such fun to describe, like a jazz pianist improvising on Beethoven one moment, Jerome Kern the next. André Bouchon would have none of that. He was nothing if not a *grand classique*.

What kind of lunch would be suitable for this French master? John leafed through his well-thumbed bible, the *cuisine* of Paul Bocuse. Something light. Something to show both technique and presentation. Kidneys? Brains, perhaps? Or a beautifully executed peasant dish given the classical touch? Pigs trotters? Or something layered in the finest filo pastry? With some kind of stuffed vegetable? A quail? A little *bouchée* with caviar to start? His mind would not focus; each possibility, after consideration, seemed better than the last.

He dressed, made his way to the corridor and was relieved to find that the pay phone, usually out of order, today managed to cough up a dialling tone. George was summoned from the depths of sleep to solve John's dilemma. As he put each idea to him, he received a minimal answer.

'Mm. Mm.'

'Come on, George. Give us a clue. Say yes to something, and I'll go straight ahead.'

'If it was me doing it . . .'

'Don't tell me. Fancy faggot food like bloody quenelles.'

'Ooh, no dear. Can't stand quenelles. They remind me of suppositories. No. What I'd do is something dreamily simple.'

'Sandwiches?'

'Not that simple. What does a Frenchman have for lunch, dear boy?'

'Omelette, chips and salad, most like.'

'That's it then.'

'You serious?'

'I am. Hang on a minute.' The receiver of the phone dropped on to the floor, and John slotted in the last fifty pence piece.

'You there?'

'Quick. Money's running out.'

'Listen while I read you a gem.' George cleared his throat. '"Something gentle and pastoral, with the clean scent of the dairy, the kitchen garden, the basket of early morning mushrooms or the sharp tang of freshly picked herbs, sorrel, chives, tarragon . . ."'

'Who said that?'

'The Queen herself. Liz David. Think about it.'

No need to say more. Good chap, George, better half asleep than most people wide awake. Something simple. That was it. But everything perfect. It was still early enough to catch the market. *Omelette à l'oseille*. He loved sorrel and so did Bocuse. The best country eggs he could find, salad leaves, the finest oils, interesting vinegar. Nothing but the best.

The brigade in the kitchen at Aphrodite's cast sidelong glances as John softened the strips of sorrel leaves in butter, compressed them into a purée, gently swirled the contents of three eggs with a fork until the liquid was deep yellow and poured it in a slow stream into the heavy copper pan where butter was turning honey gold. As soon as the liquid at the edge solidified, he placed the intense green purée in the centre, drew the edges forward in gentle folds, shook the pan, flipped the barely set omelette in half, sizzled a little butter over the surface and slipped it on to a plate garnished with a marigold flower. This he put carefully on its predestined space on the tray.

As he moved quickly away to climb the stairs, counting every nervous step, he thought everything looked fine enough for a photograph. Silver shone with not a dull mark, plates gleaming, salad with every leaf perfect, dressing just right, chips not too thin, not too thick, not too crisp, not too soft, a bottle of chilled Alsace wine and a small pottery vase he had found on his travels filled with country flowers.

'Ah!' Monsieur Bouchon removed his spectacles, tidied his desk immediately and sat expectantly on his settee. 'Put it down there and come back in half an hour.'

John left Aphrodite's, and when he returned he could not remember where he had walked, whether he had felt the warm rays of the sun or the chill wind of an overcast sky. He kept looking at his watch. Had he done right? Hanging his future on omelette and chips! He must be mad.

'*Entrez.*'

He was sitting there, the linen napkin still on his lap, sucking a peach from the cornupcopia of fruit. John looked quickly. Everything had gone.

'Sit down there. I will tell you something. When I come first to this country, I cook for the richest people in Europe. You are too young to remember. I talk now of twenty years ago. You know the hotel on the corner?'

'The Fitzwilliam?'

'Precisely. Well, in that hotel was the best casino in London. We have people in there, they can sometimes lose a million in one night. Fantastic place. My job was to cook for these people. So I am thinking, *foie gras*, caviar, you know? I prepare a menu that you cannot believe. Every night, my *chef pâtissier*, he make carvings of sugar. I am getting my ingredients from France, everything is to be perfect. And you know what?' Monsieur Bouchon paused and pointed a finger emphatically. 'Every night I am throwing away enough to feed the army of Napoleon. These people, they are not interested. Most of the time I am serving . . . Guess.'

'Omelette and chips.'

'Precisely. Sometimes even sausages. The clientele has eaten everywhere in the world, they have anything they want. So they want simple things, this I can see. So I make the Fitzwilliam Casino the best café in London. Only in this place are you getting the best omelette, the best sausage (I make myself, naturally) and I make chips too. That is how I learn.'

'What happened to it?' asked John.

'My casino? Oh, that is a bad story. The police, they close it. Not for my food, you understand! There is trouble with the management. I have to go, but soon I am lucky. Mr Beck, the *propriétaire*, ask me to come to Aphrodite's. Eh. *Voilà.*'

'Shall I remove the tray, Monsieur Bouchon?'

'In a moment.'

'Just tell me what I've done wrong.'

'Too much *oseille* in the omelette. For my taste. That is all. Now it is time for my *sieste.*' He removed his velvet slippers and curled up on the settee. John reached for the tray. Monsieur Bouchon frowned and scrutinized him from under his tufted eyebrows.

'I want to ask . . . that is, er, did you like your lunch?'

'Oh, yes. Naturally.'

'I know everyone wants to work with you, Monsieur Bouchon. I – I really don't mind what work I do.'

'Well, Mr Crabtree. I expect you in the kitchen tomorrow.' John stared, mesmerized, unable to summon up a word. 'We start at eight thirty.'

'I . . . I hope . . . I'll do my best, Monsieur Bouchon. Was it really all right? The lunch?'

114

'About this we need not speak. You are a chef. That I can see. Many young men, they come here, they cook me something *elaborée*, they try to show their cleverness. That I do not need. Many are clever. But you—' He removed the peach stone from his mouth, having sucked it clean, and placed it on the tray. 'You understand the most important thing. Simplicity.'

John ran out of Aphrodite's, looking back at the blue and gold awning over the front door and breathed in the fumes of London as though he was being infused with mountain air.

'I've done it! He liked it! I'm starting tomorrow.' Laura looked up from her pile of papers as he burst unannounced into the Sanctum. 'You'll never guess what I cooked. Omelette and chips! How about that? But it was a bloody good omelette, I tell you. All arranged just like I wanted it, saw it in my mind's eye. He loved it. Didn't say much. I start tomorrow. Hey! I start tomorrow.' He gave Laura a crushing hug. The phone rang, but she did not answer. 'Hey! John Crabtree working at Aphrodite's. How about it? Thanks, Laura. I mean it. Let me buy you a bottle of champagne. Right now.'

'I've just got something to finish.'

'No. Now, Laura.'

She sat back in her chair.

'Aren't you pleased?' he asked.

'Of course I am. You've done really well.'

John ran down the steps of a small wine bar a few doors away like a kid with a month's pocket money to spend. 'No, this is on me,' he said, as the barman presented them with a bottle of champagne on ice. 'Don't forget today, will you? John Crabtree, Yorkshire lad made good in the Smoke. Do you think they'll write about me one day in the magazines? Can I tell me Mum and Dad I'm going to be famous?' He laughed as the champagne cork flew over the bar. 'I'm joking. I only want to cook.'

*   *   *

115

'What on earth are you doing? *Here!*' shrieked Didi. 'Not your scene, darling. Or have you gone over to the other side?'

'I could ask you that,' Stephen replied. 'But I do know one thing.'

'Tell me.'

'You're not here for the men.'

Didi sniffed and glanced around her. 'Dandruff cases from Cheam. What do you think?'

'One or two from Weybridge.'

'Oh yes. That one.' Didi pointed to an anxious, spotty man with a pink tie who was scratching his neck like a mangy chimpanzee.

'What does he have for dinner?' Stephen asked.

'Well.' Didi sucked a manicured finger. 'My guess is . . . tinned gourmet hydrolysed vichysoisse with multi-grain shrink-wrapped bread and low fat spread.'

'Fine.'

'And then. I know. Overcooked diethylene packed farmed slimy salmon trout—'

'With Ready-Mix Sauce Bonne Femme . . .'

'Microwaved old new potatoes.'

'Frozen broccoli.'

'Definitely. And the whole Hygena kitchen absolutely stinking of wilting greens and desperate fish.'

'Pudding. What about pudding?'

'Does he have pudding? Surely not.'

'Oh yes. He's a pudding-twice-a-day man.'

'Apple crumble?'

'No. He's not quite apple crumble. Or only at weekends when he eats with the children.'

'How about low-fat raspberry-flavour cochineal-coloured soya sorbet?'

'Yes. With tinned mangoes.'

'Cheese?'

'No. He had cheese for lunch. He's cutting down on fat.'

'So he is. And finally?'

116

'Instant decaff coffee with a dash of ultra heat-treated skimmed milk.'

'And two artificial sweeteners.'

'And the name of his four-bedroomed, half-timbered des res with a his-and-hers garage?'

'Um. The Cedars.'

Didi giggled and then tightened her wide patent leather belt, clinching in a loose velours dress designed for the wealthy, unstreamlined body.

'See? I'm getting thinner.'

'You haven't eaten yet.'

The man with the encapsulated lifestyle looked over in their direction, seeing only two members of the press clearly enjoying the occasion. From his meet-the-press seminar he had learned that they were not all bad. Merely doing a job. He felt confident in his opening approach (Gambit One. The Introduction.) and walked towards them.

'May I introduce myself? I am Martin Brown, Assistant Marketing Director of Leone Leisure UK PLC. Miss Kowalski, Mr Boyce, we are very glad to have you with us today.'

They shook hands and Didi watched with amusement as the lumpfish eyes slipped down to her carefully unbuttoned blouse and moved hastily upwards.

'Have you had something to eat?'

'Yes, no,' they chorused in unison. Silly Didi.

Now a tray of Stockman's Reviver, Hunky Spare Ribs, Rambo's Secret Weapon, Magnum Fries and Cholesterol Corner Choice of the Day was heading towards them.

'How frightfully masculine this all is,' observed Didi, as the salivary juices in the mouth turned to ashes.

'Oh, we do cater for the ladies,' quipped Mr Brown, showing at least two gold fillings. 'Over here,' he called to the waitress in cow-girl attire, leather miniskirt and thigh boots. 'Bring us the Maiden's Blush. That consists of prawn and our own special secret formula mayonnaise in a bun. And this will interest you; the buns come over from the States every day. They're the best.'

'By Concorde?' enquired Stephen.

'As a matter of fact. No.' Was this a trick question? Quick. Change the subject. 'I do enjoy your programme, Miss Kowalski. Always provocative. My wife is an avid viewer of *Table for One* and so am I. In fact, every Thursday I have to have cold supper. She won't miss it for anything.'

'That's most kind,' Didi said, flashing her eight million viewers peak-time smile.

'Come on, Didi. Try these spare ribs. Really good.' Stephen's mouth was almost completely filled with a Hunky Spare Rib from which he was stripping the meat with well counterfeited gusto.

'Have you a napkin?' she asked of her host.

'Oh, how silly of me! I know we put out some paper serviettes. Don't move, I'll be back.' He hurried away.

'Stephen. Honestly! You're not eating those surely?'

'But of course. I'm scourging my taste buds before they feast at Aphrodite's tonight.'

'Lucky you. You are a sod. You know I hate spare ribs. I'll have to take my make-up off and put it on again now. Uck. That grease!'

'You should share the tastes of your dear public at least once a week. Good for the soul.'

'I don't have one. My soul gave up long ago. Couldn't face the competition with my stomach.'

'Sh. Here's the man of the moment.'

'Oh, they look lovely,' said Didi, delicately picking up a Hunky Spare Rib, briefly nibbling it, putting it back on the plate and dabbing her mouth with elaborate gestures. 'Delicious.'

'And now for the Maiden's Blush,' urged Martin Brown.

'It's a long time since *that* happened,' Didi said, fluttering the famously irresistible eyelashes. The Assistant Marketing Director, encouraged by such an alluring advance, picked up a spoonful of prawns and offered it to her mouth.

Didi sucked her lips round the morsel, and gulped it down. 'I imagine this is a very good seller,' she remarked, composing herself.

'Indeed. One of the most popular things on the menu. Specially with the ladies.'

'I never knew prawns were aphrodisiac,' Didi commented.

Martin Brown coughed. 'We have a very substantial female clientele.'

'You would have,' said Didi, imagining a bevy of ladies upholstered in crimplene downing the Maiden's Blush.

'In fact, we train our staff to be specially attentive to the needs of feminine requirements.'

'Fancy!' Didi sucked a finger slowly.

'We have ascertained that many food outlets ignore this factor. Our powder rooms are very thoughtfully provided, as I'm sure you will see. Now, do excuse me.' He called the waitress over again.

'I'll have some more in a minute, thank you.' Didi watched the waitress swaying away. 'Shall we go, Stephen? How about a champagne cocktail at Le Style?'

'Not today, darling. I must do some work.'

'You're not working! You can't fool me. There's no story in Hunky Spare Ribs. Come and linger with me. I don't have to be at the studio till four.'

'I wish I could.' Stephen put his arm round Didi's neck and kissed her grease-dried lips, now pale and lipstick-lacking. Then he drew back and gazed past her diminutive yet all-absorbing ear. The man he had waited a long half hour to see had slipped utterly unnoticed into the throng. For his sake, Stephen had downed the staples of Hell (doomed to eat Rambo's Secret Weapon with a double portion of French fries for every second of eternity, fit punishment for chefs who betrayed their profession).

'Who are you looking at?' asked Didi, feeling Stephen's immobile face resting against her cheek. 'Someone important? I bet it is. That's why you're here. You might have told me.'

Stephen grasped Didi's plump upper arm and pushed her forward through the chomping crowd.

'Who? Who?'

'Sh. Trust me.'

Stephen stopped pushing and Didi came to rest in front of someone who aroused a flicker of attention. Rather rangy. A touch vulgar. Beach-boy shirt. But sexy. Just exuding. Some men did, even when nothing about them was likeable. Wild hair, lots of it. Sensual lips. Looked like music business, not food business. Rock star opening his first restaurant.

'Hi.' The face crinkled in welcome, a hand shot forward and grasped Didi's chubby, ring-covered fingers. 'Well, my friend, are you going to introduce me to this very lovely lady?'

Didi looked down modestly, as one did on these occasions.

'Didi Kowalski. Didi, this is Jack Leone.'

'I love your show,' said Jack instantly. 'I really do. You know something? *Table for One* would go down really big in the States. And I mean big. Ever thought of it?'

'I can't say I have,' lied Didi, who had thought of it but was fully aware of the danger that her talent would sink in the struggling heap of British hopefuls languishing across the Atlantic glued to telephones from New York to Los Angeles.

'You know, every time I see you, I feel real hungry. That's what it's all about. Appetite. How many shows on TV make you dive into the deep freeze even when you've had dinner? I love to see you eat. You ever done commercials?'

Didi giggled. 'Oh. I couldn't possibly.'

'English girls always say no, then they have a rethink. You like my little venture?'

'Um. Oh, yes. Very well organized. Very professional.'

'So are you going to find a little prime time for me, eh? Interview on how an American is beefing up the fast-food revolution? You know something? Here it hasn't even started. You think one McDonald's in some hick town means it's happened? No way. That means there's room for at least six more outlets. Tex-Mex, tapas, pizzas, sushi, and even the good old fish and chips. Marketing. That's all you need. We're working on Hot Nosheries on garage forecourts. The opportunities are endless . . . But enough of me. Didi – may I call you Didi? – tell me something. I'm dying to know. Which are your favourite eateries?'

'Depends on . . . who's taking me,' she suggested.

'Tell you what. How about you and me having lunch? How does that grab you?'

Didi smirked at his forwardness. On the one hand, she liked out-front men but on the other . . . how one did appreciate the subtle approach.

'I'm sure Didi would love it,' said Stephen. Only she could detect his touch of affectionate maliciousness.

'Have you a business card? Or use this.' Jack grabbed a menu lying on a nearby table and extracted a gold pen from the pocket of his shirt, hand-blocked with JACK in every conceivable typographical variant. Didi scrawled her work number, and hurried towards the ladies' powder room.

'Great to see you, Steve,' Jack said when she had gone.

'A good do. I thought we might meet. I'm working on a fast-food feature.'

'Sure thing. My secretary will confirm.' Jack took out his pocket tape recorder. 'Stephen Boyce. Fix lunch. Done. Steve, you seen Laura recently?'

'A couple of weeks ago.'

'Is she in trouble?'

'Not that I know of. She seems in fine form.'

'I'm glad.' Jack looked at Stephen's reassuring, hand-some, solidly English face and continued: 'I don't want to see her mess up.'

'I doubt if she will,' he said.

Didi held her taxi, waiting for Stephen who would be too keyed-up, she suspected, to stay long.

'Toot your horn. Now,' she shouted through the partition to the patient taxi driver. 'Again.' Stephen turned and she waved furiously out of the window.

'Lost your boyfriend then?' the driver remarked leaning his head back.

Stephen strolled over, opened the door and slumped next to Didi.

'Le Style. Albemarle Street,' Didi announced.

'I haven't time.'

'Please. A quick one.'

'How can I refuse?'

'Darling, should I or should I not go to lunch with that American?'

'Yes.'

'Stephen, will you collect me from the studio?'

'Darling, I told you. I'm dining at Aphrodite's with Miss Cutbutton. My future is at stake. Or, rather, I want more space in the paper.'

'You could come round afterwards.'

'Sweetest, even my stomach has limitations. Not tonight.'

For a brief moment, Didi's face was drained of her unrelenting vitality and the bright movements of eyes and lips were still.

'I want to ask you something important,' she began, when they had arrived at Le Style and ordered their champagne.

Stephen giggled, sensing an unwelcome confrontation, then wondered if she might suddenly burst into tears. 'Come on. It's not Monday. We don't have to be serious. I was only teasing.'

'Why can't we be serious for once?' she sniffed.

'Serious? I? A journalist? The qualification for the job of journalist is being serious on paper and flippant in company.'

'But we're not working now, and I am not company. I hope.' Didi threw him one of her devastating glances and blew her nose vigorously. 'You're cross with me.'

'Of course I'm not.'

'Stephen, tell me. I want an answer. Why can't we be lovers?'

'Oh, you adorable, insatiable creature. I couldn't bear it. The longing, the expectation . . . One flaw, one maladroit manoeuvre.'

'Ridiculous! Whatever maladroit is, I'm sure you're not.'

'And you'd never talk to me again. Think of that. Sitting next to each other at a sublime meal and not talking. Waking up in some fabulous hotel the morning after and eating at separate tables. You'd be dripping tears into your boiled egg. Agony, darling.'

'It doesn't have to be in a hotel. We could do it *chez moi* over the rugs and the cushions and my gorgeous soft bed. We'd make love all night and then I'd bring you hot croissants, mulberry jam and steaming coffee.'

'Darling Didi, it's too tempting. I snore.'

'I do too sometimes.'

'I'm a slob. I leave toothpaste gobs on the basin.'

'Don't care. You're the only man I want.'

'I'm not worth your wanting. My belly is disgustingly fat.'

'So are my legs.'

'Impossible.'

Didi slowly sipped at her glass of champagne and saw them both in the mirror: elegant, fine-looking, enviable people sharing the sweet intimacy of lovers. 'I feel absolutely dreadful. Do you care?'

'If only one was an oik from Dagenham. Life would be so much simpler. I can't possibly explain. Not even to you.'

There was something he couldn't tell her. It must be appalling, tragic, unspeakable. The hidden tragedy of Stephen Boyce. Why hadn't she realized before? She took his hands in hers as though divining the terrible destiny coursing through his veins, and decided to maintain a respectful silence. She was in the presence of . . . a terrible illness. Could it be? Might there have been a brief escape in the souks of Morocco? No. Not that. The shock of thinking about it made her eyes cloud over. She prayed that he wasn't the genius she imagined he was so he would never die young. Suppose she had to write his obituary? Stephen Boyce succumbed to a tragic illness bravely borne. Everyone fought AIDS bravely. There was only one thing she could do, and that was to use everything in her power to protect his immune system. She would will him to health and together they would conquer the plague of death. Vitamin E tablets hidden inside his favourite truffles. A secret visit to that lovely doctor she'd had on *Table for One*. But now, the heavy burden of knowledge must be concealed. He must never know she knew. Pretend everything was the same as before.

'Stephen?' She heard her voice sailing too far into the cheerful upper register. 'Perhaps one day we'll have the perfect meal, every single thing wonderful, wonderful, wonderful and then . . . would you?'

'Oh, I think I might.'

Stephen turned on his bar stool and gave Didi the kiss that she had been expecting and she returned it with abandon.

As he sat upstairs in a crowded, overheated bus which would take him somewhere near his home patch of Notting Hill, Stephen was unable to compose his opening paragraph. Usually he found the labouring motion of a London bus conducive to the happily handled clichés suitable for his topic. Today, however, images and thoughts intruded which would have no place in an attack on the Minister of Agriculture's five-year plan for British farming.

Stephen idly opened *Fast Lane*, a new pictorial revue aimed at today's thinking man, hoping for inspiration. Didi Kowalski. Good picture. 'Didi cooks up a Treat.' Soft focus in the candlelight, a romantic supper for two. A male model with his back to the camera, Didi passing him an oyster. Wicked blouse. Delectable breasts. Lovely Didi. Hymn to desire, propagator of wild thoughts and wilder actions.

Darling Didi. Curious this power she had of rousing the beast in the soberest readers of the *Daily Telegraph*. Sometimes he and Didi dined unannounced but it was always an uncomfortable experience which Stephen tried to avoid. As soon as they entered even the quietest and most discreet of restaurants, there would be a lustful volley of glances from almost every man present. Some would even come up to their table. 'I say, aren't you Didi Kowalski?' 'Yes,' Stephen would reply crossly as she looked away. 'And now please would you leave us to enjoy our meal?' The anonymous admirers left their cards on her plate, offered her champagne, brushed past her in order to apologize extravagantly, stared openly, stroked her arm, her neck, whipped out cameras. Even the most outwardly respectable males, he sometimes thought, would have ravished her on the spot given the opportunity. How they hated and envied him, and the drunker ones taunted her: 'What are you doing with him? Why don't you have dinner with me? What's he got that I haven't?' He couldn't explain what it was, not to these creatures of the lower depths, nor, for that matter, to himself.

Stephen let *Fast Lane* slip down to join the assorted cardboard, tinfoil and plastic wrappings piled on the floor, and drew a face with his finger on the steamed-up window of the rear upper deck which bore a remote resemblance to his editor.

Later, much later, the phone rang.

'Steee-phen.'

She was a little drunk.

'Darling heart.'

'My producer made me cut five minutes.'

'He's a prat.'

'What are you doing?'

'Writing a really fucking boring piece. I hear the sound of knives being sharpened. It was her bloody subject in the first place. Being dutiful I obey, then doubtless she will tell me it's boring. What are we artistes to do?'

'Maybe people like being bored. Then they can feel superior.'

'I wonder if people said to Mozart, "Oh, not another boring old sonata, we thought you could do better than that."'

'*Don Giovanni*. Not that old story.'

'Yawn.'

'Yawn.'

'Stephen.' She gulped to summon courage. 'God, this wine they sent me is awful.'

'Didi, sweetheart—'

'I love you, Stephen. What a thing for me to say! How corny. How silly. How absolutely idiotic.'

'And I love you.'

Didi was instantly wafted up to paradise. She drew her satin sheets closer and put down her glass. The pink room swam round her bed and came to rest in blackness.

6

The kitchen at Aphrodite's betrayed not a crumb of its active existence. The stainless steel surfaces of cookers and preparation areas gleamed, the copper pans hung in ascending rows, the tiled floor was spotless. Only the huge stock pot gently bubbled, waiting for Monday's assault. Now that Saturday was over, this street in the heart of London was empty. Its occupants had fled to the country and those who serviced it – the refuse collectors, the street cleaners, the postmen, the parking wardens, the delivery boys – were at rest in distant suburbs. The occasional lone pedestrians could hear their own footsteps on the pavement and the chirruping of birds in the evenly spaced trees provided by the local authority amenities department.

André Bouchon's low elegant saloon had disappeared from its usual parking place outside the kitchen entrance. His wife had driven it away to visit friends, the lonely wives of other chefs. The grass widows of the kitchen kept together, gossiped, gave advice and discussed their absent men. Any woman who bemoaned her lot too frequently, who criticized or deceived her husband was shunned and soon forced out of this tight-knit society. Like most other husbands, André Bouchon was asleep, sprawled across the large heavy, rococo matrimonial bed in which he spent a few snatched hours whenever he could.

'From up North, eh, you bastard!'

John received a series of playful punches in the ribs and stood his ground. He was leaning against a matt black bar, glass in hand, surrounded by the lads who did not sleep on Sundays. There was a gathering to celebrate Mike's birthday in the Kitchen Club, which had been established in Soho by Tadeus Freeman, Tad the Lad, chef extraordinaire and photographic model when the price was right.

'Guess where I come from,' Tad said.

'South of the Watford border, I reckon.'

'Wrong, lad,' he said lapsing into the northern vowels. 'I come from bloody Leeds. Arsehole of the earth. A few tarted-up arcades, pizza parlours, hamburger joints, plastic pubs, hotels for expense-account gropers and a load of pig-ignorant cunts.'

'You don't have to stay in Leeds. That marvellous countryside . . .'

'You're a hills and sky man, are you? Even in the country, they can't bloody grow anything except sheep. Have you tried Yorkshire veg? Disgusting. No wonder they have all those pies.'

'The pies are great.'

'Absolutely,' countered Sebastian North, chef-patron of Zi-Zi's, restaurant of the year, famed for its minimalist Japanese-inspired cooking. Sebastian's voice was muffled by a fistful of nuts. 'And the Bakewell pudding is super.'

'That's Derbyshire, you prat.' Tadeus looked pityingly at Sebastian. 'I say, chaps, do you think I sound posh?'

'You posh? Give us a break.'

Mike, a kitchen junior at Aphrodite's, fought back his awe of the chef who cooked like a dream, had journalists gobbling his words and who had recently been painted in oils, full length, reclining in an olive grove, framed in gold, hanging next to Prince Charles in the National Portrait Gallery. Tad was untouchable now, could do as he liked.

'I think I sound posh anyway. "Sorry, darling, we haven't a table for weeks." How about that for a soigné accent?'

'I couldn't even introduce you to my friends. You're probably from Leeds as well. Maybe we're all from Leeds.'

'Lees?' Jean-Luc, on veg, was desperate to improve his English. 'I 'ave no 'eard of zis.'

'Fucking French. Why can't you talk fucking English?'

'Because *cuisine* is French.'

'But cooking is English, cunt. What I cook in my kitchen is English, the menu is English, the lousy clientele is English and—'

'You mean British,' said Elwyn Jones from the Sang-Froid in Fulham.

'Who cares? We're all bastardized by the fucking Common Market. It doesn't matter where we come from. You know what some cunt in my restaurant said the other day? I get better beef in Brussels. Well, I said, get back to fucking Brussels. The only thing you've given us is sprouts and where I come from we feed them to pigs. Then I threw him out. You should have seen his face. Like a turd marinated in beetroot.'

'You don't throw out customers,' said John. 'That's daft. I wouldn't do that. You've got to get them round to your way of thinking.'

'Oh, John, darling, how quaint, how positively nineteenth century,' said Tadeus throwing out his gangly arm in a theatrical gesture.

'Maybe. Perhaps I don't have the charm to do it like you.'

Tadeus laughed, looked up at the northern giant and put a heavy hand on John's shoulder. 'He's all right, this little lad.' He looked round the group, inviting them to accept his new found protégé, and ordered another bottle of champagne. 'I heard you're looking for a place.'

'Who said that?'

'Well, you're not the type to stick around as a sous churning out *filet de boeuf en croûte*. When's Big-Ears retiring?'

'Who?'

'André Bouchon,' explained Sebastian. 'Our name for André Bouchon. Cos he's always saying, "Wat eez zis I 'ear?" He doesn't miss a thing so watch out.'

'For 'is age, is a very young man,' said Jean-Luc.

'He must be fifty-three,' Tadeus continued. 'When I'm

his age I'll be retired, sunning myself by my pool on the Côte d'Azur feeling up a long-legged blonde with big tits. Or else having cocktails on my terrace. I've always fancied a yacht. Might have one of those . . . So where is Mr Crabtree going to open? Fulham, Chelsea – or Mayfair, is it?'

'I'll find somewhere when I'm good and ready.'

'OK, lads, who do we know who's going bust and deserves it?'

'There are dozens of those,' said Elwyn. 'There's two near me.'

'There would be,' said Tadeus. 'Fickle fuckers in Fulham. Say that when you're pissed.'

'Is a place near—' began Jean-Luc timidly.

'Near what?'

'Maybe is no good. An Arab man, 'e tell me is fed up, 'e want to go back.'

'Come on, tell us,' encouraged Elwyn.

'Is in the same street of André.'

'Bloody heck. Not that Lebanese joint whose name sounds like a cat being sick?'

'Is that one.'

'Well, there's your chance! Go for it.' Tadeus looked at John, waiting for an enthusiastic response.

'When I'm good and ready,' he repeated.

'For Christ's sake. In London you don't hang about. It takes months to get a restaurant on the road. That dusty old place has got potential. Right position. Good area. Get in there, John.'

'I couldn't do that to André, it's not right.'

'It'll be good for Big-Ears,' said Tadeus. 'And good for you. Keep you both up to scratch. Nothing wrong in that. There's room for all of us. I've got a little place in mind for Mike, too. How about Wembley, eh, Mike, when you're a big boy?'

'I'm not feeding bloody Pakis.'

'Don't be such a fucking racist pig. They're better than the braying stock-exchange wallies I get who spend more time in the gents pissing out the booze than eating in the dining room.'

'You can't talk. You chuck 'em out.'

'Only if their ties offend me.'

'I say, chaps, how about some grub?' Sebastian waved to the barman, who waved to someone in the dining area at the other side of the bar.

John was surprised when he sat down to eat, as he had expected rough and readiness. Two tables had been pushed together, with linen cloths, fine china plates, an array of silver carefully laid out and soft lighting. There were tapestries on the walls depicting medieval banqueting scenes, and in the spaces between were gold-framed culinary awards gained by the member chefs.

'I didn't expect this,' he said to Elwyn who was studying the menu beside him.

'Ah. That's the idea. Self-respect, that's what it is, see? A gentleman's club for chefs – Tad's idea. And he's right. We can ask anyone to come here. Even the girls. What'll you have?'

This was a menu for chefs. Steak and kidney pudding, boiled beef, dumplings and carrots, steak, fish and chips . . . food to sustain the labouring man. John ordered boiled beef, and felt a rare surge of hunger.

When the elegantly presented dishes arrived, they gathered up their knives and forks in silence and little was said during the business of eating.

'Look at that,' remarked Elwyn, cutting through the last of a large slab of succulent beef. 'In my restaurant it would be three portions. Not served like this, of course, I'd have put little garnishes around the plate, potato cages, that kind of stuff . . . *Filet de boeuf à la mode de* whoever takes my fancy. Daft, isn't it?'

'Those who eat it haven't sweated off half a stone in the kitchen, though.'

'You really going to open your own place, John?'

'Depends.' John paused. 'Elwyn, do you know someone called Laura Douglas?'

'Heavens, man, you're learning fast! How long you been in London?'

'Three months.'

'Did I hear someone mention Miss La-di-da?' bellowed Tadeus from across the table. 'Has she got her spiky little meat hooks into your tough Yorkshire skin, eh lad?'

'Ignore him,' suggested Sebastian. 'Laura keeps her knickers on. Bright lady.'

'Women should lie on their backs and stay there,' said Tadeus. 'Why do you think they find me so irresistible? Perhaps they like the smell of my sweat.'

Everyone groaned.

'Have you tried taking a bath?' asked Elwyn. 'Or do you still put coal in it?'

'Laura Douglas is the best there is,' said Sebastian. 'We all need promoting. You can't just open and wait for the punters to roll up.'

'For fifteen per cent of your turnover, which is what Miss La-di-da uses for pocket money, I'll fucking promote you!' exclaimed Tadeus. 'There's nothing to it. Fill up the arsehole journalists with grub and booze and take them on a day trip to France once in a while. Easy.'

'I couldn't be doing with that,' said John. 'I'd need to be in the kitchen. And besides, she's got contacts.'

'You must cultivate rich young ladies,' said Tadeus. 'Then they'll bring in their little rich friends. Most of them will do anything for a decent fuck in my unlimited experience.'

'You call thirty seconds decent?' countered Elwyn.

'We all know the Welsh bugger sheep.'

'Enough,' called Sebastian. 'You're not in the kitchen now, Tad.'

'Yes, indeed, Father Sebastian. Ten Hail Marys. I promise. Perhaps I should get religion. How about *Tripes à la mode des Moines*? Good, that. Monks' tripe. A whole religious menu? *Caprice des Nonnes*. Nuns' Fantasy. Holy Temptation. Let's see, cream, sorbet, chocolate sauce, meringue, spun sugar cage, and then I'd put in something bitter. Bitter. I'll have to think. You'd have to taste the bitter part at the end. Like religion. Where's the bloody waiter? Here!'

The young man assigned to their table came up, and Tadeus whispered something in his ear. The plates were cleared and the lights dimmed. Elwyn stood up, hummed a note and then it was 'Happy Birthday to You' with choral arrangement. When they had reached 'dear Mi-ike' a waiter solemnly glided in with a huge platter.

'That there birthday cake was cooked up by Jean-Luc in between turning the veg,' announced Elwyn. 'But the idea was mine.'

'Blimey. It's, it's – incredible!' Mike stared at the Harley Davidson carved out of sugar, every detail appropriate, standing in an icing green field proclaiming 'Happy Birthday' in red.

'We thought it would do until you've saved up for the real thing,' said Sebastian.

'I don't know what to say. Thanks. I mean . . . I never expected this.'

'Prize-winning Olympic gold-medal stuff, that,' said Tadeus. 'Not bad for a foreigner. Well, Mike, how does it feel to be eighteen? You'll be wanting a woman next.'

'Twenty-two feels bloody marvellous,' Mike replied. He was close to tears. He had no family, apart from his mother who was working as a chambermaid in Devon. 'Thanks everyone.'

'We're not a bad bunch, really. Even Tad has his good points.'

The brandy glasses had been filled up four times, and although no-one admitted to being tired there was a sag of energy. It was past midnight, when the kitchens would have been cleaned and the brigade on their way home to bed.

'It's getting late, Tad,' remarked Sebastian, noticing Jean-Luc stifling a yawn and shaking himself awake.

'Oh, come on. It's Mike's birthday.'

Tadeus glared round at the other diners who seemed oblivious of life outside their tables. 'Let's give 'em something to talk about. Come on, El, sing us a song.'

Elwyn sifted through his limited repertoire. 'Here's one, boys.' He cleared his throat and removed his tie. 'Welsh version of "Darling Clementine". You can all join in.'

> I'm a bastard, I'm a bastard,
> I'm a bastard, so I am,
> But a bi-igger bastard,
> Is a bastard English-man

The chefs joined in lustily, the voices came closer together, swelling in volume. Yet again they began to sing, harmonizing with abandon, until they were interrupted by the restaurant manager who came over, spoke quietly in Elwyn's ear and glided away.

'That's it for tonight, lads', announced Elwyn. 'The culinary choir will have to meet another time. Not everyone is musical, see.'

Tadeus threw a gold credit card on the table as the waiter presented the bill.

'Can't let you do that, mate,' said Mike. 'Let's all chip in.'

'I'm feeling generous,' said Tadeus.

Sebastian, Mike and Elwyn rose to go.

'Great night, Tad. Thanks a lot. See you.'

The waiter asked permission to clear while Tad the Lad and the newly christened Little John continued to down the brandy.

'Who was it didn't like the sound of music?' asked Tadeus.

'Er, those two gentlemen over there.' The waiter inclined his head towards two men in City suits sitting opposite each other, each puffing intensely at large cigars.

'Who are they anyway? Are they members? Who let them in?'

'I'm not sure, sir.'

'Find out for me.'

The waiter left to consult the manager. Mr Tadeus Freeman owned part of the Kitchen Club and had a right to information. Tadeus stared at the corner table. 'I know that bugger,' he said to John. 'From somewhere.'

'Maybe you threw him out once.'

The manager approached. 'One gentleman is Mr Leone, the other is his guest, sir.'

'Who?'

'Mr Leone, sir. An American gentleman.'

John turned his head as though he had heard a gun shot.

'What is it?' asked Tadeus. 'You know them?'

'I'd best be going, Tad. Might lose my temper.'

'Eh, up. Kiss and tell.'

John glanced again at the corner table, drew his chair closer and told the sad tale of Charlie Braithwaite, Jack Leone and the Moorland Haven.

Tadeus quietly listened, then got up from his chair and strolled over to Jack Leone's table.

'No more coffee,' said Leone without looking up. 'Give me the bill and I'll sign.'

'Good evening, Mr Leone.'

This time he raised his head. 'Hi. Do I know you?'

'Tadeus Freeman.'

'How can I help?' Leone sensed trouble and he didn't come to the Kitchen Club to be bothered.

'You can help,' said Tadeus grandly, 'by gracing the Kitchen Club with your absence.'

'I am a paid-up member,' stated Leone. 'I'm sorry we have a personality conflict here. Happens, I guess. I've nothing against you, my friend.'

'But I dislike you intensely. Are you in public relations? One of the lying fraternity?'

'As a matter of fact, I own restaurants, if you want to know.'

'What do you serve? Pancakes? Pizzas? Or baked potatoes on a stick perhaps?'

Leone rose to his feet. 'Listen, son. We're in the same business. You might need me one day. From what I hear you're undercaptialized and your lease is up for review in two years. You're heading for trouble. I spend my time rescuing people like you.'

Tadeus stretched out his long arms, seized the table-cloth in both hands and jerked it like a cat shaking a mouse. Leone and his companion backed against the wall. Brandy glasses, wine glasses, side plates, coffee cups, ashtrays, flower vase and dish of petits fours shattered on to the tiled floor and the liquids oozed and splashed in the mess of fragments.

John hurried over and took Tadeus by the elbow. The manager rushed up to Leone and ushered him with his dazed companion out to the foyer, talking, talking, trying to avoid more trouble. Never happened before, private party, drank too much, violent for no reason, nothing personal, no charge for tonight, do send your cleaning bill . . .

'Stephen, are you awake?'

'Darling, do you have to ring so early?'

'It's half past ten. Stephen, you'll never guess—'

'Laura Douglas has run off with a rock star.'

'No.'

'They've found salmonella in caviar. A junior minister is running a gourmet vice ring.'

Didi grinned. 'Listen, listen. There was a simply enormous punch-up at the Kitchen Club last night. Tadeus Freeman. Of course. He's been out of the news for at least two weeks, poor angel, and now everyone will write about him. You have to hand it to him. He's about the only chef who gets publicity without hiring Laura Douglas.'

'Come on. You're dying to tell. What happened?'

'Tadeus was knocking it back with some friends, and then Harry Wade walks in. Harry comes up, insults him, and says he couldn't cook a boiled egg and Tadeus calls him all the names under the sun and punches him. Wallop.'

'Sorry, sweetie. This one doesn't add up.'

'What do you mean? It's true. Caliope told me.'

'Harry Wade has gone back to the Watermill in Stourbridge. He's been there for months.'

'Are you sure?'

'Yes.'

'Well, it doesn't matter who it was.'

Didi put down the phone, momentarily deflated. Her large fluffy cat landed on the bed with a thump and sat close to her head, purring in anticipation.

'Salmon trout, Minou. Hold on. Let me wake up.'

André Bouchon slammed down a copper pan and beckoned to John. 'Please to come to my office.'

'Is something wrong, Monsieur Bouchon?'

'Here, no. Something wrong, yes. Come.'

'I'm sorry about the turbot but I had to send it back. The supplier couldn't get me any more for today.'

André Bouchon sat at his desk, with John opposite him. This office, which had first inspired awe, was now as familiar as the kitchen.

'OK, OK. We make something else. Maybe you like to try.'

'Oh, yes.' John got up from his chair.

'Sit down, John. What is this I 'ear? This morning, the manager of the Kitchen Club, he call me.'

John bit his lip and his heart pounded.

'You were there, *n'est-ce pas?*'

'Yes.'

'With that . . . with Freeman.'

'Yes.'

'He was drinking too much, I suppose.'

'Quite a lot. Yes.'

'For me, John, this is serious. For you, maybe, is simply fun.'

'It was stupid.'

'Not stupid. Dangerous. The papers, they will hear, then we will see a story of a chef who is drunk, who does not know how to behave. And then? Everyone will say every chef is drunk, every chef is stupid, every chef is an animal. For many, many years, I try to show that to be a chef is an honour, an important profession like lawyer, doctor or artist. I try to give our profession what it has in France. *Le standing*. If we have not this, we should dig up the road.'

As he walked back into the kitchen, John wondered if André Bouchon had ever been young, noisy, hot-headed, made crazy mistakes, felt randy and gone on the razzle with a gang of friends. Occasionally he thought this might have been so, for there were moments when he caught Le Grand Maître off-guard looking out of the corner of his eye at one of the pretty girls chopping the vegetables.

The financial update had just taken place in the Library, a terra-cotta coloured room whose walls were covered with restaurant designs placed in ornate silvered frames and whose heavy Raj-inspired furniture brought a change of ambience and displayed the flexible design approach typical of Laura Douglas Associates. The long redwood table with its shaded green reading lights gave the necessary gravitas for special occasions, such as the signing of contracts and financial assessments. The accountant had just walked out into the Studio wearing an expression of cautious optimism on his bland features appropriate to the outcome of the latest financial review. Miss Douglas, it gave him pleasure to say, was 'on course', and he could now concur with her desire to shed the accounts which had enabled her to 'gain financial momentum' and which were not sufficiently prestigious, he quite realized, to feature in the LDA portfolio.

Laura preferred to maintain a tactful silence on the accounts which, Jack had suggested, would provide a substantial bed-rock for her business. Bon Arôme bread and Icky Fingers Choc-Sticks, for example. It was such a relief, she confided, to be able to break free from the tacky world of food manufacturers whose major concerns were shelf-appeal (packaging), shelf-life (being safe to eat after a week, a month, a year), international distribution and market penetration. Now that she had a list of over thirty leading restaurants which included Zi-Zi's, the Sang Froid, the Quadrangle, les Deux Amis, Chancellor's, Le Repos du Guerrier, Minton's, La Speranza, the Minotaur and Aphrodite's under her wing, it was time to go one step further.

'I've been thinking,' said Leo, after Laura had summarized the accountant's findings, 'If we drop Icky Fingers as you suggest—'

'Thank heavens for that,' interjected Antony, who had lasted the course by willingly undertaking more tedious tasks.

'—then we need some form of sustaining account to underpin our more volatile ventures.'

Antony listened intently. It did give one an advantage having been to Harvard Business School. Still, he was younger than Leo and had time to overcome this gap in his education.

'Such as?' said Laura.

'Well, a wine account, for example?'

'Mm. That's difficult, with supermarkets buying up the best vintages. Difficult to compete.'

'There's always own label. The Laura Douglas Classic Wine selection which you could get our restaurants to stock.'

'Nice idea, Leo, but what would be in it for them?'

'Classy wines at lower prices.'

'And lower prices means lower profit margins. Not worth the problems. And it would mean a hefty set-up period of finding the right growers, and reliable supply.'

'We could link up with a quality wine merchant.'

'Might be worth looking into. Have you got those figures I asked for, Leo?'

'Nearly finished.'

'Give me an idea. What are we talking about?'

'Take a deep breath.'

'Well?'

'So far, three quarters of a million, excluding the lease. One and a half million to open.'

Laura wound a strand of her hair tightly round her finger and pulled it hard as Leo went through the figures column by column.

'We could knock off two hundred thou, but that would leave no contingency. And I haven't allowed for inflation.'

'Thanks, Leo. You've done a good job.'

'Will you go for it?' he asked.

'Maybe,' she replied, tidying back her hair and gathering her coat. Leo was impressed, and a little jealous. She hadn't hit the roof, hadn't questioned his figures, hadn't told him to go back and think again. Even after two years of being in her company, he could never be sure what she was thinking, or what emotions stirred beneath her carefully composed features.

'Are you lunching today?' she asked. 'I thought we might drop in on André Bouchon and see how John Crabtree's shaping up.'

'Nothing important. I'd love to.'

The phone rang and Laura picked it up.

'Hi Laura. It's me. How you doing?'

'Fine. Fine.'

'You sound tired. Everything OK?'

'Hectic day, that's all.'

'You seen the press?'

'Not yet.'

'You know a guy called Freeman, a Pole from Yorkshire, cooks in some overpriced joint off Brompton?'

'Tadeus Freeman. Chef-patron of Freeman's. Yes. What's he done now? Thrown you out again?'

'He did me a favour. I'm in five dailies this morning.'

'Oh?'

'Starts acting bolshie for no reason in the Kitchen Club. Too blotto for a punch-up so he clears my table for me. I think he's nuts. You represent him by any chance?'

'No thanks.'

'Steer clear. Anyway, I told the press I was thinking of buying him out.'

'And are you?'

'Wouldn't touch it. Too small. Anyhow these guys start calling from five different papers, so I decided to tell it like this. This maniac Freeman flipped, I guess because he's worried his backers have put him up for grabs. Teenie tantrums, I say. The catering industry, like the tennis business, and I quote, has had enough of spoiled brats. Read it. Then I went on to say how Leone Leisure is revolutionizing the restaurant concept. They missed out that bit, but I think they got the message. You listening, Laura?'

'Yes, Jack. But I'm just about to go out.'

'Shall we meet up? You going some place in town?'

'I've got a business lunch at Aphrodite's.'

'It's not like some of your passing throughs. Decent portions of meat, good quality too. Is it one of yours?'

'I consult from time to time.'

'How do you rate the decor? Myself, I reckon a few changes are in order. High-class clientele don't want the plush look any more. Maybe in Beverly Hills, but not here.'

'I disagree. It's why Aphrodite's is unique. No-one's mucked about with it.'

'Interesting you say that, but I think you're wrong.'

'Have you ever thought I was right?'

'Come on. You have some screwy ideas but . . . Anyhow. I might have some news about Aphrodite's, but it's under wraps for the present.'

'Oh?'

'I'm giving it thought.'

Laura bit her nail and waited.

'You still there?'

'Yes. I don't think it's the right location for a Leone Brasserie.'

Jack laughed. 'You still serious about opening a place, Laura? I've been thinking. Remember those dinner parties? Our friends still talk. Do you realize how they admired you? I could just see you, front of house. There's a sweet place going in Richmond, forty-seater, good local clientele. Could work. Think about it. I could take you down there—'

'I'll think about it.'

'Laura?'

'Yes?'

'I miss you. Every day I try to figure out why you left. What I did wrong. Maybe we should have gone into therapy. I'd have done that, but you never made the suggestion. I'd have worked to put things right, you know that. We talked about everything, so I figured it wasn't necessary. Maybe we talked about the wrong things . . . You think we should have adopted, after—?'

'This isn't the moment, Jack. I'm sorry, I must go.'

The calm of Aphrodite's was conducive to slow savouring and gentle murmured conversation with the occasional muted report of a cork being eased from a bottle. Those who dined there knew the menu, knew the waiters, knew not to betray enthusiasm. They would be eating what they always ate at Aphrodite's.

A well-known Shakespearean actor was gazing up at the sculpted ceiling. His agent was buying. The head of the Confederation of British Industry was bending his ear towards a minister who was outlining a complex policy move. A group of Japanese businessmen was elegantly cupping the rocky, gnarled shells of hand-sized oysters, with their heads turned in gestures of respect towards their leader, grey and wizened with the seniority of position. The occupants of the dining room ignored those seated a few feet away, masking recognition if they needed to catch the eye of one of the silent crowd of waiters, tacitly sharing in the studied anonymity of the truly distinguished.

As Laura sampled the foie gras, she imagined Jack walking in with the Director of Design of Leone Leisure, sizing up, taking out his remote measuring beam, his damp meter, talking into his pocket memo, stripping away with one quick glance the nineteenth-century plasterwork, the panelling, peeling back the carpet, seeing possibilities in a blank space, bidding down. Who wants a place like this nowadays? It needs a big spend, we gotta open it out. You call this a kitchen? When's the last time anyone put money in this place? Let's be serious, this decor is antique. I don't go to museums for lunch. You call that turnover? I'd double that. Am I serious? You bet I am.

'Great food,' remarked Leo, slicing delicately through a smoked salmon roulade. 'But it's about time the decor was reviewed. Wouldn't you say, Laura?'

Laura smiled and dabbed her lips wih the fine linen napkin. 'More wine?'

As she stretched her hand towards the ice bucket, a waiter forestalled her move in a second and filled up both glasses. Leo felt at ease and confident.

'Laura?'

'Yes?'

'I want to say how much I admire what you're doing.'

'Thank you, Leo.'

'I mean, the way you stick out for what you want. When I first came, I wondered if I could work for you, for a woman, that is . . . I hope you don't mind me saying this.'

'Of course not.' Laura looked at him quizzically. Leo had not put a foot wrong, but then he constantly watched his step. 'I think we work well together.'

'So do I,' he replied eagerly. 'In fact, I've been thinking. Well, I suppose the prospect of marriage does sharpen the mind.'

'Leo! I'm so pleased.'

'I was wondering if . . . it's just a thought, but—' He sipped at his wine. 'If you might consider some sort of participation. I mean, whether, in the long term, you had envisaged my . . . my becoming a partner.'

'Leo, I'm very flattered you want to become part of the company, but, truthfully, and I do appreciate all your efforts, I don't think you're quite ready. I know you have good ideas and have given me a lot of support . . .'

'Perhaps next year?' he asked hopefully.

'Perhaps.'

'I have brought in some good accounts, you see, and nowadays I'm sure you're aware that large companies, and even smaller ones, are offering long-term incentives.'

'We can always talk again. Let's see how we go, shall we?'

A waiter moved forward to the table. They both ordered coffee.

'You didn't mind my asking?' Leo said.

'No. I quite understand. It's good to talk openly.' Laura leaned back and smiled. 'But if you're thinking of leaving and taking my best clients, my dear Leo, I'll have your guts for garters.'

Leo blushed and gulped. Perhaps it was true, the rumour which said that poison flowed through the blue veins of Laura Douglas. Her level tone did not change, though, and her face maintained a gentle smile.

'You're impatient. I know how it feels. Exactly. But everyone needs a trial period. Two years is not even the length of a university course. It's a very short time, Leo.'

'I suppose so.'

Leo thought of his friends leaping up the fast City escalator, bursting into foreign markets, second homes at twenty-five. Some had gone from nothing to big something in two years. He was twenty-six and still eating takeaways when he got home and his new wife would have to make do with a flat in Chiswick. Tough when you had grown up in Holland Park . . .

'I want a quick word with John Crabtree. Could you get back to the office and see if Antony's fixed up that meeting? He does need a little prod from time to time.'

Laura rose and walked towards the door leading to the kitchen. Leo's cup was empty, and he summoned the waiter.

'And I'll have a brandy,' he said, as the coffee bubbled into his cup.

Laura greeted John, who was now preparing for the evening meal. He thought he'd better mention the do at the Kitchen Club as they stood watching the pastry chef cutting fleurs-de-lys out of dough, one after another.

'Have you thought what you want to do next?' asked Laura.

'I'll stay here a while. It suits me fine right now.'

'You're not restless?'

'I'm not even missing Yorkshire, though I'll take a trip up the next holidays.'

'I'm looking into a place for you,' said Laura.

'Great.' John gave her little attention. It was time they took the marinade out of the fridge and started the *mirepoix*. His ambition was flagging. André Bouchon was treating him too well.

'Henry Thurlow's about to open his own place in London. He wants us to handle him.'

John swung round. 'Thurlow from the Trout in Kirkbymoorside?'

'That's right.'

'He's a prat. Cooked frozen and said it was fresh but we all knew. Said he'd been cooking in France, but he hadn't. Lying bastard he is. Where's he opening then?'

'Primrose Hill, I believe.'

'Where's that?'

'Next to Regent's Park. Smart locals who never look at the bill but haggle over mangoes in the local greengrocer's.'

'Never heard of it. Anyway, never did have time for Henry Thurlow. Right place for him is Charlie's Brasserie. A chicken in a basket man is Henry. Excuse me, Laura.'

John moved over to the other side of the kitchen.

* * *

André Bouchon was snatching a moment of peace, curled up on his six-seater settee. Laura knocked gently and he answered with his eyes closed.

'*Qui est là?*'

'Laura.'

He reached for some velvet slippers, for not even Laura could see him with uncovered feet, and sat up. 'Come in.' He looked her up and down. 'Nice. I like your dress.'

'Thank you. I'm sorry to burst in on you.'

'Not at all, but today, I must say, I am in bad mood.'

'Any particular reason?'

'Last night Tadeus Freeman make another spectacle.'

'Yes, I heard. John told me.'

'You will please to stop the newspapers saying bad things?'

'I'll try, André. Tell me, how is John settling down? Are you pleased with him?'

'*Eh bien*. John, he is learning, he like to learn. He is very happy with me. Here we are always one family.'

'Do you think he's ready yet to strike out on his own?'

Monsieur Bouchon stroked his chin thoughtfully. 'He is a very talented boy. One day he can use his big imagination. Now he is doing things my way. Here there is only one way. You know that.'

'If you had another restaurant would you let John be chef?'

'Maybe. Maybe in a few months, a simple place. A little brasserie. He could try, but I would still see everything is done *manière* Bouchon. By the way, I am not intending to open another place. Is enough work here, don't you think?'

Laura looked at his lined face. He never complained, but the strain showed.

'One day,' he said, 'I must think who will take over. Who knows? Maybe Crabtree.'

'Lunch was perfect today, I have to say.'

'I'm glad you enjoy it. Now I must rest, Laura.'

He led her to the door.

John Crabtree was now blessed with something far more important than a diploma, a certificate of excellence awarded by some body within the catering profession, or even a good review from a leading restaurant critic. He had André Bouchon's seal of approval. Laura leaned back in the taxi and started to plan her next moves.

When Leo arrived home, he felt queasy. His stars, which he read avidly and in secret, had foreseen worrying times ahead under the influence of the disturber of the peace, the planet Mars. The queasiness was bound to be physical, even though it seemed to have affected his spirits. Mars, being a powerful fellow, was capable of attacking mind and body simultaneously. Not to worry, it was probably an allergy to something he had eaten. Apparently it was possible to develop one, just like that. Even at Aphrodite's. Yes, he had eaten seafood. If he had developed an allergy to langoustines, he hoped desperately it was only temporary. The doorbell rang. Standing on the step was a figure covered in thick black leather from head to toe, his face hidden in a mask spattered with raindrops. He thrust an envelope at Leo and then leapt with the jerky movements of a bolting spider on to his motorbike. Why was it necessary to appear so sinister when delivering an envelope? Another press release to rewrite. Leo opened it. Handwritten.

A few drops of rain splashed coolly on to Laura's face in the time it took to step out of the car, walk the few steps to her front door and release the intricate locks of the burglar alarm. She gave a quick look round her living room as she put down the soft leather bag bulging with her evening's work and pressed the master switch for the lighting system. A host of carefully positioned spots showed up the pale parquet floor, the rich rugs, a large canvas by Lisa Milroy, currently showing at Laura's favourite Bond Street gallery, the hard-edged black steel idiosyncratic chairs by Philippe Starck, one of which the cleaner had misplaced by a foot. This she repositioned, activated the sound system (Glenn Gould playing Bach preludes) and ran a bath. There were a few precious hours in which to finish reports, read articles and make phone calls to check the progress of restaurants she represented.

She had stepped out of the bath and was wrapped in a towel when the doorbell rang. This was such a rare occurrence, for where Laura lived was a mystery to all except a couple of friends she still saw from the Mrs Leone days, that she hesitated to answer. She pulled up a slat of the wooden blind protecting her privacy in the quiet Chelsea street enough to observe her visitor.

'I'm coming,' she said through the letterbox. 'Wait a moment.' She ran to her bedroom and pulled out the first dress she could slip into quickly. If she were to appear in a bathrobe it would give the wrong impression. It might appear as though she had planned an evening of relaxation. She opened the door to a dripping figure.

'I don't mind the rain,' he said. 'Or getting soaked.' He pressed his wet face to hers and pulled her body against his sodden raincoat.

'Why didn't you ring?'

'No time. I managed to catch an earlier plane from Milan. Can't stay long. Here. Something for you.'

He slid a small packet into her hand and she disengaged herself to open it.

'Not yet. In the bedroom.'

'Darling, I'm working tonight.'

'You can do that when I've gone.' He looked at his watch. 'I must be home by eleven.'

'To drink your cocoa?' she asked from the kitchen, where she was opening a chilled bottle of Laurent Perrier. She would save the elegantly wrapped package from Donini in Milan (he had remembered her passion for intricately embroidered Italian silk), until she was alone.

'What did you say?'

'Nothing,' Laura put the bubbling glass in front of him.

'Aren't you going to see what it is?'

148

'Later.'

He took a few sips, caressed her hair then ran his hand under her dress and down her bare back.

'Howard, I told you . . .'

'Relax.'

'I don't want to. Not tonight.'

'I've been thinking of your body all the way from Milan.'

'I'm not in the mood. Really.'

'You're just not used to a man who truly desires you.'

'You can't come here whenever it suits you and expect me to—'

'Yes, I can. And you want me, even though you try and play games to pretend you don't. I know you better than you know yourself. I'm the only man who does, Miss Douglas.'

'Do you like difficult women? I think you must.'

He stroked her slender body until he felt her give way a little, covered her mouth with his lips to forestall her objections, pulled off her dress inch by inch, insinuated his long fingers between her legs and pulled her gently to the floor. She closed her eyes as she felt his strong confident movements inside her limp body. Had he driven from Heathrow on a wet night for these few minutes of pleasure? Was she worth the effort. She opened her eyes and he folded her in his arms. He looked twenty years younger, radiantly handsome, unlined. All because of a few minutes.

'Did anything happen? Was that good for you?' he asked. 'I wish I could stay longer.'

'Beautiful,' she replied, smiling her serene smile and sitting up.

'One day you will scream with pleasure, I promise you.'

She no longer asked when that would be. He had silenced her complaints, and refused to give her either apologies or constant protestations of love. 'You know I love you,' he said.

'Shouldn't you be getting dressed?'

Howard glanced at his watch. Laura sat looking up at him as he reformed his muted silk tie into a precise knot and adjusted his crocodile belt. He could not understand why it gave her such pleasure, these mundane intimate gestures as he changed from firm-structured nakedness into the soft lines of tailored elegance.

'Tell me about your day. How is everything?'

'Do you really want to know?'

'Of course I do.'

'I want to hear about Milan.'

A meeting in Paris, then on to Milan, buying factories here, sites there, discussions with government representatives. Her day? Trivial, compared with his.

'How is the animal? Has he been bothering you?'

He insisted on knowing every time they met, or even talked on the telephone, to overcome her weakness. It was so easy to slip back into the past. He understood that so well. Good, good. He was glad someone had had the guts to give him the treatment he deserved at the Kitchen Club. Tadeus Freeman was a man after his own heart. He should have finished off the animal there and then.

'Why are you so jealous? He's in the past.'

'I'm not jealous, only curious. I'm curious about you. I want to know why you stayed so long with him. I want to know what makes you tick. I want to know your secrets.'

'You screw me. Doesn't that tell you?'

'We make love. The animal screws.'

'All right.'

'Do you screw or make love with your wife?'

'I'm not telling you.'

'I don't really want to know.'

Howard kissed her hand, then Laura stood up and started to put on her dress.

'Come on,' he said, 'You're disturbed by something. Spit it out. I promise I'll listen.'

'Do you mind if we discuss business? I need your advice.'

'I'm listening.' Howard went over to the window. 'The rain has stopped. I hate driving in the rain.'

'Leo did some figures for me. I thought I'd found somewhere for John Crabtree but, well, the cost is around one and a half.'

'Million?'

'Yes. How can I possibly raise that sort of money?' Howard remained standing by the window, calculating the time he should allow to return home at this time of night.'

'My dear Laura, give me half an hour.'

'You could do it? Really?'

'Of course. With the right location, a few letters from my friendly connections, a couple of aristocrats, your friendly connections, a couple of media personalities . . . Where would you like, Mayfair or Knightsbridge?'

'Howard, I'm serious.'

'I know. If that's what you want, I'll do it for you.' He smiled his laconic smile, noticing that Laura had sprung to life, her eyes sparkling.

'But you don't think it will work.'

'It will work. It will be the most successful restaurant in London. A sure-fire investment. Anyone who puts money in will be riding on a high for years. One thing, though: how will you maintain control? How soon will it be before you're told to change the decor, lower the prices, change the chef?'

'I wouldn't let that happen.'

'Even I couldn't prevent it. Money is easy. How do you imagine you would control the shareholders who are told by the accountant that, given certain changes, their return will be doubled?'

'I'd get the right kind of investors. People who cared.'

Howard laughed. 'Laura, darling, I love your optimism. It's charming. But I still don't understand why you want to open a restaurant.'

Laura walked round the room and adjusted a light. 'Am I asking the impossible? Do you think I'm crazy?'

'You want to raise one and a half million. Well, you'd better go into property.'

'Like Jack, you mean?'

'Didn't he start with nothing?'

Laura was silent. Howard looked at his watch again. 'We'll talk about it next time. I must be going. Are your staff behaving?'

'It happened as you said it might.'

'Ah. Did you solve it as I suggested?'

'I did, as a matter of fact.'

'I'm not going to get blamed? You don't feel guilty? No tiny twinge of remorse for getting rid of your good-looking young man?'

Laura thought of Leo's eager face over lunch at Aphrodite's, the moment when his discreet charm turned to avarice. 'No. Not at all.'

'Good. You're coming along nicely.'

Sir Howard Riley put his wet raincoat over his arm and reached for the door handle.

'Wait a moment. There's some lipstick on your cheek.'

'Don't worry. I always check before I go down the drive.'

7

Didi sat in glory way up on the seventeenth floor of Intertel's new building. She was in the midst of an earnest programme discussion in her uniquely distinctive office. Travel trophies, masks, puppets, paper birds, menus, coloured engravings of fruit and vegetables, framed letters from adulatory viewers and, of course, awards littered her walls, painted a dark, sensuous bluey pink the colour of mulberries (her favourite fruit, visually that is) at her insistence. The colour still wasn't right, but she would make do with it. An ethnic mobile made of dried African vegetables rustled in the flow of air conditioning. She hated the louvred blinds, and there had been a huge row over her maintaining her right to keep the lace curtains handmade by peasants which she had acquired in Budapest during her programme on 'Hungary Meets the Gastronauts'. The Controller of Programmes, the Director of Finance and the Head of Design had all told her that the steely blue Intertel façade had been designed to make a statement and lace curtains wasn't it. After a tempestuous battle, she had, in the end, graciously given way.

Ms Kowalski was 'in a meeting' (to external callers) and 'in conference' (to internal callers). A quiet, somewhat dowdy, modest but utterly reliable researcher, Deirdre, was passing paper plates of bacon samples for Didi's consideration across a white Formica table littered with packets, labels, photographs and sheafs of promotional, informational communications piled up and weighed down with a large paperweight labelled 'BUMPH'.

'This one is really good. One could even drink champagne with it for breakfast. Don't you think?'

Deidre, who couldn't drink champagne as the bubbles fizzed up her nose, agreed and told Didi from whence came the sample.

'I don't believe it. Stocked by a British supermarket and it comes from Israel? What will my viewers in Leeds, Manchester and North London say? They're never going to believe it! Wouldn't it be hilarious if it came out top?'

'Apparently they raise pigs outside Haifa, all kinds of rare breeds, and they've managed to find a way of lowering the dietary cholesterol.'

'Oh.' Didi frowned. 'I don't like the sound of that. They probably pump them full of nasty chemicals. Let me taste another bit.'

Deirdre felt the tension mount.

'Mm. Well, it's good, but it's got a funny aftertaste, come to think of it. Let's have the next one.'

Everyone who worked with her agreed that Didi was conscientious. She might be difficult and demanding at times, even ruthless if you didn't come up to scratch, but she was so professional. In the tough world of broadcasting to be called professional, really professional, was an accolade accorded to the distinguished few. (To be described thus with awed surprise might have seemed strange to lawyers, doctors or even soldiers, but in the language of Intertel they were not professional. They were experts.) Didi's critics pointed to her voluptuous figure and mocked her constantly, calling her the Queen of Gastro-Porn, but the ratings soared. They did not understand her commitment. Tasting twenty samples of bacon after a huge lunch at Claridge's took some doing, but it was part of the job. And she took her job very, very seriously.

'We have a responsibility to over eight million viewers. Let us not forget that we also have a responsibility to every grower of mushrooms and carrots and potatoes who tends his beds with loving care, every farmer whose animals roam free in our glorious countryside, every supermarket which strives for the highest quality in order to give our poorer families a taste of the best. I am not prepared to trivialize. I am not prepared to prostitute myself and betray eight million viewers in order to further the craven interests of the Light Entertainment department.'

This extract from a famous Kowalski memo, circulated to all heads of departments at Intertel (Stephen had helped her write it), was framed and hung next to her awards. The occasion? The Head of Light Entertainment had wanted to gobble up part of her programme by having an eight-minute beat-the-clock cooking slot for 'housewives', hosted by a northern comedian.

Sir Howard Riley, chairman of Intertel, decided to take a principled stand on this occasion. He had no wish to associate Illustra Foods, of which he was also chairman, with an unknown northern comedian whose downmarket image would be more suited to lesser rivals. As Illustra products were featured frequently on *Table for One*, and the Illustra advertising spend provided a healthy chunk of Intertel's revenue, the Controller of Programmes saw the logic of this argument. *Table for One* would not deviate from its award-winning format, he reassured Ms Kowalski in a handwritten note.

'I'm only bringing out your features.' Cindy, the Head of Make-Up, had been specially asked by Didi to drop in on the occupant of Dressing Room Ten. 'And make you look even more handsome.'

'John cringed as the powder brush flicked over his face. He was unused to having a woman stare at him so unflinchingly, appraising every tiny imperfection of his skin and hair.

'You're not putting that stuff on?' John looked in horror as a small box of rouge was taken from his dressing table.

'Just a teeny teeny bit. The cameras see differently from us. Sometimes people refuse to wear any make-up and they look dreadful. Have you seen those politicians interviewed outside Parliament? I mean!' Cindy adjusted the intensity of the rouge, stroking down his cheek. 'If they'd only spend a minute having a little touch-up, it would make all the difference. Then maybe people would believe their lies.' She giggled and flicked a lock of his hair forward. 'That's nice. I like that.'

'I don't.'

The door opened and John saw Didi's smiling face in the mirror.

'I can see someone's going to get a bag of fan mail,' she said. 'You are going to wear your lovely chef's hat, aren't you?'

'Do I have to?'

'Yes. My viewers love them. I can see you're a bit nervous but that's only because it's the first time. Television is so easy. All you have to do is be you.'

John sat up straighter in his chair and looked at the stranger in the mirror. Laura would hardly have recognized him. Didi had rung her up at the last minute as one of her usual chefs had dropped out and she was thinking maybe she should have a new face on the 'Taste for a Test' slot. Yes, someone from the North would be super, as long as his accent wasn't too thick and everyone could understand him. John Crabtree? Yes, she did vaguely remember seeing him. The tall one. Yes, at the opening of Petrushka's.

'Well, if it isn't Little John.'

Elwyn strolled into the studio carrying his tall, chef's hat and walked over to the 'Taste for a Test' set, designed like a Frankenstein laboratory with a background of retorts, jars and microscopes which were never used but lent visual interest. In front of that was the experimental kitchen, a large island of cookers, microwave ovens, a fridge and no-shine surfaces with neatly ranged dishes and pans and measures. In the foreground, to one side, was a row of cubicles so that those seated could be seen by the cameras but not by each other.

Elwyn was followed by Sebastian, then someone John did not know.

'Who's that, El?' he asked.

Elwyn whispered in his ear: 'Harry Wade. Was at the Watermill in Stourbridge for a few months. Didn't like it. Now he's got a chi-chi place in Richmond. Doesn't get on with Tad. Tad stole his girlfriend, so he says.'

'Right. Stand by for a run-through. Positions, please.'

The four chefs, in their whites and tall hats, sat down like customs men tipped off to expect dodgy suitcases in the green area. The floor manager grinned at them.

'Relax, lads. You look great. Absolutely great. And don't worry. You are all gonna be . . . *fantastic*!'

For an hour every movement was rehearsed, every shot aligned to the exacting and artistic requirements of Didi's favourite director. John wondered what you did in a studio when you had an overwhelming urge to visit the gent's, but then the floor manager called, 'Break, studio. Ten minutes.'

Didi was watching in the gallery with the director. They would soon be ready for her bit of chat over the frying bacon which, she suspected, might entail problems for sound with all that sizzling.

'Didi, love. Time for wardrobe.'

Bliss. Now she could put on the buttercup yellow Ozbek silk which plunged in a wide sweep at the back. She would turn to take the bacon samples over to the chefs, and the camera would linger over her suntanned skin.

'OK, everyone. Can I have your attention? *Please*? Stand-by studio for rehearsal of 'Taste for a Test' insert one. Ten, nine, eight, seven, six . . .'

John glanced at Sebastian who was scratching his nose. Elwyn winked. Harry Wade stared ahead, doing sums in his head, wondering if he would make enough profit on a big party tonight.

Silence. Total concentration. Didi's intro to cam. Cut, fine. Super. Great. Go for it.

Didi undulated from frying pan to frying pan, in perfect position for each camera, sniffing, prodding, giving a breathy sotto voce running commentary to her viewers, imparting the facts collated by Deirdre and giving them the urgency of a commentator summing up the runners in a race enclosure.

'I'm backing this one,' she said, bringing her nose closer to the frying pan. 'What a shame you can't smell it. It reminds me of wood-smoke drifting out from a thatched cottage.' She gazed up at Camera Three and yearned into its lens. 'When you've got out of bed to make the fire for someone you love.'

Didi moved cam right. Cut to Camera Two.

'Oh dear. What a disappointment. This looks as limp as last week's lettuce, but you never know, do you? This little fellow might surprise us! We mustn't judge by appearances. The flavour might be divine.'

The floor manager waved his hand frantically in a mystic circle. Get a move on. Twenty seconds to go and five more samples.

The director, dressed for action in jumpsuit and trainers, came out of his glassed-in gallery and ran to Didi.

'Didi love,' he whispered, 'I'm going to have to cut twenty seconds of your intro.'

'Twenty seconds?' Didi raised her voice so that the studio microphone could relay her disdain.

The director flinched. 'Do try, love, not to make quite so many pauses.'

Didi caught sight of herself in one of the monitors. 'Gosh, my face is awful. All shiny. I'm going to make-up.'

'Quiet, studio!' shouted the director. 'Ten-minute break.'

The studio audience began to arrive and the floor manager came into his own, welcoming, joking, introducing the bewildered guests to the magic of Intertel.

'Don't look at the monitors, folks. I want you to concentrate on our super chefs here tonight. Elwyn, Sebastian, John and Harry. Shall we give them a round of applause? One, two, three, and here we go.'

Restrained clapping.

'Come on, you can do better than that. They've left

their kitchens to be here with us tonight. Give the lads a good welcome. One, two, three . . .'

The second round of applause sounded better. The Head of Sound recorded it for future use, should studio enthusiasm wane.

'Good luck, everybody. We're going for a take. This is the one, folks. Ten, nine, eight . . .'

Secure in his cubicle, John tasted the first sample in front of him. He could hear Didi's voice over his headphones.

'Here is a newcomer to our team, John Crabtree from Yorkshire. He tells me he's going to open in London very soon. I can't wait!'

Who told her that? John smiled wryly and Camera Two happened to catch it.

'Wow. Sex-ee,' said the vision mixer in the gallery, bang on cue for Camera Two's offering.

'What do you think of this, John?'

John held the bacon on a fork in front of him. 'Anaemic. Flabby.' He sniffed it. 'And no aroma whatsoever. This pig has never seen daylight, I'd reckon.' He put some into his mouth. 'I'd never know what I was eating.'

'Marks, John?'

'Two out of ten.'

'That's pretty low from John. Elwyn's given it five and Harry's given it four. How about Sebastian?'

'Two out of ten from Sebastian. There's some disagreement here.'

'The numbers flashed on to the screen: Elwyn: five, Harry: four, Sebastian and John: two.

The fifth sample was due to be tasted. John realized the advantage of coming last.

'Could you ask Sebastian? I can't quite make up my mind.'

Didi took his cue like a dream. Sebastian couldn't refuse. He marked it high. Now the camera lingered on John, and he paused. 'I was going to give this one high marks, but then I thought no. Texture's fine, but I don't think it's had a proper curing. I might be wrong. Four out of ten. Perhaps someone from the audience would like a taste.'

'Good God! He's getting up. Follow him, follow him, Camera Two.' The director's frenzied voice pierced the earpieces of his somnolent crew. 'Focus. Focus, Camera Two.' The blurred image shifted to sharpness.

John walked along the front row of the audience and accosted a pretty girl.

'Right. Good. Thank you, Camera Three. Lovely. Lovely shot.'

The vision mixer pressed the buttons like hot cakes. Action stuff.

'Get a mike on to her. Sound. Sound, for Christ's sake.'

'What do you think, love?'

The director, frantically, 'Follow him, Camera One. Follow him. This is fantastic!'

The girl opened her mouth to receive John's forkful of bacon.

'I think you're right,' she said. 'Four I'd give it.'

'Cut,' said a definitive voice from the studio. The cameras held their positions, motionless. Didi walked off the set and rushed into the gallery. The master monitor went blank.

'There'll be an overrun,' said the Head of Technical Operations sourly, only too aware that he would miss the last train to Sonning on Thames which would leave in half an hour.

The director thought quickly during the time it took for Didi to squeeze past the technicians. 'Don't worry, love,' he said reassuringly. 'We'll take it from your summing up and edit round it.'

'John must repeat his assessment from the cubicle. Who told him to do that?'

'Right, studio. From shot one-nine-two. Stand by. Didi, love, are you ready?'

Didi flounced off. Meanwhile the floor manager re-assured those sitting in front of the cameras that they were

160

an absolutely super audience. Just needed one extra take. They were going for perfection.

John obediently stepped back into his cubicle, looked straight into the camera and did what was required. Didi took her summing-up position, smiled adoringly into the camera for a second, and then spoke. How surprised she was that the top bacon in 'Taste for a Test' came from Israel – pork from Israel, who would have guessed? – and stocked by Hemingway's, a small southern supermarket making a bid for the quality market. However, she really did have to point out that they used chemicals to artificially lower the cholesterol. Even though 'low cholesterol' was clearly marked on the label, customers could be misled into thinking it was healthier than traditional bacon. She personally would have rated number three, from Tesco's, as her favourite but she would like to thank all the chefs who had given their expert opinion. (Cue clapping.)

'OK, it's a wrap, studio,' the floor manager announced. 'Thank you, everyone.'

The director shook the hands of Elwyn, Sebastian and finally John. Harry Wade had rushed off. The audience was wandering towards the exit doors and Didi, meanwhile, had unlocked the drinks cupboard in the hospitality room and was already downing her bottle of champagne. The door opened.

'Laura, darling! I didn't know you were coming.'

'Didi. Congratulations. Brilliant show.'

The two women ceremoniously kissed each other on the cheek. 'I think we've got a winner with John Crabtree,' Laura said.

'He was a bit naughty, getting up like that, but don't worry. We'll edit that bit out.'

'Really? I thought he handled the situation rather well. Good television. André Bouchon reckons he's the most promising newcomer he's had for ages. In a year's time, he'll be a big name. Viewers will remember you discovered him first.'

Laura moved away to talk to John and the chefs. Didi was drained, as though her fixed studio smile was preventing her body from falling in a heap to the floor.

'Was it all right? Really?' she asked Roger, the programme producer who had emerged from the back of the studio.

'Of course, love.'

'Not boring?'

'No. No.'

He understood. Put his arms round her. Ordered her a taxi because she looked whacked. Didi wished he weren't gay. So attractive in a gaunt, haunted way. She knew he'd rather be directing drama, but he never showed any resentment. None. Nice man.

Lying in bed with a tray of delights balanced on her knee, Chopin played by that simply gorgeous Armenian pianist who won the Leeds Competition wafting through the bedroom speaker (and wouldn't she love to talk to him about Armenian food?), Minou purring, waiting, curled up on his velvet cushion beside her, Didi felt the soft fleshy folds of her stomach. If she returned to another life, she would be reclining in a harem, the white-skinned prize of some demanding sultan, stuffing perfumed Turkish delight into his mouth, her body oiled and waiting. A serving maid would be crouched beside her, attending to her every need. Why did they, the interesting men, the powerful men, prefer the spiky, whippet form of Laura Douglas?

It had been hot, the kind of heat which sank into every pore and aroused the body in waves of well-being. They were lying by the swimming pool of a five-star de luxe hotel, a warm bottle of mellow wine at their side, having toured the vineyards of Burgundy. Why, why, why? she had asked herself, as she observed her tanned expanse of flesh moulded into the shape of a Rubens Venus by virtue of a heavily boned, scarlet draped satin bathing costume. Why did finger-blown whistles and guttural shouts come her way more often than bottles of champagne and bouquets of flowers?

'Didi, sweetest, you've got the number of your hotel room written on your forehead. What do you expect?'

Sometimes, when suffering from indigestion, Stephen said things which hurt but which she sensed were wickedly true.

'Well, yours is written on your arse,' she had retorted.

'Not everyone who's been to public school is gay,' he said calmly.

'Why haven't we been to bed, then?'

'I would rather watch you suck out flesh from a lobster claw. Who needs the groping, the groaning, the bat-squeaks of orgasm, the clammy viscous outpourings of the body, the grotesque parabola of intercourse?'

'You mean you don't think I'm attractive?'

Stephen laughed and nibbled her neck. 'I can't resist you. I want to wrap you in filo pastry and smother you with *beurre blanc* fresh from one of the cows of Normandy . . .'

Didi turned over and lay on her side, one heavy breast touching the warm marble of the pool's edge, the other lolling in its inadequate cage whilst he watched her.

'Stephen, would you eat human flesh? I mean, if a cannibal invited you to a feast.'

'Of course.'

'Honestly? Bet you wouldn't.'

'I wouldn't want to try someone old and stringy, though. Only the best quality.'

'How disgusting. You've thought about it.'

'Naturally. The ultimate gourmet experience. It would be my last column. A classic. Stephen Boyce's Good Eating Guide to the Amazon.' Stephen tilted his face towards the sun and closed his eyes. '"We dined al fresco, listening to the rustles, squawks and cracklings of untram-melled Nature seeking out its prey. My companion had a twenty-two-year-old male, but I chose a sixteen-year-old female. The flavour of the male was superior, but the

163

texture of the female stood comparison with the finest home-reared pork from the Gloucester Old Spot. The method of cooking employed by the natives was reminiscent of the cruder *cuisine du terroir* but the use of unfamiliar herbs showed a surprising appreciation of culinary subtelty." Do you think I could persuade Laura to organize a press trip to the Amazon basin? We could offer Caliope as the sacrificial victim.'

Antony watched Laura arriving with large carrier bags bearing the discreetly calligraphed name of Margaret Howell.

'What have you bought? Can I have a look?'

'Later.'

She did not mind his appreciation of her good taste, and was pleased that it was no longer unmanly to be interested in clothes. They were getting along very well. One reason was that Laura had learned more of Antony's plans for the next ten years. He would eventually run the family estate when Daddy became too old, tired and feeble. Ten to fifteen years he reckoned. But now he enjoyed his little job as his sister enjoyed her little job answering the phone for an art gallery in Bond Street. She would get married and live in a cottage on the estate. He would get married and live in a farmhouse on the estate and have a *pied à terre* in Chelsea until the time came to run the twenty-bedroomed mansion, which was open to the public at weekends, as well as the surrounding acres of woodland and arable farmland. It would be a full-time task.

Leo had been too intelligent. She had learned from him that intelligence and ambition were closely allied. She ought to have known, she thought, but she had been taken in by Leo's handsome, open face, his confident bearing and beautifully modulated voice. Antony was sweet and willing. He would bring her small, stylish presents which made her smile, hand her things at the right moment and invariably impress bureaucrats and tradesmen with his seemingly egalitarian charm. A Cavalier spaniel was

Antony, bright-eyed and seeing no evil, always ready to rush out with his mistress. No-one else in the Team minded him, he always tagged along with good humour and Laura could talk to him freely, knowing he would never grasp the full import of her thinking. And if he did, it was by accident. It was by accident that he had suggested the next move for the client of the moment, John Crabtree.

'I say . . .' The Eau de Vie fired Antony's throat. He was beginning to take to unfamiliar liqueurs which Laura took for granted. 'Mummy happened to say last weekend that Lady Maclintock is looking for a chef. She's having a few people to stay at Maclintock Castle. I didn't say anything, but I thought how about John Crabtree? There'll be some fairly loaded chaps up there. Could be useful.'

'It would be fun for John.'

'That's what I thought. As long as he doesn't do too much of that nouvelle cuisine stuff.'

'But if John is going to display his talent, we really ought to have some kind of feedback. If it's merely a question of private catering . . . I suppose it wouldn't be possible to have a journalist or two up there, would it? It might amuse the guests.'

'I think that's an absolutely super idea. Why don't you come down and talk to Mummy about it?'

Antony was so happy. He had been a bit worried, inviting his boss back home, but it was a brilliant weekend. Mummy and Laura had got on terrifically and he never realized Laura knew so much about restoring old houses. Fascinating.

'You know, one is constantly surprised,' his mother remarked as she watched Laura's Lotus bumping over the cattle grid across the drive. 'She seems awfully nice. Rather jolly working with her, I would have thought. Much more than that awful person at Belinda's gallery. What's her name? Something foreign.'

'Lucia.'

'Lucia. Does one really know how much pictures cost? That's all she ever talks about. I do wish people would stop talking about money. They never used to.'

'I know, Mummy.'

The crystal glasses were wiped and put away in the cracked cupboards. One didn't trust staff with those.

The Doric Club had opened its heavy portals to the opposite sex, its only concession to the twentieth century. This would have been unheard of ten or even twenty years after women had been graciously awarded the vote in 1919, but over seventy years had passed and the committee considered the time was ripe to show equal magnanimity and voted to allocate funds for a second ladies' cloakroom on the first floor. Jack Leone, having quickly realized the advantages of bumping into the British power elite in the library, had become a member. As Mr Leone's wife, which she still was in the eyes of the club, Laura had been invited to take advantage of the amended membership regulations. Her fee alone for such a privilege paid for the ladies' cloakroom within two years but she, too, appreciated the advantages of such an institution.

The library at the Doric, Laura thought, would provide John Crabtree with a suitable introduction to the home life of the country aristocracy. There was even an oil painting of Highland cattle hanging over the fireplace. At first the idea of catering for Lady Maclintock's weekend in Scotland was met with little enthusiasm by John, but Laura had insisted. It would improve his curriculum vitae, impress the Michelin inspectors when the time came to make their acquaintance, and make him a persona grata amongst journalists who regarded titled land-owners as the last repository of the great, inimitable British tradition of taste and *savoir vivre*. Following his début on Didi's television programme, which Stephen had given a passing mention in his feature on 'The Gourmet Screen', John Crabtree had secured entry into the cuttings file on 'Food

– Chefs', the first step to eventual recognition. Following this, the *Yorkshire Post* had sought his opinion on the eating habits of the South as opposed to the North. Others would follow.

Laura sat reading the *Wall Street Journal* in the library and occasionally raised her head to see if John had arrived. A tall, elegantly suited man crossed her path of vision. Impossible.

'Laura, darling. What have I done to deserve this?'

Sir Howard Riley took her hand and pressed his lips against her fingers.

'I thought you were in Brussels.'

'Laura, have you met Viscount Alloway? This is Laura Douglas, the lady behind every top restaurant in London.'

'That's kind of you. If only I were.'

'How do you do it, Howard? Why haven't we met before? I say . . . jolly nice to meet you.'

'Will you join us?'

He looked at her with such longing, those unblinking dark eyes . . . Even in such a public place, unashamed of his love, unafraid of being seen with her, introducing her to his friends . . .

'I'm waiting for one of my chefs.'

'Never mind. I'll ring you later. Will you be in to-night?'

'Oh yes. I'm sure I will.'

He had to remember not to slouch. George had picked up on that, telephoning him after his television appearance. Wonderful show, ooh, you did look smashing, but can I say one thing? When you're a big star, you'll thank me. Shoulders back, sweetie. And chin up. Looks better on the camera. Tilting his chin upwards, John waited for the doorman at the club to address him, then he looked down from on high. 'I've come to see Miss Douglas.' He hoped he managed to pronounce 'come' as they did down South. It still bothered him, that constipated 'uh'.

'Your signature, sir.' Laura hadn't told him about this,

signing in a great leather book. The doorman handed him a fountain pen.

'It's all right. I've got a pen.' John had never written with anything except a biro. If he wrote quickly and scrawled, perhaps his illiterate loops wouldn't look out of place. Strange, the place smelt like a Yorkshire café. Fish and chips today, was it? A man stood behind him, waiting to sign. Feeling his presence, John turned round. 'Oh. Sorry.' The man stared right through him as though he didn't exist. He'd said something wrong again. 'Never apologize,' Laura had said. 'You must always assume you are right.' John wanted to leave but was ushered past the pillars, up the stairs and into a panelled room. Laura rose to meet him from a tatty leather armchair.

'Sorry I'm late,' said John. Laura smiled. 'I mean, I hope you haven't been waiting long. Monsieur Bouchon was going through a new menu. Bit of a long do.'

Laura handed him a book. 'I thought this might give you inspiration.' *The Illustrated Guide to Maclintock Castle*. 'We'll be staying in the guest wing, the part which isn't open to the public. In any case, that only happens once a month. Lord and Lady Maclintock are more interested in the shooting season.'

'Oh?'

'When the Americans come, bang away at a load of birds, eat in the great dining room, sleep in four-poster beds and line the Maclintock coffers. It pays for the drainpipes to be renewed.'

'They're not strapped for cash, surely?'

'That's putting it mildly. If Scottish bank managers didn't support the feudal system, they'd all have had to sell up years ago. Now they either build hotels and golf courses in the grounds or mortgage their sheep. They may live in castles but they couldn't afford a one-bedroom flat in London.

'Is that right? Make a good hotel, that would,' remarked John, leafing through the photographs.

'Here's who's coming.'

John read through the typewritten sheet and looked up with alarm. 'I'd need a brigade to do the kind of stuff they'll be expecting. Or have I got to think up a nouvelle haggis?'

'Don't mention haggis,' Laura laughed. 'They only eat it once a year as a penance.'

'Have I got to get myself a kilt?'

'Good heavens, no. A white jacket and the trousers you normally wear. A thick sweater will be useful. Now let's talk about the menu.'

'I feel nervous already.'

'Nervous? They'll be thrilled to bits that one of the best chefs in London is cooking at Maclintock Castle.'

'You're not saying that, are you? There's no-one even knows it's me cooking Monsieur Bouchon's menu.'

'What do you want me to say? The best sous-chef in London? You're not paying me to say that.'

'I don't like lies.'

'Exaggeration is just a short-cut. You know I'm honest with you.'

'I hope you are.' John looked hard at the relaxed face, the large grey eyes. 'If you do lie, no-one would know it, I tell you that.'

'Something to drink?'

Laura raised her arm, covered by folds of grey silk caught in at her long, elegant wrists, and an elderly man with warts on his neck shuffled over.

'Two glasses of champagne, if you please.'

'I like it here,' said John, warming to the place and loosening his tie. 'This is definitely my kind of library.'

Laura smiled, pleased that John had relaxed back into his chair. He was gradually learning to be at ease, to unbend that taut Yorkshire backbone.

8

John wondered if he looked like a Club-class man as he settled back into his seat on the shuttle to Edinburgh and attempted to arrange his long legs in the cramped space. He was wearing a blazer chosen by Laura, an Egyptian cotton shirt and tie chosen by Laura, soft tapering boots, also chosen by Laura. Soft clothes eased round his body. Cost a fortune; an investment said Laura. They felt strange, a right ponce, but he would get used to it. He looked better than the rest of them, silly prats pretending they were sitting in the office, scribbling notes, reading pages of reports on who knows what, tapping out messages on portable computers as though giving orders to an invisible army, briefcases balanced on pudgy knees. When the plane took off they didn't stir, but went on with what they were doing. Funny lot.

'On business?' John asked, seeking a retreat from his nerves, some distraction from the large, damp-faced man sitting next to him overflowing into his space. He was studying a series of graphs on the tray in front of him.

'Computers,' he replied, without raising his head.

'Interesting?' said John. Anything to avoid the uneasy sensation of being surrounded by clouds clustered like mould on well-soured milk.

'Boring, actually,' the man said.

John pulled out a crumpled letter from his pocket. He had skimmed the contents once, and now read the last paragraph with attention. He was the only man in her life, she thought about him day and night, she swore she had felt his body next to hers, quite scary, and she knew there'd never be anyone else. Mum and Dad were going down to London for their wedding anniversary, and she was going too. They'd bought the coach tickets already, and would be staying at the Russell Hotel, Bloomsbury. Was that near to where he worked? And could he have a night off? Because the plan was to have a slap-up meal. They had a band for dancing, all in the price, and they'd pay the extra for John.

He would send a card when he got back. 'Dear Cathy. Sorry it's been so long. I'm very busy at the moment and I get hardly any time off, so I'm not sure if I can make it. I hope you're keeping well. Love. John.'

Couldn't tell her he was feeling randy as hell, storing away the ones that might, the ones that didn't need to tell him he was the only man in their lives. He could ask out that pretty make-up girl. Cindy, that was it. Looked like a doll. No, he wouldn't bother. It was Laura he wanted. He had expected to be hurtling through the country in her Lotus, but she hadn't suggested it. He'd wait. Now he was wondering what it would be like to crumple that creaseless skirt, to wipe off the make-up, see the sweat on that alabaster face, and hear her panting like an animal . . .

The taxi crunched up the long drive lined with rampant rhododendrons and tall Scots pines standing upright from the tangled undergrowth. The castle appeared suddenly, like an operatic backcloth, its massive towers outlined against a windswept sky. He had been to Chatsworth once, on an outing, but it reminded him of catering college, all those rooms. This was different. A compact mass of defiance. He liked that. He imagined wild Scotsmen standing across the moat waving swords, always on the rampage like Yorkshiremen on a Saturday night. Fancy. John Crabtree staying there. Might have a four-poster bed with curtains. Always liked the idea of doing it in one of them. Rolling naked over a satin bed cover and the woman with layers of clothes on, chasing round a bed the size of his front room at home, pulling off her stockings, slipping down the rustling petticoats one after another.

'The front entrance, would it be?' enquired the taxi driver. 'Yes. That's right.'

The front door was pointed, studded and challenging. It opened with a guttural squawk as he was gathering his belongings from the taxi, and he was met by an elderly retainer.

'Mr Crabtree? I trust you had a pleasant flight.'

'I did. Thanks.'

'I'll take you to your room.'

The hall was rich and carpeted, adorned with antlered beasts and tapestries of caparisoned warriors. There was an Ali Baba pot sprouting dried, dusty tropical leaves. Once up the stone steps at the end of the hall, John felt uneven slabs of uncarpeted stone under his soft shoes. They walked swiftly down windowed corridors with damp-stained walls, chilled by an unimpeded draught which sniped at any exposed flesh. They passed dark, cracked oil portraits of remote ancestors in ceremonial uniforms posed against darker landscapes. Formerly sumptuous curtains had faded from deep crimson to pale, streaky puce as though washed with fabrics of different colours, and their tattered shreds stirred like scarecrows in the breeze.

The retainer paused by the only door which was ajar. He spoke with the disgruntled openness of those for whom tips were as rare as hot sun in December.

'There's no central heating here,' he announced, walking into a lofty room barely delineated by the dusty light struggling through thick mullioned windows. 'Hope you've brought some warm clothes, sir. The bathroom's through that door. The water in the bath comes out brown, but dinnae worry about that. Peat. That's all it is. They say it's good for the skin but it stains. We've tried everything. Moira's expecting you in the kitchen when you're ready.'

'How do I get there?'

'Down the back stairs at the end of the corridor. You'll nae miss it.'

The heavy latch was clamped down, and John was alone. Seeing an ancient fan heater, he pushed down the brass switch to which it was attached. With a clank of tired blades, it eventually emitted a thin stream of barely warm air. An iron bed leaned against an expanse of wall, struggling for equilibrium on the uneven floor. The floral, browning wallpaper topped by peeling mouldings was cold and clammy to the touch. There was a vast wardrobe which John opened. It smelt of generations of mothballs. The bathroom was equal in size to the bedroom and the marble bath, standing on dull clawed feet, was larger than his bed and stained brown as he had been warned. A rickety stool, a cracked mirror and a lavatory set on a plinth were the only furnishings. Through the window John could see a walled garden with bare fruit trees and neat rows of decaying vegetables.

John returned to his bedroom, turned back the icy cotton sheets on his narrow bed and ran his hand down the lumpy mattress. He pulled out an ancient water bottle smelling of decaying rubber and threw it on the floor. It reminded him of old ladies, bedjackets and medicine bottles.

If this was how they lived, in such cold comfort, they were foreigners to him, these Scottish aristocrats he had yet to meet. Yorkshire tycoons were the ones he knew. They had thrown out shuttles and looms along with the workforce, and sat tight on their emptied assets. Property, lad. The relics of industry monumentalized by darkening hunks of stone the size of temples abandoned by canal sides, on the hilly edges of cities, in huddled villages which had grown up to serve their needs, waiting for the time when southern property values migrated northwards with the city-suited real-estate sharks seeking out freehold building blocks for redevelopment plans, greeting each other with nervous jokes in first-class bars on the King's Cross to Leeds or Euston to Manchester Superspeed Executive. Surprising how many offices you could carve out of a mill. They would be rented one day. No-one stayed out of work for ever.

The penny-watching mill owners had been stingy with the workforce, outlawing unions and substituting their kind of random paternalism, but by God they delivered and were proud of it. In private, as John had witnessed, they knew how to spend. He had cooked for Charlie Braithwaite and Charlie's friends, and slept in a queen-size bed with built-in radio complete with snooze button and tinted lights which dimmed like they did in the Grand. He had plunged into a heart-shaped bath with gold taps, cooked in a private kitchen with two built-in ovens, a separate rotisserie and indoor barbecue, a walk-in fridge and machines he did not even recognize. The dining room had a marble floor and a full-sized bar in the corner. The gardens were floodlit, and they all had statues. John had catered a big do. *Boeuf en croute* for one hundred guests, a pianist brought over specially from Harrogate, a brass band from Kirkby Lees and fireworks which blasted into the sky with enough power to destroy a city. He'd never seen people enjoying themselves like that, not even in Blackpool when the sun shone.

Charlie would have done out this castle properly. If he ever made Charlie's kind of money, John thought he might buy a place like this. There would be a room for Mum and Dad, with en suite bathroom. And a games room – table tennis, billiards and a dart-board – for the lads. And a bar. And an Art Nouveau room for George, who liked that kind of thing. And lots of roaring fires backed up by central heating. And a palatial bedroom for himself and visiting ladies.

He laid his clothes out on the bed, changed into his whites and set out to find the kitchen.

Laura had arrived the night before John, but she had not stayed at the castle. Howard, too, was expected at Maclintock Castle but they could hardly share a bedroom there. He had surprised Laura at the last minute and booked into a small country hotel twenty miles away.

'We must have some time together, darling. I've

cancelled a couple of meetings.' A whole night lying next to him, the stillness after he had made love, waking up throughout the night, seeing his head beside hers, his arms encircling her hips, a whole night of such tenderness that Laura had wanted to cry with happiness. The hotel manager hoped that Lady Riley had been comfortable. Lady Riley. Howard had smiled. It seemed so natural. Laura Riley. One day.

'If only I had found you earlier,' he had said. 'Think of all the years of happiness.'

They had talked of nothing except the future, where they would live, which of his friends he would like her to meet, remote parts of the world they would explore. Their life together began to have a shape, a distinct and detailed form which she would cling to when events forced them apart. In the morning, he kissed her goodbye as she left for Maclintock Castle, the light, confident kiss of a husband who knows he will see his wife later that day.

'Everything will be marvellous. We'll meet before dinner.'

It was so hard to part.

She had been invited to take sherry in the library of Maclintock Castle at eleven thirty. Sherry was brought on a silver tray into the library whenever someone was expected who came from the higher ranks of those who served the aristocracy. In the days when staff swarmed like late summer mosquitoes over the estate, master craftsmen had gathered to discuss their plans to replace the silk wallpaper with carved wood panelling, painters had shown examples of their work hoping for the privilege of a grand portrait, bailiffs had laid out the accounts, copperplate summaries of life on the estate. The traditions remained, only the visitors had changed. This morning Laura was present to discuss the finer points of the evening's menu. Lady Maclintock rushed in with a breathless apology.

'Laura, I'm so sorry to have kept you waiting. One of the dogs is having puppies. They always choose such inconvenient moments. I do hope you had a good journey.'

'Yes, thank you, Lady Maclintock.'

'Do sit down and please call me Lucinda. I come in here when Jamie had his noisy chums for dinner. I say, do I look an absolute fright?'

She would pass unnoticed in the King's Road. Jeans, long, thick, cabled sweater, fine light brown hair. She would still have a slim figure under all those clothes, Laura could tell. She would look stunning with a touch of make-up.

'You look fantastic.' Laura handed her a typewritten menu.

'I thought something along these lines might be suitable for tonight.'

Lucinda poured out sherry from a decanter on the gilded Sheraton table near her, handed Laura a glass and looked at the menu.

'How awfully efficient. All typed out. I say, how grand. I keep telling Jamie we ought to have a decent typewriter, but it's another one of those things which never happens . . . This sounds terribly fancy. We tend to cook rather plain fare here. Jamie's what you might call a meat and two veg man, I'm afraid. Oh, I say, salmon. Super. One is always wondering what on earth new one can do with it and people always expect it. I simply must go now. Do forgive me. I'll see you at six for cocktails.'

Lucinda needed encouragement and attention, Laura decided; Stephen's attention. She looked out of her window at the arboretum below, with each tree placed to advantage on the hilly ground. She had learned from Antony that Lady Maclintock's passion was gardening. Place settings would be crucial. Stephen would be sitting next to her – she would make sure of that – and briefed to bring her out on the subject of Scottish gardens. And, of course, he would enthuse about this talented new chef who was soon to open in London . . .

* * *

176

The dusty back stairs wound down narrowly to the bowels of the castle, where the ceilings were low and the walls were bare. Low wooden doors led off to the right and left. One was ajar and John looked inside. A wooden bed, a jug and bowl, a frayed mat and a chest of drawers with a Formica top, a small window below ground level. It was tiny. The occupants must have been small, their needs minimal, for this restricted cell would have served for a monk, a prisoner – or a servant. Uninhabited for years, judging by the cobwebs stringing in abandon across every corner. The corridor turned sharp corners, following the contours of the rectangular architecture, then John heard heavy footsteps clattering towards him and a large woman with a weathered face stared up with surprise at this tall invader.

'Mr Crabtree, am I right? You look lost. That won't do. I'm Moira. Cook, nanny and I don't know what else. Come into the kitchen and we'll see what you need. It's years since we had a real cook. Nowadays they bring in outside caterers from Edinburgh, young gels who've done some fancy course in London and think they know it all. I'm glad to see you.'

'It's an honour for me to be here.'

The formalities over, Moira strode ahead through a large painted door and into a kitchen spacious enough to have served a medium-sized hotel.

'We don't use this kitchen often, but I've polished up the stove.'

A long preparation table stretched down the centre of the quarry-tiled floor. Laid out on platters were glistening salmon, and fresh fruit and vegetables were heaped in wicker baskets. Moira stroked one of the salmon.

'That's a good wee fish. From our part of the river. We caught more salmon this year than on any other beat.'

John frowned, and prodded the fish. 'When did you freeze it? I don't normally cook frozen.'

'It's as good as fresh, believe me. Late summer I must have put that in. You don't waste salmon like that.

177

Better than the farmed variety, wouldn't you say?'

He'd take farmed over frozen any day, but he kept that to himself. You shouldn't mix cooking and politics.

'Here's the menu. I'll check through the vegetables and get cracking.'

'*Cornets de saumon fumé d'Ecosse aux blinis*,' she read slowly. 'We always have menus in French. I don't understand every word, I must confess. Very nice. No-one's cooked that here. And salmon again, do I see? *Escalope de saumon et crème à l'aneth*.'

'Quite different flavours, so I thought I'd risk it,' commented John, opening the case which contained the tools of his trade, a series of well-honed knives. He then explored the tall cupboards where he found an array of polished copper pans, bains-marie, ancient graters, peelers and shredders.

'Our last chef left years ago when they cut down the staff. Terrible, those taxes they brought in. We used to have nearly forty people working at the castle.'

'It must be difficult for you now.' John assumed there would be dinner parties every week at least.

'Lady Maclintock has simple tastes. It's just as well. Lord Maclintock says we can't compete with smart restaurants in London. I wouldn't know. I've only been to London twice. Can I give you a bit of help?'

'You can chop me some vegetables for the terrine,' replied John.

'Terrine of vegetables? That is most unusual.'

John watched Moira take a handful of leeks over to the sink, and then he attacked a hunk of lamb, carving out neat roundels of flesh. You couldn't trust Scottish butchers with the cuts he required.

Laura appeared some time later when the kitchen echoed with the sound of Moira's slow cutting and peeling and John pounding, cutting and trimming. Then quick regular footsteps resonated down the stone corridor.

'Hello there. Glad to see you're in action, John. Have you got everything you want?'

'Could do with some more help, Laura. And the sorrel's not come.'

'I've got a couple of boys coming over soon, and I'll look after the sorrel.'

'Och, we've that in the field, if that's what you want.'

'It's another variety, unfortunately,' said John.

'Then I don't think we'd have it. You might have to make do with parsley.'

Parsley? This woman should stick to bannock cakes. John looked at Laura. 'I must have it. Even if it has to come from Bradford,' he said, thinking of his herb supplier. Didi Kowalski and Stephen Boyce were coming. They'd had lamb a thousand times. This had to be something different, something for them to talk about. The guests wouldn't notice if it was parsley. Those two would and it was them he was cooking for.

'I'll get on the phone. Don't worry.' Laura scanned the kitchen, checked each ingredient on her list and swiftly left. It would take her ten minutes to reach the one room in the Castle where she imagined there would be a telephone. Lord Maclintock's study.

'A very determined lady, I see,' said Moira.

Didi lay in a scented bath in the cold bathroom and pondered about a programme on Scotland. She would have to find a new angle. Beef and whisky had been done to death. She liked neither particularly. Then there was salmon. Oh, yes. The disastrous salmon tasting where the chefs had preferred farmed salmon to fresh, undermining her whole thesis that wild food was good food. Perhaps they had been nobbled by the Scottish Salmon Board. One never knew nowadays. Corruption was everywhere, but not on her programme. Over her dead body.

Didi got out of the bath and sat at a Victorian dressing table set out with flowered receptacles for ladies' requirements, silver-backed mirror, comb and brush and a sweet bottle of pot pourri breathing dusky floral perfume into her pretty room. The sun had emerged briefly from the clouds in time to set gracefully, dazzling through the spiny leaves of a pine tree. How lovely it was, late autumn nature, pine trees, sky, quiet private grounds, the country.

Didi wrapped her apricot silk peignoir more closely round her body. Her clothes hung round the room, suspended on a dado, inviting selection. It would be the black Armani dress, she decided, having rejected the satin suit, the frilled taffeta and the jodhpurs. Elegant starkness in the country was unusual. Didi Kowalski had no desire to be an advertisement for conformity. She would need some help with the handmade slip buttons at the back. One was missing, but they were small. No-one would notice. A discreet necklace of enamelled pink and gold leaves, small earrings to match (bought on a trip to Rome, Stephen helped her choose them) and she would be ready for Lord Maclintock. Sophistication incarnate. Strikingly different, she felt certain, from the bony, blonde, frumpily dressed aristocrats he entertained at his usual dinner parties. She curved the eyeshadow outwards from her sparkling, deep brown eyes, created a perfect deep red bow round her mouth and smiled for the benefit of her reflection. Now it was time to check up on the guests.

Gathering the folds of her extravagant wrap, Didi swished down her corridor. How thoughtful. The names had been printed on the doors. She paused at each one. Penelope Long. Oh dear. Drearsville. Still, she would go to bed early. Virginia Leroy Desgranges. Very *Vogue*. Very thin. Stephen, if he ever arrived, would invent an imaginary place which had just opened. You must go. Everyone's raving. He was good at that. They all fell for it. Dylan Tusk? Tusk? Do we know him. Hardly. Must be either from the trade press or a local consumer TV channel. Laura Douglas . . . Oh, so Stephen was coming. Or was meant to be. One never knew with him, but this was his room. He was supposed to have flown up with her but at the last minute had decided to go to Glasgow. Didi paused outside the room which might or might not be concealing the errant, unpredictable Stephen Boyce. The door was slightly ajar. She heard the sucking, gurgling sound of water making its exit down ancient Scottish plumbing and gave the door a gentle push.

'Didi, what a lovely surprise!'

Stephen emerged with dripping hair and a towel round his waist, then stepped backwards. 'I've been washing off the back streets of Glasgow.'

'What were you doing there?'

'Playing hunt the haggis.'

'You don't like haggis.'

'Ah, but my readers do. I tracked down this seventy-year-old butcher whose grandfather used to make it for Queen Victoria, and he's given me the recipe.'

'How fantastic.'

'It's not, sad to say. Like every other boring old haggis recipe. I'll have to do some creative embroidery, uncover a little secret, spice it up. How about the addition of lemon grass imported by a Thai sailor working in the Clyde shipyard? Mr McTaggart and I had an illuminating conversation about sheep's innards but I promise I won't bring it up at dinner. Did you know they ate raw ducks' stomachs in France? Marinaded, of course. *Un délice.* No worse than haggis. Glasgow's all right. I discovered a Japanese brasserie serving impeccable sushi. Pansy food but good for a hangover. My, have I got some whisky down me! Cosmopolitana, darlinks. Haggis meets the Yen in the Big Yin. Am I inebriated or is it Scotland?'

'Your room's much nicer than mine. Bigger. Are you glad to see me?'

'*Amore mio.*'

Didi went to him, stroked his damp back and pressed her body against his belly, rounded and comfortable from several years of unbridled gastronomy. They kissed. That was all they ever did. A gentle, tender kiss, lips against lips, no more. One lingering day (perhaps tonight, if the food and wine were in perfect harmony) there would be a sudden, impulsive, wild consummation of passion. That was all Didi wanted, she told herself. One earth-moving night as potent in the memory as the perfect meal of a lifetime, and she would be satisfied.

'Off you go. Mustn't be late for cocktails.'

'I can't decide what to wear.'

'Something simple and maidenly, I would think.'

'Really? Honestly?' Didi said, startled.

'Or, if you will, a vampish extravaganza in tartan. I don't know. For God's sake, I know nothing about frocks. A simple intellectual like me.'

'I thought I'd wear . . . well, it's black.'

'When women say they can't decide, it means it's a *fait accompli*. And that means black. Devious creature, I'm sure you'll look absolutely gorgeous. Why don't you go as you are? That would set the Scottish blood racing.'

'Don't be silly. Stephen, I need some help with my dress.'

'Putting on or taking off?'

'Both, darling.'

'I'm sure John Crabtree will oblige. He has lovely hands. Did you notice?'

'The chef?'

'I would have thought you found him rather dishy. Or hasn't he taken his place ticket yet in the queue of men waiting at your door?'

'Rotter,' said Didi, as she stormed out of the room.

There was a knock on her door.

'Come in,' Didi called huskily.

'Everyone's dying to meet you,' said Laura. 'Are you ready? I do like your dress. Beautiful.'

The women exchanged a quick glance of appreciation.

'I don't often see you in black. It suits you.'

(This time, thank God, thought Laura, Didi had toned down her penchant for palazzo dressing. Could be a Chanel. No, more likely to be Armani. Would have looked better a size larger. Gold tights. And stiletto strappy sandals. Oh dear.)

(Draped chiffon. Jasper Conran last year, and not sure about the colour, thought Didi. But yes, she can get away with it. Wonder if I could wear that shade of pink? Pearls a bit boring, though.)

'Oh, Laura. Could you be a darling? There's a button I can't reach.'

She turned her back, breathed in and felt Laura's cool, delicate fingers manipulating the fabric and pulling the tab over the button. Ah, the relief. Now, buttoned up and ready to go, she would deliver her performance.

The Great Hall dwarfed the people clustered like parched animals at a desert oasis, drinking in the warmth of the blazing trunks and branches piled up in the Gothic fireplace. Didi walked in as though she had a Great Hall at home in Kensington. Being so well known, such a public person, it was not necessary to be surprised – or impressed – by anything. And not one person stared. Such wonderful manners, the aristocracy. One did appreciate it.

John was examining the *terrine de légumes*. Slowly he dribbled a light layer of walnut oil over each one. Nearly every one a perfect shape, thin layers of leek, a shaving of truffle, blanched black radish (homage to André Bouchon). A commis imported from a hotel in Edinburgh was looking at a pale sauce in a copper saucepan.

'How is it?' asked John.

'Looks fine.'

'Have you tasted it?'

'Not yet, chef.'

John went over, dabbed a finger. 'More cream. Too thin.'

Then he remembered. 'Where are the canapés? They should be out by now.'

'Not quite ready, chef,' replied a slow Scottish lad from the Welcome, a restaurant serving steak and Black Forest Gâteau by the edge of a loch.

'I want them ready. In two minutes. Move. Something's overcooking. What is it?'

John rushed over to one of the ovens and a plume of smoke surged up into the kitchen.

'Oh dear,' said the lad.

'That oven always gets too hot,' said Moira as she polished the silver for the table.

'Throw those out. Make some more. Use the other oven,' barked John.

'And don't soak that sorrel,' he yelled, noticing his precious leaves, miraculously found by Laura from a local supplier, swimming in water. 'Why d'you do that?'

'We always do. Hygiene.'

'Fuck hygiene. Wash it I said, not drown it.'

John felt the perspiration starting to trickle down his back. Nerves. It was not that hot in the cavernous kitchen. Every time he wanted something he had to think. Started to get irritable. He wanted to throw the voluble Moira out and lock her in a cupboard. You didn't need women in the kitchen. Was the lamb ready? What time was it? Get a move on. Were the flowers out? Tables should be laid by now, Moira. Almost finished. All right. Everything has to be timed right. I know it takes five minutes to get to the dining room. You told me. What time did you say it was? We'll put layers of cloths over. No, I don't bloody use warmers . . . His tension spread and the kitchen fell silent, apart from the rustlings of human activity.

The cluster of people turned slowly outwards, like summer flowers pivoting to receive the sun. Lady Maclintock came forward. Taffeta, Didi noticed. What a wise decision not to wear taffeta.

'Miss Ko-wall-ski. I'm so pleased to meet you.'

She said it as though she meant her to curtsey. Didi shook her firmly by the hand.

'Hello.'

Didi stood immobile at the centre of the group, a champagne glass pressed into her hand. She shook hands with a succession of black-tied men and their simpering wives.

'Will Lord Maclintock be dining with us?' she asked in a relaxed, low, worldly tone, so different from the enthusing, energized television personality eight million viewers knew and loved.

'He's been in town but we're expecting him,' explained Lady Maclintock, as though this was an unusual event. 'No doubt the plane was late.' She glanced over Didi's shoulder. 'Oh, you look super.'

Two men advanced down the hall, Stephen following a few yards behind. He looked so distinguished from a distance, Didi thought. He gave her a watery smile (media people on duty did not betray their affinities) and took up a position on one side of the fireplace.

An elongated stringy man in a flapping suit strode towards his wife. He had buck teeth, frayed, balding hair and he leered. Lady Maclintock pecked him on the cheek.

'Well, Lucy darling, everything looks pukka tonight. Good show.'

'Didi Ko-wall-ski. This is my husband, James Maclintock.'

'Jolly good of you to come. Lucy tells me you appear on the television. Never watch it myself but I might start now. You never know.' He gave Didi a wink and ogled her breasts. 'Gather we've got some good grub tonight. Hope there's some decent meat, eh? We Scots like to get our teeth into a bit of flesh.'

'It's all frightfully professional stuff,' said Lucinda uneasily.

'Long as it's not nancy food!' Lord Maclintock laughed like an ancient car engine juddering in the cold. 'Good cook, my wife. But chaotic. Absolutely chaotic. I'm lucky to get dinner at ten o'clock. But I don't mind. Couldn't boil an egg to save me life.'

Didi looked at him. This man owned a castle and he also owned the nervous pretty woman. He was kiltless, sporranless, daggerless and as exciting as thick-cut raw onion in a mixed salad. Lady Maclintock moved away.

'Do you live in London?' Lord Maclintock began.

'Yes. But it must be wonderful living here. I do so love all this space.'

'I spend more time in town, you know. I decided I should do my bit. Go to the Lords. Remind them of the tartan.'

'Do you know, I've never been to the House of Lords.'

Lord Maclintock was not so ugly when he was talking. When he was animated, the mobility of his features covered the structural short-comings of his face and neck.

'I hear the food's improving.'

'Prefer Rules. Or Simpson's. What's your favourite eating hole?'

'It depends.' Didi paused and drooped her eyelids. 'I usually seem to end up at Aphrodite's.'

'Do you, now?'

Lord Maclintock, too, paused and scratched his neck. 'Met a chappie who was after that place. Ought to give it a try. Would you, er, would you accept an invitation to lunch one day? Then you could tell me, you know, what's what. And so on.'

Didi gave him the candid fleeting smile, formal interest, no more. 'I would be delighted.'

'You might like to drop in at the House beforehand.'

'Charming gel,' said Lord Maclintock, grabbing a handful of nuts from a table and inclining his head towards Didi, who was now talking to somebody he didn't recognize, probably some reporter. There were some coming, Lucy said. Sir Howard Riley's attention, however, was elsewhere. 'Hah. You've noticed Laura. Damn good looking. Organizing for Lucy. Shall I introduce you?'

'No, no, it's quite all right.'

Sir Howard continued talking to his good friend Jamie Maclintock and waited until Laura turned in his direction.

Dylan Tusk decided to charge. 'You must be Lady Maclintock. Pleased to meet you.' He proffered a chubby hand. 'Dylan Tusk. Cars, food and travel, that's me. Here, have a card. I tell you something. This place is much better than those French castles. I was at Versize last week. No taste. Honest. No taste whatsoever. They gave us sausage on sticks. I mean . . . You bin there?'

Lady Maclintock kept a fixed smile, the radiant one which so entranced the American guests. Laura had advised her to smile at journalists who wrote regularly in popular journals.

'I can't say I have,' she said, lying politely.

'Don't bother,' said Dylan Tusk Esq, as he liked to be known on envelopes. He was at ease everywhere.

'Oh, really,' said Penelope Long, on being informed that Sir Howard Riley was the Chairman of Illustra Foods. It was hard to mask the distaste she felt at being in the presence of this Lucifer who ruled the world of manufactured nectar and tinned ambrosia.

The flamingo-legged, hair-swinging Virginia Desgranges sailed in to the rescue, untroubled by qualms about what the Working Classes ('WCs', a term restricted to the office and editorial conferences) ate during the gross calorie intake of mealtimes. Mealtimes, or the precise time to which these referred, were thankfully outside her experience as she brunched vaguely and lunched vaguely, but rarely dined. Parties took up so much of one's time.

'I know I'm frightfully ingorant,' she began, 'but do tell me about Illustra Foods. It sounds awfully grand.'

'Big rather than grand,' said Sir Howard Riley. 'We own the Prima group. Supermarkets and subsidiary industries.'

'I demonstrated once outside the Prima supermarket in Islington,' retorted Penelope, hoping Sir Howard would rise to the occasion. 'You were stocking irradiated prawns.'

'I take it you disapproved?'

'Of course I did.'

'I understand your feelings. Believe me, we gave the

matter months of consideration. But with a turnover of five million pounds worth of prawns and prawn recipe dishes – very popular lines – our concern is to protect the customer. If one of our eighteen million customers has to be hospitalized through contamination, we regard it as a catastrophic failure. And I'm happy to say, our record is clear in that respect.'

'I'd like to take you up on that,' said Penelope, opening her capacious handbag and fishing for a notebook. 'I was talking to an environmental health officer only last week and he was telling me . . . .'

Laura was listening to Stephen explaining his views on the come-back of Savoy cabbage as a serious vegetable in the repertoire of Nouvelle Cuisine Rustique (he had noted its re-emergence at Aphrodite's). She appeared not to be listening, as she swept a distracted gaze round the room like a lighthouse beam signalling hazards to shipping. The hazards, in this instance, were Virginia Desgranges, Dylan Tusk and Penelope Long, whom she did not yet know well enough to trust with a room-full of distinguished guests. Those who failed to understand Laura's odd behaviour attributed it to arrogance and boredom, but Stephen was used to it. Some of his colleagues, he acknowledged privately, were grossly insensitive and needed surveillance. Some had to be gently pushed, some even mildly threatened, into adopting the appropriate behaviour for occasions such as this. The press, other hacks that is, were rarely muzzled, but frequently nudged.

He was in mid-sentence, expounding on the progress of the Savoy cabbage from peasant soups via Russian-French Tsarist cooking to the Troisgros' Chou Vert au Lardons, when Laura left his side abruptly.

'Excuse me for interrupting, Penelope. I must have a quick word, Sir Howard.'

She led him to an empty stretch of the room. 'I didn't think you would relish a full frontal from Penelope Long.'

'She's doing what she's paid to do. Sell newspapers. But

I can't understand why the left is convinced that we are sinister bioengineers creating death potions in micro doses to poison the population. My aim is simple: To provide variety and excitement to pep up the desperate British diet. Is that wrong? And why would I wish to poison my customers? Hardly good marketing strategy.'

'Everyone is afraid of hidden cancers taking root in their bodies. Unknown, destructive chemicals collecting in the digestive system, and destroying the cells. They have to blame someone.'

'Shouldn't we be praised for protecting the masses from slovenly hygiene? I'd rather eat irradiated prawns than meat and two veg in a semi in Wigan. But then I have a sensitive stomach. Unlike Ms Long who is probably killing herself with an excess of All Bran and filthy organic carrots. I can't understand why two things I detest, dirt and roughage, should be so highly valued.'

'Is that a reason for irradiation? If something isn't fresh, why pretend it is? Why have it at all?'

'No-one's pretending. It makes food cheaper and safer. Isn't that what the lefties want? Or would they prefer the unemployed and impoverished to starve? Maybe they would. It's easier to start a revolution with a starving population.'

'That's not the argument. They think you use your millions to influence government policy, to dictate what farmers should grow.'

'If only we could. How do you see me, Laura? Do you think I abuse my power? Do I force you to do things against your will?'

'Do you have to turn everything into a personal issue?'

'You're cross with me.'

'Why do you hate the left so much, Howard? They're pretty harmless.'

'They take up time and they irritate me, and I don't like being irritated. It's a waste of energy.'

'I think you're disturbed by people with convictions.'

'In my experience, convictions lead to poverty and war,

destroy marriages and breed hypocrisy. I prefer to be free of them. You look gorgeous tonight, darling.' Howard moved closer. 'I shall resist the temptation to take you in my arms.'

He gave her the look he had given her as he slipped the dress from her shoulders in the hotel bedroom.

'Serve the terrines now.'

'OK, chef.'

'Not yet, John,' said Moira. 'The bell hasn't rung.'

'What bell?'

'The bell they ring from upstairs when they're on their way to the dining room. It takes a while.'

'Do it now.' John looked at his steel watch. 'They're late.'

'They're never on time for dinner. This isn't London, you know.'

'Run out of sour cream, chef, for the blinis.'

'Get some yoghurt. And some double cream. Move. I want to get these garnished. Are they ready?'

'Not quite, chef.'

'What have you been doing for the past half hour?'

'The pastry. I had to do it again.'

'Stop giving me fucking excuses. That's all I need.'

Moira was arranging small slices of smoked salmon around a filling which looked like Crowdie cheese. She didn't like hearing that word. No-one, in the old days, used it in front of female staff.

'Ten minutes I want the blinis.'

I'll not do this again, thought John. All this bloody work for what? So that a few pissed Scots folk could boast of dining with the Maclintocks.

'They like a few drams before dinner,' remarked Moira.

'And breakfast too,' added John.

'Och, no. Never before twelve,' came the rejoinder.

He was beginning to loathe Scotland, personified in the rounded figure and trunk-like legs of this former nanny. She'd be better selling corsets in Rackham's. She was like

Auntie Doris who lived in a semi in Leeds and washed her curtains once a week. Lived for ever, that sort.

Stephen was now singing for his lordly supper, rehearsing arias dedicated to Lady Maclintock.

'It's a brilliant idea having a fantastic chef cooking in one's home.'

'Do you think highly of this young man? I know nothing about him. One has problems eating out well around here, so there are no standards of comparison, I'm afraid. And, quite frankly, we can't afford it. Running a place like this gobbles up money. Not that I'm complaining. Inheritance is a privilege for which one must be prepared to suffer, don't you believe?'

'Certainly,' replied Stephen. He would certainly suffer for his. One day Mummy's bungalow in Bournemouth, smelling of cats and lavender cologne, would become the sole asset of the Boyce estate.

'Where does your family come from?' asked Lady Maclintock, wondering if she might know the progenitors of this delightful young man.

'Sussex, actually.' Mr Boyce was neither known in Sussex, nor to his mother, nor to the Registrar of Births, having absented himself a month before Stephen's entrance into the world. 'Has John Crabtree put his famous salmon dish on the menu tonight?' enquired Stephen, cutting short a threatened diversion concerning the relative location of well-born families residing in Sussex.

'Oh yes. We are having salmon. Our own, actually.'

'Crabtree has a unique understanding of fish,' continued Stephen. 'He can do something simple and make it sing. Without doubt he shows *un grand flair*. I personally think he will go far.'

Lord Maclintock edged into the gap between Stephen and his wife. 'Did I hear salmon?'

Didi approached, and made a space between Lord Maclintock and Stephen. 'Salmon is ab-so-lutely my favourite,' she sighed, modifying her London tones to resemble a parody of the upper-class accent and blinking her heavily mascaraed eyelids in time with each syllable. 'Especially Scottish salmon. Such a . . . masculine fish.'

She presumed Lord Maclintock had noticed that she was well versed enough not to say Scotch salmon and breathed in for his benefit, so that her breasts would expand even further from the plunging neck of her Armani dress to expose a provocative partition. Laura strolled over with Sir Howard Riley to complete the group.

'I do hope you and Lucinda will be my guests when John Crabtree opens in London. It should be early next year,' she said.

'As long as it's after the pheasant season,' said Lady Maclintock.

'Any excuse to escape from the Yanks,' boomed her husband. 'We have them staying here, don't you know, but the buggers never eat game. Bang bang all day and then they ask for a low cholisterol dinner. What is cholisterol anyway?'

'Cholesterol, Jamie.'

'My lords, ladies and gentlemen—' A strong Scottish voice (hired for the evening) soared above the rising volume of conversation. 'Dinner is served.'

9

Laura had spent as much time pondering the intricacies of the Maclintock Seating Plan as she had in discussing the menu with John Crabtree. One wrong guest in proximity to another could ruin the finest food, bring conversation to a halt and rain down unhappiness like a storm interrupting a summer picnic. It was a question of assessment and balance: interspersing guests whose behaviour would be safely predictable (the amiable, acquiescing kind) with those of unpredictable tendencies (irritable, explosive temperaments, chips on the shoulder, passionate obsessions, irrational personal dislikes).

The stage would be set immaculately for the performance of John Crabtree's Menu Gastronomique. When it was completed the notes might be forgotten but the sensation of harmony would remain. Laura Douglas with the conductor's baton giving the beat to her audience.

Fifty guests seated at two long tables in the sombre dining room unfurled the scroll of vellum wrapped in dark green ribbon placed beside each plate and studied the gold calligraphy by the light of tall candles, of the same green, which stood rigidly upright in an array of silver candelabras like close-packed trees in a newly planted pine forest.

MENU GASTRONOMIQUE PRESENTED BY
JOHN CRABTREE AT MACLINTOCK CASTLE

*

Terrine de Légumes, Vinaigrette aux Tomates

*

Cornets de Saumon Fumé d'Ecosse aux Blinis

★

Escalope de Saumon et Crème à L'Aneth

★

Noisettes d'Agneau, sauce à la Menthe à L'Oseille

★

Petite Sélection de Légumes

★

Tarte aux Framboises d'Ecosse, crème Chantilly,
caramel au beurre

★

Sélection de Fromages

★

VINS:
La Fourchaume, Premier Cru, Albert Pic, 1990
Vieux Château Certan, Pomerol, 1983

★

Lord Maclintock, at one end of the table: 'Good gracious.
I need specs for this. Ah. In French. Where's the meat?'

Didi, sitting to his left: 'Here.' She ran her best
varnished finger down his menu.

'Jolly good.'

'Shall I translate?' enquired Penelope, on his right.

'Perhaps Lord Maclintock likes surprises,' said Didi
quickly.

'Rather.'

He pushed the cumbersome menu aside as a frilly
aproned waitress moved forward bearing the terrine de
légumes, a small square of striped green edged by a pool of
red.

'Ah. Green stuff. I shall eat it up like a good boy.'

Lady Maclintock, at the other end of the table: 'Do you think it matters,' she said in a low voice to Stephen, sitting to her right, 'that the china doesn't all match? It is Sèvres, of course.'

'Not at all,' he confided. 'Mismatched china is the height of chic. A family heirloom ravaged by time is far more attractive. I have nothing which matches. Except, perhaps, my socks.'

She laughed. What a charming man. Sensitive. How nice. As the hired-in waitresses carefully put down the plates in front of them, she wondered where he might live. Most likely it would be in one of those lovely little pink-washed Chelsea houses with clematis clinging round the porch and rooms full of first editions in mahogany bookcases, chiming clocks and Staffordshire china. Stephen thought of his collection of disparate cups bought over the years from raucous stallholders in antique markets and now stacked up stained and disordered in his ancient sink.

'I suppose you live in London,' she said, delicately cutting the terrine.

'Are you from these parts?' articulated a senior member of the judiciary, smiling toothily as though addressing an unusually pretty member of a jury, in this case the lovely Virginia.

'Gosh, no, but my uncle has an estate not far away.'

'I might be mistaken, but I seem to detect an Alsace wine in the gêlée.' Sir Howard watched Laura as she slipped a portion with one graceful movement into her mouth. He liked wide mouths.

The terrine was removed and the *saumon fumé aux blinis* took its place.

'How amusing.' Lady Maclintock speared a fragment of blini on her fork. 'It tastes like a pancake.'

'The Russian version. They have them for Shrove Tuesday, as we do,' said Stephen. 'But not very good for tossing.'

'It must be wonderful to know so much about food. I

know so little about anything. One has so much to do.'

'I've heard that you're a horticultural expert,' objected Stephen 'I'm longing to see the subtropical trees you manage to grow.'

'I love growing things but I'm no expert. Goodness, no. Do you have a garden?' she asked.

'A couple of window-boxes.' Stephen was about to comment on the food, but Dylan Tusk, on Lady Maclintock's left, foiled his attempt.

'I'm a dahlia man. Anything as long as it's a dahlia. Funny that. I've never wanted to grow anything else. Got this tiny garden. Full of blooming dahlias. Drives the wife potty.'

'Are they difficult to grow?' asked Stephen.

'Depends on the compost. I don't get the sort in bags. That doesn't work, you see. My favourite is the pompon dahlia, s'matter of fact. Willo's Violet and Mary Paterson. You seen them, Lady Maclintock?'

'Indeed.'

'And if you're looking for table decoration, there's nothing to beat Doris Rollings. That's a cactus one. Pink and purple. In candlelight, it looks unreal. Go a treat in that vase there. Mind you, speaking personally, I grow Cheerio mesself, got a prize for that one . . .'

She smiled. Mr Tusk did have an amusing way of putting things. Rather like her gardener.

'Do you imagine this salmon has been smoked over oak?' Penelope asked intently of Lord Maclintock, who had been giving most of his attention to Didi. He turned abruptly in Penelope's direction, his eyes popping slightly, his neck muscles strained and tautened so that he reminded Didi of that strutting bronze turkey she had observed on a visit organized by the Traditional Farmfresh Turkey Association.

Lord Maclintock appeared to be listening to Penelope, who was ignorant of the lascivious thoughts dancing in his head. Had he seen her exclusive interview with the Minister of Food in which he had resolutely refused to admit to what she knew to be true, that even the best hand-cured smoked salmon could possibly be subject to carcinogenic residues? Smoked salmon was most commonly – and she had witnessed it herself – cured slowly over smouldering wood which was largely confined in a barrack-like box. The wood was oak. This was significant. And then. She had been sent, from an impeccable scientific source, some absolutely conclusive research on the potentially toxic effects of barbecue smoke in southern California. She could show him the paper if he so wished. It was not yet definitively proved that oak smoke, as opposed to birch, hickory, pine or elm, was carcinogenic, but wasn't it time the government did some research? The Minister of Food was totally unaware that smoked salmon could be a hidden time bomb threatening the lives of innocent consumers.

'Lord Maclintock, you really ought to raise it in the Lords.'

'I say,' said Didi to Lord Maclintock with such a tone of urgency that he happily abandoned all hope of following Penelope's discourse to its bitter, lugubrious end.

'Yes, my dear?'

Didi put her face close to his ear. 'Do you know the man sitting next to Virginia Desgranges?'

'Sir Howard Riley? Splendid chap.'

'No, no, he's sitting next to Laura. Next to the blonde girl on this side.'

'Oh. Him. Viscount Alloway. Giving you the eye, is he? Ho. Bit of a one with the ladies. Chairman of the MacCrae Banking Group. We were at school together.'

'He didn't eat his terrine,' Didi said, shocked.

'Dear me!' He roared with laughter. 'Naughty boy. What's this? Pancake? Where's the lemon?'

The general was sending out the battalions from the kitchen. The waitress cohorts were shifting from one foot to another, giving shy glances at the handsome chef as he moved round from pan to pan.

'Lamb ready?' barked John.

'Coming, coming.'

He went over to the copper saucepan, smelt and dipped in his finger. 'This doesn't taste of sorrel. Too much mint. Get some more.'

Moira went over to the fridge.

'You didn't have to put it in there. What's the idea? Come on, come on. We can't hang about.'

'There's no need for haste,' she said. 'They're not used to courses coming like the chimes of a clock. This is Maclintock Castle.'

'I'm not spoiling my lamb for anyone. Understand?'

'Oh, yes. I understand,' replied Moira wistfully. 'But you're wasting yourself. With enough alcohol, they don't care.'

Laura shifted uneasily in her high-backed chair. Where was the next course? Was there a problem? Would it be better, or worse, if she slipped out to confront it? Or was it preferable to ignore the delay? She looked round the table. Divisions had formed, some talking across the table, some behind the backs of others, some speaking low to adjacent partners. The volume of conversation was rising, ebbing and rising again, with Lord Maclintock's laughter booming through the noise like a kettle drum in a symphony orchestra.

'Is anything the matter?' asked Sir Howard, replenishing her glass from a nearby bottle of one of his favourite wines. 'I thought the salmon was excellent. Almost up to Aphrodite's standard, I'd say. I can see why you think so highly of young Crabtree.'

Laura turned to him. His voice and his presence gave her reassurance, and the waitresses were bringing in the next course.

'Ah, that's the stuff,' said Lord Maclintock, ogling the

plates of meat set down around him. 'Do you girls eat meat? Lots don't these days. My children won't touch it but I've told them both I want them to marry meat-eaters. Never trust a veggie, that's what I say. Are you a meat-eater, Miss Long?'

'Just now and then.'

'Jolly good.'

'It's an interesting question. *"Dis-moi ce que tu manges, je te dirai ce que tu es."* I wonder if Brillat-Savarin was right. Are people what they eat? I wonder?' reflected Penelope, as she cut timorously into a small portion of lamb.

'I've never met a Frenchman who was right. They speak the wrong language. Never could get the hang of it.'

'I eat everything,' said Didi towards Penelope. 'What would that make me?'

'Plain greedy, like me.'

When Lord Maclintock's guffaws had died away, Penelope continued, 'I suppose you could define someone by their favourite and most frequently consumed food. But it would have to be through choice, of course. You couldn't say, for example, that the Irish were potato-like at a period when potatoes provided their sole nourishment.'

'Or that the Scots were haggis-like,' said Didi.

'Yet,' pursued Penelope, 'we do tend to define nations by what is perceived as the dominant food. Curry eaters, spaghetti eaters, frog eaters. Usually, I might add, in the pejorative sense.'

'Good chap that chef.' Lord Maclintock smacked his lips loudly.

'Exactly how I like it. Bloody in the middle.'

'What do you think of the sauce?' enquired Penelope.

'I think . . .' Didi raised her eyes to the fleur-de-lys on the ceiling. 'I think . . . it works. Just. Yes.'

'A little strange. There's something I don't like.'

'Could have done with a dollop of mint.' By now Lord Maclintock's plate was empty.

*   *   *

199

Dinner conversation with strangers was like a long series of starters where the main course never arrived. It paled in comparison with the complex experiences of seeing, smelling, tasting, feeling the myriad inventions of an inspired chef, and recalling it course by course the morning afterwards. Stephen would have liked to have been the gourmet monk of some silent order, reaching the Almighty through contemplation of the edible. If only chefs, too, yearned for the divine experience, instead of lusting after fame, fortune and young ladies from the suburbs.

'I hope you are not disappointed by the food,' said Lady Maclintock, disturbed by his silence.

'Far from it. It is superb. I'm considering this sauce.'

Then she too ate in silence, hearing the wash of Tusk's conversation about cars, about which she knew nothing, and the laughter of her husband from the other table. She was relieved that he was enjoying himself, and hoped he might think she had contributed to his enjoyment. Just some little acknowledgement. She had, after all, created this dinner for him, she realized, looking down the rows of animated guests.

The corridors of the castle had lost any remnants of heat they had absorbed during the day and Laura shivered, having left the warmth conjured in the dining room by fifty people and a regiment of candles. Then she broke into a run, up some stairs, down some more, around a corner, through a small door and to the kitchen. John was sitting alone, eating some bread and cheese.

'Where's everyone gone? What's happened?'

'Don't panic. Moira's taken them to the staff sitting room. Did they like it? Was it all right? How was the lamb?'

Laura gave him a quick kiss on the cheek. 'A triumph. You're on your way.'

'Didi and Stephen?'

'Raved.'

'So I can get some kip now?'

'Not yet. You've the bouquets to collect. Come on.'

'No, I'm all sweaty and past chatting up. I can't be doing with that at the moment. I'm the chef. You do the talking.'

Laura took his hand. 'You needn't say much. Everyone's half plastered anyhow.'

'No thanks.'

'John, I'm afraid you must.'

'Not even for you. I can't be doing with fancy manners. That's your job.'

Laura tossed back her hair. 'Do you want me to look a fool? They're expecting you to make an appearance. If you can't even walk upstairs and shake hands with a few people . . . Don't give me a hard time, John.'

John poured himself some of the wine he had used for cooking. He stayed seated. Laura stood by the door, poised to leave.

'Why are you being so bloody difficult?'

'Mebbe you're not used to men saying no.'

'I'm not making a pass at you, I'm trying to help you, for God's sake. And stop looking so cross.' She paused a moment, then walked a few steps nearer. John got up, put his arms round her, and felt her flinch.

'You don't have to be so perfect all the time,' he said. 'I like you. I think of going to bed with you. Who wouldn't? But don't worry. I get the message. Strictly business. OK. Strictly business it is. You go. I'll finish this, then I'll come. And just as I am. On my own.'

The assembled company retired, mopping brows, surreptitiously loosening belts, and followed their hostess to the Macintosh Room. Charlie Rennie Macintosh had taken sherry in the library with his wife Margaret Macdonald at some time in the late 1890s. Commissioned to create a room in the new style, they had stripped away the panelling and in its place created a stencilled wallpaper with grey stripes and a furled wild rose. The imposingly simple white fireplace was inlaid with the wild rose motif. It was the only room in the castle which Laura would remember, the only room which showed the designer's hand. Stark perpendicular lines redeemed by that rose. Laura had made a quick sketch to remind herself of its structure. The minimally delineated shape of this romantic flower pleased her but it could scarcely have pleased the Maclintocks, for otherwise they would not have placed such an unsuitable picture over the fireplace.

'Lovely picture,' remarked Dylan Tusk, standing with his legs appropriately spaced in a position of appreciation, taking in the details of the dark canvas. A young barefoot girl wearing a rough cloak was sitting on a wild-eyed pony, her head thrown back, gazing mournfully at a stormy sky. In the distance, he could make out the jumbled turrets of the castle.

'Is she a relative?'

'As a matter of fact, she was the daughter of the estate manager. A sad life,' said Lady Maclintock. 'She fell in love with a stable boy whom she was not allowed to marry, so she hanged herself in the stables. Her father wore mourning for the rest of his life.'

'Marvellous. All that history. I suppose they're haunted, the stables I mean. Do you have ghosts here?'

'Not in the castle itself, but we have had servants who claim to have seen her riding a horse bareback in the moonlight.'

'Fantastic.'

Lord Maclintock approached. 'Funny thing. People always start talking about ghosts after dinner. Had some Americans here who come to Europe just for the ghosts. Damned weird if you ask me, but it gets us on the ghost list.'

'Good one,' said Dylan. 'I like it. Make a good piece.' He lowered his voice. 'You'd never guess, but between ourselves, I'm a bit psychic, as a matter of fact. But I don't let on. They're a cynical bunch, the lot at work. Think they know it all. Do you know anyone else around here with ghosts?'

'I'm sure we could rake up a few.'

'By the way, I'd be grateful if you didn't mention it, that I'm . . . you know. Some people think you must be bonkers. Make it a casual sort of enquiry, will you? Can I give you a call from the office when I get back?'

'Certainly, old chap.'

Bearing a tray of tiny bone-china cups, Moira came towards Stephen and Didi who were sitting together (at last) on a yielding sofa, each with a glass of five-star brandy.

'Coffee, madam?' she asked. Didi turned away scornfully.

'Miss Kowalski takes it black,' said Stephen. 'And I'll have a tiny drop of cream.'

Moira performed her duty, slowly, and walked away.

'You must understand, sweetest, that in these heathen parts anyone over the age of puberty is addressed as "Madam".'

'No-one has ever called me "Madam",' said Didi haughtily. 'Do I look as though I wear boned corsets and directoire knickers?'

'Suspenders, perhaps, stretching down your delectable thighs. Edging their way through some lacy fragment immodestly covering your modesty . . .'

Didi whispered in his ear. 'Do they make you quiver with desire?'

'Yes. Yes,' he replied, discreetly licking her earlobe. 'Now tell me, wild creature, what's your opinion of—?'

'Of whom, darling?' she said, imagining Stephen pushing her gently towards her bed.

'What did you think of dinner?'

Penelope Long stood over the lolling pair, handbag to the fore, making it quite clear that she intended to sit beside them, space or no space.

'I think,' said Didi, pushing her hair back, 'that John Crabtree is heading for one star.'

'Do you?' said Stephen, with the utmost gravity.

'He's not quite there yet. Some of the flavours were slightly discordant.'

'*La sauce à la menthe à l'oseille,* do you mean?'

Didi stared over Penelope's head, gazing up at the ceiling as though receiving words from a divine source and ignored her interjection.

'The terrine was very accomplished. The cornets – well, fine. Salmon super, I thought, and thank God he's using cream instead of the interminable butter. Blinis rather too Russian for my taste.'

'Really?' said Stephen.

'Thick.'

'I like them thick.'

'Should one use authenticity as a criterion?' Penelope asked. 'My point is, if you call a pancake a blini it should partake of its origin. A thin blini is hardly a blini. The dividing line between a pancake and blini bespeaks an entire culture.'

'You have a point there,' said Stephen.

'Anyway . . .' Didi regained the floor. 'Overall, it was a distinguished, well-executed menu. And he's not even French. A Yorkshireman coming up trumps. I think that's super.'

'We could do with a three-star British chef,' Stephen added.

'I give him five years. With the right opportunities and encouragement.'

'Mm. Interesting you should say that.'

'Have you made up your mind?' Penelope asked Stephen.

'I always like to sleep on it,' he replied. 'I'll tell you over breakfast.'

Stephen had no intention of sharing breakfast with Ms Long. By that time he would be well past the Scottish border, tucking into the best breakfast in the country: sausages, black pudding, two eggs spewing deep yellow yolks sitting on chunks of shiny, hot, golden fried bread – ah bliss! – listening to the vivid conversation of long-distance lorry drivers.

* * *

'Excuse me,' said Stephen, rising slowly to his feet.

'You're not going to bed already? So early?' asked Didi, unable to disguise her alarm.

She pulled down her skirt (why did every fabric manage to ride up her thighs), left Penelope writing longhand notes in a book entitled 'Shorthand Notebook' and set off to find Lord Maclintock.

Viscount Alloway's hand relaxed its grip on the neat, barely covered, enticing buttock of Virginia Leroy Desgranges.

'You're a disgusting old man.'

'It was only a . . . f-f-fatherly j-j-zsheshture,' he pleaded.

'Fatherly? Who are you kidding? You're not old enough to be my father. You're old enough to be my grandfather. You should know better.'

'You're – how frightfully pwim.'

Virginia pointed to a chair behind him. 'Sit there and don't move until I come back.'

Dutifully he slumped backwards into the cushions. Everyone at this dinner party was a crashing bore, and it was no fun at all. No-one under thirty. Virginia ran off to her room. It was time she had an early night. Dinner was OK. She'd eaten a bit. Funny how old people went on about food. That's what you did when you couldn't dance any more. Yawn. Yawn. Three parties tomorrow. Great.

John stood at the entrance of the Macintosh Room with his arms folded. What was he meant to do? Good evening, ladies and gentlemen, your chef would like to have a few words. What words? Everyone looked either sleepy or slewed, strewn around like turned vegetables on a large plate. He caught sight of Laura in the corner talking to a smooth-looking bastard. She noticed him. Did nothing. See if he cared. There was Didi, sitting on her own. He walked towards her.

'Good evening, Miss Kowalski.'

'Please call me Didi. Sit down, sit down.' Didi attempted to straighten her back.

'I've not changed my clothes. I'd best not.'

She looked at his stained white jacket. 'Who cares? Half these people won't even make it to their rooms. Have you enjoyed cooking here?'

'I suppose so. I'm a bit knackered now. Tell me, did you like it?'

'It was simply wonderful.'

'You don't have to say that.'

'Supposing I'd said, "Ghastly". What would you have done?'

'I'd have known you were lying, or didn't know about cooking.'

John's entrance went almost unnoticed. A few heads turned slightly. John sat down decisively next to Didi and tried to look away from the skirt riding up her thighs. He liked a girl you could feel.

'Being on the tele, I suppose, you can say anything you like. Folks can't answer back, can they? Chefs can't answer back either. Stuck in the kitchen and everyone going on afterwards, pulling everything to pieces.'

'Most people don't have any opinions at all. "Like it" or "Don't like it" is the farthest they get.'

'I'm not bothered about *them*.'

He liked her scent, concentrated aromas singing together like a good sauce.

'The brandy is irresistible. I think I've had rather too much,' said Didi. 'Lucky I'm not in the studio tomorrow. Time to smooth out the lines.'

'I like the way you look.'

'You're sweet.'

'Are you going to tell me?'

'Do you really want to know?' she said, her head on one side, looking at him like a cheeky robin.

Was she playing hard to get? Was he meant to seek her opinion while she lay in his bed? Not easy to tell the difference between a woman teasing and a woman asking.

'I'll get us something to drink.' He left her and went to a side table. Lady Maclintock was pouring coffee.

'Super dinner. Everyone was frightfully impressed.'

Laura approached with an empty cup. She should have told him to bring a clean jacket. Why did she have to think of everything? Paid to, yes, as John would no doubt remind her.

'Are you talking to me, then?'

She flashed the practised, serene smile. 'I didn't want to interrupt. You seem to be getting on very well with Didi.'

Laura moved away. Was there a hint of jealousy? Maybe, but it wouldn't show. Never mind. He'd done what she wanted. He was, after all, playing her game.

'You're good,' Didi said, when he returned to her.

'Yes, I know. But how good? Michelin star good?'

Didi sucked her finger. 'Mm. You must have your own place. And work on the menu.'

'What do you mean?'

'Make it simpler. Too many flavours, too much sauce.'

'You mean more controlled?'

'Yes.'

'Laura wanted me to show off. So I did.'

'The lamb was perfect.'

'I thought so, too. It's right what you're saying. You know something? I didn't think I was that ambitious. I'm beginning to change my mind.'

'There's nothing wrong with ambition.'

'What's yours?'

'Oh.' Didi dropped her eyelashes. 'To find a gourmet millionaire.'

'I don't believe you.'

'All right, I'll try again.' She glanced over at Stephen. He was sitting alone, his head leaning towards his chest, a book open on his knees. Not reading, but sleeping.

'To eat and eat and eat, and have the bathroom scales stay the same.'

'I've never met anyone like you.' John took Didi's left

hand and kissed her fingers. No wedding ring. 'You're fantastic.'

Didi received so many words of admiration, mostly expressed in the illegible cramped handwriting of her regular viewers, that compliments became as meaningless as printed circulars promising millions in prize money. She had perfected two reactions, copied from silent late-night movies, which dispensed with the need for responding with the usual trite verbal clichés. One was a slightly vulnerable, faraway, dreamy look, directed at a forty-five degree angle from the ground. This pose translated as: 'I'm so used to compliments.' The second reaction involved moving her head downwards until eye contact was reached with the speaker. A smile quickly followed, held for a few seconds, dispensing with the need to murmur, 'How sweet of you to say so.'

'I do mean it, Didi.'

Even if he didn't, thought Didi, with those kind of looks all he had to do was lean on a bar and any girl would topple.

'It's hard talking to you. You must be able to have anyone you want,' John continued.

'Like choosing from the sweet trolley, you mean?'

'No. I wouldn't say that.'

She giggled, remembering her piece on party patisserie when she had said straight to camera, 'I'm a sucker for cream horns.' The studio had laughed so raucously that the tiny mike concealed between her breasts had ceased to function. Cut, of course. They always cut the best bits.

'What's funny?'

'Something that happened on the programme. Not funny really.'

Surely she had done her duty tonight. She didn't need a protracted bid for her favours. It wasn't necessary. A good old-fashioned lay, which he looked likely to deliver.

'It's time I went to bed. Oh dear. Too much to drink. Heaven knows how I'm going to find my room. All those corridors . . .'

'I'd best be going, too,' said John, but was unable to move his body away from the soft cushions and the warmth of Didi's leg pressed against his. Throughout the conversation, he had been wondering. Well, it was that kind of weekend.

Didi looked around the room. Brandy bottle at his side and glass in hand, Dylan Tusk was sprawled on a rug. Lady Maclintock sat neatly cross-legged next to him, allowing his ever-flowing fountain of stories to wash happily over her. The book had dropped from Stephen's hand. Laura was saying goodnight. A golden retriever, which had earlier crept illegally into the room, was groaning in its sleep, stretched out proprietorially in front of the dying fire.

'If you meet me by the main staircase,' Didi found herself saying, 'you can be a darling and point me in the right direction.'

Somehow she arrived gracefully in the upright position and went to say her goodnights. No-one except Stephen would have realized she was a *tout petit peu éméchée*, that her enthusiasm was a little too profuse, that her vowels were stretching to meet the consonants. But Stephen would say nothing on this occasion, as he was snoring gently like a replete cherub on the lap of Venus. Dreaming of his distant love? Perhaps. This would not be the Destined Night . . . Oh. Where was John?

He was standing nervously looking at the great balustrade of the main staircase, wishing his own bedroom door was shut safely behind him. Silly prat. He had delivered himself up on a plate. Another in the long queue of candidates who had succumbed to Didi's charms. He could be trapped if he wasn't careful. And he wasn't being careful. Whatever he did from this moment on, there would be repercussions. What if Didi told Laura. Did they talk? Would Laura mind? If she set against him, she would be dangerous. And if Didi set against him . . . No more television appearances. Wasn't Stephen Boyce meant to be her boyfriend? Suppose he found out? That would mean bad reviews for ever more. He wasn't used to thinking about girls lately.

He walked a few steps up the stairs and inspected the full-length dark portrait of a tartan-draped woman with a pale, set face, backed by threatening clouds. A Maclintock – he could tell by the chin – untroubled by storms or repercussions.

John had decided to retreat to his room when a hand touched his arm, and he started.

'I've taken my shoes off, they make such a clatter on these floors.'

What would happen when they arrived at her door? What did she expect? Should he go in? Should he suggest she come into his room? Was it a goodnight kiss? Or more?

They reached Didi's room first and she opened the door. 'There. How do you like my little room?'

He stepped gingerly on to the threshold, marvelling at the instant metamorphosis of an anonymous neat guest room. Silk underwear was draped over the chair. On the dressing table stood tiny bottles with gold letters 'KW' entwined on the glass, a hair-drier, a hair-curler, a gold beribboned teddy bear seated at the top of her pillow, a miniature portable television by the bed, the dresses queuing along the wall.

'I always watch something idiotic before I go to sleep.' She switched channels, then sat on the bed with her knees up, hands cupping her chin, watching the tiny screen.

'Nothing but talking heads. Yuck.'

John sat down on the edge of the bed. After a couple of minutes, Didi switched off the TV and wriggled to the floor.

'This dress is so tight. All your fault. Oh, that dinner! . . . Must get it off. Won't be a moment.'

He didn't dare move. If he asked to help, she might think he was taking advantage. She sounded so natural, but it wasn't clear what he should do. She had a funny way of undressing. Underwear first. She unhooked her stockings, slipped them off her legs and dropped her suspender belt to the floor.

'Bloody button!' She came over to him. 'This one. I can do the others.'

John's hand was on her naked back, and he trembled. The black dress was attached to Didi's body by one remaining tiny loop clinging to the fabric button like a limpet.

'It's difficult.'

'Dreadful when you're in a hurry. Typical male designer. You pay hundreds of pounds for a dress that you can't get into and you can't get out of. Still, I do love the feel of it.'

'I might tear it.'

Then came the moment when John could no longer stand the vertiginous spin of emotions pulling him this way or that as he tried to puzzle out what he should do. He abandoned the button, pulled the dress down over Didi's shoulders until the loop gave way, then kissed her lips forcefully. He felt her struggling. Was she resisting, pretending to resist, accepting him or rejecting him? No matter. He grasped the top of her voluptuous thighs, opened her mouth with his, and gently and sensuously caressed the most influential taste buds in Britian.

Her body became limp as he slowly concluded the ritual of the first kiss.

'Didi.'

'Yes?'

'Open your eyes.'

'Take me to bed.'

'No. Not now.'

Didi opened her half-closed eyes, and stroked his face. 'It's all right. No-one will know. We can watch the dawn come up, and then you can creep out.'

'No. If we . . . I can't tonight. Not with you. I mean, I want to and I would but—'

'But?'

Didi held her breath, praying she was not about to relive

211

her worst nightmare. For weeks she had rushed off every weekend to meet a swoonily poetic lover (he gave the wittiest dinner parties in Oxford as well as the best lectures on the Lakeland Poets) whom she had succeeded into driving to such a pitch of wild desire that his physical means of expression was unable, only temporarily unable he explained, to live up to the strength of his unbridled lust. One evening, over oysters ironically enough, he had told her. Surely she had guessed? Just because you kiss a woman, it doesn't imply that you need to travel full throttle all the way. Didn't Didi realise that? No. No. Not bisexual. Yes. Of course he was gay.

'Can I see you in London?' John said.

'I'm sure we'll bump into one another.'

'That's not what I meant.'

'Don't worry. You'll get your restaurant before long, and be written up by absolutely everyone, my dear.'

'Didi, listen to me. You don't understand.'

'Of course I don't. I'm not too bright. Everyone knows that.'

'I fancy you like crazy, but I'm not going any further tonight.'

'I have a lot of gay friends. Lovely people—'

John put his hand over her mouth. 'Quiet. It's simple. I respect you.'

Didi squeaked and took his hand away. 'Are you serious?'

'Dead serious.'

'John, what on earth . . . ? *Respect*? What do you think I am? Some kind of Mafia Momma waiting for the sons to kiss her hand? Do you think you'll defile my honour and ruin my life for ever?'

'Where I come from, that's how it is. I don't care what you think. Lust gets forgotten. Love lasts.'

Irresistible, the way he said it. That northern accent. The 'u' sound was so . . . determined. Couldn't possibly be gay.

'I could fall in love with you.' He kissed her lightly. 'But it wouldn't be sensible, would it?'

Didi pulled her dress back over her shoulders. 'Why can't we just be friends? Love is such hard work.' She sighed. 'All I want is . . .'

'Everything.'

'No. Someone to lie in bed with, love and cuddle with, eat smoked salmon sandwiches with, share my chocolate truffles with, drink a glass of champagne with, giggle with. My ambition is ordinary.'

'You couldn't be ordinary for five minutes,' said John.

'I only want what everyone else wants.'

'No, you don't. Any more than I do.'

'I'd like to be married, have two children and give nice dinner parties.'

'Can't see you queuing at Sainsbury's check-out.'

'Oh, really, darling. Not Sainsbury's. Hyams and Cockerton, Boucherie Lamartine, and Harrods food hall if I'm really pushed for time.'

'One thing.'

'Yes?' she said hopefully.

John reached in the pocket of his white jacket and pulled out the crumpled typed menu on Laura Douglas Associates paper.

'Phone number. Write it here.'

Didi reached for her tiny gold pen, scrawled on the paper and opened her bedroom door. When John had gone she carefully left it on the latch, in case he should decide to return.

The lights in the guest wing were extinguished, relieving the uncertain electricity supply of its unaccustomed burden. Lord Maclintock was snoring in his dressing room. His wife was studying a botanical text in the room adjoining. Stephen Boyce awoke with a start in the darkened Macintosh Room, looked at his watch and decided to stay where he was, exchanging his armchair for a deserted settee rather than risk the unknown, chill corridors of the outer world. Two alarm clocks within easy reach at her bedside, Laura Douglas was asleep, correctly positioned on her side, creamed and prepared for the next day's endeavour, her arms stretched out across the pillow, reaching towards her man sleeping several thick walls away.

Only two guests were awake in the two hours which remained before dawn, punctuated by the distant hoot of owls announcing themselves to their prey. Penelope Long sat up bolt upright in her small room at the end of the corridor and switched on her bedside light. She was feeling decidedly nauseous. Pulling out a mirror from the ever contiguous handbag, she looked at her face. Goodness! Bloated, puffy and was it redder than usual or was it the light? She pulled down her lower lids. Eyes red, too. Then pressed a hand to her forehead. It was hot. She got out of bed and felt the sheets. Hot and moist. She must have been sweating for some time.

It had happened once in Delhi, also shortly before dawn. Or had her pupils been yellow then? She had suspected malaria, yellow fever, typhus, kala-azar or even a new, as yet unnamed disease, a ghastly hybrid of nature gone wrong, a deadly bacterium, a rampant spore flourishing unchecked in a hot climate. An Indian doctor had nodded sagely, told her to take to her bed for six days with a box of pills individually made up for such a rare case of Delhi fever. On the seventh day, she would arise better than new. And she did. Only the truly healthy such as herself, an ardent practitioner of preventive medicine, could catch serious diseases. For many years she had escaped the clutches of the unspeakable ravages of modern man, but given the laws of chance it was inevitable that some attacking microbe was planning revenge.

This was England. Or, rather, Scotland. Home of Robert Burns and heart disease. No, that much she knew: her symptoms could not be categorized as the effects of atherosclerosis. She stared at length in the mirror at the puffy caricature of her pre-dinner self. Of course. Food poisoning. Dreaded by those, such as herself, who acted as watchdogs for the British food supply. Obvious, had she only thought. The vellum menu, borne away to be studied at leisure, was unfurled. She pondered every ingredient and was unable to nail the culprit with total certainty. One had to be certain to point the finger. Should she tell Laura now? Suppose all the guests were swelling up to the size of pumpkins, too terrified to admit what had happened, gazing horrified in the mirror as she was? Her face seemed to have increased in size within the last ten minutes. And she was shivering.

Pure nerves, Penelope old girl. She remembered the filthy fly-ridden places where she had eaten without a thought. Algiers. Saigon. Belfast. Had she thought about food poisoning as the helicopter swung its way over the Vietnamese jungle? Of course not. She remembered meeting a fellow foreign correspondent on a sabbatical from a posting in Jerusalem, reliving old times when they covered the same beat, knocking it back in El Vino's. 'I come here,' he said, 'and everyone's worried about their diet. Out there, they're worried about survival. What has happened to my beloved country? Has everyone gone crazy?'

Perhaps she was suffering from mental deterioration, the first symptoms of brain disease, multiple sclerosis, Parkinson's, aluminium poisoning seeping into the cells. Penelope went into her icy bathroom and splashed cold water over her face. Then she had a revelation.

Noisettes d'agneau, sauce à la menthe à l'oseille. Oseille. Sorrel. She had remarked that the sauce tasted strange, she remembered. Potassium hydrogen oxalate. A component of sorrel. She must be suffering from oxalic acid poisoning. She returned to her bed and wrote in her notebook: research the occurrence of oxalic acid in sorrel and its effect at different temperatures. Fresh sorrel could be obtained in health food shops, and even Sainsbury's were selling it nowadays as a substitute for the more perishable spinach. Sorrel on the danger list – the hidden perils of Nouvelle Cuisine. Stephen Boyce and others could write drivel about some new chef. Penelope Long had a better story.

She left the notebook open on her bedside table, in case she failed to live until morning. As she wound the alarm of her ancient, wheezy clock, she started to salivate at the thought of kippers and scrambled eggs for breakfast. What a piece of unhoped for luck, coming away from a ridiculous jaunt like this with a story . . .

'Sleep all right?'

D. Tusk Esq was riding on a wave of optimism aided by thick fleshy sausages, fried eggs, mushrooms and tomatoes which he had garnered from the heated trolley in the breakfast room. He and John were the first to arrive.

'Fine, thanks,' replied John, fastidiously lifting the backbone from his kipper, wondering whether Didi had already left or was sweetly sleeping in an abandoned posture. Laura had booked his car to the airport. He would be back in London in a few hours, and tomorrow in a real kitchen among people he understood.

'I'll be writing this do up on the plane. Two thousand words between Edinburgh and Heathrow. You don't believe me? It's a fact. Last week, you'll never believe, twenty thousand words,' continued Dylan Tusk. 'Off to the Nevada desert tomorrow night. Car launch. Don't worry, you'll come out good. Don't believe in knocking copy. What's the point? If you say it's bad, there's sure to be some Charlie writing in saying, how dare you, I had the best meal of my life et cetera, et cetera. But if you write positive, who's going to complain? Only the whingers. Get my point?'

'Sounds logical.'

'My whole aim in life is to be positive. Why spoil things by being negative?'

His knife and fork crashed in a straddled position on the plate and he jumped to his feet. 'Good to have met you. Two *es*, one *b* is it? Crabtree?'

'That's right.'

'*Hasta la vista*, mate. I've got to go like the clappers. Plane to catch.'

They would be on the same plane. At least he would be writing, so there was no need to babble. What a relief. He'd done pretty well, considering. A good dinner, even though it had been a struggle. One dinner. That was all it was. Had he lost the knack? Used to do lunch and dinner, lunch and dinner at the Moorland Haven, think nothing of it. What was Laura up to? This talk of him getting somewhere in London. A load of fancy chat, he suspected. Wonderful, smile, super, smile, delightful, smile, fantastic, smile, aren't we doing well? What southerners did to make themselves feel good. Didn't things go wrong? Was the phone never cut off? Did the bank manager never say no? Perhaps they were just the lucky buggers, the ones who brushed past him on the way for a refill of champagne. Oh well.

Moira came bustling into the breakfast room as he was leaving. 'I'm so glad I caught you. We did enjoy your food. Lady Maclintock asked me to thank you for your good work. She's busy at the moment.'

'Thanks for your help, Moira.' He smiled, he was practising now, imitating, starting to lean emphatically on certain words, keeping his shoulders back, his stride long and relaxed. John picked up his bag, headed for the main entrance and on to the front terrace, past the gold Mercedes, the navy Ferrari, the dark green Bristol, the white Jaguar, Laura's Lotus and a few BMWs parked carelessly on the expanse of gravel. A mud-spattered Ford was waiting, his airport taxi. For a moment John saw himself lowering himself into that Ferrari, driving off with car phone at the ready – and Lady Maclintock coming out to wave goodbye. He wouldn't mind that. No. Be honest, he wanted it. If you fucking want it, Tad the Lad had said to him, fucking get it. You're worth more than all those stupid bastards. Time to get off his arse. Do it his way. Talk to Monsieur Bouchon. Have it out with Laura.

10

John was surprised at André Bouchon's thorough acquaintance with his menu. Yes, he admitted, Laura had asked his advice as, of course, he was familiar with the dining tastes of the aristocracy. Elaborate for a chef with little experience, perhaps, but it was right in order to make a big impression. His talent was beginning to flower and for this reason, Monsieur Bouchon solemnly declared as he sat behind his desk with both hands resting on a mound of papers, he would like John to take the position of *chef de cuisine* at Aphrodite's. To be in charge of the most prestigious kitchen brigade in the country.

John approached the desk, and shook him by the hand. 'I'm very happy to accept. And it's an honour. I didn't expect it, not this soon.'

The celebratory bottle of champagne was placed on the table, glasses filled and raised.

'To our collaboration!'

When he thought about it later, while taking his afternoon break, John missed the feeling of elation he'd had when he first started working in the kitchen at Aphrodite's. The kind of honour he wanted didn't mean bossing the lads and reproducing the menus of André Bouchon. He was good while you were learning, but once you became critical about what you did you didn't need to be told. Different generation. Treated you like a head prefect. *Chef de cuisine*. Head chef. Sounded more important in French but what would that mean to his friends up North? Still meant working for a boss even if the money was better. Not good enough for a flash car, but good enough to buy an Armani jacket and take Didi

218

Kowalski to tea at the Ritz (Laura's suggestions). Cathy was still writing week after week and only got a card from him once a month. She kept saying she could catch the coach to London, and why hadn't he told her when he'd come up to visit his Mum and Dad for the weekend? She'd heard a week later . . . How could you tell a pretty girl you weren't in love? He'd tried, several times, then torn up the letters. One day, surely, she'd get the message.

'Come. To work. Many important people tonight. My *propriétaire*, Mister Beck, is coming. I introduce him to you.'

Monsieur Bouchon was of the old school which believed that cooks should be kept in the kitchen. The restaurant was the stage, the diners the audience, the waiters the modest ushers of the spectacle. In all the months at Aphrodite's, John had never seen the faces of those whose stomachs he filled each night. The momentum in the kitchen slowed at the late hour when appetites waned, glasses were drained, and coffee cups filled and refilled to accompany the slow descent to repletion.

'Here. Take a clean jacket.'

When he had splashed water over his face and combed back his hair, John followed Monsieur Bouchon upstairs. As they passed over the velvet carpet of the dining room, he greeted occasional guests, forming this seated *tableau vivant* of well-cared-for opulence. John felt the weight, the heavy perfume of money, saw a façade of smooth faces burnished by sea breezes and mountain air, ageing monuments serviced by hidden hands which staved off ravages, cavities, aching joints. He caught glimpses of pampered flesh displaying the glint of jewels on throats, wrists and fingers, fine fabrics hanging in hand-tailored folds or giving corpulence the graceful lines of dignity. Definitely *la crème de la crème*, as George would say.

André Bouchon stopped at the centre table reserved for favoured diners. John gave a start on recognizing the heavy features of his former boss, but merely gave a slight smile and a nod of the head. He had learned by now that all reactions should be toned down, a mark of breeding he had imitated from listening to Monsieur Bouchon's measured cadences on the telephone and Laura's seemingly dismissive way of conveying enthusiasm.

A wizened, mole-covered hand stretched forward to take John's. Mr Beck, *le propriétaire*. John could not see his eyes hidden behind the tinted glasses.

'Working hard, young man?' The cracked voice articulated slowly, with effort.

'You might say.'

Monsieur Bouchon pulled up a chair and gestured at John to do likewise as Mr Beck delivered the names of his guests in a monotone.

'Well, lad.'

Charlie Braithwaite. Charlie Braithwaite down South. Charlie Braithwaite putting down his fat cigar. His exuberant style of dress had given way to a pinstripe suit and a white shirt.

'Good to see you. Fell on your feet, eh? Knew you would. Give him his first break, I did. I tell you one thing, Charlie Braithwaite knows a good thing when he sees it. Knew he'd come South. And he's been on TV. Not hanging about, our John. Waiter, bring us another bottle of champagne. Cold, mind. John, sit by me. Let's have a chat.'

'You look well, Charlie,' said John, staunching his resentment with a smile.

'Meet my colleague and friend. Jack Leone, John Crabtree.'

'Jack stubbed his cigar vigorously to extinction and looked at John. 'We've met. Can't think where. Know the face.'

'Like I said, Jack. He's been on TV.'

'Everyone stares at you. I can't go shopping any more.'

The dazzling young girl sitting beside Jack in a high-necked diaphanous silk blouse which clung to her nipples pouted at John and opened her shimmering eyes wide in the light of his barely concealed wonder. She was perfect. Skin, eyes, teeth, lips, all perfect.

'Zoe's starring in her first movie. Isn't she cute?' Jack stroked her leg under the table. 'You know that, Mr Beck?'

The shaded eyes moved and peered forward. 'Very beautiful.'

'It was a good-class restaurant, that Moorland Haven,' began Charlie Braithwaite, addressing John with an attempt to lower his voice. 'I understand why you left, lad. Would have done the same in your shoes. This place . . . well, it's a different cup o' tea.'

John wrenched his eyes away from Zoe's china perfection as Charlie Braithwaite brought back Yorkshire, good times, glowing pink on the snow, the keen moorland air, friends.

'I hope you don't hold it against me.'

'Course not, lad. We had our ups and downs but I'm glad to see you. If I can help when the time comes and you're looking for a place of your own . . . My card. Put it safe. Don't hesitate to call me. I mean that.'

'I liked your food, Mister Bouchon,' said Jack. 'I ate at the Quadrangle yesterday and every damn thing was cold. Would you believe? You know something, your cooking makes a man feel warm inside.'

'Thank you for the compliment, Mr Leone.'

'You been here a long time?'

'Nearly twenty years, I believe.'

'André has cooked for the Royal Family. Many royal families,' said Mr Beck as he slowly rose from his chair. 'It is late and I am tired.'

A waiter was sent to alert his driver and another brought his coat. Charlie followed him for a few paces towards the entrance.

'Think about what I said, Mr Beck. You'll not be having offers like mine every day. I'm being generous because I like this place. It's got character. And I'm realistic enough, being from up North to know that character costs. I'm willing to pay for that.'

'You're most kind. Unfortunately, Mr Braithwaite, I am unable to sell.'

Monsieur Bouchon rose quietly from the table and gestured to John to follow. As they left, John was perplexed. His mentor, the great Monsieur Bouchon, had seemed like a court jester with no joke to tell. He had never seen him so subdued. A man serving his masters, knowing his place. Humble like his Dad meeting the boss in church. And who were they? Braithwaite and Leone. He wouldn't even let them swab down his floor.

'So that is Monsieur Leone,' said Monsieur Bouchon, as he checked round the kitchen with John. 'Very charming. And a beautiful lady.'

'Too young for him,' said John.

Monsieur Bouchon laughed. 'She spend in five minutes what I give you for a month.'

'Not with me, she wouldn't.'

'One time, John, I have a girl from the Folies in Paris. I am in love like a slave. For one year I can just pay the rent. No more.'

'Before you were married?'

'Oh that.' He winked. 'I don't tell you.'

A shy face peered round the glass door of the Sanctum. Nigel, fresh from labouring in the port business, was learning the ways of the Grey Men. 'Excuse me, Laura, Mr Crabtree is in reception.'

'Fine. No calls for half an hour,' said Laura.

'Should I show him up now?'

Laura nodded. Nigel was proving himself by effecting graceful exits and entrances, taking off and putting on visitors' coats at the appropriate moments, distinguishing the recipients of champagne from those meriting a cup of tea. He had also demonstrated a sensitive if conventional palate, fine discrimination of wine vintages and an ability to learn, although his shadowy personality needed a little encouragement as Laura found herself unaware either of his presence or his absence.

'John!'

'I want your opinion, Miss Douglas.'

The butterfly had crawled out of the chrysalis. John Crabtree paraded round the office in a bright red silk polo-neck shirt, grey and white checked slubbed silk jacket, royal blue trousers and dark blue suede shoes. Laura blinked.

'Real silk is this.'

'It's incredible how . . . different you look.'

Ready for the golf course in Marbella, thought Laura, to be seen accompanying the kind of girl who wore strapless cat suits, stiletto heels and a gold chain on her ankle.

'This is John Crabtree, *chef de cuisine* at Aphrodite's. How about that? So I thought, time for a new image.'

'I'm really pleased. You deserve it.'

'We're celebrating at the Kitchen Club later tonight, me and some of your chefs. Will you come? We're friends now, I hope.'

Laura smiled. 'Of course. I'll try and drop in.'

'I know you won't,' said John, 'but I've asked you. You'd come if it was the Doric Club and I was toffed up.'

'Don't be—'

'I don't mind.'

'It won't always be like this.'

'Going well then?'

'Fantastic. I'm turning down clients, we just can't cope.'

'So you haven't time to find me a restaurant. I understand. As a matter of fact I was thinking, if I put it to him right, Charlie Braithwaite might give me a hand. He was in to dinner last night.'

'I thought you hated his guts.'

'Oh, Charlie's different now. Very friendly he was. And there was that American, Leone, with him.'

Laura pursed her lips.

'They're in together. Big plans. Charlie said I was to keep in touch.'

Laura looked away.

223

'Funny how you bump into people in London. It's a small business is this. Leone's got a very big company. Restaurants all over the country.'

'Yes, John. I know about Jack Leone. So what was he offering? Johnnie's Brasserie in Earl's Court?' She opened her desk drawer, pulled out a folder and tossed it towards John. 'Why don't you look through that? I've got to go next door.'

John glanced through the glass. Clever the way you could see everyone, all angled for a good view. He pulled out photocopied sheets of paper, date and source labelled in red ink, 'Crabtree – Press' written in capitals at the top.

Stephen Boyce, *Daily Reporter*. A short paragraph. John skimmed quickly. Did he or didn't he? Breathe, lad. Ah, he said something good: 'It is rare to find an aspirant chef of whom one may confidently predict a place amongst the top twenty, but I will put myself on the line with John Crabtree.'

And another one. The *Weekly Herald*. What was Penelope Long on about?

The constant search for innovation is taking its toll on the beleagured digestive system. How many chefs have paused to consider the toxic properties of exotic ingredients which have no place in the daily diet? John Crabtree, latest in a line of chefs addicted to unnecessary embellishment, chose to mar a perfectly good sauce by using sorrel. Sorrel, said Professor Martin of the Lancaster School of Dietetics (author of *Nature Beware*, Linseed Press £10.95), has toxic properties and could lead to vitamin B depletion, particularly if given to the under fives.

John tossed Ms Long's contribution across the desk. 'Unnecessary embellishment.' What rubbish! It was obvious she'd not eaten at Aphrodite's. Embellishment: What did she mean? What did she want? Food thrown on the plate any old how?

He picked up the next sheet. *Freewheel*, the weekly magazine for the motoring enthusiast. 'The Maclintocks Go Gourmet' by Dylan Tusk. John scanned the first paragraph. He hadn't cooked this meal. How could the man mistake beef for lamb? John read on: 'I watched the long-serving ghillie lay the garnered fish carefully on the oak table which had seen service for generations of the Maclintock family, rugged members of a proud Scottish dynasty.'

The phone rang on Laura's desk and she swept into the Sanctum to answer it. 'Can I ring you back later?' she said. 'In a few minutes?' She put the phone down. 'Three write-ups and one television appearance. Aren't you pleased?'

'Do you pay them to write this stuff?' asked John. 'Some of it's made up.'

Laura stared at him coolly. 'What do you expect them to say? Their job is to make someone want to read about you. It's called presentation. You should understand that by now, John. And if you think you can bribe the press, go ahead. I'd be delighted to learn how to do it, and so would every advertising agency in the country. Has it entered your thick head that journalists might trust my judgement? I've had a lot of chefs sitting where you are, and I've shown them the door after ten minutes. Why do you think Stephen Boyce and Didi Kowalski took two days off to go to Scotland when they could have been in Paris or New York or Tokyo? It wasn't because of some unknown chef called John Crabtree. Why did Lady Maclintock choose you, and not a bonny Scottish *chef de partie* from the Caledonian Hotel in Edinburgh? Or the titled daughter of a friend who'd done cordon bleu in some Swiss finishing school?'

John stood to leave, but Laura continued the tirade in the same, even tone, like a teacher putting the fear of God into an unruly class. 'I have chefs ringing me every day, begging for an appointment. I don't think you'll find journalists queuing up to interview the new *chef de cuisine* at Aphrodite's.'

225

'OK. That's the way you see it, Laura. I see it different. I'm not bothered one way or the other what people say, not really. I don't sweat about it. I know I'm good. I just want to cook.'

'Well go off and cook. I'm not going to stop you.'

John swung open the glass door and strode past the supercilious Grey Men planning their next onslaught, pouring messages of well-tempered enthusiasm down the receivers, tapping it out in fantasias of eulogy. All this activity, computers clicking, telephones ringing and buzzing, yes-men jumping – for what? Not for John Crabtree. Miss La-di-da thought she had it all tied up, thought he'd come running at her convenience. He'd have to show her that he didn't do that for anyone, not even for Charlie Braithwaite. He wouldn't show his face in there again. Not likely.

Laura took the Crabtree file and threw it into the drawer. He had made her irritable, and usually only an incompetent member of the Team caused her irritation. If she wasn't careful, John Crabtree would fly the nest she had feathered so carefully. The gauche fledgling was flexing his wings. Without even saying thanks for your help, Laura.

A few words on the phone and she was herself again. Extraordinary the effect he had, his low confident voice bringing her back on course.

'Present him with a *fait accompli*. Force the issue. You, my dear, are in control. Aren't you?'

'You're right, Howard.'

'Of course I am. Can I go back to my meeting now?'

'Will I see you tonight?'

'I'll try, darling.'

As Laura sauntered, just late enough, into Aphrodite's, she looked through the stares and made her way to her corner table. Viscount Alloway attempted to rise to his feet.

'Please don't get up. I'm teribly sorry I'm late,' she gushed.

'Worth every minute, my dear,' he said. 'Not often a chap gets to have lunch with such a vision of loveliness.'

There was a splendid room booked at Claridge's should she care to take coffee in more intimate surroundings, and she looked the kind of girl who would. A smart girl, friend of Howard's, oh rath-er. He could recognize that kind of friend. Dark horse, Howard. More than a bit on the side, this one. Going to open a restaurant? Hah! Rather small beer for MacCrae, but he wouldn't rule it out of court. She talked a lot of sense. Not like most women. Didn't realize at first it was a business lunch. By golly, it was, so no Claridge's. Facts and figures. She was on the right lines. Done her homework. No harm in giving a helping hand. He guffawed at the thought as he strode down Piccadilly towards Pall Mall.

Laura emerged from the ladies boudoir at Aphrodite's having changed back into her grey tailored dress. Were she to arrive at the Studio in uncharacteristically riotous clothing, the staff might get the wrong impression. She looked up and down the street before hailing a cab to Mortimer Street.

With a great scrawl in the visitors' book, Jack Leone immortalized the presence of Charlie Braithwaite who stood with his hands in his pockets admiring the sweeping marble staircase of the Doric Club.

'You want the lift, Charlie?'

'Not bloody likely. It's only youth has to be carried upstairs.'

His admiration of the marble sweep changed to the challenger's contempt, and Charlie measured the steps with an upward and downward glance. 'You watch this, Jack.'

He took a deep breath and projected his portly body up each marble tread, his small patent leather shoes tapping out his progress. Burping and gulping he reached the summit. Daft bugger, he thought, running after a five-course dinner. Jack climbed slowly, rhythmically, easily, like a cat on the prowl.

'I don't know how you do it, Charlie. You got some kinda engine inside there?'

Breathing heavily, Charlie followed Jack into the library.

Braithwaite Holdings PLC, as the Leeds tax inspectors now knew, was no longer trading. Ceding gracefully, and profitably, to the superior economic power and buoyant share value of Leone Leisure, Braithwaite House had given over its floorspace to Leone Leisure Northern Development, of which Mr Charles Braithwaite was chairman.

'OK, Charlie. Fire.'

Charlie leaned forward in the unyielding leather chair and sipped his brandy. 'It's a keen proposition, Jack. I'll say that. You don't know till it's well and truly rodded, if you understand me.'

'Meaning?'

'Probed, Jack. How shall I say? – entered into. What is the freehold situation?'

'Checked out. Straight. Clean site.'

'S'pose some bidder comes up with development plans? Then the price would rocket. Wouldn't be economic.'

'Listed, Charlie.'

There was a pause.

'Quiet here,' remarked Charlie, taking another reflective sip. 'Tell you what, Jack, that structure's a worry. I noticed a few cracks. I bet the old man shuts his eyes. Could be major replacements, a clean-out job. Know someone who'd do the look-over? Quietly.'

'Easy, Charlie. Electricity board doing a wiring check. Never fails. This guy's got the uniform, the gear. He can smell rot through a keyhole. What do you reckon, space-wise?'

'Plus fifteen.'

'I'd give it plus ten.'

'Let's be conservative. Say ten.'

'You gotta be realistic, Charlie. This is high style. Older-set guys, they don't want to be crammed.'

'Squeezed up's cosy . . .'

'Not for lunches, it ain't. Let's say ten more tables. We'll be aiming at block-booked concessions for high-finance clientele. We gotta get them out of the in-house dining syndrome back into the midday spend.'

'So how we get the old boy to shift his asset? You think he meant it? No sale?'

'Oh, yeah. Old guys get sentimental and they don't need money.'

'But if we don't act soon, he'll turn up his toes and, bang, we won't have a property, we'll have a bloody inheritance and cousins coming out of the woodwork.'

'You know when old guys stop being sentimental? When they're insecure. That's what we gotta do. Keep old Beck awake at night.'

Charlie gave Jack a hard look. 'You're not thinking of a chip pan setting fire by chance?'

Jack grinned. 'Not my style, Charlie. You don't need a bulldozer to crush a mouse. Just a little personal data-check. Background info. Give me two months. He'll sell, and he'll sell rock-bottom.'

The scales juddered, then the needle came to rest and Didi, enveloped in clouds of scented steam billowing from her hot bath, peered downwards to take a reading. How was it possible for her weight to have increased by one whole kilogram since yesterday, particularly as she had set herself a challenge and walked up all seventeen floors to reach her office at Intertel? She stepped down, allowed the needle to rest at zero and then stepped on again. It seemed to have crept up a fraction more. She would have to replace her scales with a more accurate register. Wiping the steamy mirrored wall, she stood regarding her blurred imagine. In profile, it was remarkably sleek, once she had tensed her buttocks and pulled in her stomach, but one could hardly maintain a slim profile in every long-shot. It was all very well her beauty consultant telling her to think thin, but she preferred a more practical approach.

Once again, Didi rehearsed the possibilities, sitting on her velvet bathroom armchair waiting for the heat to subside. She had tried: the fruit diet (with mono-variations like the kiwi fruit diet, the grapefruit diet, the banana diet), the vegetable diet, the bread diet, the brown rice diet and Mu tea diet, the steak diet, the foie gras and champagne diet, the combination diet, the liquid diet, the no-fat diet, the no-sugar diet, the high-protein diet, the yin and yang diet, a multitude of dietary pills, the diet in a pill, starch blockers, the fat burners, appetite reducers, even the Eskimo diet and the no-diet diet. Her many-shelved fridge had at different times resembled a half-empty Eastern European foodstore.

There was a logic in the mysterious process of losing weight, Didi decided. The more difficult the diet, the more effort required in its accomplishment, the more mystery surrounding its practice, the more it was likely to succeed. And, of course, it had to be costly. Tomatoes and grapefruit were all very well for the lower categories, but Didi Kowalski needed something as rare as a Fabergé egg and as difficult to attain. She would embark on a long journey, by air, by train, by bus, by camel, perhaps. The journey to an undiscovered guru of slimness had to be full of rigours, discomfort and privation. She would submit to blinding sun (swathed in virginal linens) while the sand from desert storms whipped her face. Or she would be staggering across snowy wastes (long, white mink with a hood, permissible at sub-zero temperatures), fording rivers, clinging to narrow mountain roads (gaberdine jodhpurs and tight-fitting safari jacket). The jungle, Stephen's favourite landscape, she would avoid, for she had no desire to plunge into primitive, sweaty, serpentine depths. Didi preferred civilization, by which she meant ancient civilization. An ancient culture would yield the secrets denied to Harley Street consultants who had failed to understand that the determination to become the ideal shape, the ideal weight, had nothing to do with centimetres and kilograms or being size eight in six months' time. Didi wanted to become imbued with the spirit of slimness, to be comparable with the sinuous Egyptian priestesses undulating across ancient libation cups.

The quest would have to be made alone. Stephen would inevitably insist on some gastronomic diversion. He still featured in Didi's thoughts, although her attitude to him had changed. Over the months she had observed his swelling belly and changed her tragic assessment. There might be some distant amour languishing in a foreign clime, but he would not, she was now sure, fade away in her arms as a skeletal reminder of his former self. That gorgeous Harley Street expert doctor had reassured her on that point. The wasting effects of AIDS would have made its mark by now.

Didi pulled on her leopard-skin tights, and threw over a wafer-thin black silk smock which clutched at her breasts and then swung free in myriad, camouflaging pleats. She evoked the contents of her fridge and made her mental selection. Quails' eggs. A tiny jar of caviar. Smoked salmon pâté. Bruschetta. Fresh-made capeletti. A truffle she had been hoarding from the trip to Périgord. Lightly shaved, flecking a cream sauce. Foie gras as well? No, that would be *de trop* and, besides, that was for Stephen. She slipped two large jewelled hoops through her ears, and went bare-footed into the kitchen.

Minou was making ecstatic figures of eight round Didi's ankles, and emitting staccato miaows as she pulled the delicacies from the fridge and arranged them on fine china bowls and plates, which she dotted with nasturtium petals.

'Nothing special. Just something to nibble on,' she would say, as she opened the champagne. Damn. The vintage. Forgotten to put it in the fridge. She managed to tread heavily on the feline tail as she rushed out to the terrace wine store.

'Skedaddle!' she screamed at Minou, who screeched off

into the night. At that moment, the telephone rang and the doorbell sounded in a dissonant chord. 'Damn!'

The machine was on answer, thank God. 'Didi darling,' the faintly slurred voice began, 'I'm back from Alexandria. Absolutely stunning . . .' She turned down the volume and tripped over to the door.

'John. How lovely. You look gorgeous.'

(How sweet. He was trying, but that could be remedied. They could always go shopping together.)

'Hope I'm not too late. It was packed tonight.'

'Come in. Have a drink.'

John stood marvelling at the red flowers careering across the satiny curtains, the red silk wallpaper, the frilled settees, the marble nymph posing in the fireplace, the gilded clock gently ticking, the small chandelier dripping with glass.

'Sit down. I'll get something to nibble from the fridge.'

'You don't have to bother, Didi.'

'No bother,' she said. 'I usually have a little snack at this time.'

She disappeared for a couple of minutes, and John heard clinks and clatters from the kitchen down the corridor. Should he ask to help? No, better not. Girls didn't like men in the kitchen.

Didi emerged again, bearing her little snack on a huge tray. She arranged the dishes on a low table, and looked up at the long figure on her settee.

'You've done me proud. I appreciate it,' said John.

It was the second time they had met in London, but this time Didi was apprehensive. He had invited her for tea at the Ritz, which delighted Didi as occasions came rarely when she could wear her adorable wide-brimmed hat from Paris, and she had received her usual homage from ardent watchers of *Table for One*. ('My viewers coming to the Ritz!' she had exclaimed. 'I must be having some effect.') And she had noticed with pleasure the envious looks directed at her handsome escort.

Didi experienced a pang of guilt. He was sitting on the

settee where Stephen should have been reclining, expecting her usual invitation on arriving back in London after an exhausting expedition abroad to evaluate the emergence of Egyptian cuisine from 'peasant to posh' as he put it. Why did she feel guilty? Would they or would they not go into her bedroom? As he asked her polite questions about the source of the capeletti, and commented on the flavour of the black truffle, she kept putting the confusing question to herself. Should she? Or should she not? Tonight? Too soon? Was he expecting it? And if he was, should she delay? It was different at Maclintock Castle, easier somewhere strange; she would have done it there. And if they did, would he stay? Should she ask him?

Supposing, most ghastly thought, he were to boast next morning in the kitchen that he had bedded Didi Kowalski. And supposing, even worse, that he spilled the beans to some jealous girlfriend who imagined she had claims on him – women always knew – and she came storming up to Intertel to make a scene . . . What if Stephen got to hear? Or Caliope. ('Guess what? Didi Kowalski is having a scene with guess who.') Or Laura Douglas . . . She could imagine Laura's look of contempt. Going out with one of my chefs. Extraordinary! Didi's desire which had been fanned by expectation now subsided like an undercooked soufflé.

'Is anything wrong?' asked John. 'You've not said a thing for a while.'

'I had a few problems today. Sometimes I know the programme isn't going to work and I can't quite see how to put it right. That's all. Boring. Isn't it silly, caring about food?'

'Not to me.'

'I wanted to go on the stage, but my father said over my dead body. It wasn't a proper job. My parents still don't think I've got a proper job.'

'What do they want? There can't be many women who are as successful as you.'

'Oh, success isn't having a career. Not for them. Success is having a nice husband who's got a good job, has a nice pension plan and two children who do well at

233

school. What do you expect? My Dad's a bank manager. They keep waiting for me to settle down. They wanted me to be a nice girl and I'm not. According to them, that is. My sister has two kids and lives in Purley with an insurance salesman. She's nice. Girls are meant to be nice. It's all right to be ambitious at school. What are you going to be when you grow up? they all ask. Then you grow up and you do well, and they don't like it.'

'They're mad.'

'I don't know why I'm saying all this.'

'Do you see much of them?'

'I try not to. Every time I do, my Dad says, "Time you got engaged, Dorothy. I was married at your age." Oh dear. Don't tell anyone. Promise?'

'Promise.'

'Dorothy Dean. That's my real name. If the press found out, I'd be finished.'

'It's just a name. Don't be daft.'

'Dorothy Dean sounds like a nice girl, don't you think? Plaits and clean underwear. I had a Polish grandmother who had lots of lovers, so I changed my name to hers. Kowalski. Grandma Irena had men at her feet when she was sixty.'

'And so will you. Come here.'

She went and sat next to John and tucked her bare feet under her ample buttocks.

Her resolution was wavering. Even Stephen didn't know about her Polish grandmother. Or the existence of Dorothy Dean. Perhaps she had only mentioned it because John, for some reason, made her feel like Dorothy Dean.

Play hard to get. Men only want one thing. I'm being boring, she thought as the adolescent phrases rang in her head. Like my Dad. It was so close to the surface, that stifling suburban background she had tried and tried to disguise, mock and deny. Bromley, Kent, where the cupboards might be clean, but which still held dirty secrets, and everyone mentioned the weather as they walked down the shopping parade and tore reputations to shreds over the sherry in the front parlour. Dad hitting the whisky bottle and, occasionally, hitting Mum. Or Mother, as she preferred to be called. Mother married beneath her but had lace tablecloths and bone china and did good works to meet a nicer class of person than Father.

The clock chimed and Didi sat up.

'Goodness. Is it that late? I must be going to bed soon. Early start tomorrow.'

John did not move and held her more tightly. 'It must be terrible being a star.'

'That's what they all say.'

'All the boyfriends?'

'Yes. They say poor Didi, never being able to go out and not have people stare. Such an awful strain. Make-up and mirror.'

'I'd like to see you without it. I'd like to see you as Dorothy Dean getting her first break.'

'Forget I told you that. I don't know why I did. Perhaps I invented it. Everyone's so curious, you've got to tell them something.'

She started to resent this stranger sitting so comfortably beside her.

'Would you like to taste my favourite truffles before you go?' she asked, in her second attempt to remove the handsome intruder.

'Love to.'

Didi went to the small escritoire in her bedroom and unlocked one of the tiny drawers. There, wrapped with a gold bow in a black box, was Stephen's present from Belgium which she fingered hesitantly. Should she? There was another, less orgasmic box in the fridge, but John was sure to know that he was being given inferior visitor's truffles. Ghastly to give away one of Stephen's lovingly selected truffles but the thought of yet another night in bed savouring the dark rich chocolate swimming round her teeth after she had cleaned them, then sinking back into solitary sleep, fortified her decision.

'Those are too precious,' said John, standing at the

235

doorway to the bedroom, watching her hesitation and her look of regret as she pulled the golden bow. 'Save them for a special occasion.'

Didi turned towards him. 'My bedroom's in a terrible muddle. Don't look. I meant to tidy up today, but—'

'Nice girls are tidy?'

'Nice girls put their clothes on hangers immediately.'

Didi started to make for the door, balancing the small box in her hand.

Next morning, as she waited for the early morning car to take her to Deirdre and the Monday programme meeting at Intertel, she tried to recall each step of the night before. What had happened precisely? She looked in the mirror. Would everyone know? Was it showing beneath the mascara, the blusher, the glossy lipstick, the eyeshadow? She couldn't remember how he had diverted her, but there she was lying across the bed. And he had been inside her for a long time, the soreness reminded her of his desire. Her eyes had been closed, he had grasped her hips, she had been still. Farther and farther until she had screamed. Didi smiled. He had thrown her upwards, downwards, manipulating her hesitation, drawing out liquid cascades. Then at last, he had kissed her, plunging into her mouth with his tongue, withdrawing it slowly.

'I love you, Didi.'

'What a sweet thing to say,' she had said politely. How gorgeously gauche. Like her first date.

Love lived in the suburbs, had a white wedding and grew into silent boredom, Didi knew that. She preferred to stick with lust. A few months of lust, if it lasted that long. So rare nowadays, genuine, energetic, calorie-absorbing, full-frontal lust. Her face flushed at the thought, and she relived the long night with the lingering trickle dampening the satin sheets beneath her legs, evoking his male scent, the heady smell of sex which thrust through the heavy perfume she had splashed over her naked body.

Outside, she heard the familiar toot of the horn. She lifted a corner of the lace curtain and waved. Picking up her large bag, packed full of programme ideas, she languorously greeted the day, bent her yielding body into the back seat of the car and settled in a feline position against the mock leopard of the Intertel limousine as the driver pulled away.

The headquarters of Illustra Foods soared brazenly above more modest towers, stamping its unmistakable mark on the river line. From the wide sweep of his office windows, Sir Howard Riley could look down on the wind-rippled muddy waters of the Thames and follow the pleasure boats, like children's bath toys, chugging their clockwork way past sights deemed worthy of attention by the Tourist Board.

At eight o'clock each morning Sir Howard Riley cleared his throat and began dictating letters to his secretary, who had followed his upward progress for twenty years and guarded him with the ferocity of a starving tigress. It was now quarter to six in the evening, but she was still devotedly at work.

'Forgive me for disturbing you, Sir Howard,' she said, pressing the communication button from her tiny but exclusive office. 'But there's a person to see you in reception. Says he has an appointment.'

'Find out what he wants,' he answered, looking at his diary. 'Ah, yes. Get the head of personnel to deal with him. Tell him I've been unavoidably called away. Yet another food technologist who reads the *Guardian* and thinks we owe him a job.'

'Thank you, Sir Howard.'

He was thanked many times a day, for his ability to make decisions, the quality most admired by the devoted and the modestly paid. Burying himself in an extract of the month's EEC directives, Sir Howard would get round to giving his views on the outlined marketing policy and advertising strategy for the launch of Whammo Ricicrisps in

237

Japan at approximately – he checked his watch – six p.m.

'Forgive me for disturbing you again,' came the careful tones of the oiler of the wheels of power, 'but Miss Long from the *Weekly Herald* wishes to know your policy on secondary irradiation in convenience foods.'

'Send her our policy statement.'

'Certainly. And, Sir Howard . . .'

'Yes?'

'Laura Douglas, a little early for your seven o'clock meeting. Shall I tell her to come up?'

'Why not?'

'Thank you, Sir Howard.'

Laura observed the paintings hanging round the sparsely furnished waiting area. A Picasso drawing? Surely not. And a small Matisse? And a Miro? She examined them more closely. They seemed genuine. Why? How many visitors sitting here would even have noticed? One in a hundred, perhaps, but one in a hundred would be impressed. Justification enough, she supposed. A framed poster caught her eye. 'Illustra Foods Exhibition at the Royal Academy.'

'Well, Laura. You've hunted me down at last.'

Howard stood in the doorway, smiling. He looked at her, then came quickly towards her, clutched her waist and kissed her neck, sinking his teeth gently into her flesh.

'Howard, I need to talk to you. I want you to see the prospectus before the meeting.'

'Of course, of course. You're not worried, are you? Come. Have a drink first.'

She followed him into his office, ten times the size of the Sanctum.

'Wasted space, but people insist . . .'

Laura felt awe in his presence. Jack could never dominate in such an effortless manner. Who could say no in such a room? Then she noticed his desk. Two silver-framed pictures. A girl laughing, her hair tucked into a scarf tied

238

peasant fashion, flowered blouse, long full skirt. Too young to be his wife, but surely too grown up to be his daughter? Obviously taken on holiday. And the other picture: two boys sitting on a log in a garden. They were there in front of his eyes as he telephoned to say he would be late.

'Aren't you going to show me?'

Laura gave him a delicately patterned folder and went over to stand by the window, gazing at the lights below muzzed by the light rain.

'Cecil, Jamie, make yourselves comfortable.'

Viscount Alloway and Lord Maclintock shook hands with Laura and introduced the investment manager of the MacCrae Bank, Henry Mathews, who was short, wiry and given to stress attacks natural to his position.

'Do sit down, Henry.'

Howard was pouring out the Scotch as the three men settled back into the creaking leather of the heavy black sofa and looked expectantly at Laura.

'Why don't you sit at my desk, Laura? There's more room.'

She moved to behind the shining expanse of wood and felt like a general observing a distant battle. She opened her folder, stretched her long legs in front of her under the desk and took a deep breath to calm her racing pulse.

'I've told the others a little,' Howard said, breaking the silence. 'I don't know much about restaurants.'

She turned slightly in her chair to banish the silver-framed photographs from her line of vision and to face Howard who was leaning back, one leg crossed elegantly over the other. She began her introduction hesitantly, and heard her low modulated voice as though it was echoing back to her in a half-waking dream. Then she noticed Howard lean forward, cup one hand under his chin, intently listening, half smiling, and she talked to the men in front of her as she talked to Howard at home while she was dressing after they had made love, and he sat like that on the bed.

She described her vision – the emergence of the new British cuisine, spearheaded by Laura Douglas. She would draw from the traditional to create the new, and she had found the man uniquely capable of understanding the clarity of her vision: John Crabtree. And she had found the ideal site.

'Let me show you.'

Architect's plans. Beautiful drawings. Did she do those herself? How clever!

Now for the figures. More Scotch, and the conversation began. Looked right on paper. Query here, query there. She answered. Knew the figures. Business sense there. No major hole. Cash flow slightly above expectations. Not too pessimistic. Not too optimistic. On paper.

For the next hour, the four men threw themselves into heated discussion. High risk or medium risk? Medium risk or high risk? While Laura listened. Dream or reality? She could not tell.

'We'll give your proposal positive consideration, Laura. Can't say more.' Viscount Alloway winked at her. They all shook hands, the room emptied and Howard was leaning against his desk.

'Well?' said Laura.

'You've got your restaurant, darling, if that's what you want. This was just a formality. Cecil and I had already discussed it. Mathews and your accountant can work on the fine points.'

'But—'

'It's a little diversion for the MacCrae Bank. More fun than petro-chemicals and oil rigs, I should imagine. Are you happy now?'

Laura flung her arms round him. 'I don't know how to thank you.'

'You don't have to. I'm glad to help.' He stroked her face and ran his fingers across her lips. 'I want to have you on the floor,' he said. 'Right here.'

'Where you screw your secretary?'

She pulled away from him but he pushed her down,

pinning her to the carpet. 'Let go of me. At once! Don't be ridiculous.'

It was undignified to struggle. Howard pushed up her skirt, parted her legs and savoured her thighs with his tongue.

'Do it, if you have to. Go on. Quickly. If that's the price.'

He moved his face upwards and pulled aside the thin silk in his way, moving upwards until he felt the needle point of desire which he sucked until she quivered like a compass driven into disarray by a nearby magnet. When her body came to rest, she opened her eyes and he quickly removed her knickers, unzipped his trousers and plunged inside her.

'No, Howard. Please I don't want it. Not here.'

Then she heard only his low, insistent voice, as though it, too, had entered her.

'You like it, don't you? . . . you do, I can feel you do. You want to be taken like a slut. That's what really excites you. Am I right? I know I am. Little Laura's secret. That's what you've wanted all along. But no-one saw that, not even Jack. I should have taken you outside and done it against the wall. Is that what you did with the boys in the school playground? Dirty little Laura.'

He was filling up the empty space inside, pounding and pounding until Laura screamed and her body seemed to liquefy, releasing torrents, crashing through the dam she had built up in the pursuit of perfection.

'You can get up now.' He threw her her knickers, adjusted his trousers and tie. 'I didn't hurt you, did I? It was only a game. But it worked, didn't it? Don't look so serious, darling. It's not the end of the world, having an orgasm. Shall we go and eat something? I'm starving.' He pulled her to her feet and kissed her forehead.

'I can't go like this. My dress—'

'You look lovely.'

Howard took her by the hand and led her towards the lift.

11

In her womb-like cubicle at the House of Beauty, Laura thought only of Howard. As she slipped off the fine silk which only he would see and gazed down on her pale skin whose delicate softness only he would feel, she saw his handsome face, whose fleeting expressions were sometimes haughty, sometimes melancholic, sometimes remote, sometimes sweetly, regretfully tender. His portrait went through a myriad changes, resisting pen and brush. Yet he was never distant. He looked at her as few men ever did, piercing her with his intense, passionate eyes, or mocking her with his world-weary, seductive smile – the man who had cracked open the façade she had constructed over years. Howard had forced her to see beyond the kitchen window, had shown her the world where she really belonged.

Once again, the hot wax oozed over her body. She allowed herself to flinch, as though it was being placed by his hand. And when the smooth movements of the masseuse's touch caressed her, she was giving herself to Howard. As she was leaving, she caught sight of herself in the softly lit mirrors. They had all said how radiant she was, how happy, which she accepted as the customary homage given in such a place, but today they meant it.

The front of the Moukkhadem was boarded up and inside a regiment of workers was attacking the fabric with every ear-piercing device known to the building trade. They were a week behind schedule and each day Laura entered the chaos, refusing to be deterred by the daily problems which threatened to delay the work still further, trying to convey the urgency of an opening date which could not be changed. Confronted with an architect for whom the builders had scant respect, Laura had changed herself into a whirling virago, whipping up activity until even a tea break had to be accounted for and drawing forth reluctant admiration from the sweating men.

Every night, she dreamed of falling masonry, water gushing from broken pipes, men dropping from scaffolding and being crushed like beetles, beams cracking, debris raining down on white tablecloths. China shattering, guests fleeing and screaming . . . Then, after the nightmare of chaos, came the gentle swish of brush on plaster and woodwork as the decorators took over from the wreakers of havoc and the overflowing skips had been lifted away.

Laura sat on a stepladder, breathing in fresh paint, gazing round the space which she could now measure inch by inch, visualizing the expanse of carpet, the deep blue rose-flowered wallpaper, the curtains swathed lightly in harmonious contrast. As soon as the undercoat covered the stripped wood, she placed the square wallpaper sample against the wall, still wondering after all these weeks, whether she had made the right decision or whether she should have opted for the sparse modernity of the nineties, the cool grey of her trademark.

'Do you really like it?' she asked the senior painter, whom she had already asked a dozen times.

'It goes a treat, Miss Douglas,' he replied, puzzled at the indetermination of this determined woman.

Antony was growing used to Laura's frequent absences. She came in late every evening, and every evening Antony waited for her, making sure the champagne was cold, the flowers fresh, the studio was tidy and the day's checklist was on her desk. Everything had to be just right. He, too, was learning to sift through the constant demands on her time, the deluge of calls and correspondence, and could determine what needed urgent attention and what could go the way of office garbage.

*   *   *

As John struggled to park in the tightly packed street meandering round the back of the King's Road in Chelsea, George stood on the pavement assessing the area.

'Quite the right part,' he said, 'for a town house, that is. So unspoilt.'

John looked up at the creeper-clad houses mimicking the cottages of a country lane. 'It's one of these, George.'

'Haven't you been before?'

'No.'

'There's one for sale. It would just do you.' George took hold of John's arm, and sleeked back his hair nervously. 'How do I look, John?'

'Fine.'

'At first I thought jeans. Then, no. Not on a Sunday. One doesn't, except perhaps for gardening and I've never been one for the earth. Do you like the scarf?'

'Divine! There's no need to worry, George.'

'One gets out of touch. Another week in Jeannie's Bistro and I swear I would've been wearing a medallion round my neck. I don't want to let you down, dear boy.'

'Say you were in France some place after the Moorland, if you're asked.'

'I've done the day trip to Boulogne.'

'OK. Say you were working for Lady Chevening in York.'

'Are you sure? It's a bit of a fib.'

'Folks down here aren't that bothered, I've noticed. Long as you're good, which I know you are.'

'What did I do for Lady Chevening?'

'We'll think of something.'

'I could say we brought over a French chef . . .'

'From a two-star restaurant outside Boulogne.'

'I feel better already.'

'Here. This is it.'

George threw back his shoulders, adjusted his neckscarf and followed John with a springing step through the wrought-iron gate.

'Miss Douglas! Of course I remember you. You sat at table sixteen in the Moorland Haven.'

'Did I make such an impression?' asked Laura.

'Indeed you did.' George stood in the middle of Laura's room. 'Beautiful. I love the chairs.'

'Philippe Starck. My extravagance.'

'They'd look wonderful in a restaurant.'

'Come downstairs. I've some things to show you.'

John had never seen her like this, dressed in jeans and a shirt, no make-up, bursting with enthusiasm.

'Here. Look.'

From a long trestle table Laura held up a large sheet of heavy white paper. In the centre was a wild rose of the palest, dusty pink, trailing across the page, petals ruffled by a breeze, delicate thorns bristling along the stem.

'Who's the artist?' said John.

'Who do you think?' Laura smiled. 'Do you like it?'

'You did that? All that fabulous detail. It could be Redouté,' added George. 'Honestly, Miss Douglas.'

'It's the symbol of our restaurant. Now guess the name.'

'Restaurant de la Rose?' suggested George.

'Not quite. It will be called the Eglantine. Or, as the French would say, Eg-lan-teen. It's the old English name for a wild rose.'

'Eglantine,' repeated John. 'It's strange . . . But I like it. I think I do.'

'John Crabtree. Chef at the Eglantine. Oh, yes. Very distinguished.'

'And George Hollings, restaurant manager of the Eglantine. Yes?'

'Well, Miss Douglas, I thought you might want . . .'

'Do call me Laura. I noticed you, too, at the Moorland. You're far too good for Jeannie's Bistro, whatever that may be.'

George glanced at John who pursed his lips slightly. Say nothing.

'Now look at these,' Laura pulled over a sheaf of

245

drawings. 'Deep Venetian blue wallpaper with very faint pink eglantines, made to my design copied from an Italian palazzo. Pale gold tapestry chairs with a rose on each one and a deep gold carpet with a tapestry effect. Tables with gold linen, white plates with just one rose on the rim . . . And the chairs. You should see the chairs. Inspired by Chippendale but in light wood. And this will be the kitchen, taken out into the courtyard at the back. Do you like it?'

John was overcome. Doing all this for him. He could hardly believe it. And her not saying a word about it.

'I never imagined . . . I didn't think . . .'

Laura put her arm on his shoulder.

'You're the only chef who will make it work.'

'I'll do my best.'

'We must start talking about the food. I've lots of ideas. Can you come to the Studio tomorrow afternoon?'

'I shall have to see Monsieur Bouchon.'

'Of course.'

'Have you said anything?'

'No. I thought it would be better for you to talk first. Just tell him you've accepted an offer. There's no point in saying any more. He'll only get upset.'

It was a quiet Monday, for the May weather had suddenly turned from temperate spring to summer heat. Even regular diners had forsaken the thick, muffled decor of Aphrodite's and the kitchen brigade worked at a leisurely tempo, escaping outside whenever they could to turn their faces to the sun. It was like playing a matinee to a half-empty theatre. All the preparation, all the care and a handful of people who would only eat grilled fish and salad. André Bouchon came into the kitchen to whip up enthusiasm.

'Every day is an important day, *voyons*!' he said to a slow-moving sous-chef who had failed to stuff the poussins in time.

'Yes, Monsieur Bouchon.'

'Maybe one person he come in and this is the most important day of his life.'

'Yes, Monsieur Bouchon.'

Mr Beck, the proprietor of Aphrodite's, struggled out of the ancient Daimler helped by his chauffeur. His daughter Juliet stood on the pavement cradling a white Lhasa Apso dog.

'Shall I take Sushi, Miss Beck?'

'No thank you, Pierre. This is his special treat.'

The manager noted with horror that a dog was about to enter the portals of the august monument to the genius of André Bouchon, and was going to suggest that the animal might like to have a special menu in the office when he recognized the bent figure coming hesitantly towards him and changed his mind.

Mr Beck groped for his chair, which was quickly placed beneath him, and stared at the familiar menu as he prepared to disobey his doctor's orders.

'My eyes are not good today,' he remarked to Juliet, who sat erect on her chair, nervously observing the expanse of empty tables around her.

'There's hardly anyone here.'

'It's early for luncheon. Is it Monday today?'

'Yes.'

'Lobster Newburg as usual, Mr Beck?' said the waiter.

He nodded. 'Is André expecting me?'

'That's why we are here, father.'

André Bouchon removed his white jacket, came over to the table, inclined slightly towards Juliet Beck and shook the hand of this frail old man who had devoured the lobster heightened by butter, cream, brandy and marsala wine.

'Please sit down, André. Are you well?'

'*Très bien*, Mr Beck.'

'How is the young man?'

'I am very pleased.'

'Good, good. I have a letter to show you. The letter, Juliet, the letter. Is it in your handbag?'

'Just a minute, father.'

Juliet completed peeling a prawn and offered it to the dog, seated beside her on a velvet stool. 'Nicely, Sushi.'

'It was delivered to my home. I don't remember giving my address.'

Juliet took out an envelope from her bag which she handed across the table. Monsieur Bouchon read the letter once, then again, and the three sat in silence until he handed it back.

'Why is this Mr Leone offering me so much money? Do we have an oil well under the kitchen?'

'A freehold property is valuable, Mr Beck,' said Monsieur Bouchon, trying to mask his apprehension.

'Is that the right price, André? Is it enough or is it perhaps too little?'

'Father is curious. That is all.'

'I merely wanted your opinion.'

'You . . . have the intention of selling?'

Mr Beck gave a slight cough. 'Selling? Selling Aphrodite's?' He laid his hand on Monsieur Bouchon's arm and tapped it gently. 'I have no need to sell. Or to buy, for that matter. When you get old, André, you are indifferent to money. When I die, I will leave Aphrodite's to Juliet.'

'This is my second home,' she said, peeling another prawn. 'Do you remember when André first came and he made me a cake for my thirtieth birthday?'

'She remembers everything,' said Mr Beck, smiling proudly at his daughter, now fifty-two and unmarried, having never met a man who was the equal to her adored father.

Later that afternoon when the brigade had left John decided he could wait no longer. The moment had come to confront André Bouchon. He knocked, entered the office and found him poring over his portfolio of menus.

'So. Today we are quiet. *Ça arrive*. You must not be preoccupied because of this. The English, who have not much sun, when the day is fine they must sit and burn themselves outside. Crazy! You think we should make a little garden in the yard? Then we get people?'

'They don't like strong light,' said John, considering the predominantly ageing clientele. 'Never mind. I'm sure things will pick up. We're three quarters booked for tomorrow.'

'Good. That is good. Now, John, what are we going to make for the French ambassador? I am thinking of some ideas. Maybe we should—'

'Monsieur Bouchon.'

'Something is wrong?'

'No, no.'

'Perhaps we should do a banquet of classic Escoffier, style Bouchon. Even the French do not realize he is thinking in a very modern way. We—'

'Yes, you could do that.'

'We, John. You and me, we make the decisions, *n'est ce pas*? Now you are understanding so well the *manière* Bouchon, you must not feel I am always saying what to do.'

'No, I don't. Not at all.'

'Then. Everything is OK?'

'You're a great chef, Monsieur Bouchon.'

'You and I, we know each other well. We understand. This is a rare thing. Many people come here. They are good, but they don't speak my language. There is something not quite right. But you, you are understanding my thoughts, what I am wanting. Maybe, I say little. But I appreciate you, John. Maybe sometimes I am busy, I am *préoccupé*, I say not enough. *Eh bien*. You are happy here?'

John looked away. It would have been so much easier if they had had an argument, a blazing, kitchen-shattering row.

'You must tell me if something is wrong. There is no need to be afraid, John.'

'It's hard for me, this,' began John. 'But I hope you understand . . . I thought I'd better tell you now.'

'Ah.' André Bouchon stared at him intently. 'I knew it was something. You are leaving me.'

John heard the French clock on the mantelpiece ticking, which he had not heard since he sat on the edge of his chair at their first meeting. 'I've had an offer, Monsieur Bouchon.'

'Ah, yes. Of course.'

'To have my own restaurant. It's taken me a long while to decide. Working with you has been the best thing that's ever happened.'

'Yes, yes.'

'But I knew it couldn't go on for ever. I'm getting older.'

'How old? Twenty-four, twenty-five maybe?'

'I'm twenty-five.'

'You are still *petit garçon*.'

'Maybe, but I know I'll only be creative for perhaps a few more years. Time is running out.'

'Who is saying these ridiculous things?'

'The other chefs. Tadeus, Sebastian, Elwyn. You work like crazy while you can, eighteen hours a day, thinking up ideas, making them work . . . Then you get to thirty, thirty-five, and there's nothing new. You've experimented, you know what works, what doesn't and there's nowhere new to go. Unless you've got your own place. Then you start training another young man. I don't want to be clapped-out at thirty-five, Monsieur Bouchon, resenting you, trying to make out I'm doing what I want.'

'I assure you this is not right. You have mistaken ideas.'

'I've seen it happen. Being a chef's like being an athlete. Past thirty, you've got to be looking for another career. I'm not the type to go off and run a country pub in the middle of nowhere doing lunches and dinners because I've no energy for anything else.'

'So. What is it you want?'

'I want to be John Crabtree, one-star Michelin. John Macintyre had one when he was three years younger than me.'

'But here we have three stars. You want to go backward, John? Is this what are you saying?'

'No. I want it for myself.'

André Bouchon walked slowly over to a table and poured himself a cup of coffee, forgetting that the pot had been cooling for over an hour. 'Coffee?'

'No, thank you.'

'Tell me. If I give you more money, you decide not to go?'

'It's not that—'

'But they are paying you more, *sans doute*.'

'Well, yes.'

'And you are telling me where is this restaurant?'

'I can't. Not yet.'

Monsieur Bouchon went over to his desk, sat down and put on his glasses. 'I think you are making a very big mistake, but it is your decision. In France the great chefs can still cook at fifty, at sixty. They are not afraid of work. You British, you are afraid of work. You want to make money and then go outside and burn yourself in the sun and do nothing.'

'That's not what I want.'

'So? You stay with me. I promise you in ten years' time you will be ten times better than you are now. And recently, I must say, I was having the idea to send you for a time in France, to one of the best restaurants. *Eh bien*, I must find somebody else.'

John gave a regretful smile and then took a deep breath. 'I'm giving you a month's notice. Here. I've written you a letter.'

He went and put it on the desk. Monsieur Bouchon took it and instantly tore it up, dropping the fragments into the waste bin.

'This is not necessary. I pay you one month. But today you go. Is better this way.'

'Thank you. That's kind. I'll be needing the time as a matter of fact.'

'I cannot stop you making a big mistake, but I tell you

251

something: if your cooking is not good I will forget that John Crabtree was working in my kitchen.'

John rose from his chair, shook Monsieur Bouchon by the hand and walked quickly down to the kitchen to resume his duties.

'I wish to speak to Laura Douglas.'

'I'm sorry. She's in a meeting.'

'I do not care. This is André Bouchon. I must talk with her. Immediately.'

Laura dismissed the Grey Men congregated in the Sanctum and leaned back in her chair as the familiar voice shouted down the telephone.

'I take in this young man because I am a friend of Laura Douglas, and now he is leaving. You know this?'

'John did mention he'd had a couple of offers.'

'So you did know?'

'I didn't know he had accepted.'

'You think this is right? He learn everything from me, and now he will go and make my recipes, copy my dishes and say look what a wonderful chef is John Crabtree.'

'I don't think he would do that,' said Laura soothingly.

'I am not stupid,' thundered André Bouchon. 'Why are *you* not stopping him?'

'He's over twenty-one.'

'And he is going where? Tell me that!'

'If I knew, I'd tell you. You know I would.'

'Huh. You think I believe that? You make money from this young man and you make money from me. This is finished now. I do not like the British way of doing business. Everything polite and nice and then you behave like somebody from the gutter. You I believed to be different.'

'Listen. André—'

'I have nothing more to say and I do not wish to see you. Goodbye, Laura.'

He slammed down the phone and Laura continued doodling on the pad in front of her. André Bouchon was taking up far too much time and it would be quite convenient if they were not on speaking terms by the time the Eglantine was open . . .

She caught Antony's eye and beckoned him into the Sanctum.

'I think we covered everything, didn't we?' he said.

'Oh yes. By the way, if André Bouchon calls I'm not available.'

The small flat in Earl's Court, now home of John Crabtree and temporary home for George, was awash with carrier bags and potions and strange objects acquired by George in his perambulations round Knightsbridge, Fulham, the King's Road and Bond Street. London, pure heaven! Even better than he had imagined. And the boys! Those gorgeous little shorts which no-one dared wear in Leeds, at least in public. Walking down the streets in droves. Bliss! He adored the traffic, the crowds, the smells, the noise, the colour. George Hollings, soon-to-be manager at the Eglantine, the best restaurant in town, was now sitting in a taxi cab with a telephone inside it bound for the Kitchen Club and an introduction to the darling of the glossies, the legendary Tadeus Freeman.

'I don't believe it. Not another one from Leeds, the arsehole of the universe?'

'Not exactly Leeds,' said George.

Tadeus leaned forward and pinched the fine tweed of George's lapel. 'Good bit of schmutter, that. I don't imagine you're a beer man. What'll it be?'

'George likes champagne,' said John. 'It's what they drink in Bradford, where he comes from.'

Tadeus called out to the barman of the Kitchen Club. 'Bottle of champagne, then. Bradford's better than Leeds. Anywhere's better than bloody Leeds. If David Hockney had been born in Leeds instead of Bradford, he'd have ended up painting and decorating. And if I'd stayed in that god-awful catering college, I'd have ended up grey and spotty in a Happy Eater.'

Sebastian North strolled over to the bar.

'Have a glass, Sebastian old chap. This is George from Bradford, friend of John's. Meet chef-patron Sebastian from Soho. He has an upmarket little café called Zi-Zi's. His speciality is rice and seaweed. Had any bookings yet, eh?'

'Full till next week, Tád.'

'You can buy me out the week after, then. I'm thinking of retiring. Little John, do you fancy buying me out? Three million and I'm yours.'

'Prefer something in a smarter part of town.'

'But it's so far away from the shops, darling.'

'What is?'

'Buckingham Palace.'

'Won't catch me cooking for royalty.'

'You will, John, you will. But remember, Princess Diana doesn't eat much, so no Yorkshire pudding thank you.'

'She loved my *sakemeshi*,' said Sebastian.

'Name-dropper. At Zi-Zi's, George, the whole menu is in Japanese and everything is garnished with chrysanthemums and *tokiki*, which is, so I am reliably informed, the extracted roe of the flying fish flown in from God-knows-what polluted heathen country.'

'Sounds good to me.'

'I'm closing for a week for a refurb.'

'Sebastian's putting different mats on the table,' said Tadeus. 'And, believe me, with his staff that takes a week.'

'Come after that, George, if you're still in London.'

'He'll be in London,' said John. 'He's going to be restaurant manager at my new place.'

'What?'

'I'm opening.'

'You serious?'

'In Mayfair.'

'You crafty sod! When?'

'Next month.'

'Well, well, well. Is it true what they've been saying? You getting your leg over with Miss La-di-da?'

'No way.'

'It's true, then, that she's bought the Moukkhadem?'

John grinned. Tadeus got down from his bar stool and shook him by the hand. 'Congratulations. You fucking deserve it.' He then climbed on the rung of his stool and shouted out to the Kitchen Club in general: 'Watch out, boys. John Crabtree is going solo.'

Faces looked up, and an earnest young man came over. 'Paul Stephens. *Hotel and Caterer.*' He shook him by the hand. 'Congratulations. Where's it to be?'

'Mayfair. Can't say more at the moment. Opening in a few weeks.'

'Do you think I could have an exclusive?'

'S'all right, Paul. You'll get your invite to the press lunch.'

'Come on, Paul,' said Elwyn. 'How about a round?'

'Sorry, I've got an interview. Must rush.'

'Mean bugger,' muttered Elwyn as the newshound moved away to collect his raincoat. 'Here!' he called across the bar. 'Another bottle of champagne. And we'll have a decent one this time. Not the house muck.'

Tadeus whispered in John's ear. 'You told Big-Ears yet?'

'He wasn't happy about it, but I couldn't be staying for ever doing the same things.'

'You'll have to take elocution lessons, darling. We all talk posh nowadays, don't we Sebastian? How about Melissa? She'd give him lessons all right.'

'She's rather busy at the moment,' said Sebastian.

'Oh? You naughty boy!'

'Working for me, as a matter of fact.'

'Then she'll need some extra money, won't she?'

Sebastian turned away.

'Must be giving her one,' Tadeus said to John. 'Everyone else is. Come on, El. Pass that bottle. Well, Little John, who's losing her knickers in your bed now you're rich and famous? I think we should be told.'

'No-one you know, Tad.'

'Don't tell me you've run off with Lady Maclintock's daughter? You crafty bugger.'

'Didn't know she had one.'

Tadeus chuckled. 'Annabel Maclintock. Has lunch *chez moi* every time she comes to London. Fancies me to distraction, but I said no. Scotland's too cold. Prick-shrinking country.' He took John by the hand and addressed George and Elwyn. 'John's in love. How adorable! Did you know that you can only make soufflés when you're in love?'

'Give over, you Polish nut-case.'

As he lolled in the cab – oh, they knew how to put the drink away, and he wasn't used to it – George leaned towards John. 'Would I like her?'

John laughed. 'You'd better.'

Didi tossed restlessly from one side to another, then lay back on her crumpled pillows and tried to change the direction of her thoughts. It was so hard. Sprawled in abandonment next to her was John, taking up far too much room and breathing heavily in deep sleep. Tomorrow he would be up early, working in her kitchen to serve a foretaste of the Eglantine to a select group of flattered guests who would be only too happy to give their invaluable comments. An intimate candlelit supper in the grand style for the cognoscenti with Didi Kowalski presiding as the Spirit of Goodwill.

Could she resist temptation? She peered at John and gave him a gentle prod, but he did not move. If only he had grunted, but there he lay a satisfied man. Oblivious. Didi, on the other hand, was not swooning with satisfaction, even though she had no cause to feel disappointed. Why did the subdual of one desire excite another? She turned on to her side but the urge, instead of declining with drowsiness, grew ever stronger. Very slowly, she placed her feet on the floor, turning to observe John by the light of the street lamp outside. A car passed by, music blaring through the stillness. Didi's heart pounded and she froze. She really ought not to but, well, why not? She crossed the room and groped for her shawl which was buried under a mound of clothes slung over a chair, then she let out a short, anguished squeal. She had stubbed her toe against the clawed foot of her dressing table. Limping over to the bed, she looked at John again. How could anyone sleep so deeply? Minou the cat brushed past her legs. Didi picked him up, put him on her shoulder and crept to the door.

She would just have a look, a long, long look. She opened the heavy fridge door and ran her eyes up and down the crammed shelves, ogling the phenomenal display. Fish terrines, meat terrines, pâtés, a tin of foie gras, ballantines, a coral-coloured side of smoked salmon, cheeses from pale gold to deep orange resting on straw, heart-shaped, barrel-shaped, oval, square, a jar of Russian caviar, scallops, langoustines, oysters, then the neat rounds of tournedos, noisettes of lamb . . . and in the next fridge, riotously coloured fruits, some macerating in liqueurs, and vegetables and sprays of fresh herbs and *petits pots à la crème* and tubs of Jersey cream and gulls' eggs.

Didi closed the doors, and sat at the wooden preparation table, listening to the heightened hum of the fridge motors. Soon all these riches would disappear down the gullets of educated palates, never to be replaced once John had taken up his rightful place in the kitchen of the Eglantine. Didi wished he would cook everything and then leave her surrounded by a banquet which she would consume dish by dish by dish in glorious solitude. Then she would call Stephen and send him into delirious envy as she described the lot . . . How could the complex layers of sensation, the kaleidoscopic changes of colour, smell, taste and texture tumbling together, the succulent wonders of the earth and the sea permeating her body and sinking to rest in her belly, compare with the simple, brief act of sex? Only men were obsessed with sex. Women

257

knew better. Perhaps Stephen was right. Better to suck the flesh from a lobster.

Once more Didi opened the fridge. I'll just have a taste, she told herself, taking out the side of salmon. Then, her appetite whetted, she had to try one of John's pâtés – he was good at those – and then perhaps a little of the fish terrine, and an oyster, perhaps another, and oh, the creaminess of the cheese, and that one she didn't recognize, ah, perfect ripeness! Her shawl slipped to the floor as she tiptoed backwards and forwards from fridge to fridge. A bottle of wine, too. Chilled and ready. And the irresistible velvety, throat-caressing pudding. A spoonful of deep golden cream, yes. And oh, she'd forgotten to see how the caviar tasted. Ah. Heaven.

The dawn light grew stronger through the kitchen window and the birds began to chorus. Didi lay with her head on the table amidst the debris of delights and the juice from a ripe mango trickled between her breasts and splashed on to her thighs.

'Have you gone mad?'

She awoke to find John standing over her. Unable to move, she merely fluttered her eyelashes. 'I've been a bit naughty.'

For a few seconds he was speechless, his face contorted. 'You fucking crazy cow.'

'There's no need to be vulgar.'

He raised his hand.

'If you hit me, I'll call the police. And then I'll call all the gossip columns.' She giggled. 'It's all right. I'll tell everyone you've caught a nasty bug. Dinner postponed.'

'Why? For fuck's sake, *why*?'

Didi put her head to one side, in mock apology. 'Because it was there.'

'I think you should at least put some clothes on. Don't you feel sick?'

'I don't suffer from bulimia, if that's what you imagine. I won't puke over you, darling.'

'Have you seen a doctor?'

'Frequently.'

'And what did he say?'

'He said I was in perfect condition.' Didi stumped off to the bathroom, showered, slapped on some perfume and returned to make coffee. 'I feel marvellous. Oh well, I suppose I'd better put everyone off till another day. How about Thursday?'

'Didi, how can you shrug it off like that? It's – it's not bloody natural.'

'Natural?'

'And you're getting to look like a turkey fattened up for Christmas.'

'Charming. Why don't you find a nice bony beanpole then? There are plenty of them around.'

She ground the coffee beans longer than necessary, enjoying the high-pitched, cranking whine.

'That's long enough.'

There followed an extra burst. John took away her hand.

'Leave me alone.'

'Perhaps I should. I can't stand this, Didi.'

'You take everything so seriously, John. I put off a wonderful trip to Australia the day before you open. Never mind, I'm sure they'll find room for me. Stephen was dying to go, but I said sometimes a little sacrifice was in order, and after all we want to help that talented young man. He will be pleased.'

'I don't understand how you can stuff yourself like that. It's disgusting.'

'I was hungry.'

'Greedy.'

Didi laughed. 'Everyone's greedy. What's wrong with that? You're so ridiculously puritanical. It must be a strain coming from the North.'

'No more than being Dorothy Dean down South.'

Didi turned and sank her teeth into John's arm. As she drew blood, he pulled her face away and slapped her hard on the cheek.

259

'Don't ever do that again.'

'Get out!' she screamed.

'When I'm good and ready.'

'You fucking northern ape!' Didi yelled from the bedroom. Tears ran down her face as she examined herself in the mirror. Her cheek was swelling noticeably. She heard the front door slam shut, dried her face and put an urgent call through to her producer.

'Roger, darling,' she sniffed. 'Something awful's happened. I tripped and fell down the front steps and my face is a terrible mess. You know how clumsy I am . . .'

The dinner party was cancelled as Didi had caught a mysterious virus. That evening Stephen tapped on Didi's door. She might be in bed, but she had summoned him to see her, he must come, it was urgent, now, now, something she had not done for many weeks. Didi ill. Bonking someone, more likely, going on a Kowalski bender with yet another unsuitable man.

Didi opened the door in a white shift. 'Darling, oh, darling!' She flung her arms around him, pressing her face against his chest. 'The most dreadful thing has happened,' she stammered through her sobs. 'And I've missed you so much.'

'I haven't been away. Well, only for a couple of days.'

Didi drew back her head crossly. 'You haven't rung me for ages.'

'I left several messages. Who was it? Anyone I know?'

'What do you mean?'

'Never mind. I trust it was thrilling and wonderful.'

Stephen took his place on the settee while Didi headed for the kitchen. He noticed that a couple more pictures had been squeezed into the tiny wall space still remaining. Hardly Didi's style, they were black and white photographs, and not an edible substance in sight. He looked more closely. Ah. Fay Godwin's northern landscapes. Must be some young cameraman from Intertel who still retained an interest in pictures. A couple of bottles of Famous Grouse were competing for space on the over-crowded shelves.

'Are we off champagne, then?' Stephen asked as Didi appeared bearing a small, gold box.

'Just a few samples.'

'"Taste for a Test" for the discerning alcoholic?'

'Certainly not.'

Didi held out the box. Stephen fingered the velvety truffles and placed two in his mouth.

'Mm. Not bad. Two star. Italian, I'd guess. Too sweet.' He took another, sucking his fingers.

'Stephen, life is awful. It's never been so awful.'

'You do look a little pale.'

'My face. Does it still show?'

'You can't expect to hurl yourself into debauchery and still look like a freshly painted Botticelli cherub, sweetest. I know it's unfair—'

'Stephen.'

'Yes?'

'Nobody knows, but I've got to tell you.'

Didi turned away and dropped her head in shame. 'I've been naughty again.' Curiosity getting the better of her, she quickly turned back to see how Stephen would react, with an expression of the tragic martyr waiting for the first javelin to pierce flesh.

Stephen took another truffle. 'Anyone I know? Not another muscle-bound cameraman, is it?'

For a second Didi glared angrily, then she howled and wept and sniffed. Stephen handed her a grubby handker-chief.

'He – he . . . hit me.'

'The brute.'

'Oh, why can't everyone be like you, Stephen?'

'One can't have a world full of failures, sweetest.'

Didi's face brightened. 'Stephen, I shouldn't tell you, but – don't mention it to a soul – well, Caliope says you're up for the Glenfiddich Award.'

Stephen laughed. 'How truly exciting. I can't wait to get a case.'

'Aren't you pleased?'

'I hoped you were going to say the Nobel Prize for Literature. I wouldn't mind that.'

He was being difficult. Didi started for the kitchen. 'My fridge is full of wonderful things.'

'Not now, darling. I've just had dinner. Later. Well, in half an hour or so.'

She sat down again beside him. 'Aren't you going to ask me?'

'What?'

'Who it is.'

'Which butch slob is it this time?'

'He's a chef.'

'Then I'd say he has a fifty-fifty chance of not being a slob . . . Not Tadeus Freeman?'

'John Crabtree.'

'Oh, that's all right. I rather liked him.'

'How can you say that? He's the most incredibly chauvinist, uncouth lout I've ever met. If I see him again, I'll kill him. You're laughing at me.'

'No, no. I'm sure you're right. We chaps are awfully bad at judging other chaps.'

'Stephen.'

'Yes?'

'I've made up my mind. I'm not going to the opening of the Eglantine. Not after what happened. Look' – She pressed her cheek – 'it's still swollen . . . You won't go either, will you?'

'Didi, be sensible. We can't miss that. You needn't see him. He'll be going bananas in the kitchen.'

'He's bound to come out sooner or later. Shall I tell Laura, then, that unfortunately we can't be there?'

'Rise above it, sweetest. Forget it happened. Viscount Alloway will have a desperate evening if you don't go.'

Didi pondered.

'And Lord Maclintock will be there, so Laura said. And none of your eight million viewers.'

'You go. I can't possibly.'

'On my own? How can you do this to me?'

'I'm not going to let him get away with it. I mean, one has to stand by one's principles.' Didi bit into a truffle. 'Do you realize something?'

'What?'

'We could go on that Australian trip instead. We could take a gourmet survival kit to the outback. You'd love it, and there's a wonderful diet doctor in Melbourne.'

'I promised Laura.'

'Do you still love me?'

'Of course I do.' Stephen gave Didi a light kiss and smoothed back the curls straying over her eyes. 'What did you say was in the fridge?'

Le Style was crowded now that the spring to summer season was gathering momentum and the ski-broken legs had pieced together. John sat in a corner surrounded by a group of young men and women who talked across him, and even poured wine into his glass without noticing that he was not one of them. He got up when he saw Laura struggling to the bar and attempted to grab her attention with a wave. He climbed over the bare legs surrounding him and joined her.

'I've a wonderful list of acceptances,' she said.

'Have you invited Monsieur Bouchon?' asked John.

'Yes, but I don't expect him to reply.'

'I still feel bad, Laura.'

'So? In a few months' time he'll have calmed down. Specially when his next book comes out. I'm not worried about André, but I've had a refusal from Didi Kowalski. She said she had an Australian trip planned months ago, but I know that isn't true.' Laura paused and looked hard at John. 'Do you know why she's not coming?'

John avoided her eyes.

'If she decides against somebody, she won't hesitate to

stick the knife in,' Laura said. 'A few phone calls and Didi can bury a reputation and empty a restaurant overnight. I want to make sure her decision wasn't based on anything personal.' She noticed John's cheeks heighten in colour. 'Everything counts on the first night. If there's one sour note, it can be disastrous.'

John swallowed, unable to decide whether he should cross the boundaries which separated the professional from the private. You didn't talk about girls, not where he came from.

'What's wrong? Please tell me.'

'It's difficult to say. It'll come out daft.'

'We all get involved with the wrong people,' Laura said. 'I suppose everyone does who turns down the safe and predictable for something . . . someone, that is . . . who makes you feel alive.'

'I can't handle it,' said John. 'I'm seeing Didi and . . . well, we had a row, and now she's not talking to me. It makes me . . . Oh, I can't say.'

'Can I suggest something?' Laura asked tentatively. John nodded. 'Send her a box of her favourite chocolate truffles – I'll tell you where to get them – with some flowers and a short, warm note.'

'Saying what?'

'How upset you are, how you didn't want to hurt her.'

'I'm no good at writing.'

Laura composed a short letter which John copied carefully.

'I'll get Antony to bike round the flowers and truffles tomorrow,' Laura said. 'I'm sure you'll see her at the opening.'

Laura went home and did some work. She was on edge, waiting for the phone to ring. Howard was in New York and had promised to call. She put on some music, but heard nothing, her ears attuned to the first low-pitched ring of the phone. It might be four in the morning when he called; it was always so difficult for him to get to the phone, she knew that. Having fallen asleep a couple of

264

times and jerked herself awake she eventually went to bed at dawn. All the receivers were correctly in place on the telephones in every room of the house. He had not rung. She clutched her pillow, then dug her nails deep into her hand as uncontrollable tears escaped from her closed eyes. Laura Douglas, who spent her day warding off callers, cutting short conversations, being unavailable and controlling the lives of others, was waiting for her phone to ring.

12

George Hollings, restaurant manager of the Eglantine, his status confirmed by a visiting card designed by Laura, looked down the guest list and was infused with warmth, as though all these people of distinction whom he was about to greet were dear friends personally invited for his own private celebration. Very much his kind of place, he thought, as he examined his newly acquired chestnut maroon suit for the minutest signs of dandruff or escaping hairs. And the menu! John was excelling himself, reaching new heights of refinement and originality.

Copied carefully into George's pocketbook were Laura's notes explaining the professional standing of each guest and even the occasional witty description where relevant. Some names and notes were underlined in red.

Two editors from rival newspapers must sit on opposite sides of the room as each was in the ungentlemanly position of suing the other. The Programme Controller of Intertel was not to sit too near Didi, preferably adjacent to Lord Maclintock, as one could never gauge the temperature of their uncomfortable relationship. Viscount Alloway's glass, please inform waiter, only to be replenished by halves. Didi Kowalski, of course, next to Stephen Boyce. Magnus Shaw and Sigmund Halberstadt, senior columnists who nowadays only ate at Michelin-starred restaurants and disassociated themselves from the rank and file scribblers on food, but who were making an exception by coming to an untried restaurant, were to sit at tables of equal but not contiguous prominence. (Difficult that: better put one in the alcove section.) Near them, George could place any number of titled persons or holders of the CBE or, indeed, anyone who had received official, financially rewarded recognition with the exception of award-winning authors, frequently too outspoken in their bid for attention. Bankers were not a problem as they were not known for expressing, or holding, strong views on anything except currency, loan rates, and Third World debts. Oh, and if Sir Howard Riley should arrive, Laura had said, a little tensely George thought, he can sit at my table. The journalists would be at adjacent tables on the farthest side of the dining room, as no-one should be made to feel that this was an occasion engineered for the benefit of this tolerated, but seldom trusted, species.

Half the restaurant had been cleared of chairs and tables to provide an opportunity for guests to be introduced, and for those of similar standing to recognize one another whilst sipping a choice of champagnes and being offered some exquisite *amuse-gueules*. The exact moment when dinner was about to be served would be given appropriate dramatic impact by George's announcement.

George surveyed the garlands of wild roses hanging over the small wrought-iron balustrade leading up to the foyer.

'I hope you don't mind my saying so,' he said, his attention caught by Laura's pink and grey silk chiffon dress iridescent in a shaft of evening sunlight, 'but your dress is exquisite. Very Gainsborough.'

'Is John managing all right? Have you been down to the kitchen recently?' she asked.

'The brigade is super. Everything is going to plan, Miss Douglas.'

Laura moved away and went to inspect the dining room yet again, nerves taut as fiddle strings, wishing that it was all over, wishing that Howard could have been there, not next to her, but somewhere near.

'You don't need me, darling,' he had said, when he eventually telephoned two days ago from Zurich. 'It will be your evening. I should merely be in the way. We'll meet as soon as I get back.'

'But I want so much to share it with you!'

He laughed. 'Don't be silly. I'll be thinking of you.'

She had started to wonder, during sleepless nights, if he still loved her or if he had found someone else, but dared not ask. Doubt was entering her mind for the first time like a thorn edging under the skin. He sounded indifferent, which she had not known before. There were times now, when she was drained and disappointed, that she would have given away everything she had fought for with such single-minded determination just to have Howard all to herself.

'Laura, you're brilliant. It's a dream.'

Didi swept in first, like a yacht leading by miles in the Fastnet race, peacock blue flounces clinging for all they were worth fore and aft, plunging neck, plunging back, white ribbons streaming from her curls, and dripping with diamante jewellery. Stephen, behind her, was golden brown, immaculate in a dinner jacket, and beaming.

'So looking forward to this,' he said, kissing Laura.

'I cancelled Australia specially,' Didi announced.

Laura smiled, still a little apprehensively, relieved to see the guests begin to throng through the door, and record their presence on the wide pages of the Eglantine Book Day One. She watched them gaze round the deep blue, pink and gold dining-room like tourists who had arrived at a scheduled stop for art and beauty.

'Can I get you a drink, Laura?' enquired Sigmund Halberstadt, bearing the prestige of his paper with appropriate arrogance, and gesturing towards the array of champagne bottles sitting in ice on the bar as though he had provided them from his own pocket.

'In a moment, thank you,' said Laura.

He was soon to be followed by his arch-rival, Magnus Shaw, who took up a position at the opposite end of the bar.

'Magnus always has to have an extra cushion because he's so small,' whispered Laura into George's ear, observing his entry.

268

'Hello, Laura,' boomed Lord Maclintock. 'Everything super. What a super place! Jolly well done! Where's Lucy? Oh, you're there. Come on, let's fight our way to the bar.'

Viscount Alloway followed closely behind. 'You've done us proud, Laura. Hope there's some proper red meat for me and Jamie, eh?' He stroked Laura's slim behind, and launched himself towards the bar.

'Most interesting,' remarked Sigmund Halberstadt to the shy waiter, grabbing enough *amuse-gueules* (mussels and oysters bathed in a champagne sauce contained in the thinnest, perfectly formed pastry shell, caviar in miniature brioches, deep fried prawns with a dipping relish, tiny buffalo mozzarella pizzas) to serve at least ten guests. The young man waited until Halberstadt had removed his thick fingers from the plate and hastened away to the other end of the bar, summoned by an imperious gesture from Magnus Shaw.

'I presume this is a foretaste of Crabtree,' he said, scooping an equally large handful. 'What's inside?' He took a bite. 'Decent quality oysters for a change. Colchester are they?'

Didi steered Stephen towards another part of the room.

'Stephen,' she whispered loudly, 'someone told me that Magnus Shaw writes for porno mags, not under his own name, of course, gets loads of dosh. Do you think he does?'

'Why don't you ask him?' said Stephen rashly. 'No! No, Didi. Cut. Stop. For Christ's sake . . .' But she had eluded him.

'Mr Shaw, it's so long since we've met. Didi Kowalski.'

'I don't have time to watch television,' he said mournfully, looking above her head.

'Shame,' Didi said. 'I was about to invite you to an incredibly expensive lunch but I'm sure Sigmund would like to come.'

Lord Maclintock ignored the paltry figure of the man

apparently capturing Didi's attention and grasped her hand. 'Well, I'll be damned. Didi, Didi—?'

'Kowalski.'

'That's it.' He lowered his voice. 'You're a magnificent girl, Didi. I'm in town for a few days. Lucy's going back.'

Didi pressed his hand briefly and departed in search of Stephen, pausing to give a glacial smile to the Programme Controller of Intertel and a gracious inclination of the head to Viscount Alloway. Later, she decided, she would have a stupendous night of passionate love with John Crabtree. Must, must, must, she noted to herself, hold back a little, must remember to leave something on the plate. It was time to make up and how sweet of him to send her that huge box of her favourite chocolate truffles.

'Dinner is served.'

George walked round the clusters of guests, handing each one a card on which a numbered table plan had been beautifully drawn by Laura with formalized seated figures in pink, green and gold, and an alphabetical list of those present together with their table number at the side. Later, he would frame one.

The form of the menu had been discussed on many fraught occasions by George, Laura and John. John insisted that if Laura had her way it might spoil their chances. The Michelin inspectors would be horrified, he was sure. They might interpret it as a slap in the face, an insult to the grand tradition, might be provoked to condemn the Eglantine out of hand. André Bouchon would not eat in a place with such a menu, let alone take it seriously. George could see both sides, but took Laura's point. In the end John gave way, confronted by Laura's unshakable belief that she was right. The hotly debated menu would be in English.

Stephen and Didi were both in a trance, conjuring up each dish, each ingredient. For a long time, during which everyone else had made their selection, decision eluded them.

Terrine of Foie Gras, Muscat Jelly, Toasted Brioche

Stephen: How can I not eat foie gras?

Didi: You don't have to have it every time. Try something different.

Stephen: One ought to taste John's Brioche.

Mozaique of Marinated Seafood and Summer Vegetables with Saffron Vinaigrette

Didi: Oh, that's André Bouchon's speciality. We should try some, to see if it's the same as his.

Stephen: But Aphrodite's mozaique is so perfect. We should retain the perfect memory. Shouldn't we?

Didi: I don't know. I don't know . . .

Ravioli of Truffles, Celeriac and Parsley

Didi: Truffles, Oh, Stephen, I must, I must.

Stephen: Try something else. Be hard on yourself, sweetest. I could have that, couldn't I?

Didi: No, no. I want it. I want it.

Lobster and Scottish Salmon Terrine

Didi: John's terrines are absolutely fantastic. You must have that.

Stephen: Or you could have it.

Didi: Oh, lobster. I can't resist that.

Salad of Home-grown Speciality Leaves with Warm Norfolk Duck confit, Woodland Sussex Mushrooms and Lentils

Stephen: How can I deprive myself of duck confit?

Didi: And wild mushrooms . . .

Stephen: One of us has to have that.

Didi: Me.
Stephen: No, me. I will.

Harmony of Baby Vegetables in a Warm Coriander
Vinaigrette

Didi: We really ought to try the vegetarian dish.
Stephen: Ought we?
Didi: Certainly. Tiny calories, darling.
Stephen: You can get tiny calories at home. Which
          reminds me, shall I tell you a joke?
Didi: Quiet, I'm thinking. Oh. Yes. Go on.
          (A WAITER TAKES THE ORDER OF THE BANKER AND
          HIS WIFE SITTING OPPOSITE)
Waiter: And you have decided on . . . ?
Didi: No, no. Not nearly ready.
          (THE WAITER LEAVES)
Stephen: What's the similarity between foie gras and a
          blow job?
Didi: Honestly!
Stephen: You get both away from home.
Didi: (LAUGHS) Who on earth told you that?
Stephen: Who d'you think? Tadeus.
Didi: (SERIOUS) That's not funny. It's filthy.
Stephen: So what are we having to start then?
Didi: How about a little of everything?
Stephen: No, sweetest. A decision.
Didi: I can't. I can't. Let's look at the main courses.
Stephen: Here's one decision. You have fish, I'll have
          meat.
Didi: Must I? There might be a really fantastic meat
          dish.
Stephen: Yes. You should stick to fish. Does wonders for
          the hormones.
Didi: Does it? Honestly? Here, let me choose some-
          thing from the fish section. Crown of pan fried
          scallops with a lime and basil butter sauce.
          Scallops. I adore them. Fillets of Dover Sole

272

with caviar and champagne. What? Oh, utterly wonderful. I must, must, must, have that. Nage of various seafoods with coriander and ginger.

Stephen: Baked wing of skate with Wiltshire herbs and a red wine sauce. Earthy and gutsy. Should I have that, I wonder? John is terrific with fish. (THE WAITER RETURNS.) I haven't decided yet. (THE WAITER LEAVES.)

Didi: My turn, my turn. Listen to this! Tournedos of Scottish beef with a nest of crisp vegetables, grain mustard and pepper sauce. Mille feuille of calves' sweetbreads, summer vegetables and madeira. Ah . . . oh. Rosettes of Herefordshire lamb, prunes and port wine sauce . . . Glazed Mignon of organically reared veal with artichokes, celery and Beauty of Bath apples. Variations on a theme of Mrs Bradfield's home-raised duck: breast, legs, a port stuffing and, and (THE WAITER RETURNS), just a minute, an onion confit in an orange sauce. I can't bear it, I can't bear it!

The waiter decided that he would have to conclude the anguished scene enacted before him.

'Excuse me, but would you allow me to make some suggestions?'

'Yes, do,' sighed Didi, putting down the menu and gazing thankfully at the waiter who had released them both from their agony. He suggested one thing, then another with such authority that, finally, the order was written.

'What an ordeal, but how delicious.'

'The anticipation . . .'

'So much better than . . .'

'Satisfaction.'

'Excuse me,' said the banker sitting next to Didi, who was now tucking in to his starter, 'but I couldn't help overhearing. Are you by any chance in the restaurant business?'

'In a way,' replied Didi. 'We tell people what to eat.'

As the first dishes were placed in front of them, Didi and Stephen became taut with the concentration of a long-distance runner waiting for the starting signal, envisaging every stage of his allotted route in order to maintain the proper pace. They ate in silence, seeing nothing except the delicately displayed foods in front of them, occasionally taking a morsel from each other's plate and solemnly exchanging forks. Each mouthful was reverently pondered. At intervals, they gazed thoughtfully at the ceiling. When knife and fork were finally laid to rest, came the ritual response.

'What do you think?'

'What do you think?'

And then, as another menu was set in front of them, there was the renewal of expectation and yet another arousal of appetite . . . Dark Belgian chocolate truffle with orange, caramelized mousseline with mango, a Grand Marnier soufflé with chocolate embellishment and macerated blood oranges, brandy snap leaves layered with ice cream, seasonal berries and raspberry coulis, a praline mille-feuille mousse with mocca sauce, and Mrs Beeton's treacle tart.

By now, Didi and Stephen were oblivious of those around them. They heard nothing except their own sounds of delight and saw nothing except the objects of their desire.

There would never be another evening to compare with this, for the guests seemed to be joyously trapped in a repeated bar of time, a vivid allegro of movement, eating, laughing, talking, gesticulating, drinking.

Laura rose from her chair, unable to sit still for more than a few minutes. The puddings were starting to be set down, and she wanted to see the reaction at every table. She felt like a magician who had conjured up the impossible, doves fluttering out of silken scarves, breathtaking images created from nothingness.

'Laura, darling. Absolutely spectacular.'

She stood by Stephen and Didi. A small table had been squeezed in beside them on which was an array of plates.

'We had to try every single pudding,' explained Didi, quivering her eyelashes. 'It's so impossible to judge with just one, don't you find?'

'Here.'

Stephen pressed a spoonful of diaphanous soufflé into Laura's mouth.

'If only one could start all over again. Right from the beginning.'

'Do you think the portions were too small?'

'Of course not.'

'Wouldn't it be impossibly wonderful if we could—' Stephen frowned at Didi, but she continued. 'Laura, would you be terribly shocked if we ordered again? Then I could have everything I wanted and Stephen had, and he could have everything he wanted and I had.'

'Didi, darling,' Stephen objected, 'I was only joking.'

George dimmed the lights imperceptibly lower, drawing the evening into closer intimacy amidst the tawny glow of brandy glasses and the chinking of tiny coffee cups.

For a while, Laura had forgotten about the kitchen, unable to believe that on her first night there seemed to be no hint of anything to mar the ease with which each elaborate course made its appearance. Not being of a superstitious nature, she even went so far as to congratulate herself on the outcome of months of work, months of pondering every detail. There were one or two things still to work on, but they were minor. Unused to such unstinted praise, such evidence of appreciation, her first reaction was to disbelieve it, imagining that it was merely politeness which drew it forth. Then, as the generous compliments flowed, it struck her that this was unusual. How could she possibly merit such accolades?

She went through the swing doors into the kitchen, where the brigade was starting to tidy and clean, and John came forward, mopping his brow.

'I'm so unbelievably happy,' Laura said, throwing her arms round his neck. 'You've done it. Everything was superb. Don't you feel proud? I do.' She laughed. 'I'm a little drunk.'

'The dressing on the salad wasn't quite right. Such a simple thing and it shouldn't have been like that. There was too much balsamic vinegar and it destroyed the balance. I wasn't sure about the onion confit with the duck. The onions were slightly overcooked. Did you have that?'

'Oh, John.'

'Next time it will be correct, I promise you. I could kick myself. Fancy fucking up on a simple thing like a dressing.'

'There's not been a single word of criticism. Didi is ecstatic and wants to hang the menu over her bed.'

'And Stephen?'

'Says he'll take the whole column.'

'It's happened then! Will you be coming to Le Style when they've all gone?'

Laura seemed doubtful.

'Why don't you bring your friend? Table for two, George said. Or are you keeping him to yourself? Lucky bugger.'

She took John by the hand. 'Didi's waiting for you. Come on.'

Very few had left, for there was little reason to depart. Yes, Laura told the wine waiter, he could open some more bottles of champagne. Sigmund Halberstadt appeared to have fallen asleep at his table and was emitting a low, growling snore. Should he be awakened? asked George. Gently aroused with a fresh pot of coffee, Laura suggested, a discreet tap on the shoulder. And then, he said, there was someone who wanted to see her, come late, surprise visitor, wanted to congratulate her. Wouldn't give his name but she'd know soon enough.

Laura suppressed her impulse to run from the dining room and throw herself into his arms.

'Hello, Laura. I thought I'd come and surprise you. Wish you luck.'

'How kind. Do go through.'

Laura barely took Tadeus in. She looked quickly around her like a rabbit seeking out a bolthole, then she rushed to the cloakroom, brushed powder on to her flushed face, combed her hair and stared blankly at her image in the mirror. With trembling hands, she searched for a small diary in her handbag, turned over several leaves, found the number she was looking for and ran out.

There was no-one in the bar. She picked up the telephone on the counter. Her fingers hovered over the buttons and then pressed out a long sequence of numbers. Someone was in.

'Good evening,' she said, a little breathlessly, 'this is the Eglantine Restaurant. Is that Lady Riley?'

'Speaking,' replied a clipped, frosty female voice.

'Sir Howard Riley booked a table for tonight and we wondered if—'

'Really? I think you must have made a mistake. Sir Howard is out of the country.'

'He definitely booked a table for two for this evening.'

'Impossible. He's not expected back until tomorrow.'

'We kept a table free for the entire evening.'

'I shall inform him.' Laura was abruptly cut off. Then she caught sight of her stony expression in the muted, artificially aged mirror behind the bar. I shouldn't have done that, I mustn't let myself hate him, she thought as she walked back into the dining room.

John was sitting with Didi and Stephen. Only Magnus Shaw and Sigmund Halberstadt had expressed their praise. One or two had looked up briefly as he came through from the kitchen, but that was all. In the months ahead he would have to make his mark. No good staying in the kitchen all the time. He wanted everyone to think

Eglantine, Crabtree. Tonight it was Eglantine, Laura Douglas. That needed changing.

He seemed all right, Stephen.

'Sorry I lost my temper the other day,' John said to Didi, feeling bold enough to stake his claim.

'Oh? Did you? I don't remember.'

Stephen's eye was caught by a familiar, gangling figure heading towards their table.

'Do you like my suit? Hand-made, darlings. I've been spending hours in conference. My conference suit. I'm getting very good at it. And I cut half an inch off my hair. Did you notice?'

'I prefer it long,' said Didi.

'I bet you do,' said Tadeus. 'Women say it doesn't make any difference, but they're lying.'

'Behave yourself, Tad.'

'Give us a bite, then. Not a bad place, this. Tasty bit of decorating. I hear Miss La-di-da did it herself. How is the *Daily Reporter*, Stephen? I notice you haven't mentioned me for at least a month. You could always write about my suit. It seems that food writers write about anything nowadays, so why not? You writing about Little John then?'

'Wait and see.'

'Well, lad, you'll be as good as me in a few years' time.'

'Better, Tad. Better. Hey, George, make up Tad a plate.'

'Good evening, Mr Freeman. How are you?'

'I'm starving. Give me anything that's not fish. Who do I see over there? The Ichneumoniforms. Magnus Ichneumoniform and Sigmund Ichneumoniform. See how sober I am?'

'Come on, Tadeus,' said Stephen wearily, 'translate the insult.'

'You might use it. I want a credit. All right. The cuckoo, as you well know, goes broody in other people's nests. The Ichneumon is a nasty little insect which lays its eggs on top of someone else's and when the larvae hatch they gobble them all up. Anything which resembles the Ichneumon is called Ichneumoniform. I only reserve it for very special people, darling.'

Tadeus jumped like a grasshopper off a leaf and was away.

'For God's sake, John, get him back. Oh dear, I can't move. Who invited him here anyway?'

'I said to drop in later,' replied John. 'He's a mate.'

'You're mad,' she said.

Tadeus walked up to Magnus Shaw and blocked his route to the door.

'I understand you enjoyed the meal you had in my restaurant, Mr Shaw.'

'Indeed. Most innovative. The venison was excellent.'

'Thank you for the compliment. Could I ask one thing?'

'Certainly.'

'I wonder if your paper would mind paying my bill? Over five hundred quid, Mr Shaw.'

Magnus Shaw looked into the distance and deftly moved towards his destination.

'If I don't get a cheque,' shouted Tadeus, 'I'll break your fucking legs.'

In a moment, Tadeus had returned. 'Ah. Here's my dinner.'

A waiter barely had time to set down a plate of samples from the menu before Tadeus was wielding his knife and fork. He ate fast, taking in the ingredients, estimating the cooking techniques with quiet concentration.

'Who've you been having a go at, then?' asked John.

'Just having a piss. I find the need to pass water occasionally, don't you?'

'Shall we hit Le Style?' suggested Didi. Stephen groaned. 'We could walk there.'

'Walk?'

'Why not?' said John. 'I'm game. I'll check the kitchen's cleared.'

'I'm going to bed,' announced Stephen. 'Sleep is the best aid to the digestive system I know.'

Didi looked hurt.

'Right.' Tadeus wiped his plate with a piece of bread. 'I liked that. Now, boys and girls, let's go.'

'I'll get Laura.'

John found her in the deserted bar, sitting alone. 'You all right?'

'Fine, fine. I couldn't have hoped for better.' Her voice sounded flat.

'Really?' John put his arm round her. She looked up at him, her eyes clouded, and then she tossed back her hair.

'I'm tired, that's all.'

'Come with us to Le Style. Me, Didi, Stephen, George and Tad. We're going to get arseholed. Come on, Laura.'

'I've got to go home.'

'It's our first night. You can't leave just like that. We want you to come.'

Laura sighed and stood up. 'Another time.'

George came over. 'Miss Douglas. Your car.'

'Thank you, George. You've all been fantastic.' She gave them both a peck on the cheek and walked away.

It was like the first day of moving into a new home. John could not quite believe that tomorrow he would walk through the same door and re-create everything anew. And he could not quite believe that he had been able to order whatever he wanted, to do everything in the particular painstaking, elaborate way which, he was beginning to see, was his own particular style. He cast his mind back to the opening of the Moorland and remembered the gauche youth who had interviewed him, his Mum and Dad (who this time refused to travel to London), Charlie, the Mayor, the overspilling of generous humanity . . .

'Do you realize we northern lads have entered the beau monde?' remarked George as he poured out the remains of an unfinished vintage. 'I took one look at the dining room, and I thought, George Hollings, you have arrived. We are now among people of consequence. Aren't you thrilled? I wouldn't be surprised if we get little mentions in famous memoirs. You know the kind of thing: "I first met Sir David Hockney when I was sitting in the Eglantine." And everyone with lovely manners, and so well spoken. And some of the clothes! Ah! It's tragic. They wouldn't have a clue in Bradford. Not a clue. Moorland Haven? I'll say. You call that a restaurant?'

'Even so,' said John, 'I'd like to see this in Yorkshire. No reason why you couldn't.'

'Dear boy,' said George disdainfully, 'I hate to say so, but they wouldn't know what to do with it.'

At night, if you could get through the doors, you went to Le Style to 'show your face' and to maintain the illusion that the drearisome business of earning enough money to spend on champagne was a hangover to be suffered in the cause of enjoyment. Didi was greeted like a reclusive actress who only made rare stage appearances, even though she came at least twice a week, and meaningful smiles were directed at John, Tadeus and George. Having been tutored by George in the art of high-class casual dressing, John felt the equal of the loose-limbed young men throwing out witty gobbets of gossip to admiring girls. And he was with Didi Kowalski.

She would insist on throwing her arms round unknown men, who seemed to be on intimate terms to judge from their choruses of rapture at seeing her, but Tadeus, too, was greeted by similar delight. He had only to stand moodily at the bar, and flocks of barely dressed girls pressed forward.

'Hello, darling, why haven't I seen you for so long?'

Tadeus repeated his stock phrase as he kissed the queuing hands and then, gazing into their eager eyes, threw his head back in his much-photographed and favourite posture. George, too, appeared to be making an impression on a smaller and less extravagant scale, swaying his hips fractionally as he approached a group of young men who assumed that he, too, doodled at graphic design in his spare time. And that amazing accent. Was he really from Bradford? He sounded like David Hockney. As a matter of fact, came the modest reply, as George reverted to his native accent, he's a close friend.

Didi chatted away, her voice swooping through the full register as she confided her intimate impressions of the most exclusive opening in London, to which she, and not her listeners, poor things, had been invited. Had they heard about the Eglantine? No, well, that kind of place did not need publicity. Very low key. Cecil Alloway, Viscount Alloway, head of that bank in Scotland, you know, the MacCrae group, a great friend of hers, was behind it; he was there, of course, and then that wonderful character, Lord Maclintock. They had both agreed to come on her programme, an absolute coup as they never watched television, of course, those kind of people don't, but absolute naturals, not at all snobbish.

John put his arm around her neck, but Didi removed it. 'Not in public,' she whispered in his ear.

'Why not?'

'People will gossip.'

The food? Oh, the food. Absolutely divine. To die for. Well, after all (inclining towards John) he is the best chef in London. You don't know him? Oh! This is John Crabtree. I discovered him. You remember, 'Taste for a Test' on bacon? You did see it? Thank you, it was quite a good programme. Lowering her voice: I think he's going to overtake Tadeus Freeman, but that's just my personal opinion. Sigmund Halberstadt agrees with me, as a matter of fact . . . By the way, have you heard what Magnus Shaw does? You'll never guess. He writes under an assumed name, really wild, apparently, unbelievable descriptions of gay orgies . . . goodness, no, I don't read things like that! Do forgive me, there's someone I've got to say hello to . . .

Didi slipped away from John's side, and the group surrounding her dispersed. He decided not to follow her.

'Well, Little John, which one are you taking to bed? I fancy that redhead over there.'

Tadeus had removed the jacket of his suit, unbuttoned his shirt and was flaunting the downy hairs on his chest.

'I'm spoken for, Tad.'

'You devious northern bugger. Secret rendezvous with Miss La-di-da? Don't say she's dropped them for you?'

'You're way out, Tad. It's Didi.'

Tadeus slapped John on the back. 'Smart move. I bet she's a girl who likes cock.'

'Cut it out.'

'Allow me a touch of jealousy. Here stands a spurned man, John, whose invitation was cruelly rejected.'

'Get this straight, Tad. It's serious. I'm not fucking around, and I don't want you blabbing about it.'

'Ah.' Tadeus contemplated John and frowned. 'A relationship?'

'That's right.'

'A word of advice from a young roué, John. Give her a hard time. And I don't mean in bed. Unless they see the beast, girls won't respect you.'

'I'm more romantic than you.'

'Romance is for the birds. Have a good time, but don't trust her. I don't. If anything goes wrong, it'll be John Crabtree? *Who?* The Eglantine? Shame about that place. And you've got to get your star.'

'I'll bear that in mind.'

Didi swept into vision and put her lips against John's ear. 'I've got a car waiting. See you outside.'

The only thing he could think of was slipping into her bed and keeping her awake all night.

Laura had imagined herself walking through her door with Howard and into a room full of flowers, her public happiness awaiting private recognition. Had a small note been pushed through the door, perhaps? The letterbox held only brown envelopes. How she hated brown! Flinging down her silk wrap, she noticed her Answerphone aglow with messages. Seven. Lucky seven? The tape spun backwards, compressed into a stream of harassed screeches. One, two. Dear Stephen. Three . . . four, Antony. Three more to go.

'Hi. Just got back from Hong Kong. You OK . . .' Two more to go. 'Oh it's one of those machines. Are you there? Never mind. Do I talk now? Laura dear, hello? Hello?' And the last, the fatal one: 'Hello, Mrs Douglas. I think I left the light on downstairs in case you was wondering. Margaret here. Bye.'

There had been a choice. She could have gone to Le Style, basked in the admiration she always commanded, drunk herself into happiness surrounded by the vitality of those who came to life in the dark. And why not? He had mentioned he would be returning tonight. She went to the window. Sometimes if she did that, by one of those curious coincidences experienced in love, his car would draw up at that moment. The street was quiet. Love, she decided, was more akin to a debilitating virus than a disease. It crept up, clouded your judgement and ate into the logic of everyday life before you realized what had happened. Why, after all, should Howard care about the opening of the Eglantine?

She would savour the memory alone. Laura poured herself a large glass of brandy, kicked off her shoes and stretched out on her sofa contemplating the white roses and lilies populating the sparsely furnished room. It would be there tomorrow, the Eglantine. Her place. And she could go whenever she wished. Her business would grow and grow, she was sure of that. Laura Douglas, the success story. Laura Douglas, darling of the City pages.

What would grow around her? She tried to see herself leading the life of wealth. Money to spend, money to invest, money to create the world she wanted. Her own house in the country. Perhaps a working farm. House parties. Lunch with friends in Paris. An apartment in New York. She must open in New York, once the Eglantine was established. Plan ahead, babe. Money breeds money. Antony would handle the mundane routine of her business. Holidays on remote tropical islands. She would have time to take holidays . . .

Perhaps I am doing all this, she thought, to prove that

Howard was right. But suppose he was wrong? Suppose he had misjudged her? Laura Douglas, promising art student. There were hundreds of promising art students every year. Laura Douglas, an interesting minor decorative talent. Hardly genius. Why devote one's life to pursuing a minor talent, to become part of the regiment of women familiar throughout history but undocumented who were good at cookery, good at gardening, good at languages, played the piano a little, painted pleasing water colours and were given inordinate praise by their doting family? Ah yes. Minor talent was the excuse for burying oneself in marriage. But like a small mole displacing huge clods of heavy earth in order to surface, she had crawled her way out.

Lady Riley? Was that really what she wanted? For the moment, she rejoiced in the absence of husband. No husband in the background taking the business decisions and waiting for his dinner as a reward. No-one to say sorry, we can't accept your invitation, I'm playing in a golf tournament. No-one to say not Thursday night, babe, you know I've got a tough day on Thursday . . . No-one to say could you collect my suits from the dry cleaners? No-one to say what's got into you, babe?

Laura went downstairs to her studio and looked at the drawings still spread over the table. She had wanted to make her mark. That seemed to be the explanation. It was all there, the genesis from sketch, to watercolour, to scale drawing, to specifications. It had nothing to do with Jack. Or Howard. She had done it alone.

It was difficult to adjust to seeing herself in space with nobody else. Alone, she could see more clearly, the tiniest things; her senses were sharpened, her body free, her direction clear, she could work until fatigue overwhelmed her and could start again like a missile heading for a distant planet when she awoke.

When she saw Howard the world was no longer hers, but his. If he had been at the Eglantine, she could not have acknowledged his presence as she would have wished. He would have left early. Better that he did not come. He should be no more important than a client, a special client with whom she had a particular rapport. She had dreamed up love, she decided, in a moment of weakness and she could, with enough strength, redress the balance. Jack needed no replacement. She was merely seeking to replace one trap with another, enclosing her existence in the existence of another, in the way that women did.

Now calm, her balance restored, Laura slipped into the freshly laundered sheets, spread herself over the bed and abandoned herself to sleep. She did not know how long it was before a disturbing noise invaded her dreams and drove her into half consciousness. The telephone. A wrong number, no doubt, or Didi arriving home and longing to engage her in conversation. She turned over. The noise became clearer and she realized it was the low buzz of the front door bell. Her decision was taken, and even if it was Howard – for who else would have the effrontery to demand her attention at this hour? – she would ignore it. The buzz was repeated, and this time her curiosity overwhelmed the decision she had taken only an hour earlier. If it was Howard, she would throw defiance in his face. He had no right to invade, and she would tell him so.

Laura lifted up a slat of the blind, then opened the door even though a voice said, don't, don't, don't.

'I had to see you. I've had such a terrible day.'

Howard stepped over the threshold and held her tightly as though he was a soldier whose leave had come to an end. 'I've been ringing the bell for ages. Were you asleep?'

She pulled herself away. 'Yes,' she said angrily. 'I was exhausted.'

'I can stay with you till the morning.'

'I'll make you some coffee, and then you can go. I have to be up early tomorrow.'

Laura heard her own voice, firm and efficient. She had

286

not betrayed herself and went to the kitchen. Howard followed her.

'Laura.'

'Yes?' she said, filling the kettle.

'I tried to ring the restaurant.'

'Really.'

'It was engaged. Constantly.'

She shrugged.

'I managed to get an earlier plane. I wanted to come to your opening, but it was delayed. I was waiting for hours, and I couldn't get through to you.'

'There's no need to apologize.'

'I'm not apologizing. I'm telling you what happened, for Christ's sake.'

She ground the coffee as though she was grinding his emotions into powder so that she could scatter them to the winds.

'Why are you so angry? I've come, haven't I? Illustra Foods are facing a potential catastrophe. It could mean a loss of millions. I shouldn't be here, really.'

'You can stay if you like, or go home. I don't mind. Do as you please.'

Howard said nothing, but she saw him walking towards the sitting room. He would be collecting his coat, opening the door, getting into his car . . .

'Howard!'

'Perhaps it would be better if we stopped seeing one another for a while,' he said. 'We're both under strain. I shouldn't have come. I'm sorry.'

'Please stay.'

'I know when I'm not wanted.'

'You haven't even asked if it was a success.'

'I presumed it was. I was eating stale cheese sandwiches at Zurich airport. Did you receive masses of compliments? Did your young man do what was expected of him?'

'Yes, yes.'

'So what am I meant to say? Laura darling, congratulations. Congratulations. You've done it.'

'I couldn't have without you.'

'You'd have found someone. I just happened to be there at the time.'

'I have to tell you something.'

'Go ahead.' He looked resigned.

'I was so worried when you didn't appear. I . . . I rang your home from the Eglantine. Your wife answered. She didn't understand why you had booked a table when you were abroad.'

Howard burst out laughing.

'What's so amusing?' asked Laura.

'Laura darling, I would have expected that from a girl on the checkout counter, but hardly from you. Couldn't you have thought of something more subtle?'

'I felt utterly desperate.'

'It could be that you enjoy behaving like a business-man's tart.' He walked over, gripped her from behind like a dog taking a bitch and pushed her against the wall.

'Leave go,' Laura said coldly.

'Am I hurting?'

She felt his fingers digging into her thighs.

'No. I don't feel anything.'

With a sudden movement, he lifted up her silk nightgown and pierced her, entering deeply with the full length of his erection. Laura screamed with pain, but he covered her mouth and continued. Then the pain became muted, bearable.

'Come. Damn you.'

'No. I won't,' she cried, but then something inside her gave way. The pain grew in intensity, she could feel it again, and her body slipped away from her control like a kite caught by a sudden gust of wind, careering across the sky. She was sinking down, into blood-warm depths, only to be driven upwards, forced to the surface, and then dragged deeper and deeper down into blackness.

'No more.'

Her whisper merged into a groan as her body flailed in drowning spasms. Then the slow withdrawal gave way to emptiness, as though he had left a gaping wound.

Howard lifted her, carried her out of the room and laid her carefully on the bed, waiting for her eyes to open.

'I love you. You know that.'

'Sometimes I'm not sure.'

Then he turned away to occupy the space on the far side of the wide bed. 'What more do you want? I'm here, aren't I?'

She scarcely heard him, her exhaustion giving way to deep, dreamless sleep.

13

The manager of Aphrodite's had his face anxiously pressed to the window. It was almost impossible, he told Monsieur Bouchon, to find somewhere to park and the clientele was becoming irritable. Not good for the atmosphere. The Moukkhadem restaurant had reopened with a new name. Today there was quite a crowd.

Monsieur Bouchon shrugged his shoulders. 'So, you will telephone to the police and tell them to find some parking for my clients,' he said loftily.

'I don't think they will help,' said the manager, doubtfully.

'Well. You find a solution.'

'Have you seen what they are doing in this place?' enquired Monsieur Bouchon later that afternoon.

'I believe they are aiming to provide English cuisine,' said the manager.

André Bouchon guffawed. 'This kind of restaurant will not be successful in this area, *n'est-ce pas*? Mind you, perhaps they will find some lunch trade. That is possible.'

There was always somewhere to go for tea. Mr Beck, the proprietor of Aphrodite's, wandered into his restaurant at precisely half past three, well aware that within the next five or ten minutes he would be sharing a pot of Assam with André Bouchon, and a plate of petits fours left over from luncheon.

'Cucumber sandwich, Mr Beck?' enquired the waiter, grumbling to himself as his solitary guest took up his accustomed position. 'We have some delicious marinaded wild rabbit in sauce *indienne*.'

'In a sandwich. In a triangular sandwich, no crusts.'

'Of course.'

He felt his salivary juices come into their own and sucked at his cheeks. He would keep Aphrodite's open if only to provide him with the delights of a properly presented English tea. Fit for the leisured classes, of which he was now a member. Opening the *Financial Times* at the appropriate page to keep tabs on old friends and old enemies in the neat percentages of rises and falls, Mr Beck sat motionless like a satisfied frog on a water lily.

'*Bonjour*, André.'

'*Bonjour*, Mister Beck.'

Mr Beck lowered his paper, folded it carefully and placed it at his feet. 'You look a little under the weather. Too busy?'

'Unfortunately not. Is difficult for me to say this. Recently we have not enough customers. I am sorry, very sorry, but I think I have a solution.'

'André, my friend, don't worry.'

'But I do.'

'I don't fire people at my age.'

'I am thinking perhaps I shall start to cook new things, lighter things.'

'I like your cooking. Why change? Fashions come and go, but that needn't concern us.' André Bouchon bit his lip, thinking of his dispirited brigade who had gone home early. 'I must tell you.' He tapped his finger on the teapot. 'We do not make money.'

'Our Lord threw out the money-lenders, André, and He fed the multitude on loaves and fishes.'

'*Mon Dieu*. I am not Jesus Christ! I 'ave to pay the man who bring me fish, and my chef *pâtissier* who makes bread.'

'Are they not paid?'

'No, no. I do not make complaint for this. I am concerned for you, Mister Beck.'

'You are a good man and I thank you, but the Lord has blessed me. I am fortunate. Aphrodite's does not have to make a profit. You run a restaurant for pleasure. This is my pleasure, my hobby. When I die, you will be provided for. A small pension, but adequate.'

André Bouchon looked at his patron with disbelief. 'I am still a young man. I am not thinking yet of pension.'

It was as though Mr Beck had laid the hand of death on his shoulder. André Bouchon shivered.

'Now I must get back to the kitchen. I have some things to do. I see you soon.'

André Bouchon had nothing to do and he sat staring ahead of him in the deserted kitchen, gloomily contemplating his future.

Laura was preparing herself for a major confrontation. She had come in early to the Sanctum, as usual, and as the last Grey Man took up his position and opened up his neat file, she was preparing to depart.

'Will you be long?' asked Antony, who now monitored her exits and entrances to decide the precise moment at which an important client could call back to be rewarded with a few minutes of her attention.

'This one is open-ended,' she replied. 'I'll take anything urgent between six and six-thirty. And if those lazy so-and-sos leave at five thirty, it can't be that important.'

'Quite,' said Antony, who would spend the evening perfecting a press release which described the next menu at Zi-Zi's as though a new galaxy had emerged in the heavens.

The sickly, heavy floral scents washing through the House of Beauty on waves of air conditioning reminded Laura of the feminine world she had put behind her. Women with towels draped round their heads and tucked around sagging breasts wandered around aimlessly waiting for the next in the line of appointments carrying glasses of ill-defined health-giving liquids prescribed to 'cleanse their insides'.

Miss Douglas was looking remarkably well. Had she

been on holiday? Was she going on holiday? Would she be taking her usual massage?

'Are you quite sure?' Yes, she was sure.

'You're very brave. Very few of our customers manage that. I'll heat up the wax for you, Miss Douglas. Won't be long.'

Today her skin felt sensitive, like newly opened spring petals assaulted by a wintery shower.

'Would you like some music, Miss Douglas?'

'No. No, thank you. Just do it.'

The wax seemed hotter than usual. Laura held up her long arms and steeled herself as the scalding cover sealed the translucent down of her armpits. She imagined the inhabitants of Pompeii overwhelmed by laval cascades of glutinous wax, then, to avoid such thoughts, she looked up into the doll-like face which was frowning with concentration.

'It'll be lovely when it's done. Then you can go out and buy a strapless evening dress, can't you? Shall we do the next bit?' She pulled down the sheet further, then spooned out the wax and smoothed it like icing on a cake.

'Ay . . . eee!'

Laura dug her nails into her hands as the hairs under her arms were ripped from the roots. There was no going back; each strip had to be wrenched away, bit by bit. She realized her body was as rigid as a board, fighting back the assault. Each second lasted a day, every nerve was sensitized from her sclap to her toes. At last, as though the torturer had decided to give a respite so life could continue, the ripping stopped, giving way to a stinging as though a swarm of angry bees had fastened on to her armpits. She slowly inhaled, exhaled. I can bear it, she told herself. The girl held down Laura's stomach as she made the first rip across the pubic hairs, leaving a pink stripe of wounded flesh. Laura shut her eyes, and abandoned herself to pain.

'It's over. Would you like a cup of tea? You've been ever so brave.'

Laura didn't hear her. Instead, she heard Howard:

'Are you all right? Did you enjoy that?'

Now renewed by the overcoming of pain, Laura felt like a swan drifting along the slow current of a sleepy river as she stepped lightly over the threshold of Aphrodite's, walked up the stairs – which needed cleaning, she noted – and knocked on André Bouchon's door precisely at the time he had requested. She had, in the end, graciously conceded an appointment.

'*Entrez.*'

He gestured to a chair and stood against the mantelpiece. Today there would be no champagne, no coffee, nothing to stand between *le grand chef* and what he had to impart.

'Well, Laura, since I cannot speak to you on the telephone, you will now listen to what I have to say. Then you may go.'

He had thought it all out, she could see that, like a headmaster giving the appropriate rebuke to a transgressing pupil. It was the hour appointed for anger.

'OK. Three, four years ago you come to me. You are sitting in that chair. Before that, I see you sometimes for dinner with Mr Leone. He is a good client. So when you say you are making a new business for yourself, I listen. It is good sense. I am impressed. Everything is promotion, you say. Actors, writers, sportsmen, they have promotion. And you have the idea to promote restaurants and chefs. I like you. Your idea is a good one and you even have a nice piece of paper to say what it is. I spend lots of time talking with you. This girl is serious, I am thinking. Beautiful girls are often not serious. And she understands my food. You remember what I do?'

'Of course.'

'I agree to be the first person for you to represent. André Bouchon. You understand what I am doing for you? Now you can go to the television, to the press and say, I am the voice of the best chef in England. And, *en plus*, I pay you something. Today you have a nice business. Everyone wants to be with you. But remember, you do it on my back. All the times we have spent together when I tell you what is in my heart and in my mind, that is something precious.' He clenched his large hand. 'Now you behave like a *putain*.'

Laura looked at him. 'André, please. You didn't ask me here to remind me of how I started. If you think I've let you down, I am prepared to waive my fee for the rest of the year. Admittedly, I can't give you as much time as I did at the beginning—'

'This is not the question,' he interrupted angrily. 'The question is the Eglantine. You tell me nothing. I hear this news from my supplier. He also supply your restaurant. Well? Have you something to say?'

'If you find it upsetting to have a competitor—'

'No, no, no.'

'Let me finish. It happens all the time. I didn't imagine you would be bothered. After all, Didi is filming your dinner with the French ambassador. That alone is worth twice what I charge you, believe me.'

'Ah. You learn quickly. Now you become like the others who feed off us. Who are you promoting? *je me demande*. Laura Douglas. Now you open the Eglantine, you take my clients, you take my best chef and you are not decent enough to let me know. I learn from my supplier. Everyone is frightened to inform me. *C'est bien ça*. And what are doing these young men in your office? Telling me to get off the line! I am paying so they can insult me. Mrs Leone, we have no longer anything to say to one another. *Adieu*.'

André Bouchon turned his broad back and waited for Laura to leave.

'André, I know you're upset. It's understandable, but that's no reason for us to fall out. Aphrodite's is still the best restaurant in the country. The Eglantine is quite different. We have different customers.'

'Ah yes.'

He turned to her and smiled bitterly. 'My customers are

old. My restaurant is becoming like the grave. The young people in the kitchen, they do not stay. You remind me of this. But still, I am writing another book. I don't need you, Laura . . . One thing. The money I pay you is nothing to me. Why I am sad is when I make a mistake. And I make a mistake with you. Now you do not feel about anything except for money. Perhaps you never did.'

André Bouchon stormed out of his office, and Laura felt the vibrations of his heavy descending footsteps. Before she left, she looked in the gilded mirror and admired her unruffled countenance.

The Grey Men in the Studio looked up, gave nods of recognition and continued the work of the day. It was no longer necessary for John Crabtree to be announced. He hovered outside the glass partition of the Sanctum, and Laura beckoned him in.

'It's going marvellously. We're getting the best stuff in London, and the suppliers are giving me first choice. They didn't at first, but I sent back a few things and they've stopped playing silly buggers. They give me best over Aphrodite's now. Get a bigger order from me, so stands to reason. Well, I know it's not right, but that's Monsieur Bouchon's problem, not mine. He shouts at them. They don't like that.'

'Do you ever see him?'

'No. He knows he can come in any time, I told him that. I still respect him, but he's too old-fashioned. That's why he's not doing well.'

'He's doing all right, John.'

'I know for a fact he isn't, but who's going to say things are bad? No-one in this business. Now if he'd opened another place . . .'

'What?'

'You can't keep still nowadays. You've got to keep everyone at it, you've got to create excitement. We might even start thinking of another site.'

'Hold on. Let's get the star first.'

'By the way, we had someone in yesterday, all on his own. You won't believe this.'

'Yes?'

'Spent six hundred pounds. For lunch. Paid in cash. How about that? George was killing himself.'

'It's one way to launder money, I suppose.'

'Do you think it will keep going like this? I couldn't be doing with a failure. Didi says people soon get fed up in London, move somewhere else for no reason.'

'But *she* still comes.'

John smiled. 'She would, though.'

Laura caught his expression, a mixture of pride and momentary vulnerability.

'Why not keep it that way?'

'You mean marriage? She might say no.'

'The first time, perhaps.'

George was about to have a seizure. The phone rang constantly and each caller had the most pressing reasons to book a table. What do you mean, fully booked? exclaimed incredulous voices, hurt voices, arrogant voices, threatening voices. George was forced to admit that his knowledge of London society was not as comprehensive as he had led Laura to believe. How was he to establish an order of priority to safeguard the exclusivity of the Eglantine? How was he to choose between a lord, a politician, a film star and someone called Brown, worth millions only you'd never know unless you followed the City pages? It was a problem, but Laura sweetly suggested a few guidelines. Keep back two or three tables every day, she advised, and anyone who says they're a friend of Lord Maclintock's or Viscount Alloway can have one.

'That the Eglantine? Hi.'

An American voice. On a car phone. George was experienced enough to realize that not all Americans were rich.

'Table for two Friday.'

'Friday, sir?' intoned George, with practised incredulity.

'I'm afraid we're fully booked on Friday. Could I suggest another day, perhaps?'

'This is Jack Leone.'

'Ah yes, Mr Leone.'

'OK, so find me a table.'

'I'm terribly sorry—'

'Listen, don't give me that crap.'

'Just a moment, Mr Leone.'

George pressed his panic button. 'John! John!'

'Yeah?' came a voice drowned in the clattering of the kitchen.

'John, it's Leone. Wants a table. Yes or no?'

'Yes, you daft bugger. And put twenty per cent on his bill. He owes us.'

'Mr Leone? Sorry to keep you. It so happens we've had a cancellation for Friday lunch.'

'One o'clock. Two of us.'

The line went dead and the phone immediately rang again, as it would all morning.

The doorman at the Ritz blinked as a passing cloud of strawberry pink and pistachio green interrupted his field of vision. Caliope Fortescue gave him a cheery smile, as though she was personally importing the summer season into the foyer, and charged off to find a prominent table. Didi, as usual, had found the prime position in which to be observed, and was now displaying a stretch of thigh to an unknown admirer who backed off at Caliope's approach.

'Hello, my dear. You're looking ravishing.' She took in Didi's poppy-red silk suit with plunging neck. 'But we clash.'

'Are you going skiing?' asked Didi.

Caliope lowered her chin to examine the quilted volume of her attire. 'Far better on a motorbike. Are we drinking a little bottle of something chilled? I fancy pink. I'm feeling very pink today.'

Didi summoned some pink champagne and Caliope

downed her first glass of the afternoon with surprising rapidity.

'Have you tried the champagne diet?' She cocked her head to one side. 'You've definitely lost weight.'

'Can you tell?' Didi beamed.

From past experience, Caliope knew that such a remark would elicit a second bottle of champagne.

'Actually, I'm not dieting. It's . . .' Didi looked over her shoulder coyly.

'You mean activities of an amorous nature? I thought everyone had given that up. Far too exhausting, and dangerous. Who, my dear?'

'Promise not to tell anyone.'

'Cross my heart and hope to die. Not a word.'

Didi whispered in her ear, but Caliope could not resist a loud guffaw. 'A chef? How awfully original, my dear. And his name?'

Didi put her fingers to her lips and whispered again.

'Petrushka's. I remember. The one with a sense of humour who's related to Lady Cynthia Crabtree from Darlington.'

'Did you see Stephen's piece on the Eglantine?'

'Slightly excessive, my dear. Without being unkind, I did think the prose was a tiny bit . . . promotional. Very nice for Laura, of course. Very nice. Does he – Stephen – know?'

'About?'

'About the chef, of course.'

'I think he must. Oh, yes.'

'And does he object?'

'Stephen isn't possessive.'

'I don't know how you do it, my dear. Having two men on the go. How does one remember what one has said to whom? Or which one takes two sugars in coffee and one in tea and vice versa? Isn't it dreadfully confusing? And it must make for horrendous laundry bills.'

'Every time I see Stephen I want to be with John, and every time I'm with John I think about Stephen. It's dreadful.'

'Stop thinking, my dear. It spoils the appetite. You have different dresses for different occasions. Why not different men? One wouldn't dream of attending a dinner party given by Lady Knowles and the opening of a tapas bar with the same escort, after all.'

'But which one should I marry?'

'Marry!'

Caliope roared with laughter. 'That is only for girls with insubstantial means. Marriage is for the lower orders, except where property is involved. Has Stephen property?'

'I don't think so.'

'Has he proposed?'

'Not yet.'

'What a lucky girl you are. Two men who adore you, and millions who would like to do so. Cheer up! Let's have another bottle.'

'The thing is, Cal—'

'Ah. He's coming.' Caliope gesticulated and pointed with a grimace to the empty bottle.

'I want babies.'

'Didi!' She spoke in a sepulchral tone. 'You're not pregnant?'

'Of course not.'

'Thank God. You almost gave me a nasty turn.' Caliope ripped off her ancient paisley silk neck scarf and mopped her brow dramatically.

'But I do want to be. Desperately, Cal.'

'Oh, really! Imagine us sitting in the Ritz and talking about breast-feeding and nappy rash. My dear, I couldn't bear it.'

'Didn't you ever think you might want a baby?'

'Never. Isn't one of me enough? I even got rid of my cat. It was always after my food. Too much competition, my dear. You and I are one-offs, exclusive models. Beware of imitations.'

'Am I wrong, Cal?'

'For the girl who has everything, my dear, a baby makes

absolute sense. Now shall we talk about what is really happening? I heard a great piece of gossip last night . . .'

The waiters were collecting plates and gliding in and out of the kitchen as though taking part in a frantic relay race. This was what John had dreamed of. Frenzied activity with him at the centre, every nerve strained in total concentration as the written orders steadily mounted on the spiked holder.

'Table twelve want a portion double of Beluga with ze salmon mousse and ze Chateaubriand flambé without garnish,' shouted a waiter.

'Fucking hell.'

'And 'e order a wine for zree 'undred pounds!'

'Jesus!'

'You make flambé?'

'No, I bloody don't.'

'What I tell 'im?'

'Give him the Beluga and regret no flambé.'

'*Très bien, chef.*'

The pot of coffee tipped and the thick, dark, earth-coloured liquid pulsed over the papers on Laura's desk. She grasped the pot like a drowning child and stood it upright. Splatters of liquid had fallen on to her lap and sullied the colour of her freshly pressed pale almond green linen dress. She looked down with horror. Brown stains. Laura Douglas never had stains on her clothes. The mark of the slut. There was no time. She ran down to the dry cleaners and stood there as though she had just witnessed a bloody road accident.

'Look, look,' she said to the puzzled Greek who had left his steaming press. 'My dress. I've spilled coffee over it. Please. Can you do something?'

He shrugged his shoulders and said he couldn't guarantee success, but he would try. Ten minutes later she left, pressing a twenty pound note in his hand. Thank you, thank you, thank you.

George was about to tell Laura that Mr Leone had booked a table and was spending like you wouldn't believe, but it was obvious that something terrible had happened. Fatal illness, death even, was written on her face.

'George, George, please come outside a moment.'

He followed her hurriedly and she stood in front of him on the pavement.

'Can you see anything?' she asked.

'Gorgeous, as usual. Love that dress.'

'Look! Look at me properly.'

George gave his attention to the mirror-polished court shoes, the long, ivory-smooth legs, the pale linen dress, the newly washed hair framing a face without blemish.

'A couple of tiny creases, but linen always does. Just that little human touch.'

'I spilled some coffee down my dress. It's stained. Can you see?'

George peered. 'Honestly. I can't see a thing. I'd tell you if I could.'

'You're not looking properly,' she said impatiently.

He took her by the arm and steered her inside the doorway. 'Your guest has arrived. I know I've seen him somewhere. I always remember a face.'

'Sir Howard Riley,' she snapped.

The dining room was crowded, but he stood out like a black and white image in a sea of colour and Laura saw nobody else.

'Hello, darling.'

'Have you been here long?'

'I know you like to keep me waiting, but I've been admiring the dining room.'

Laura hurriedly sat down and placed a napkin over the tell-tale stains.

'Won't you sit beside me?'

'No, I'll sit opposite.'

The room jarred. The pink roses were the wrong shade, too dominating in natural light. She should have thought of the different effect produced by daylight and artificial light. It was too late now, and would needle her until she could afford to change it.

Howard stretched out his arm and placed his hand lightly over hers. 'This must have been a great strain for you, darling. I'm sorry I had to be away. I've been looking forward to this. Since I last saw you, I've been to meeting after meeting.'

And going home to your wife, she thought. But no. She didn't care.

Two photographers, known as 'paps' or 'papparazzi' – who could be distinguished by their doleful waiting-weary features, and their loose jackets bulging with cameras and film – sat slumped in the front seat of a fleet car watching the entrance of the Eglantine in the mirror from the opposite side of the road.

'Right. Let's hit.'

They worked synchronously, like two computer-linked clocks in a railway station. Two doors opened and clunked shut. The two men, one tall, one short, both sporting tread-bare trainers, jogged across a gap in the traffic.

'You get him. I'll get her.'

This was going to be dead easy. No-one at the door. An in and out job. The fastest draw on the Street. The zoom lenses pointed and they fired.

Jack leaped up, but not before he had flashed a smile, and ran out in pursuit.

Laura swung round in her chair. 'What's happened?'

'A couple of photographers after a couple over there.'

She saw faces looking round in disapproval.

'You should have someone on the door.'

'I do. Oh, how dreadful.' She started to get up.

'Sit down. There's nothing you can do.'

'How dare they? Half the people here won't come back now. Oh, Howard!'

'Sit down.'

'I'll find out who they are. I'm going to ring every single

303

paper when I get back. I'm not having those oiks from the gutter in here.'

Howard laughed, 'I thought you knew how to handle the press.'

'They're not press. They're scum.'

The waiter arrived with the first course.

'Aren't you eating today?' asked Howard, as she picked at the garnish surrounding meltingly tender scallops. 'This is superb. Shall I tell you my news?'

Laura gave a start. Was this the moment he had chosen to inform her that he was going to leave his wife? In the space it took for Howard to finish his mouthful and break a crusty roll, she had raced through every possibility. Would they live together or would it be better for him get somewhere in London first? Would she be dragged into a messy divorce? What would it be like seeing him all the time, when he was not abroad? Did she want to? Suppose it turned out to be a terrible mistake? Another marriage in ruins. Her responsibility. Would she be glad or terrified?

'I thought it might amuse you to know, anyhow.' His wife had gone off with somebody else. No, of course not. 'Strictly between us. And I mean that.'

At first, there would have to be the utmost discretion. Even today there was still a vestige of shame when the marriage of a prominent figure was seen to be crumbling. It would probably be a while before they could be seen together, officially. But she could introduce him to a few friends . . . Howard leaned forward over the table.

'We're thinking of taking over Leone Leisure.'

'Why on earth are you doing that?' she said, with all the vehemence of disappointment.

'It makes perfect sense. As a minor adjunct to Illustra Foods, it would be a useful asset. Leone has chosen his sites well. Not in the high streets with escalating overheads but sound secondary sites in improving areas with fixed long leases. He's been shrewd.'

'How have you got on to this? Jack's company is private. Even I don't know everything he's done.'

'That's the easy part. Finding out is always easy. No, the interesting idea is to have a chain of outlets for Illustra products to keep the brand names high-profile. We've been thinking about this for some time.'

'What products?'

'Oh, the usual things. Our best-selling fast-food lines, but maintaining a high standard of quality control. We can be more reactive than Leone. We have the back-up facilities for far greater market penetration. The concept of fast food interests me. No-one has really thought it through.'

'Do you think Jack will roll over on his back and let you take away his bone? He's not like that. He's had offers in the past. Jack plans ahead. If you think he's a quick-buck merchant, you're wrong. And he won't sell. Why should he? Jack is dedicated. You and I might criticize him, but he'd fight to the death to keep what he's built up.'

'I like a fight.'

'Has this anything to do with me?'

'Good heavens no! What makes you think that?'

'You won't succeed in buying up my past, Howard, although I know it appeals to you.'

He stroked her hand. 'Eat up.'

'I'm not hungry.'

'It must be hard for you living in the shadow of your former husband, but isn't it time you saw him objectively, Laura? What did you see in him? I always wondered. Never understood it. Still, I suppose he's not unattractive to a certain sort of girl.'

'You seem to have forgotten that I left Jack for you.'

'No, let me correct you. You had moved out two months before and were staying with a friend in Fulham.'

'We shouldn't be talking like this here, Howard.'

The main course arrived and the rich aroma rising from the plate sickened her. She lowered her voice and leaned towards him.

'I was still living in the farmhouse. Don't you remember? We were introduced at Aphrodite's. You were having

305

lunch with a junior minister and I was alone. André Bouchon introduced us. We sat down and had coffee and liqueurs. You had an Armagnac.'

'You're making it up.'

'I thought then that something has passed between us, that we both knew. I didn't care who you were, or where you came from.'

'Oh?'

'Without saying anything. You looked at me very hard, you stared as though you had recognized something. And I thought about you for days afterwards. I used to lie awake in bed, at our country house, waiting for Jack to come home. Often he didn't. Sometimes I'd sit at the bedroom window listening to the owls and the bats and willing myself to pick out the distant headlights of the Ferrari coming down the road, turning into the drive. And then I thought of you and that things could change. After a few days I plucked up enough courage to ask you to lunch.'

'That awful Japanese food you made me eat. What was the name of the place? God, it was noisy. I couldn't hear myself speak.'

'Zi–Zi's. You shouted at me.'

'Did I?'

'"I love you. Damn you." That's what you said.'

'Yes. So I did.'

'Then you kissed me on the pavement outside. In the middle of the afternoon. You didn't care if you were recognized. I asked you why you swore at me. You said, "Because you will never leave your husband. I want you. I would never be satisfied with having you as my occasional lover. This has never happened to me before. What have you done to me?" . . . You refused to go back to your office. It started to rain so we went to the Museum of Mankind and stood by that strange Easter Island statue.'

'Hoa Haka Nana Ia.'

The waiter removed their plates, but Laura continued, unaware of the movement behind her, unaware of anything except Howard's face. He was looking at her with great tenderness.

'You said, "Laura, do you feel the same as I do?" "Yes." "Would you do anything I asked? Do you feel that strongly?" I didn't answer. Everything was wild confusion. Then you stared at me, as though the statue had moved, and you said, "I'm going to ask you to leave your husband. To live with me."'

Howard looked up as the waiter approached again. 'Just coffee. Do go on, darling.'

'We saw one another several times after that. Sometimes I left early in the morning, with Jack, saying I had a dental appointment. We used to have breakfast together at the Savoy. How I envied the couples coming down from their bedrooms. We must make love, you kept saying. But you couldn't bear the idea of booking a room. It was too sordid.'

'Quite right.'

'Then I decided to leave Jack. You had made me realize that I was using my marriage with him as an excuse to bury my talent.'

The waiter set down the silver coffee pot.

'Listen to me, Laura.' Howard's voice suddenly became harder. 'I never suggested you should leave Jack. Your marriage was no better and no worse than most others.' Then he smiled, his large brown eyes softened and he leaned forward to take her hand. 'You may not remember now, but you were very disturbed at the time. Alone, with your husband hardly ever there. Unable to distinguish fantasy from reality. It's not uncommon. Unhappiness led you to re-create life as you wished it to be, and then you believed your fantasy. I can understand. You really are an artist, Laura. I wish I could invent as you do. Unfortunately I have to live in the real world. In many ways I wish I had said those things. I'm sorry I've disappointed you, but I've done my best. I've given everything I could. And I'm proud of you. I really am. I don't know what you see in me. After all what am I? A perfectly humdrum corporate man. Rather ordinary. I have no illusions about that. You deserve better . . . I've changed my mind. Let's have a pudding. Waiter? Shall we have a sorbet?'

The blanket of resentment dissolved away. She opened her mouth and Howard inserted a spoonful of fondant, mango sorbet, withdrawing it slowly as the coldness drew the heat from her mouth, leaving a delicate, scented flavour.

'Hi Laura.'

She felt a hand on her shoulder and whipped round in her chair.

'Thought I'd surprise you and then those goddamn snappers came in. I gave 'em a real hard time outside.'

'Sir Howard Riley. Jack Leone.'

Howard stood up and Jack grasped his hand. 'An honour, Sir Howard. I've a lot of time for Illustra Foods. Bought a few shares myself.'

'I appreciate your confidence, Mr Leone. I hear good things too about your company.'

'Give me a couple of months. You'll be hearing more.'

'Going public?'

'No, never. I'm strictly a one-man big band.' He laughed. 'Play everything. Ask Laura.'

'Really?'

'She made the mistake of walking out on me, but I love her anyway. Great place, babe. Love the flowers. I'll give you a call. Bye, Sir Howard.'

It had happened, the meeting which Laura had rehearsed so many times. So easy, the laying of ghosts.

'Well, what did you think?'

'He's more attractive than you led me to believe. Not the kind of man I'd have imagined you with, but—'

'Who would that be, Howard? Or doesn't he exist?'

'Someone intelligent, sensitive, but forceful. You need that. Someone who cuts through the conventions but plays the game. And he'd have to be kind. Women respond to kindness in men, I've noticed.' Howard smiled regretfully. 'I don't know why you are so tolerant with me, but

I'm sure you have boyfriends who fit the bill better than I do. I wouldn't presume that I'm the only one.'

'Is that your way of avoiding jealousy? Or avoiding the pain of being in love?'

'You're free to do as you like, Laura. I've never wanted to restrict you. After years of marriage, anyone would want to break out, explore, take different lovers. I wouldn't blame you for that. It would be unnatural if you didn't.'

Laura stretched back in her chair. 'You know Howard, sometimes I think you should have been a surgeon. When you put the knife in, you do it with such elegant precision.'

She could find no expression in his face which betrayed the slightest awareness that he had caused her pain. He was right, probably she did imagine things.

Howard reached again for her hand and pressed his lips softly against her long slender fingers. 'Can I come round tonight? Or are you working? I don't want to disturb you if you are.'

She had blotted out the (imagined) wound, like the mother who forgets the pain of childbirth with the baby in her arms. The house would be filled with fresh flowers, champagne in the fridge. Her preparations made that morning would not have been in vain. And she could look forward to the reward of a few more precious hours in his company. He did love her, she knew. Why did she try and make herself hate him?

'Forgive me for being so unpleasant today,' she said. 'It's the last thing I wanted.'

'I didn't think you were unpleasant. It was a wonderful lunch. I'll remember it always. I'll come tonight as soon as I can.'

14

There is always one day when the warm, rich smell of summer is tainted by the first sharp note of approaching autumn, like a minute brown patch on a ripe peach heralding the change from juicy ripeness to sour decay. John was aware of an autumn tang faintly penetrating the benzine haze on this warm, dry summer's day at the beginning of September and his spirits lifted.

Hot summers were bad for the kitchen. Despite the air conditioning, the body heat of seven men in a small space made working uncomfortable and the brigade resented their absence from the sunlit, scented gardens and rippling water when they caught sight of the tanned bodies of passers-by who, unlike them, had long lunch-hours to spend basking on walls, in courtyards, or seeking out the scrubby patches of brownish-green grass dotting the city. The windows of the Eglantine were tightly closed and the summer flowers adorning each table breathed in the deadness of coolly circulating purified air and kept their perfume to themselves.

John looked forward to summer's decline. He had grown up in cold, sharp air, relishing its vigour, and all through the hot summer months he had sweated to serve the stream of diners crowding through the doors of the Eglantine longing for the light menus which demanded so much work – the mousses, the *gelées*, the delicate sauces. The raw ingredients always had to be minutely checked and rechecked for the deteriorating signs of heat and bruising.

'I never want to see another sea food salad.'

John threw down a box of lamb's lettuce starting to lose

their dark green lustre and screamed at his supplier of scallops and langoustines for making up the weight with ones whose freshness had peaked the day before. His cheeses either oozed ripeness or cut hard, over-chilled and flavourless. Still the diners came, though, thronging through the holiday season when other restaurants were mausoleums of empty tables.

'Anyone would think the Eglantine was the only restaurant in London,' remarked George, as he made the last booking for the week ahead. 'It must be *my* manner. You know the American lady with pink hair? "George," she says, "you make me feel like a billion dollars." All she ever has is mineral water, a salad and a sorbet. Doesn't look at the bill. I've got my answer for those that do, mind . . . Healthy ingredients are so expensive! Did you know we personally import our produce from California? All grown bio-dynamically in the right organically manured magnetic field. The animals are inspected by a vet and guaranteed happy and free from stress. And they're not slaughtered. Oh, no. They're put to sleep. Did you know that, John? I thought it might appeal.'

'Bullshit.'

'They love it.'

'You won't catch me saying that.'

'It keeps bums on seats, dear boy. Not my kind of bums, but bums none the less.'

George ran his finger down the booking list.

'Anyone I know coming?'

'Couple of MPs. I wish they'd buy proper suits. The usual lot from the MacCrae bank, Mrs Partridge and friend. Don't know them . . . nor them. Oh. Listen. Last night. I meant to tell you but—'

'Tippling again.'

'Merely disposing of surplus to requirements, dear boy. My memory is intact. I'm willing to bet fifty pounds we had two Michelin inspectors in. Well ten pounds.'

'What were they doing. Inspecting the toilets?'

'Two men on their own. Not in business, I thought,

311

wrong haircuts, wrong suits. Not journalists. Only the financial ones wear suits. They read the menu like mother reading a hire purchase agreement, ordered more than they could eat, ate ever so carefully and left the minimum tip. If those aren't inspectors, I don't know who are.'

'Do you think they were impressed?' asked John.

'No idea. They didn't exactly stand up and clap.'

'They gave Elwyn Jones a star. If they give one to that Welsh git, they can give one to me.'

'You seeing the girl of your dreams tonight?' George asked. 'Do I have to make my own cocoa again?'

'Probably. I think I should tell you, George. I'm going to be moving out.'

George's face fell.

'I don't much like Earl's Court.'

'I do,' said George, imagining the small flat peopled with prints of David Hockney's poised young men, and the real thing, an Australian hunk, stretched out on the couch.

'Maybe you could take over the rent.'

'If the tips allow.'

Without thinking about it, John had made a decision, but he couldn't determine whether it had been forced on him or whether it was the consequence of having found the girl he had been looking for all his life. That's what you were meant to do, to keep on searching. The hard part was judging when to stop, like finding the perfect holiday place where you could happily go year after year.

He was going to live with Didi.

Sometimes he thought he was being led gently into a trap, but then he wavered. Didi gave not a hint of long-term plans for a white wedding, and showed no inclination to take him to tea with her parents. There were no complaints that he worked the night away. If they had a row, she stormed but never sulked. There were no dark corners he had yet to discover. Gently Didi persuaded him along the route she had mapped out for him.

Surely John didn't intend to stay in Earl's Court? Not

that there was anything wrong with this area, apart from a remarkable lack of noteworthy restaurants and an infuriating lack of parking spaces. But wouldn't it be much more sensible for him to remove himself to Kensington? To her spacious flat? If he would like to, of course. And wouldn't it be an appealing idea to give the occasional private dinner party (her kitchen was large) for very special and very influential friends? She'd love him to tell her what to do about her kitchen, had never got round to planning it properly . . . and she had decided to be absurdly extravagant. Should she or shouldn't she make a bid for that divine four-poster bed in the catalogue of Sotheby's sale?

'If you say no, I won't do it,' she said on numerous occasions.

Most Sundays they spent the day together, for Didi had always planned a joyful event – a picnic on the river with a hamper crammed with delicacies, or a visit to wealthy friends who had gourmet barbecues at the poolside, or chamber concerts in stately homes whose owners she vaguely knew. If he said little all day, half listening to the tattle of who was reading what, who had seen what, who had eaten what and where, who was out and who was in, who was underrated and who was overrated, whose marriage was breaking up, he knew he would come into his own at night.

'I cook and I fuck. That's what I do,' he said.

'Both divinely,' she said, with such a look of radiant satisfaction that he wondered why any man bothered to become chained in marriage.

This Sunday, John was alone. Didi had taken off to France because she had heard that some forest warden north of Amiens had discovered a way to breed truffles, and George was visiting friends in Brighton. It was a time to sleep, to ignore the outside world, to let one day slip away unmemorably. Around midday, he might go for a pint or two.

'Cathy!'

She was standing there, heavy make-up, hair softly

rollered, chains and bangles showing beneath a raincoat clinched in at the waist, high heels, with an overnight bag.

'Shall I come in? I was just passing. I'll not stay long. I'm visiting relatives.' Without pausing to look round the gloomy entrance hall, she followed John up the stairs.

Plumping herself down on the edge of John's divan, she took a deep breath. 'Three hours, that's all it took to come down here. And I'm working now, like I wrote, good job, but I'd have taken time off. I didn't mind waiting. Well I won't say I never enjoyed myself.'

'It's not as though—'

'No need to say anything. I'm not blaming you, never would. But I suppose I knew when you got to London things would be different. Tried to tell myself they wouldn't. You've changed, and I haven't. I couldn't love anyone else, but I think it's better we stopped writing. You look tired, you work too hard.'

'No choice.'

'I know.'

Cathy wiped away a tear. 'Mum and Dad send their regards. Didn't mean to cry. Didn't want you to see me like this, the last . . .'

John went over, about to put his arms round her, but Cathy took hold of her bag, rushed to the door and ran down the stairs.

For two days after her visit, John shouted in the kitchen and raged down the phone at his suppliers. He noticed puzzled, hurt faces and sharp glances.

'You OK, chef?' enquired Jean-Luc.

'I'll get over it,' he replied, giving a smile for the first time that day.

George's cheerful voice came over the intercom. 'Table six is waiting for John.'

Didi's guest had left. An awfully boring man, she assured him, who was the world expert on mushrooms, but essential for her *Magic of Mushrooms* programme. Needless to say, he had no magic whatsoever but he could talk for one and a half minutes on the death cap. And now, she would tell him the amazing story of how to clone a truffle. While she was speaking, John became aware of two men behind her.

'Excuse me, Miss Kowalski,' said the bolder of the two. 'We just wanted to say . . .'

Didi turned round instantly, said 'Thank you so much' and flashed the pain-of-being-a-public-personality smile.

'Does it worry you?' she asked.

'As long as they don't touch you. If they did, I'd—'

'What?' said Didi, enthralled.

'Crack their fucking jawbones.'

She leaned across and caressed his face. 'You're so wonderfully possessive,' she sighed. 'What a shame I have to go off and talk about mushrooms. The smell. Mm. It reminds me of when' – she lowered her voice and put her mouth to his ear – 'I suck you.'

'Don't,' he said, longing to pull off her dress and have her right there, down on the gold carpet in front of the braying tight-tied, brandy-flushed businessmen. 'I must get back to the kitchen.'

It was nearly time for the exhausted brigade to take their break, to lie for a few precious minutes in the afternoon sun. John was giving them their notes, praise and criticism delivered with calmness after each service. That had been George's idea. Artistes are always given notes, dear boy, so you can keep the bolshie ones down and encourage the shy ones. Shows they can't get away with anything.

Before he had finished, George appeared in the kitchen and gestured urgently for him to come upstairs. As he approached ground level, John heard an almighty clanging and then he saw lights flashing through the voile curtains.

'Not our building?'

'No, no.'

What they dreaded most. Suppliers might fail to appear, dishes might unaccountably be overcooked or undercooked, staff might burn themselves, cut themselves, leave without warning, rows might erupt in the dining

315

room, but there was only one thing which could spell ruin. And that was a fire.

John and George stood on the pavement watching hoses snaking down and firemen rushing into an entrance. Black smoke billowed out, filling the streets with an acrid smell.

'I'll go', said John. 'Look after the shop.'

There were four fire engines nose to nose and John ran to the one in front. 'Where's the fire?'

'Kitchen,' came the shouted reply.

A familiar old Jaguar came tearing down the wrong side of the road. André Bouchon. At least he was alive. He jumped out of his car, ran past John without seeing him, hurtled up the front steps of his restaurant, but was turned back. John saw him gesticulating, shouting, and then his hands dropped to his side. He stood watching, his mouth open, his eyes fixed on the black clouds of conflagration as John walked towards him.

'It always looks worse than it is,' John said, placing his arm on André's shoulder.

'*Un désastre. C'est fini. C'est tout fini. Je ne comprends pas. J'étais pas là. Y avait personne.*'

'Perhaps something overheated. The air-conditioning unit.'

'Perhaps. Perhaps. Is done. Now we close. *C'est fini.*'

'You're not finished, André. In a couple of weeks you'll be open again. I can get you some great builders, they work all night.'

'No. Is finished.' A Daimler drew up next to the Jaguar. 'Now I must go.'

'Come over to the Eglantine, Monsieur Bouchon. Let me offer you a drink. They'll get it sorted. Don't worry.'

The chauffeur from the Daimler supported Mr Beck as he crossed the road with hesitant steps and the chief fire officer approached him.

'You the owner, sir?'

'I am.'

'Lucky thing. Someone was passing by, smelled burning and phoned us. Could have been much worse.

Nothing's collapsed. It's nearly under control. Bit of a mess, though.'

'What is the cause? Does anybody know yet?'

'Could be any number of things. Faulty wiring . . . They'll find out in the investigation. Don't worry.'

'In my kitchen we only have fire once when a commis heat too much the oil,' said Monsieur Bouchon. 'I put it out myself.' He looked anxiously at Mr Beck. 'What are we going to do?'

'Examine the damage,' he replied, drily.

'Not yet, sir,' said the fire officer. 'In any case, I wouldn't go in dressed like that.'

Mr Beck turned to his chauffeur. 'I will wait in the car. André, you will go home and I will telephone you.'

'No, no. I stay.'

'There is no point in being here. This is not a sinking ship, André, and you are not the captain. I will deal with this.'

André Bouchon looked at the debris as he opened his car door, then changed his mind and walked swiftly down the street towards the Eglantine. It was the first time he had crossed the threshold. Scurrying waiters were clearing the soiled plates from table after table.

'Hello, Paul,' André said, noticing one who had previously worked at Aphrodite's.

'Afternoon, Mr Bouchon.'

John poured out several measures of brandy. 'I don't know what to say, Monsieur Bouchon. If I can do anything for you, you know I will. Till your kitchen is ready again.'

'How many weeks? You know what it is not to work? It never happen to me.'

'I'm so sorry.'

André looked round the bar, he turned towards the dining room and murmured, *'Elle est jolie, cette pièce.'* He scratched his forehead and glanced up at the ceiling. 'John, you think there is someone who does not like me? Some crazy person who maybe worked in the kitchen.'

'You're a tough boss, but you're never mean. Anyway, it doesn't happen in our end of the business. In Chinatown or some dodgy Italian joint, maybe. Most like it was the wiring needed renewing. The insurance will cover it, don't worry.'

'Ah, yes. I must ask Mr Beck about that.'

'Why don't you take a holiday? Go back to France and have a good time.'

'Perhaps. Have you heard of this little place in the Alpes-Maritimes, Jean le Clerc? The Michelin give him a second star. *Extraordinaire*.'

Soon the two chefs were gossiping, exchanging notes and talking about new dishes as though they had grown up together, served their apprenticeship together, and John no longer remembered that there were nearly thirty years between them. As the liquid in the brandy bottle sank slowly down, André Bouchon ceased to think of his burnt-out kitchen. Their passions were the same.

There was a message on his machine. It could wait. Mr Beck slowly removed his suit. It was covered with blackened marks and smelling like a putrid kipper, the odour of the fire's aftermath was embedded in his nostrils so that it appeared to have permeated every room in his flat. He made himself some tea, and he had now insisted Juliet spend a few weeks in the country cottage outside the remote East Anglian village of Long Paxton. He liked the village, liked the taciturn inhabitants who minded their own business. He had even persuaded André to buy a retreat nearby. He would escape there too, as soon as he could.

He switched on the 'play' button. First, there was the sound of chinking glasses, hoots of laughter, distant conversations, the bleeping of a computer game. No-one addressed him. A pub, probably. There was no way of identifying it. Then it came, the voice. A Cockney accent? Who could tell? All London accents sounded the same.

'Sorry about the fire, Mr Beck. Done a bit of damage,

has it? Someone must 'ave bin careless. What a shame . . .
I'm runnin' out of change, Mr Beck.'

The line went dead. His heart was pounding, he could
feel the blood frantically pumping through his veins. His
throat constricted and he was gasping for breath. In the
drinks cabinet. His pills. He reached for the container and
shovelled several into his mouth. Then he found his Bible,
opened it and started reading the dancing letters until the
drumming inside his ears faded enough for him to hear
the slow rhythm of the ticking wooden clock.

'A fire at Aphrodite's?'

John had rung Didi. Didi had rung Stephen. Stephen
had rung Laura. Half an hour later she was gazing at the
blackened doorway. André Bouchon and John were still
sitting at the bar of the Eglantine as she walked in.

'I must go,' said André, and Laura realized she had
never seen him drunk.

'It's dreadful, André,' she said. 'If there's anything I
can do . . .'

André ignored her and addressed his remarks to John.
'Fortunately, we were not busy,' he said. 'John, thank
you. My wife, she will be wondering . . .'

'Will you talk to the press?' Laura said.

'Why? For what?'

'Publicity, André. Then when you re-open, we'll do a
big launch. It's the kind of boost you need.'

'When I want to talk, I talk. Goodbye, John. Soon I
come and eat with you.'

'Tomorrow?'

'Soon.'

They shook hands and André Bouchon departed,
walked a little too carefully with his eyes fixed on the
outside door.

'He's so stubborn,' Laura said. 'I told him time and
time again he should bring his prices down a little. How
many people will pay thirty pounds for a starter? No
wonder he was half empty. Now he's got the chance to

start afresh. I'd love to get my hands on that place, design it properly. I can just see it working in the French country house style, restrained grandeur. It's so frustrating. I could really help him.'

'He doesn't need you, Laura. And he doesn't care what's on the walls. Monsieur Bouchon could start up anywhere.'

'He does need me. You're wrong.'

'You mean it's a challenge.'

'Well, yes.'

'And if it's not you get bored, don't you?' Laura smiled and smoothed back her hair. 'You'd better not get bored with the Eglantine. It's time I had my name in the paper again.'

'You don't need it at the moment. It gives you an opportunity to consolidate, get known amongst people who pay.'

'You know,' said John, 'I've noticed down here that folks don't talk much about money, but if they say something's wonderful it means one thing. Profit.'

'Surely you're not upset because our turnover's better than anyone else's?'

'Your turnover, Laura.'

'Don't be silly. It reflects on you.'

John shrugged.

'You think I'm doing this for the money?'

'Yes,' he replied. 'But I don't mind. I think different, though. I'm after a star.'

By the time Laura had walked through the Studio, smiling briefly at the new recruits, and taken her place behind the grey desk in the Sanctum, she had forgotten the moment of doubt aroused by John's hostility.

'Hi, Laura. Can you hear? I'm in the car. Just wanted to tell you. Great place, great food. I'm proud of you. Why didn't you say you did the decor? The floral motif hits you in the eyes like bare tits in a church. What is it? Some kind of a tulip?'

'Roses, Jack. The Eglantine. It's a wild rose.'

'Close. Hey. I heard about Aphrodite's. Terrible. Just terrible. Friend of mine was taking a party of ten tonight. Oh well, he'll have to book at your place.'

'We're full, I'm afraid.'

'Hold on a second Jack, will you? The other phone's going.'

While Laura answered her call Jack travelled the length of Park Lane, dictated a letter and was heading towards St John's Wood for a quick interlude with Miss Tuesday Nightdate who got a kick from being screwed from behind while she watched a video and ate Milky Bars.

He drew up at some traffic lights and found himself parallel with a red-haired beauty in a large hat who was resting a long manicured finger on the wheel of a convertible BMW.

'Sorry to keep you waiting, Jack.'

'Gotta go, Laura.' Jack said. 'Talk soon.'

He put his foot down, releasing the guttural mating call of the Ferrari and chased her tail up the Edgware Road.

'Are we going to do anything about Aphrodite's?' asked Antony, placing some fresh roses in the vase on Laura's desk. 'We still have the account, don't we?'

'He takes up so much time. That's the trouble. And he refuses to listen.'

'If I were you I'd give him the elbow, Laura. I mean it's all right for the old crowd, I suppose, but who wants to write about Aphrodite's? It's like writing about the Tower of London. Nothing to say. For a few thou it's not worth it. That's my opinion, anyhow.'

'You may be right. If anyone else rings about the fire, will you please deal with it?'

She had given sufficient time to André Bouchon. Every second was now measured along the scale of productivity and she was able to reach decisions almost before she was aware of having a decision to make. Far better to concentrate her efforts on the Rialto Hotel Group, who were majoring on cuisine and acquiring majestic toeholds in the States, Canada, Europe and the Far East. When she swept into stately boardrooms followed by her Grey Men, she was greeted with deference. It was as exhilarating as leaping from wave to wave on a power boat when a roomfull of men listened to her every word with the attention of cabinet ministers deciding the fate of the economy. And as the cheques and bankers' orders rolled in, she acknowledged their reward for her services at the tables of the Eglantine, thus demonstrating her taste, style and business acumen. Chefs were like the members of a tribe, and she did not intend to be a tribal ruler. A boardroom queen. Yes, that suited her well.

The intercom buzzed.

'Keep them waiting for fifteen minutes, Antony. I'm not quite ready.'

Laura escaped to her private bathroom, dug her hands into a pot of cream and removed every inch of make-up. Stripping down to imperfect features and building up to the image which satisfied was a process which was more than a familiar feminine ritual. The little-girl face grimaced in the mirror. No-one saw her like this, not even Howard. No-one saw this reminder of the small person who lied about where she was going for her summer holidays. This face was masked out and she drew upon it the face of the woman she felt she was, brushing over the imperfections, the tiny lines, with a shower of translucent powder. Eyes, cheeks, lips were etched and shaded to assume the clear-cut aspects of command. She blotted her lips in the mirror. Serious perhaps, this time.

'Go on. Give us a smile, Miss Douglas.'

Laura blinked into the photographer's lights and raised her chin. She was looking through a glass case, an angular metal form was cutting the image.

'No. It would be wrong for this kind of shot.'

The photographer twitched.

'And I don't feel like smiling today.'

Laura Douglas, the subject of a profile in *Harper's*, knew that the rarity of an unsmiling portrait of a woman would gain attention. Her smile was becoming too well known.

'Just one. We won't use it.'

'No.'

She stood in the position she had established, immobile, until the reel of film was finished.

'Thank you, Miss Douglas.' The photographer moved the vase of flowers on her desk.

'Could you sit here?'

'Yes. But no flowers.'

The stark grey wall would be behind her. She liked that. Unbuttoning two buttons of her rich purple blouse, she relented. A hint of small, firm breasts. Legs stretched out, crossed to one side. A half smile. The photographer completed a second roll of film.

The following day the fire at Aphrodite's warranted a few lines but its importance had been noted. A theme, a subject, dropped from heaven on to the blank pages of this week's word count. Sigmund Halberstadt's mind raced, obliterating last night's indigestion. Magnus Shaw forgot about his back pain and unscrewed his fountain pen. Penelope Long let out a sigh of inspiration and hammered at her ancient typewriter. Dylan Tusk stopped chewing gum and expleted. Stephen Boyce tapped furiously on his keyboard, as lucidity streaked through the haze of last night's vintage like a rainbow in a slate-grey sky. Even Virginia Desgranges casually brought the event to her editor's attention. Didi reached for the phone, brimming with commiseration. A peg for a story, for high and low.

The words devoted to Aphrodite's and delivered by Sigmund Halberstadt and Magnus Shaw would have a certain similarity, not because they communicated with one another but because they shared the same lofty feelings towards the Masters of the Art. Their unanimous theme was the neglect of our finest chef. When will the

British break out of the Philistine mould and appreciate greatness? Both columns were peppered with the names of the great to reinforce this argument and to reinforce their reputation for being on intimate terms with every three-star Michelin chef in the world.

'André Bouchon confessed to me on one occasion' occurred in both appraisals. Penelope Long demanded a centre-page position before she would commence her consideration of whether such a high-priced restaurant deserved her readers' attention, and whether the fire at Aphrodite's should be viewed as a blatant neglect of fire regulations or an unavoidable tragedy. Stephen Boyce flung aside his dirty laundry, hunting for the file where he had kept the menus from Aphrodite's which would enable him to give an overview of André Bouchon's culinary style.

Dylan Tusk charged into the ailing cuttings 'library', a cupboard in the overcrowded offices of *Freewheel* and rewrote a former interview with a new opening paragraph beginning, 'As I gazed in horror at the smouldering remains of London's most celebrated restaurant, I felt a momentary shudder. My blood ran cold. Then I remembered. This building, constructed in 1869 ('Check', he noted on his draft) was once notorious. A former coffee house, it was visited by a mysterious presence . . .'

Sitting surrounded by exotic fruits in her Intertel eyrie, Didi Kowalski searched through her card index. What would André Bouchon have to say about papaya, guava, feijoa, granadilla? It was several months since he had filled the screen of *Table for One*, and that shelved sequence of the Ambassador's dinner was a yawn a second. Could she fit him in? It would be nice. Dear old – well not so old – André Bouchon.

'Why don't we have him for the butter tasting?' suggested Deirdre.

'He's a bit too grand for "Taste for a Test",' retorted Didi.

'Have him doing a *beurre blanc*, then. Little end-piece.'

Didi sucked her finger and delayed her reply.

'I'll see whether I can fit it in,' she said. Why hadn't she thought of that?

'Amazing, the coverage on Aphrodite's,' Antony said. 'I wouldn't have thought they'd give all that space to a chef.'

Laura smiled. 'I care about André. He's his own worst enemy. I told him a couple of years ago he should buy into Aphrodite's. But no. He preferred to take his wife on some ludicrously expensive holiday.'

'Talking of holidays, Nigel—'

'Where is Nigel?'

'Seeing a client.'

'Why isn't that in the diary?'

'Last minute. Sorry, Laura. Anyway, he was wondering if he could take a week off.'

'When?' asked Laura sharply.

'He thought January, when things were less busy. Getting over Christmas and all that.'

'That is precisely when *we* will be more busy catching up. He should know that by now.'

'So what should I tell him?'

'I'll let him know when I can spare him.'

Laura sounded irritated, as she did whenever the subject of holidays was mentioned. Bank clerks and check-out girls took holidays.

'He really needs some time off, Laura. Been working late nearly every night.'

'I've said he can come with us to Bombay for the Rialto opening. That'll be at least a week.'

Antony did not pursue the subject. If you were taken on at LDA, it was reward enough to have a monthly paycheck. Without dedication, one might just as well be a bus driver.

He walked out of the Sanctum and stood looking round the Studio like a prefect seeking out the shirkers. Simon appeared to have nothing to do. He was leafing through a magazine.

'I say, Simon, would you mind awfully making two copies of this lot?'

He put the cuttings in front of Simon, and walked nonchalantly back to the imposing desk which Laura had chosen especially for him.

Laura looked at her watch and calculated her schedule. Two more appointments. Then leave. Howard was coming. What dress should she wear? The one Howard had bought her in Paris? It would show rather too much of her body, which, she supposed, was his reason for choosing it. It was something Didi might have flaunted herself in. What had led him to imagine that she would wear red satin, or something slit up to her thighs? Was that how he saw her? He was hardly the kind of man to advertise the fact that he could afford a mistress. Anyhow, that was not how she saw herself.

What husband ever talked to his wife as he talked to her, with such self-deprecating openness? She hid nothing from him, could say anything to him and no subject was taboo. One night as they lay peacefully in bed he had talked of his wife, not because she asked, but because he wanted her to know.

'You can't go on lying, at least I can't. It was hard to do, but eventually I told her there was another woman who meant a lot to me. Just that. She became completely hysterical. She howled, rolled on the floor like a rabid dog and then she threatened suicide. I thought I had married a strong, independent woman and instead here was someone who was totally dependent on me. It had never crossed my mind. She couldn't accept that I love you. She wouldn't let me go. And I couldn't do it. I can't do it. I just can't. Not at the moment. I quite understand if you would prefer us not to meet. I can offer you nothing.'

If only he knew how much he did offer, if only he knew that she had, really, come to accept his impossible dilemma, if only he could be convinced that she would not have changed places with his wife for the world, that having his confidence and respect was all she wanted.

Tonight they would be appearing in public for the first time, and he wanted her to leave the Studio early.

The Grey Men were tapping at keyboards, answering calls, preparing reports but his hand was resting between her wet legs and she lay swooning and floating in the darkness.

When she dredged herself up from semi-consciousness, Howard was lying on his back, his arms folded behind his head.

'Can we talk now?'

'I want to remember, how wonderful it was.'

'I'm flattered.'

'Don't you sometimes wish we could stay here all day and all night?'

'Come, darling. It's time you got dressed.'

She wondered if he had noticed that her cheeks were damp, as tears of relief and exhilaration escaped between her lashes. As her body slowly awoke, she wanted him again.

'Again?'

She would not answer, but lay on top of him, pressed her tongue down inside his ear, moved her fingers inch by inch down his long body and rested them on his cock, which stiffened under her touch.

'You do? Come on. Tell me what you want.'

Her voice was stifled, and she was unable to ask. She did not ask men. They gave. She received.

Howard pushed her to one side, and sprang off the bed. 'You're becoming insatiable. Go and get ready. We'll be late.'

Laura stood under the shower and shuddered as the icy cold jet of water washed away the smell of sex, numbing her open pores, then seized her bottle of body lotion and rubbed the familiar perfume over herself which, as she grew warmer, would exude a distinctive aroma recalling closed panelled rooms hung with silk tapestry, dust scented with strange potpourris, Eastern rugs on cedar-wood floors. Her smell.

'You're not going to take all night, are you?' Howard called from the living room.

The white dress. Hastily pulling up the sheets on the disordered bed, she unwrapped her treasure from its chrysalis cover. Each dress was a mark in her history. This one she had bought when Howard had been silent for a week. Utter extravagance. She had no occasion to wear it, but for this evening it was absolutely right. She slipped it on, and the silk Fortuny pleats billowed round her as she opened her bedroom window to let in the cool evening breeze. Then she piled up her long hair, encircled her head with a gold knotted cord and examined herself in the mirror. The goddess Athene on a temple frieze. Yes, she thought, that is me. Scudding across Olympus.

'Oh,' said Howard.

'Don't you like it?'

'Why aren't you wearing the red dress?'

'I love it but not for this occasion.'

'You look as though you're about to play a harp in the foyer at Claridge's. It's the kind of thing my wife would wear.'

'Charming. I thought you said she had no taste.'

He ignored the sarcasm. 'I've been so looking forward to seeing you wear it. If you didn't like it, you should have said. I could have changed it.'

'No, it's beautiful. Really.'

The disappointment on his face was more than she could bear. As she exchanged white for red, she scarcely looked in the mirror. How vivid it was and how it clung, revealing her long thighs, her small breasts. Titters would greet her as she ascended the everlasting staircase, she was sure.

'That's better.'

He moved quickly towards the front door and could hardly have observed her. The smooth satin was as slimy as a fish wrapped in plastic. She picked up her long skirt and navigated herself into Howard's black Mercedes. When she bent her leg the slit parted like a yawning grin.

'It makes me feel like a Parisian tart in the Bois de Boulogne,' she said. Howard laughed and started the engine.

Laura said little as they drove from Chelsea towards the Rialto Hotel. The pale, delicately coloured cosmetics she had carefully applied to accompany the white dress were quite wrong for this dramatic colour. Her face would look strangely detached from her body. Perhaps she could borrow some red lipstick from Didi.

'I understand your ex-husband has some megalithic plan, big Spanish development. Golf course, leisure complex, something like that.'

'Really? He suggested I join him on a boat trip off Spain.'

'Spain's a very open market now. They're falling over backwards for foreign investment.'

'Do we have to talk about Jack, Howard?'

'Of course not. Just idle thoughts. I'm interested in the way he operates. Only from the business point of view. I'm curious to know what he's doing with the twenty million he's raised from the MacCrae Bank.'

The gold-lettered notice in the foyer announced 'The Illustra Foods/MaCrae Awards of Excellence'. The reflection in the sheets of mirrors lining the way to the ballroom showed a streak of blood-orange red as Laura moved gracefully down the wide stairs, looking ahead of her.

Chefs and restaurateurs, wine-merchants, journalists, radio and television producers, bankers, stockbrokers, property developers, lawyers, accountants – an assembly of the faintly great, the sometimes good, the worthily mediocre and the shoddily bad; but they did not rub shoulders. They stood by the white-robed tables holding long-stemmed glasses discreetly fizzing with champagne, unaccustomed to the vast space, huddling near, but not too near, with stiff backbones like a collection of newly planted young pines set in geometric rows to replace the untidy straggle of natural growth. Rarely did they see one another from a distance, full length, and some who bumped into each other regularly at crowded receptions took a moment to establish recognition.

It took Didi, flanked by the two delectably dinner-suited men in her life, a moment to recognize the occupant of a long heliotrope-coloured gown with a spray of orchids pinned to her henna-dyed hair.

'It belonged to my grandmother. Isn't it splendid?'

Caliope stepped back to allow Didi to appreciate the extent of her transformation.

'Stunning colour, Cal.'

'You're looking unusually virginal, my dear. In a decadent way. It rather suits you.' Caliope chuckled and then gave a quick intake of breath. 'Tell me, dear, who's going to get the main award?'

'I swore not to tell,' said the always-knowing Didi.

'I loathe being kept in suspense. It gives me hot flushes. Tell me if I need to put on some more face powder. I wouldn't want to accept an award with a shiny nose.'

'Your nose is perfect.'

'Bound to be Sigmund or Magnus, but perhaps I'll receive a consolation prize. Which, of course, is no consolation at all.'

Caliope turned her head from side to side as though scanning a crowded airport terminal for a dear friend. Could that be Lady Knowles? No, she never wore green. Remarkable resemblance.

'You know John?'

'Naturally. And Stephen.' She grasped his hand. 'Tell me which restaurant I should be seen at. I've been so busy. Quite out of touch.'

'It's not a bad start, being here,' he replied.

'Oh, but the whole world minus his dog is here. Gracious. Do my eyes deceive me?'

Didi turned round, trying to avoid spiking her gauzy skirt with the stiletto heels which kept her rooted to the spot.

There was a moment of hushed silence, raised eyebrows and then there was nothing for it but to stare.

'Even I wouldn't wear that,' exclaimed Didi.

'You have rather more to show than she has,' said Caliope.

'Not slit up to my fanny.'

Didi took in the tall, imposing man at Laura's side.

'Gawd!'

'I beg your pardon?'

The voice of Dorothy Dean had involuntarily taken over, and sweet sixteen briefly occupied the white muslin dress with puffed sleeves and heart-shaped neckline ready for the first 'Excuse Me Could I Have This Dance?' until Didi Kowalski returned with a clutch of vowels which would have been greeted with approval by her elocution teacher.

'She's with Sir Howard Riley. You must know him.'

'I don't know any Rileys, dear.'

'Chairman of Illustra Foods.'

'You don't say?'

Didi whispered close to Caliope's bejewelled ear. 'Married.'

'Ah. I see. One of those,' boomed Caliope reflectively.

'She is being rather blatant about it.'

'About what?'

'Bonking him.'

'How on earth can you tell?'

'Oh, Cal, honestly. The dress! Girls always go shopping when they've had a good lay and buy something they regret.'

'Do they?' said Caliope, fixing her beady gaze on Didi's white muslin. 'I don't.'

The banqueting manager of the Rialto announced to the lords, ladies and gentlemen that they could now be seated.

'Shame you're not on our table, John,' said Stephen. 'It would be much more fun if you were. Come and join us for coffee.'

'Thanks. I will.'

John was beginning to enjoy the threesome Didi created

around herself and was no longer jealous. He was the one who was going back to her bed.

Laura was sandwiched between Magnus Shaw and Sigmund Halberstadt. On the opposite side of the wide round table was Didi, with Howard on one side and Viscount Alloway on the other. Before the first course arrived, Howard strode up to the flower-bedecked platform and took the microphone.

'Ah,' thought Stephen, salivating at the printed menu.

'Caviar. Your favourite,' said Didi, leaning across the table, breasts to the fore. 'Although it's hardly likely to be Beluga. Not with all this lot.'

Sir Howard Riley was effortlessly broadcasting his opening address. Laura was entranced. There was no-one who remotely matched him.

'Sh, sweetest,' said Stephen to Didi. 'Behave.'

'Do I have to?' she said in a low resonant voice.

Laura gave her a momentary, barely perceptible glare.

'Do you find it rather hot in here?' Sigmund Halberstadt said, addressing his rival.

'No. If anything it is rather chilly, I would say.'

'I must be getting ill.'

'Perhaps you've eaten something,' said Magnus Shaw complacently. 'Or have you forgotten your pills?'

'Banquet food. Ugh! Does one have to sit through this?'

Laura turned away. How despicable they were. All of them. Flaunting their masks of boredom, their private preoccupations. Perhaps she had organized the evening badly. Howard had wanted to give the prizes first, but she had insisted that if he did so the evening would go downhill.

She heard the muffled clapping of inattentive spectators as resounding approval, but before he sat down Howard whispered, 'We should have given the prizes first. I hope they don't start leaving.'

'It was a wonderful speech,' she said.

Sir Howard Riley appeared to have made little impact

on a table near the back of the lofty room, built for ballroom orchestras and stately quicksteps.

'Your place must be crawling with famous people,' remarked Dylan Tusk to John, as he cut vigorously through his mousseline. 'Hot-bed of gossip, I suppose.'

'You don't hear much in the kitchen.'

'All the same, if you get to hear . . . I'm doing this gourmet social column. *Freewheel*, natch. Thousand words they give me. You like cars?'

'I'm thinking about getting a Porsche.' Or, rather, Didi was thinking about a Porsche.

'Porsche? You must be joking. Tell you what, I can do you a great deal on a Nissan lookalike. Fantastic motor. I just come back from the Pyrenees. Goes up mountains like a knife through butter. Vroom! Jus' like that. Took the wife. She was sick. Doesn't like heights. Bloody marvellous, isn't it? You don't want a fuckin' Porsche, mate. Honest. Take it from me.'

'Are you insulting my motorcar?' said Sebastian North loftily.

'Cor blimey! You got a Porsche? Zi-Zi's must be doin' all right then. Is it true Princess Di drops in for raw fish?'

'It has been known,' replied Sebastian.

'She came with her brother to the Eglantine last week.' John was learning the art of the throwaway.

'Must have been slumming, then,' retorted Sebastian. Failing to recognize the traditional chefs' banter, Dylan narrowed his eyes at the prospect of lead columnfodder. 'Top chefs fight over royals.' Or how about 'Vying for Di'?

'Oh!' Didi looked in disbelief at the white muslin veiling her breasts on which a large blob of *tomate concassée* had landed with the force of an aerial bird dropping. 'How on earth did that happen?'

Before Stephen had time to extract his crumpled handkerchief, Didi's neighbour had sprung to the rescue.

'May I?' Sir Howard dipped his napkin into a glass of

mineral water and handed it to her. Stephen was mildly irritated.

'I can't help feeling worried, Sir Howard. If one is concerned about the highest standards, it is rather dispiriting to see that you're expanding the fast-food division.'

'Does it show?' cried Didi.

'We are up-grading that section. I can't really discuss it now, but why don't you come round to Illustra House and talk with some of the directors? We would value your comments.' He turned towards Didi. 'It hardly shows. Really. Such a pretty dress.'

'Have you been to Maclintock Castle again?' began Didi. 'Such a divine place.'

'I'll be going with my wife next weekend as a matter of fact. The fishing is superb. Do you fish by any chance?'

Didi laughed. Sir Howard glanced briefly at Laura. Her face was pale and she had left most of what was on her plate.

'Only one more course to go, Laura.'

Strange how she could hear his voice through a mêlée of conversation. 'You didn't tell me your wife liked fishing,' she said.

Now Didi knew. That look. It was unique. A man might miss it but not Didi.

'Laura, you must come to dinner next week. John's cooking for me on Sunday. There's an absolutely gorgeous man I want to introduce you to.'

The pudding was solemnly distributed round the table, a riot of chocolate nestling against marinaded oranges which Didi and Stephen spooned into with abandon.

'You must try this, Laura,' said Stephen, directing a portion from his plate towards her. 'It's the only decent thing so far.'

She opened her mouth a fraction, and then shook her head. 'I couldn't. I've eaten so much today.' She gave a forced smile and brightened her voice. 'Howard, I think it's time for you to . . .'

Sir Howard said he would be brief. During the minute

334

or so of his introductory remarks to the announcing of the award-winners, the two elder statesmen of gastronomy were both looking down modestly at the overly patterned carpet below them and having further thoughts as to the most gainful way of spending the ten thousand pounds prize money. Didi was preparing her congratulatory smile. A five-minute slot had already been apportioned on *Table for One* for the winner and she did so hope it would be Magnus Shaw and not Sigmund Halberstadt who was prone to an unfortunate on-air stutter which drove the finicky man in the editing suite berserk.

'And now I would like to ask Stephen Boyce to come forward and accept the first Illustra Foods/MacCrae Award for Outstanding Achievement.'

Didi let out a gasp, a shriek and immediately put her hand over her mouth.

As Stephen pushed back his chair and made his way past the tables towards the platform, her heart pounded so violently it was as though a pneumatic drill was vibrating at full power and splitting her in two.

'Curious choice,' murmured Magnus to Sigmund.

'I suppose one should encourage the younger generation. How much longer do you suppose this is going to take?'

Magnus looked at his watch. 'My car's coming in half an hour.'

Stephen took the microphone, clutching his envelope and his framed award.

'Usually when one has reached the stage of satisfaction after a wonderful meal,' he said, 'there is only one thing to look forward to. The bill.' (Laughter.) 'I can honestly say that this is the first occasion when I have been rewarded for eating. This is totally unexpected and I'm sure there are those who deserve this award more than I. However, I would like to thank Illustra Foods and the MacCrae Bank for honouring the *Daily Reporter*, and my humble efforts.'

'I'm going to cry,' Didi said to Laura, dabbing her eyes. 'It's too, too wonderful.'

Once Stephen had returned to his chair, she sat through the descending categories of awards, neither seeing nor hearing.

'Your turn, sweetest.'

'What?'

'Your name is being called.'

Didi sprang to her feet and realized she was shoeless. Everyone in the room turned to look towards her as she fumbled to squeeze her hot feet into the tortuous stiletto sandals, and she then walked in a trance towards the platform. Didi Kowalski, recipient of the Illustra Foods/ MacCrae Special Award for Outstanding Achievement in Visual Communication.

'Thank you, thank you. I'm so thrilled. For once in my life, I can't think of a thing to say.' She gazed round at her smiling audience and went on: 'This award isn't just for me. It's for my fabulously talented team at Intertel who put up with me every day. And my eight million viewers who care. Thank you, Sir Howard. Thank you, Viscount Alloway.'

Ten awards later, Sir Howard and the cheery Viscount took their places for the last brandy.

'That went beautifully,' remarked Laura.

'I suppose they'll all get sloshed now,' said Alloway. 'By the way who was that fierce lady in blue?'

'Penelope Long.'

'She a leftie? I can sniff 'em a mile off.'

'She's a good journalist,' said Laura.

'Never does any harm giving the odd hand-out to the left,' said Howard. 'She might lay off Illustra Foods for a while.'

'I don't know how you can write for a left-wing paper without a private income,' said Didi.

Stephen laughed.

'Not being able to afford silk knickers wouldn't worry her,' Stephen said. 'We do need someone to be serious, darling.'

'But I am serious!' Didi protested.

'You don't have to be serious tonight,' said Howard. 'You know something, Didi? You remind me of the girl I first fell in love with. A long time ago.'

'Do I look like an old-fashioned girl?' Didi turned to give Stephen a knowing smile.

Howard started to rise from his chair. 'Well, everyone, I have to be off at the crack of dawn, so I must say goodbye. Laura, thank you so much for your help. Wonderful evening.' He pecked her on the cheek and murmured, 'I'll ring you from Brussels.' He didn't turn round on his way out.

'Don't say no, Laura,' said Didi. 'You're partying with Stephen, John and me.'

The constricting shoes were kicked off. 'I'm going to get John. Stay there.'

In a flurry of white muslin, Didi ran across the ballroom.

Stephen sat down next to Laura, and put a stray chocolate truffle on her plate. 'Try it. Seven out of ten. Or take it home for the cat.'

'I don't have a cat.'

Stephen studied her for a moment. He tried to steer clear of the intimate intricacies of other people's lives but tonight he saw Laura differently. It was as though she had given up making the effort to please, and he had never observed this before.

'Will you make me a hamburger? I really fancy one.'

'Stephen! Where on earth do you put it all?'

'I would like it cooked under the grill with lashings of butter, a few capers, seed mustard . . .'

'All I've got at home is cottage cheese and radicchio.'

'Then we'll go to Freeman's and get Tad to make hamburgers. It's not too late. He never knocks off till one.' Stephen took her by the hand and pulled her to her feet. 'It must be the award. I'm ravenous.'

'I'm sorry, Stephen. I really should go home.'

'Oh, forgive me. Is he – or rather are you – has he, um . . .'

337

'You heard him.' Laura bit her lip. 'He's off to Brussels at dawn.'

'So what are we waiting for?'

'Very well, let's go and see Tadeus. I'll go home first and take off this ghastly dress.'

'Absolutely not. I love it. With your hair . . . Very Augustus John. Anyway. I shall enjoy spending Mr Illustra's money. I've already started planning the ultimate trip.'

'Which is?'

'Not telling you till I come back. I'll write you an enigmatic postcard and you can guess. Did you have anything to do with the selection for the awards?'

'I made one or two suggestions.'

He kissed her hand. 'Thank you, my dear. You're an angel.'

For the few hours until dawn, Laura, Stephen, John, Didi and Tadeus were the closest of friends, like members of a touring company who have lived together for several months, having forgotten where they came from, or where they would go to next. They kissed, teased, confessed, bitched, giggled and made grand resolutions which would be forgotten by the next day.

Laura was leaning against Stephen, and the dining room was moving slowly round like the restaurant in the Post Office Tower once did. 'I'm drunk,' she said.

She was carried into the taxi, she thought by John but it might have been Tadeus. Yes, didn't he lurch in with her and say he was coming home with her, and that he fancied her like mad? And now she was at home and the cushions still bore the imprint of Howard's body. The bed was smoothed over, but still the sweet smell lingered. The white dress draped over a chair, the half-full glasses with flat champagne they hadn't had time to finish, the whole room breathing his presence as though he would walk in any moment and say, 'Are you ready? Let's go.' And he had left a message. Stopped at a phonebox on to the way back to . . .

'It's me. Stephen. Drunk and desperate. Laura. Oh, God, I didn't mean to start like this. Don't switch off. When I was twenty they said I was going to be a great British writer. They published my poetry, and put on my play at the Royal Court. I was twenty. New Osborne. Fuck Osborne. Is he writing still? I've just won a prize. For being second rate. In my business, they like . . . failures. Who else would write about the contents of their stomach? My place stinks. I'll . . . I'll . . . No, I won't. Honestly, I won't. Life is good. They say it is. You see, what . . . I can't . . . Don't switch off. Didi. That is . . . Didi. Listen. Listen. Didi thinks I am touched . . . with genius. She's fucked off with John. She. To, to, spin around on his cock. That's what girls do. They adore crea- creativity. Fas-cinated by it. Stephen, you're so, so talented. Loves me. Oh, why am I talking? Why? Why? Yes. I do mind. I mind. And she thinks I don't. I want to kill that smug, muscle-toned, hard-packed . . . prick. Laura? He doesn't have to try. Why am I saying this? Oh, God. I'm drunk. I should tell you a joke. Are you all right? Really? Speak to me. Why are we all in such a fucking mess? I should have said . . .'

The tape ran on. Nothing else. Bleep. End of message. Stephen had put down the receiver.

I will make myself some coffee. Instead of howling. Coffee. Lots of mineral water. I hope you stink of my perfume. I hope she wakes up and cuts you with her razor voice. I'll give your red dress to the cleaning lady.

There was a memo pad in the kitchen and Laura scrawled, 'Ring Stephen.' She wondered why she had filled the kettle. Peeling off the red dress, she aimed it at the waste-paper basket and flung herself on the bed.

15

'I'll have a Danish pastry.'

The waitress knew the kind he liked, the one with royal icing and a cherry scattered with chipped almonds. Old Mr Beck was looking cavernous, his complexion was parchment yellow, and when he removed his spectacles to rub his eyes, she noticed deep aubergine-coloured circles as though he had been resurrected that very morning in some laboratory.

'It's got cold again. Are you well, Mr Beck?'

He nodded. There he was, seated outside under the canopy, watching the world from his usual wicker chair, anticipating a frothy coffee and a sticky bun, wishing he had the energy of youth. Why should anyone wish to bring terror to an old man? Sending his restaurant up in flames? . . . His memory lurched backwards, trying to dredge up faces, conversations, but all he could recall were evenings, of laughter, pretty girls being handed presents, the pâtés, the sausages, the suckling pig, the *tartes*. How ravenously they had eaten! And how well! He had never tasted such cooking. And the wines, dusty from the cellar, the ribald songs, turning over the tables, dancing, showering coins . . . He did not remember hatred.

A mirror-polished red Ferrari squealed to a halt, two wheels on the pavement, and a tall, tanned man in a cream suit jumped out.

'Hey, Mr Beck! Mind if I join you? Jack Leone. We met at Aphrodite's.'

'How do you do? Yes, I remember you.'

'I just couldn't believe the fire. Guys get careless in the

kitchen, I guess. Terrible for you. How many years you had that place?'

'Over twenty.'

'You know, it's my favourite place in town. Done more deals there than any place else.'

'We are fortunate to have a loyal clientele.'

'They'll all come back when you reopen, believe me.'

'That may be some time off. We have to find the cause. It may take months.'

'Needn't take that long.'

'Depends if it was arson, Mr Leone. One can't rule it out nowadays. Someone gets dismissed because he can't get along with André Bouchon. Who knows?'

'Is there much damage down there?'

'The kitchen will have to be refitted. Complete re-decoration.'

'But nothing big, nothing structural?'

'I believe not.'

'Could have been worse then. Take you no time to reopen. Why don't you go on a vacation, get the hell out for a few weeks?'

Mr Beck dropped his head towards his chest.

'You OK?'

'I must go home. I forgot my pills.'

Jack insisted on driving him back. As they both entered the gloomy, musty hall of the Beck residence, Sushi came running towards them.

'Cute dog.'

'It belongs to my daughter.'

Beck sank into a chair while Jack brought him some brandy and sat down opposite him. After days of silence, Mr Beck was slowly coaxed into conversation. The Lord moved in mysterious ways, and this young American was a true Christian. Beck liked Americans.

The sky-blue pool of the Palm Springs health club was the perfect antidote to that musty apartment. Jack plunged into the water and did a flailing crawl up and down, splashing the portlier members whose preferred method of locomotion was the more leisurely chin-above-the-waterline breaststroke. He covered more lengths in a day than they would in a week. No time for a work out. Shower. Wash hair. Meet Charlie.

The last time Charlie Braithwaite had been in a place like this was in Italy. Elaine would remember where. Same kind of style, rococo she called it. Like their en suite bathroom at home. Gilt and marble and mirrors and twiddly bits. As he walked to the poolside bar in his navy blue pinstripe suit, costing the decor (all white marble and palm trees, real that, he touched one, and a fountain, high-class gold plate), he wished he had worn something more casual.

Practically naked they were. Two girls, in glitter bathing costumes cut so high at the side and low in front he wondered why they bothered, sat side by side on exercise bicycles pedalling in unison, long brown legs, endless thighs, gold chains round the ankle, cherry-red fingernails, cherry-red lips, cherry-red toenails. Their eyes were glued dreamily to the middle distance, somewhere between the rosewood doors of the changing rooms and the large wall mosaic of nymphs clustered by a river bank. What figures! Charlie blinked. They must be there for something else, those wafer-thin-hipped bodies. Pedalling that slow wasn't exercise and they weren't counting calories, either. Pretending they weren't watching every man that came in, but he knew they were. You couldn't help but stare.

'Can I get you something?'

The barman in a black satin singlet embroidered in gold lettering with *joie de vivre* over a pair of red-sequined Marilyn Monroe lips leaned over the black marble bar. Real veined marble.

'Would they like something too?'

'Oh, they don't drink, sir. They'll be giving swimming lessons in a minute.'

'Swimming lessons? That right? Gin and tonic, lad. Double.'

He was only distracted for a few minutes, for he felt he was making a spectacle of himself in the tight crumpled suit, hand tailored by the best man in Leeds, which had hung loose in the spring and now strained over him. Beads of sweat appeared on his wide fleshy forehead which he wiped away vigorously with his silk handkerchief.

Jack had rushed into that Spanish development as though he'd discovered a bed of oil. Charlie would have held back a little longer but Jack wanted to be up and running before the competition. If things chanced to go wrong . . . Charlie hadn't slept last night, had to wake up Elaine.

'I'm not saying I don't like him, but he's not my type. He'll always be the boss, Charlie. A bit too clever.'

'I call it business sense. Gerry thinks the world of him.'

'Women see things differently sometimes. Anyway, what's good for you is good for me, so what does it matter what I think?'

When Charlie Braithwaite first flew out to Algeciras and was greeted by that blast of heat, he felt as happy and ebullient as the day when he had opened the Moorland Haven. Walking round the stretch of land with the architect beside him, he could imagine the plans starting to take shape – the barren flatness tamed, soon to be transformed into a golf course of verdant green, plots of land measured out, for the construction of Spanish-style villas, lovely style that, with white arches leading to a shopping arcade and a pool in the shape of a sombrero. Even a play area and a pool for the kiddies. Much better than his idea for a theme park in the Dales, which had failed to attract the necessary investment. Spare cash was going abroad these days, you couldn't trust the economy. When could you ever?

Charlie had kept his eye on trends and scoured the holiday supplements. Nowadays, people weren't so keen on paying good money to bake in the sand. Bad for you, sun was. Gave you cancer and wrinkles. Young folks, maybe, but not the ones with money to spend seeking refined relaxation. Play a round of golf and come back to a frosted margherita and the smell of giant prawns roasting on the barbecue as you sit by the temperature-controlled pool. The fountain splashing, the resident guitarist softly plucking Flamenco airs . . .

And this development would be spotless. Spain without litter and flies and inadequate toilet arrangements. Spain with air-conditioned bars, and boutiques with French resort wear, and fresh whitewash gleaming against the azure sky, and flowers everywhere. And no need for a weather forecast.

When the flattening and excavation had begun, Charlie took a trip down to the port at Algeciras and sat in a bar wondering where all the women were and how those little garlic-ridden men, who spoke as though they had constant phlegm like in the bad old days in the mill towns, could live as they did, all that squalor and stinking oil and rubber rings on little plates. If that was their dinner, no wonder they were such runts. Leone Leisure would show them what life was all about. Charlie had been convinced of that in the early days.

The changing room door swung open, and Jack appeared with a towel round his neck and a pair of tight trunks. You didn't see male bodies like that often, not up North anyway where the norm was small legs and big bums, powerful on top, like Charlie. The two girls turned their heads together like well-drilled cygnets in *Swan Lake*, still pedalling *lento*, *lento*.

'Hi, Jack.'

'Hi, girls.'

As he sat down and stretched his well-honed legs in front of him, Jack waved at the barman.

'Good to see you, Charlie. Ah. That's better.' He tilted his head in the direction of the two girls. 'If you take them to see a fight, it's on the house. You like wrestling?'

'I could do.'

Charlie's briefcase was out of place amongst the potted

palms and yukkas, and the marble and the velvet-upholstered chairs. He lifted it on to his knee and opened it with a loud click.

'Well, how's it coming along? You got the pictures, Charlie? 'Cause I'm gonna need them. And I'll want the new brochure. The guys in MacCrae are giving me a hard time over the top-up loan. They're not too "happy" – how about that? – not too happy about the fact that Leone Leisure is a few points down on pre-tax profits this year. Whadda they expect? Everyone's down. So Pizza Palace has a blip? Some years you get that. No-one in this goddamn country understands about money. They give with one hand and claw back with the other. I guarantee that when we'll have cleaned up in Spain, they'll all have their noses in the jam pot. Ten years too late. They're sticking over the extra five mill, Charlie. Crazy. I'm gonna have to work real hard to loosen them up. Alloway says he can't do anything. Board decision. Fucking board decision. There are times when I wonder why I hang out in this Disney land.'

'Here. Some's a bit out of focus, but take a look.'

'They solved that drainage problem?'

'Oh, yes. Look at that road. See them trees? All along. And the clubhouse, that'll be over there. Don't you love the tiles? Hand-made, they are, Jack. The photo doesn't do them justice.'

'How far behind are we?'

'Only a couple of months.'

'Christ! Every month we hang about MacCrae eats us alive with interest charges.'

'I'm doing the best I can, Jack.'

'Let's get outta here. I need some lousy London air.'

Being in one place for more than an hour or so made Jack restless. Walking the streets gave him ideas and when Charlie visited London he made sure his shoes were comfortable. Jack received his update on Leone Leisure (Northern) Developments striding down Park Lane, with Charlie taking two steps to his one. He was becoming used to the constant distraction, the comments on the changing façades as developers moved in and developers moved out . . . And now. Lunch in the best, the most exclusive place in town.

'You like the design?' Jack led Charlie into the dining room of the Eglantine and stopped by the door. 'Isn't it just beautiful? Smart girl, Laura. Did it all.'

Charlie thought it was too dark, needed more lights on the walls and you didn't need that much space for a table, but he decided to withhold his comments.

'Like my wife. She designed the Moorland Haven by herself as well. No help whatsoever, not on the design side. You remember how it was before Charlie's Brasserie? Elaine would go for those pink flowers. Oh, she does love pink.'

'What do you reckon on turnover?'

'Turnover?'

'Here.'

'I'll ask George. Used to work for me, you know.'

'Should be over a mill.'

'You think?'

'Charlie, look. See these people?' Jack lowered his voice. 'These kinda people we need. Hundred a head, that's nothing. When I've gotten hold of Aphrodite's—'

'Jack, I think that should be on a back burner.'

'It won't be like this, though. I'm gonna go for a lighter feel. Something atmospheric. Needs opening out. Yeah. Make all the difference.'

'Hold your horses, Jack. We can't be doing with another big project. Not with Spain.'

'You advising me, Charlie?'

'No, I wouldn't do that. But it's not the moment. Maybe when we've halfway sold the villas . . .'

'And I want waitresses in casual clothes. But sexy. Chic. Silk shirts, unbuttoned down to here. Well-spoken but none of that snotty aren't you lucky to get service.'

'Jack, listen.'

'No, you listen. Sit down. Our table, this one. OK. You wanna know why I'm gonna take over Aphrodite's? We'll

346

take the set menu and I'll give you the story.'

The waiter was over in five seconds. Charlie timed him. When the first plates arrived, he hadn't even had time to read the menu. Must remember to take one for Elaine.

'I'm a kid of twenty-three with my own take-out food business in New York. My uncle Luigi asks me to cater a gallery opening in New York. Son of a friend of his paints, an artist written up in the *New York Times*. He wants a real nice occasion, so I make a fantastic buffet and do it at cost. Lobster, oysters, salmon en croute, rib of beef – the lot. You never seen anything like that with galleries 'cause they act real mean when they entertain. It was quite something. The people. Every one you'd notice. Used to money. They could have bought a Picasso like they were going shopping for a pair of shoes. And then I see this young girl. She's in a white dress, long gold-coloured hair, pale face. And I tell you, Charlie, I just knew. Don't ask me why, but it was like I'd seen her before, in a dream. That's the one, I said to myself. And I'd had girls. But she was—'

'Love. I know. Happened just the same to me when I met Elaine.'

'I could see she was aristocratic. Family going way back, you could tell by the face. But I didn't care. That girl was going to marry me. I dated her twice and then I followed her back home to London . . . Sound crazy to you? That's how I am. If she was in England, so be it. I'd make it in England. Didn't faze me. I came over and we both knew then. Romeo and Juliet. That's how it was. I worshipped her, Charlie. Still do.'

Jack paused to gulp down a few prawns.

'I go down one weekend to this cottage. (I thought she lived in a great house, my mistake.) So her Ma comes to the door and you know the first thing she says? "You are exactly as I imagined, Mr Leone." That's all. Then she goes out into the garden. I watch her through the windows and she starts pruning the fucking roses. Snip, snip, snip. Like she was cutting off my balls.'

Jack speared an asparagus head.

'Later, Laura cooked supper and her mother looked straight past me. Like I was some garbage collector. Then she asks would I mind "awfully" getting some wood for the fire. "Chilly," she says. "It's getting chilly." Yeah. Chilly. And me, sweating.'

'Was her Dad there as well?'

'Oh no. He ran off with some chick when Laura was five. Do you know, she never invited me there again? She didn't need to say I was trash. Now you know why I'm gonna get Aphrodite's.'

'I'm not sure I see the connection.'

'That woman said it all. In this country, there's those that count and those that don't. I didn't.'

Charlie put down his knife and fork. 'It's skin deep, Jack. If they need you they treat you right, believe me.'

'I want to come in, sit by the phone and tell those bastards that we're fully booked. I want the most goddamn snob restaurant in London. And I'm gonna say who comes in. And we will be fully booked. You think I wanna be remembered as a pizza man? Never. If I could buy out this place, I would. But this is Laura's baby. And my wife doesn't sell. Me neither. I buy.'

'I have to say, Jack, doing business is not to do with an emotional attitude. I don't go along with that. Let's think this one through. I'll skip the main and have a pudding. Always did like John's sweets. You don't mind me being blunt?'

Jack sat back and took out a cigar.

'Is your wife, Laura—'

'Ex-wife.'

'Are you sure it's not because of her? If she didn't have this place, would you be after Aphrodite's?'

'I want class, Charlie. Leone Leisure needs a flagship restaurant. Leone Leisure needs to have a Mayfair presence. Like I've told you before. A solid base for future plans.'

'Just wanted to make sure, you understand.'

Charlie looked at Jack for a few moments, like a

348

seasoned trade union negotiator weighing up the mood of the bosses before putting his offer on the table.

'Has it got to lawyers yet? Are you in bed with Beck?'

'Soon, soon.'

'Well, might I suggest a few delaying tactics until we've a better cash-flow situation?'

'So the old guy dies and leaves it to his daughter? He could go any minute. Lives on pills. No, I gotta do this fast. Leave it to me.'

'And the price? What do you reckon he'll take?'

'One and a quarter, with the quarter cash.'

'It's worth double. If he doesn't realize that, his lawyers will.'

'He likes me, Charlie.'

Now he was talking. You never let the bank stand in the way of a good deal.

When someone entered dressed in white against the dark glow of the Venetian blue walls, it made an impact. Charlie gave a broad smile. 'How's my lad then?'

'Fine thanks. Are you keeping well, Mr Braithwaite?' John shook hands with both of his guests.

'Elaine often asks after you. Soft spot for you, John.'

'I trust you enjoyed your meal, Mr Leone?'

'Great. As ever.'

'I can't stay, but would you accept something on the house? A brandy, perhaps?'

As John left, Charlie wrinkled his nose reflectively.

'Started to get London ways, I notice, our John. Mr Braithwaite he called me. Huh! What d'you think he's up to in that kitchen? Is he getting his hands dirty or is he cooking the books?'

'It's called hosting, Charlie. Customers like it.'

'There's none of that in Spain. And, quite frankly, I didn't want to see who was cooking the messes I got. I wouldn't give tuppence for the hygiene, either. We'll have no flies on the counter and the only clean water in the country.'

'See over there, Charlie? Just getting up? Look at those legs.'

George could sense Jack raising his finger in the middle of a crowded room, like an auctioneer spotting a bid. He was over in an instant.

'Yes, Mr Leone?'

'That girl going out. I've forgotten her name.'

'Melissa Desgranges. Sister of Virginia, who writes for *Vogue*. Used to work for Sebastian North and is now with Tadeus Freeman. Not for money, I assume.'

'Freeman. That son of a bitch at the Kitchen Club?'

'The same.'

'Bastard.'

Jack threw down a gold credit card. 'Come on Charlie, let's go. We've got a site to inspect. And you're gonna find a whole load of trouble.'

The front gates of Aphrodite's were locked and the curtains drawn but there was no outward sign of neglect. Charlie left Jack's side to walk across the road and stood with his legs apart, shading his eyes against the sun, checking the roof, the stone facing, the window frames, looking for signs of subsidence, imprinting the exterior on his developer's mind. Jack was already striding down the street, turning a corner so that Charlie had to break into a trot to catch up.

'Mr Beck? You remember Charlie Braithwaite? He knows more about buildings than anyone. Expert on fire damage. He'll take a good look and give you an honest opinion. That's what you need. The insurance company are gonna lie all the way to give the minimum payout.'

As they went down the back steps, Charlie took out his notebook and adopted an expression which was equally appropriate for funerals, redundancies, dry rot, woodworm or the ravages of wind, flood – or fire. He examined every burned-out corner of the kitchen, thumped his foot down on charred floorboards, poked in walls and barked out detailed questions, which the old man was unable to answer.

'It's not great, Mr Beck, I'll tell you straight. Would you like me to write it down in a report? As you're a friend of Jack's, I'd be pleased to do it gratis.'

'Tell me the worst please.'

'Houses like this are like old people. Anything major happens, it's a shock to the system. And you can't do anything piecemeal. No good mending a leg if the heart isn't pumping the blood round. Major surgery, Mr Beck. That's what I would advise. To be on the safe side. How much is your insurance cover?'

'The whole building—'

'Just a moment. Contents cover first.'

'Two hundred and fifty.'

Charlie looked down at the ground then turned on his heel. 'Two hundred and fifty would cover the major structurals. What do you reckon, Jack?'

'New floors, fire regs. Yeah, at least that.'

'Then there's the refurb. Top class job would be—'

'You're talking at least another quarter of a million.'

'I think – and this is only an estimate, you understand – total renovation to the standard required, we'd be talking. Oh. Million and a quarter.'

'I'd go along with that. Mind you, Charlie, I'd like a second opinion.'

'Naturally.'

'I know a first-rate surveyor. Like me to send him round, Mr Beck?'

They stood in the dining room gazing at the blackened gilt, the debris still on the floor, the peeling strips of deep crimson and gold wallpaper.

'It makes you weep,' remarked Jack. 'This place meant a lot to me, Mr Beck. Coming back from abroad and coming straight to Aphrodite's made me feel I was home. A certain kind of perfection created by someone who cares. We're losing sight of that, Charlie. I do believe we are.'

Charlie shifted his weight from one foot to the other and they both looked at Mr Beck, who was fingering his heavy set of keys and clinking them together.

'I will go home and assess the situation. Thank you for coming here today. Goodbye, gentlemen.'

He locked the back door and shuffled away down the pavement, keeping to a straight line like an old crow making his way along the branch of a familiar tree.

'He doesn't have the cash. We're in business.'

'I'm not so sure, Jack. He might keep that place as it is. Do nothing. I've known that before. Dog in the manger stuff. Keep it a ruin and sit on the asset. I had a place in Bradford I was after for years. Magnificent site with period features but the bloody man who owned it didn't give a damn. I watched the roof cave in, the windows broken one by one, the vandals taking everything of value. When I eventually got it, I had to gut the lot.'

Jack grinned and patted Charlie on the back. 'This place is mine,' he said. 'Right. Now we'll show the Spanish commercial attaché how to do business. Ready?'

The Bavarian clock positioned in a corner of Mr Beck's sitting room wheezed and emitted an end-of-season arhythmic 'cuckck . . .oo' five times, even though it was half past six. He stirred from sleep and settled back in the large winged chair, his pale, blotched hands dangling over the arms, waiting until Juliet came home to make his supper. The door bell rang. He hated the metallic sound but he did not think of replacing it, any more than he thought of taking the clock to be repaired. Everything was coming to an end of its natural life, including himself. Perhaps the restaurant, too, had had its day. To be able to cease caring was one of the minor consolations of old age, living in the grey tranquillity of the here and now. The bell rang again. He had forgotten to check that her key was in her handbag which meant she would have locked herself out yet again.

When he opened the door on its chain, he was startled.

'It's Jack. Can I come in?'

The chain was slowly released. 'I brought some orchids

for your daughter. She admired the ones in Aphrodite's, so I thought—'

'How very kind. Forgive me. I was taking a nap.'

Mr Beck tied the sash of his silk morning jacket more tightly around him and accepted the bouquet whilst Jack stood waiting. As he moved off down the hallway towards the kitchen, Jack called out, 'Can we have a word, Mr Beck?'

'Do come in. I beg your pardon, I have only just awakened. Will you accept a glass of sherry? Go into the sitting room. I will join you when I have put the flowers in water. Juliet will arrange them.'

It was the first time Jack had had the opportunity to be alone in this room. He sat accustoming his eyes to the gloom. The furniture was heavy and ornate: a large scrolled chest, a desk large enough to have hidden compartments, faded rugs, fluted wooden standard lamps with silk-pleated fringed shades and a small tree made of semi-precious stones standing in the fireplace tiled in dark green. The pictures, in over-ponderous gilded frames, seemed as though they were painted to be ignored – dark oils of stiffly arranged flowers, a stormy seascape with a distant galleon on the horizon. And there was Juliet as a young girl holding a puppy, long hair in pigtails tied in blue ribbons. The cuckoo clock was out of place, a rustic memento of some holiday, perhaps. The *Encyclopaedia Britannica* of an ancient vintage was lined up perfectly in a ponderous glass bookcase. Jack sat flexing his muscles, reminding himself of health, strength, and young, soft bodies.

'I've been thinking about Aphrodite's, Mr Beck. Charlie's assessment could be a little optimistic. He comes from Leeds and doesn't understand southern overheads. Your place needs a lot of work. Six months, I reckon.'

'Six months.' Mr Beck sipped slowly from his crystal glass.

'And that means six months of constant supervision. Then, at the end of that time, you'll need to woo back the clientele with a big promotional spend. Needs very careful handling.'

'If one were to continue with the undertaking, how would you envisage the total cost?'

'No change out of two million, Mr Beck. Minus insurance pay-out. Say one and a quarter million. Whatever way you work it. You wanna see some figures?'

'There is no point. I don't have the capital. Everything is in trust for Juliet when I die. It will enable her to live in certain comfort.'

Mr Beck stared at the glass, balanced on the arm of his chair.

'Can I make a suggestion?' Jack said.

'Certainly.'

'The way I see it it's a lot of hassle for you. Nowadays, you have to sweat your guts out to get guys to work. They'll rip you off, take every short cut they can . . . I'm used to this kinda thing. I'm gonna make a suggestion. Just a suggestion to see what you think.'

'What kind of suggestion?'

'Suppose I take Aphrodite's off your hands? Even if you were thinking of selling, no-one would take it in that state. Not at what I'm prepared to offer.'

'And what might that be?'

'One and a half million. And I'll give two hundred and fifty thousand in cash.'

Mr Beck gave a slight cough. 'I thank you for your offer. But whatever I decide, I'm not selling. You might as well ask me to sell my home. It is the same. If Aphrodite's no longer belonged to me, it would be the same as cutting off one of my arms.'

Jack took a sip of the Amontillado. Not his favourite drink. 'It was only a suggestion. On the other hand, you could buy a beautiful retirement home. A small castle on the Rhine, or maybe a farmhouse near a quiet little place like Belley. I hear it's ideal for retirement. Peaceful, nice mountains and a fine cathedral, so they tell me. Vineyards, orchards. You can even drive over to Lyon for dinner.

You ever eaten in Lyon? Best food in France, Mr Beck. Eat there and die. That's what they say. You ever been? Rich food, but what the hell? You'd like it, I know that for sure. If you're interested, I could get you a good deal on a property.'

Mr Beck spluttered and clutched his chest. Jack went over to the cupboard and took out a bottle. He shook the contents. 'Trinitro-glycerol. I guess that's what you need right now. Here.'

The old man grabbed the bottle with a shaking hand and tried to undo the cap.

'Allow me. Four be enough?'

Beck shovelled the pills into his mouth and sat staring blankly whilst Jack walked slowly round the room as though he was carrying out an evaluation. He stopped by a picture and peered at the signature.

'Oh, German. I thought it might have been French. Juliet would have been around two at the time? That right? Have I done my sums right? Nineteen forty-three. Yeah, she must have been toddling by then. The Jewish kids you had shot were a little older than that, weren't they, Mr Bachthoven?'

'I think you have mistaken me for somebody else.' The old man's voice was barely audible.

'What did you say?'

'You . . . have made a mistake.'

'Nowhere like France for learning about the joys of food. Must have given you a thrill, too, when the folks around were starving and living on pigshit. But they always brought the best for the SS Obersturmführer, right? Yes, a unique experience and a unique education. I envy you, Mr Bachthoven. I grew up with burgers and dogs. And somehow I never got to acquire a lovely English accent like yours.'

The lock on the door clunked back and a voice called, 'Papa? You've left the chain on.'

'I will see you out. There is no need for us to meet again.'

Jack waited, listening to a low exchange of conversation in the hall, then Juliet walked into the room followed by her yapping dog.

'Sushi, quiet.'

Jack went forward and took her hand. 'You're looking fantastic. Know something? I've been thinking about you.'

'Father wants you to go.'

'I guess he's always been jealous of your young men.'

'I didn't tell him.'

'Of course not. Would you like to take tea with me again? I would be most honoured.'

As Mr Beck re-entered the room, he failed to notice that his daughter's cheeks were flushed, her eyes sparkled and her half-apprehensive, half-joyful expression echoed that of the portrait behind her.

'You will be late for your next appointment, Mr Leone. Come this way.'

Jack followed the old man towards the door. 'For the sake of your daughter, I advise you to accept my offer,' remarked Jack as they walked down the hall. 'The one thing missing in the Mossad records is your exact address, but that only takes a phone call.'

Without pausing to allow the ancient lift to rumble up, Jack ran down flight after flight barely touching the threadbare carpet, out through the swing doors to where the hall porter was standing on guard proudly warding off predators from the bright red car of his dreams.

It was too late to take the alternative route. Sir Howard Riley had heard the traffic warning but he was trapped on the M4.

'How do I cope with the stress? I think women are used to it. We have the advantage because it's second nature. We worry about our husbands, our children, our houses, our friends . . . It's the same with a company. It's another sort of family, really.'

'You make it sound so easy.'

Howard heard the slight laugh, could see her pushing back her hair.

'I can't imagine working in a vacuum, as men do. And it makes us care more. Running a business is all about caring – a successful business that is . . .'

'And listeners. I should tell you Laura also manages to run one of the most famous restaurants in London. In her spare time, I suppose I should add.'

'My restaurant, the Eglantine, started as an idea, a dream. Then it happened. I suppose I've been lucky. My chef, John Crabtree, is absolutely brilliant. I know I'm biased, but I think he serves the best food in the country. Have you eaten there?'

'I have to confess, Laura, that I haven't. But it'll be top of my list. One last question: have you any advice to give those of our listeners who are returning to work after having their families?'

'Wake up in the morning, look in the mirror and say, "I can do it". And learn to like yourself. After that everything is easy.'

Howard felt irritable. He had tried to make Laura understand the intricate workings of commerce, the subtleties of successful enterprise, the strategies of achievement, and now she was reducing his teaching to the level of a knitting pattern.

He had put her out of his mind for several weeks, wearying of the lies and the diversionary journeys to Chelsea, the intensity of their meetings, preferring to spend every minute ensuring that Illustra Foods was set on course for the year two thousand, keeping in the lead, set to dominate the new markets and restlessly pursuing innovation, removing those who could no longer take the pace, giving bonuses to those who proved that they would lay their lives on the line for Illustra Foods, hectoring, urging, addressing . . . There was hardly a moment when he was not pondering some aspect of this vast enterprise. When he returned late in the evening, he merely went through the motions of being at home.

He was thinking about Laura again, wanting her, wanting her young body beneath him, wanting to feel his blood race, wanting to be twenty again.

Laura was trying to adapt to the constant nagging pain of Howard's silence. It was hard to put it out of her mind, despite the daily impetus of events, each replacing and pushing down the other into oblivion like a mounting pile of autumn leaves.

Sometimes, when she arrived early at the deserted Studio or sat curled up on her sofa waiting for exhaustion to change into drowsiness, she found herself staring at the telephone, willing it to ring, willing it, willing it until she jumped, convinced that she had heard the first note of the trilling tone. Could she but transfer her thoughts to him, make him stretch out his arm, pick up the receiver . . . In the night, her dreams ended in the echoing ring and half asleep she lunged for the telephone.

How dare he make me feel like this? said Anger. How dare he send me back to the time when I had washed my hair ready for a date and had to ask my mother why he didn't ring when he said he would? He may be ill, said Concern. Something may have happened. No, it would have been in the news. They would have given him a full-page obituary. He is trying to get hold of you, but he can't. In a hospital bed or feverish at home guarded by his wife. Of course he will call as soon as he can. You know he will. Why not ring his office and speak to his secretary? She will put you out of your misery. The last thing you should do, retorted Anger. Then he will know that you are worried about him. The office will gossip. That dreadful girl who's always pestering. If she rings again, tell her Sir Howard Riley is in a meeting. You weren't seriously thinking of calling Lady Riley again? Are you out of your mind?

Howard lurked behind her thoughts when she briefed Antony or berated Nigel, when she had discussions with the accountant, even when she rushed out to buy a dress. What would he have said? Would he have liked it? When she made a successful bid for a difficult account, he was saying, 'Well done, Laura. I knew you could do it.' And at night. At night, she heard his low resonant voice in her ear as she spread herself over the bed, imagining his body over hers as she ran her hands down her thighs, down over the hairless mound, tracing the sweet-smelling resinous liquid of her unfulfilled desire. He loves you, said Concern. He despises you, said Anger.

'Stephen on the line. Are you taking calls?' asked Antony as he brought Laura her freshly roasted, freshly ground morning coffee. He was becoming more and more protective, an assiduous Cerberus who was never off guard. The Laura Douglas empire was growing on his well-tailored shoulders and he was building up a lucrative business in Laura Douglas wines which were now featured as best buys for the discerning oenophile. Having for some time attended classes to consolidate his knowledge of the superior vintages, as well as extending his acquaintance of obscurer small growers known only to the cognoscenti, he was a familiar figure at more exclusive wine-tastings. Most of the talked-about restaurants now featured on their menu 'Wines personally selected by Laura Douglas' followed by the LDA rose-entwined logo. Antony had even suggested broadening their penetration by marketing a Laura Douglas perfume, an idea which she was considering.

'By the way, Mummy heard you on the wireless. She thought you were super. I recorded it. I thought it might be useful for presentations.'

'That's very good of you. Yes, do put Stephen through.'

The manager of the Rialto, Mexico City, one of the world's most exclusive and least written about hotels, set back amongst the palms, poinsettias and bougainvilleas surrounding the well-spaced colonial mansions of the Coyoacan, talked of nothing but L'Inglès. So charming. So modest. So much knowledge. So much gentleman. As Laura had commanded, Stephen had been given the most luxurious suite, unlimited champagne, a fax machine should he require it and his own private swimming pool which was strewn with flowers every morning by dark-eyed Indian maidens who hitched their skirts around their thighs and undulated their slim hips to perform this religious task, casting smiles at his balcony in case he should chance to be awake. Ravishing young girls fulfilled his slightest whim, by day and night, but he always acknowledged their gifts (sweetmeats and posies) with grave respect. A gentleman. Señor Bo-is, everyone love him.

'Laura, darling. What had I done to deserve that?'

'I hope everyone looked after you.'

'The hotel, perfect! The people, so kind! The food! A revelation. Have you ever had Mole Poblano? Only to be eaten in Mexico. And when I went to La Merced – remember, the market you told me to visit? – and saw the spices, the chillies, the heaps of banana leaves and prickly pear, the mounds of tomatoes and mangoes and the old women bringing in their little piles of produce, it was bliss. I'm not so sure about the rows of pigs' heads hanging in formation round the meat stalls, but I took a photograph for Miss Cutbutton, naturally. And the Oaxaca cheeses. The colours! The smells! My senses are reeling and my taste buds are on hold. I shall eat nothing. Until tomorrow anyway. You know, I'm here looking at a blank screen and seeing nothing but blue sky. Miss Cutbutton is the colour of a green banana, trying to hide her jealousy. I wanted to miss the plane back. Can I come and share Mexico with you? Tonight? Before it fades? Before I get on my bicycle and clog up in this bastard climate? Tonight. I'll be round at nine. I've got a present for you.'

'Stephen. I—'

'Expect me. Or else I will chain myself to your railings till morning.'

When Laura let him in, his sun-drenched face was like burned toffee against the softly lit walls. He had bought her a silver Mexican ring in which was mounted a large moonstone. Trying each finger in turn, she found that it fitted neatly over the one from which she had removed her wedding ring.

'I can't wear it there. Don't worry, I'll have it enlarged.'

'Why not? What's in a finger?'

'Silly. No reason why not, I suppose. I had to have Jack's ring cut off. If only I could reproduce that chameleon colour. So beautiful. Hovering between blue and grey and white.'

Stephen rubbed the watery moonstone. 'Look hard. If it goes cloudy, you must go and meditate to calm the turbulent spirits.'

Laura put on the tape which Stephen had brought and a cocksure rasping tenor threw out the words of a favourite Mexican song backed by a competing accordion.

> *Con dinero o sin dinero*
> *Siempre hago lo que quiero*
> *Sigo siendo el Rey.*

'Oh, if only I had been born in Mexico instead of Bournemouth. "With money or without money, I always do what I want. I am always the king. *Sigo siendo el Rey*".'

Stephen started the tape again, and the strong slurred cadences of a voice which had broken in hard Mexican sunlight pushed back an interval of silence in which the voice of Howard still threatened to intrude.

'One day I wandered off from the hotel and found myself in Plaza Garibaldi. Behind the Plaza there are all these back streets crammed full of tiny bars. I went into one, hearing singing. There were three *mariachi*, itinerant musicians who come to sell their songs. Crowding round them in the small, dark room were about a dozen young men. They stopped when they saw me. All these gleaming eyes staring out of mahogany faces. I started to back away, then one said, "Americano?" "No," I said. "Inglès." Then, would you believe, I got out my phrase book while they gawped at me as though I had parachuted down from

361

an empty sky. I read the phonetics for "I am a stranger here. I would like to try your local speciality." They roared with laughter and beckoned me over. They put something in front of me on a small pottery plate which I could not recognize. Then a man, the proprietor I guess, went to a shelf at the back and took down a bottle. I gave him a handful of coins, he gave me the bottle and I pointed to the men. We all drank and they cheered and waved at the musicians calling for another song, then another. "*Echate unos tragitos mas*", they kept saying. Have more to drink! Apparently someone called Juan was getting married. I had stumbled into a Mexican stag night. It was the best night of the whole trip.'

'All human life?' said Laura.

'Mexico isn't just about murderous politics and poverty and wealth. It's about men living it up in stinking bars and fruit and vegetables piled up to the sky. Everything that makes you want to get the hell out of England. Of course it's fascinating to see strange and marvellous places and rub shoulders with the people, but occasionally you also find what you're really looking for. I have this strange quest to seek out the most outlandish, edible substances known to man. I'm always searching for the freakish, the unheard-of, the impossible. It's the only challenge there is – once you've tasted every refined variation of the chef's art, and can detect the faintest ingredient in a symphony of flavours, you eat with pleasure but you stop being excited.'

'Perhaps you expect too much.'

'You know the dream of every food writer? To have been the fourteenth guest at the Last Supper. Imagine . . . On extremely rare occasions you are suddenly hurled out of the familiar orbit.' Stephen took a bottle from his carrier bag and put it down in front of Laura. 'This is the finest tequila, distilled from the blue maguey or agave, the *agave tequilana*, commonly known here as the century plant. Mistakenly described by the careless members of my profession as a cactus. The agave does retain water, like a cactus, but it is a member of the aloe family. However. Get two glasses, a lime and some salt and we will celebrate Mexico in darkest Chelsea.'

Stephen smoothed some salt crystals round the rims and poured some clear liquid into Laura's delicate glasses. She took a sip and shuddered.

'Ugh.'

'The first moment of initiation. Have some more.'

Laura allowed the fiery spirit to trickle down her throat. He patted his pocket. 'And now. I will provide the traditional accompaniment.'

She heard him moving round the kitchen. 'What are you looking for?'

'I've found it. If you shut your eyes, you can find anything in a kitchen.' When he returned he was carrying a small dish. 'Here. Drink! *Echate unos tragitos mas!* Drink!' He grasped the thin stem of the glass and threw the contents back down his throat. 'Like this.'

Laura followed suit. She would imagine herself far away from him. Sitting with Stephen in a fly-ridden bar, an invisible presence amongst the odour of sweating men bent on survival. He handed her the dish.

'What is it?'

'Taste first.'

'A little crunchy. Faintly reminiscent of peanuts.'

'Yes? Yes?'

'But hardly any flavour. Is it meant to be a delicacy?'

'To the Mexican palate. Yes.'

'Some kind of water chestnut?'

'No.'

'From the land or from the sea?'

'It looks down on the earth. Come. You must drink with it to obtain the full effect.'

'Is it a bird? It doesn't taste like a bird.'

The music grew more frenzied, as though chasing wheeling flocks and scudding clouds. The liquid seemed to sweep through her veins like a torrential flood smoothing out the stony bed of a river. She was nowhere, intoxicated, flying into nothingness and there was Stephen, leaning back, content and smiling.

'I think you should serve it at the Eglantine. With the addition of a little walnut oil, perhaps.'

He was about to take the last piece from the dish. 'Laura. I was forgetting. Will you . . . ?'

'No,' she murmured. 'But are you going to tell me?'

'What you have eaten?'

'Tell me. Please.'

'In the morning.'

'I want to know now.'

'It's only of interest to us would-be academics, dredging up the soggy mantle of respectability to disguise our gluttony. Look.' He patted his stomach. 'The one part of the body which is capable of infinite expansion. When I die, it will be in a coffin made for two. Hah. Poor mother. I hope she is saving up.'

'Stephen!'

'*La muerte*. I'd rather contemplate death than deadlines. Do you think I could master the art of Spanish prose? Darling Laura, you have just been initiated into the Confrerie des Gourmets. You are now about to digest the worm from the agave plant in Oaxaca. Alas, it was tinned. I couldn't get the fresh ones. I would have to go back to that bar where they had brought a bucketful of small, white grubs writhing amongst the agave leaves, fit delicacy for a man about to be married. They threw them into a deep pan of olive oil. I watched them cooking. Quite extraordinary and quite delicious. But, of course, the Aborigines, too, have a liking for worms . . .'

The bathroom was bright with the lightning sheets of a summer storm. Both her hands were supporting her frail frame against the basin and the bitter taste of vomit was burning her throat. Laura retched again but only a trickle of sour liquid escaped from her mouth. When the spasms and the coughing stopped she stared at her white reflection in the mirror, then turned on the shower and sat in the bath cross-legged as the water coursed over her, over her hair, her uplifted face, her dress and the long smooth legs.

'Laura!' Stephen opened the door, raised her up from the bath and enfolded her in a towel. 'Stupid of me. Mad Señor Bo-is. Misguided desire. We have to share.'

Laura opened her eyes and felt the warmth of his arm round her.

'Why should it be different from eel or squid or snail? Ridiculous. Do you feel all right now? Am I allowed to finish my discourse?'

'You'd better.'

'Brave girl. Now. The famous Mescal worm. This is a grub which only inhabits the agave and is honoured by being pickled in alcohol. A brilliant idea from the public relations consultant of the distillers of Mescal. The worm in the bottle. A bitter reminder of death?'

'Or a test of manhood?'

'Which I could never pass.'

'Do you want to stay? It's late.'

Stephen kissed her forehead. 'You do me too much honour. I don't deserve it. I will unchain my bicycle and be away. If my cleaning lady finds me absent from my bed, she will ring the police.'

Gradually Howard's presence grew dimmer and dimmer so that it became an effort to remember the things he had said, where they had been, even the exact contours of his body. Only his sardonic, gently mocking smile remained distinct. After that evening with Stephen something had been overcome, although she was not sure what it was. A strange exorcism she could not explain.

The Eglantine had become the place for celebration of success, real or imagined, and each evening became a soirée dedicated to the display of achievement.

Laura watched John spread his wings, for, unlimited by the constraints of lesser kitchens, he could indulge his taste for the exquisite, the highly wrought and the rare. They would only have to wait until March, she was sure, before John would be rewarded with his longed-for star of excellence. Laura Douglas rode over her competitors with serenity and charm, and gave her clients less and less of her time. Sometimes she smiled wryly, for they paid handsomely for the mere privilege of being a name in the Laura Douglas book. She flitted in and out of boardrooms like a peacock butterfly going from flower to flower accompanied by her increasingly elegant young men carrying slim folders and slimmer computers for instant information retrieval should the occasion arise. Her name had become a mythical harbinger of good fortune.

Peter Henderson had reappeared in her life. Long ago, before she met Jack, he had been her steady boyfriend and one night there he was, at a table in the Eglantine. He did not kindle any great fires, any more then he did then, but when he wrote asking if they could meet, as he was now respectably divorced, she responded with pleasure. A solid stockbroker, which everything about him proclaimed, made an acceptable companion and he was proud of her achievement. The storms of passion behind her, Laura Douglas was taking her company smoothly where she wished to go.

The tidal wave of Christmas was approaching. Laura was sending out a bottle of vintage champagne with a handwritten note to her favourite clients. The chairman of Rialto Hotels would receive a specially designed solid silver sculpture, a replica of their latest venture in Abu Dhabi.

Didi had prerecorded her Christmas programme in order to make time for the purchase of innumerable gifts. It was the season of excess, the season of forgiveness – and the season of guilt and foreboding. Where on earth should one spend Christmas? Did one have to submit to the penance of exchanging banalities amongst the drooping bosoms and creaking limbs of the family? Or should one throw nagging duty to the winds and retreat to some country hotel to lie in a lover's arms?

The dilemma kept Didi awake at night, even though John had rejected the country house suggestion. He was working until Boxing Day when he would be returning to his family in Yorkshire, and, no, she didn't fancy downing ten pints in the Packhorse pub. Didi came to the same reluctant conclusion she arrived at every year around the beginning of December. Everyone has a family. Didi Kowalski would, after all, perform her annual duty and Dorothy Dean would be nice to Mummy, Dad and Gran and have tea and mince pies (how loathsome) with Auntie Maureen, Uncle Stan and the cousins (equally loathsome). And she would have to sing along in the local pub because that's what they always did, with Uncle Stan banging out 'Silent Night' on the jangling piano. Then they would watch her Christmas programme in the front room with the neighbours, sweet sherry and Mum's fairy cakes, and the neighbours would keep looking from the screen to Didi and back, unable to believe that they were sitting with that famous lady from the tele. Ghastly, predictable Christmas. There was nothing for it but to grit one's teeth. It was a bit like going on a diet. Poor Stephen. Mother in Bournemouth who couldn't understand the fuss people made about cooking. Frozen turkey breast, tinned peas, burnt roast potatoes, a brick-shitting Christmas pudding with aerosol cream and a bottle of Liebfraumilch in honour of her son's visit, all courtesy of the Prima Supermarket in Sea View Parade. On 28 December they had made a date to make up for the period of penal servitude and pig themselves into oblivion at the Eglantine.

'What do you think of the tree?' Jack put down the suitcases in the hall.

A giant fir shaped like a many-forked candelabra extended a welcoming array of branches garlanded with silver streamers, red and green silk flowers, silver painted balls, tiny replicas of vintage cars, round-bellied miniature Father Christmases, crackers, jovial gnomes and replica candles which blinked in rhythm with 'God Rest Ye Merry Gentlemen', chorralled through hidden speakers with enough power to fill the Royal Albert Hall. Looking down on the hurly-burly and the heap of presents piled up like a landslide was a long-legged doll in a white fur bikini, wielding a star-spangled wand, whose lash-fringed blue eyes opened and closed in unison with the lights.

'Electronically controlled. Isn't that something?'

The house had changed little. Any minute now, Mrs Leone could have come running gracefully down the stairs dressed for dinner, ready to give the table a last-minute appraisal. Laura walked through this museum of the past as though it had been invented for her like a false identity. Christmas was a time for banishing pain and the test she had set herself was less fearsome than she had imagined.

'I figured you might like your own room, babe. But my door is always open,' said Jack as he placed Laura's cases in one of the spare rooms.

'This'll do fine. I always liked the view from here.'

Jack put his arm round her shoulders. 'And see that? I remembered your favourite flowers. Come down and have a drink when you're ready.'

The heaped logs were crackling and spewing out sparks into the wide chimney breast by the time Laura went downstairs. Everything seemed unusually calm. Now that she was no longer part of it, she thought she could come to accept his friendship. When his frantic movement stopped, when he was in repose, his handsome, muscular body at rest, his face had dignity and strength.

'I've been thinking about . . . us,' he began reflectively. 'I always loved you, but I guess it was in my way. Trouble is, I never knew what your way was. You know that?'

'Jack, you don't have to—'

'Always wanted to help. I guess I did it wrong. Things are different now.'

'Are they?'

'I respect you. No, I always respected you. You made it. You really did. It's an honour for me to have you here.'

'Thank you, Jack, but you don't need to say anything.'

'But you had to do it alone. I understand that, babe. Really I do. Now. You, er . . . you serious with someone?'

'There is someone. Yes.'

'You thinking of settling down?'

'I haven't the time – we're expanding so fast.'

'Anyone I know? . . . OK, OK. None of my business. I want to ask you something.'

'Yes?'

'How come you didn't bawl me out?'

'You mean, scream at you?'

'Yes.'

'Not my style, Jack.'

'Sometime a guy needs a come-back. I figured you didn't give a damn. Or else I was some kind of scum floating on a pond.'

'You mean you wanted me to give you the added thrill of making you feel guilty as you screwed your way through London?'

'That's unfair, Laura. You know me. Some guys play golf. I screw. Like having a work-out. You and me is quite different.'

'Was.'

'OK. Was. Were you unhappy? Because if so, I couldn't see it. Neither could our friends. Did I ever treat you badly? Did I ever look at another woman when I was with you?'

Laura smiled. 'I wouldn't have minded.'

'What did you mind? Not having a child? Did everything change when—'

'When I lost the baby? Afterwards, I couldn't imagine myself being a mother. It was like losing something I wasn't meant to have.'

'You know how much I wanted it. We should have tried harder. You should have gone to that clinic.'

Laura looked away. 'I couldn't see you as a father. Where's Daddy? Working late. I couldn't lie.'

'If you'd have told me then.'

'Jack, you can't talk back a marriage. I've changed.'

'And I haven't?'

'Jack—'

'Listen. Let me finish. I want to put things right. So we can have the best Christmas ever, like I said. I want to do a turnaround on our marriage, Laura.'

Laura crossed her legs and sat with her head slightly to one side, as she did at her grey desk in the Sanctum, anticipating the weak points of a wavering client. 'I'm not open to negotiation, as you know.'

'Everyone is open to negotiation. Including you. And including those Spanish bastards.'

'I don't see why you have to upset yourself. Is it because I'm the only woman who said no to you, who said no to that giant, hyperactive cock of yours?'

Jack laughed. 'You're really something. No wonder that company of yours is going great guns. I'm proud of you, Laura. I hear what you're saying. But if I couldn't do anything about your little problem, no-one could. It made me sad, babe, but it didn't worry me, some girls are just made different, they never . . .' Jack got up and thrust the poker into a greying log, smashed it open and watched a flame arise from the embers. 'I'm gonna make you a proposal. You don't have to answer, but I'll say straight. I am prepared to . . . to quit screwing around. If you want me to prove it before you decide, I'll go on probation.'

For a moment, Laura hesitated. 'I'm not sure that—'

'No hurry. Take it easy.'

'Jack, I'd rather tell you now. I'm glad to be here. I'm glad everything is going so well for you and I don't feel bitter any more.'

Suddenly, Jack sprang up and came over to sit beside her. 'Sometimes I think there must have been another guy.'

Laura stared intently at the fire. 'Would it have made it easier if there had been?'

'I'd have broken his balls.'

'It's late and I'm tired, Jack.'

He rested his hands lightly on her neck, pulled her face towards him and kissed her tenderly, as though it was their first date.

'Good night, babe. Breakfast at nine. I'll bring you tea.'

At twelve o'clock on Christmas morning the friends started to arrive, bringing children and dogs and gifts, and the house burst into life with running feet, joyous shrieks, the rustle and tear of paper and tributes to the kindness of the Leones. 'You like it, you like it?' Jack kept repeating as he watched the rapt faces of children and adults dissolving into smiles as they opened the packets and boxes he had piled up as he swept through everything Harrods had to offer, regardless of cost, spending away the memories of penny-pinching childhood.

'Hey! You've forgotten this, Laura.'

She sat on the floor, witness to his generosity, swathed in blond cashmere, her neck encircled by thick ropes of pearls. Soon they would all head out into the surrounding countryside. Come on, come on, it was time to get moving, breathe in the keen air, rouse the Christmas appetite because there was a helluva spread like you've never seen, cooked it all himself.

'I can find my way around a kitchen. Never knew that, did you?'

As they straggled across the fields, the women who had once sat round Laura's dinner table murmured to one another. 'So good to see them together for Christmas . . . So civilized. They seem so happy. Why on earth did she want to leave?'

And when, later, they were alone together and Jack was pacing round the room with the telephone greeting all the people he always used to greet on Christmas Day, Laura found herself drawing pleasure from the familiar rituals. He handed her the telephone. 'How about calling the Eglantine?'

There was a cacophany of voices, clinking glasses, waiters being called as George answered. 'Happy Christmas, Laura. You've never seen anything like it. Packed. I've pushed together a few tables. It's chaos here but wonderful. Can you her that noise? And the chestnut soufflé. Raves! Want a quick word with John?'

There was a long pause then, 'Laura? Good to hear you. Having a good Christmas?'

'Yes, yes. Are you coping all right?'

'Just about. It's bloody murder in the kitchen but the lads are knuckling under. I'm giving them dinner later . . .'

'I wish I could be there . . .'

'You'd go crazy. Just a moment. I'm going to the other phone.'

The torrent of noise became muffled.

'Laura. You still there?'

'What is it?'

'André Bouchon. He was supposed to come here for a drink yesterday. Never came. He's dead.'

16

The winds of East Anglia swept ferociously across flat, frost-caked fields. The vicar of St John's church in the village of Long Paxton stood looking down the road pondering his unusual assignment. A few black and white cows swinging their mud-splattered tails ambled from one side to the other, and when they had passed on to the farm track a queue of cars was released which moved slowly up the village high street. They were coming from London. At least there would be a turn-out for this man whom he scarcely knew, in whose rarely frequented cottage he had taken tea and discussed the decline of religion. Mr Bouchon prayed to God, that he knew.

Mammon had despatched a host of representatives. A limousine emblazoned with the Intertel logo led the procession. Then followed long-bonneted, thick-tyred vehicles, black ones, silver ones, white ones, town monsters built for country speed, but rarely seen in these parts. By now a cluster of villagers had emerged from their wind-tight doors to watch where these foreigners were going to park. The vicar waved them towards a field by the church and they bumped over the stiffened tufts of coarse grass.

Didi took up her position in a pew halfway back, the better to observe who had made the long journey instead of going to the champagne tasting at the Garrick Club or a Taste of Provence luncheon with a three-star Michelin chef flown over from France. Only old people went to funerals. Death was a peripheral event, a statistic culled from periodic reports on mortality rates from diet-related causes which occasionally passed from Deirdre's desk and plopped into Didi's waste basket. They were a cue for another attempt to cut back on cholesterol and alcohol, an incentive to walk upstairs instead of taking the lift. Death was like some distant country at the back of an exclusive travel brochure which she would visit when the time came but which she never thought about. Old age and death. Ugh. Didi shivered and noticed that Laura was wearing navy blue. One didn't have to wear black nowadays but, as Didi had explained to Stephen, who was wearing his usual much beaten about leather jacket, she believed in tradition, or she supposed she did.

There was a light tickling on her leg and Didi looked down to observe a determined ladder edging from its hiding place under her high court shoes and leaving a flesh-coloured line like a vapour trail up her sheer black stockings. Damn! How could one enter into holy contemplation with a ladder in one's stocking?

She hardly recognized them. Was that Caliope? Penelope? Who had brought children? Dylan Tusk. Good heavens! Must be doing a story in the area. Gloria. Jean. Cynthia. Joan. The round-hipped, droopy-breasted nice nice nice contingent from the women's magazines ('eckies', or home economists, with minds measured in millilitres and grams, whom Stephen positioned on the borderline between Purgatory and Hell). They had regularly beseeched André to please please do us a little easy-to-follow recipe so his face and tall chef's hat could urge their readers on to the nursery slopes with Quick 'n Easy recipes from the French master. Lionel Goldman, oh yes, André's publisher. How different they looked, bereft of the smiles and festive clothes, gazing straight ahead with barely blinking eyes, listening to the glassy upper register of the church organ. Sounded like the awful scales she had to practise at school. How nice of them to make that dreadful journey. But then they were . . . nice. We are all nice really, thought Dorothy Dean, who had forgotten on this occasion that all she ever wanted to be was not nice.

There was the shuffling sound of leather on stone and

Didi looked round, as did John sitting straight-backed beside her.

'Do you think those are the relatives? Aren't they amazing? Like the little men who were making cheese in—'

'Sh, Didi,' hissed Stephen on her other side.

Low voices murmured in the sing-song burr of a French dialect as the small group settled at the front. Mr Beck, his daughter and the brigade from Aphrodite's walked in solemnly and sat behind them, heads bowed. Sigmund Halberstadt and Magnus Shaw took up their respective positions near the front, but on opposite sides of the church, and both fixed their gaze heavenwards as though the congregation was a backdrop for their exclusive communing with the Lord. Neither noticed the French ambassador slip into the back row, otherwise they would have acknowledged his presence with a lofty nod of the head they reserved for superior beings worthy of attention.

Laura mouthed the doleful hymns, having left her singing voice behind at school, whilst Antony threw himself lustily into each verse, a former choirboy she imagined, and the halting voices followed him half a beat behind the organ. She had to get back for her four-thirty meeting. Antony would have to phone to check the road reports. The church was uninteresting, except for a small stone carving of a dove. Eleventh century . . . It never worked, making a restaurant from a church. She had once toyed with the idea. One or two people had done it. She had forgotten to cancel her appointment at the House of Beauty. She really had done all that was humanly possible for André Bouchon. Who would take over at Aphrodite's when it reopened? Whoever it was would be younger. Ambitious. Ready for the Team. Raring to go. The renaissance of Aphrodite's. The cuisine would still be traditional. There must be no competition with the Eglantine. She would see to that. Even if Jack succeeded in his bid.

Sigmund Halberstadt spoke fluently, Laura paid her tribute, John said how André Bouchon had taught him everything he knew. Another hymn. It took eight sturdy, straining bearers to lift the shiny wooden box with do-it-yourself all-purpose, heavy-duty brass handles. They had placed his chef's hat on top, together with the medal of his Légion d'Honneur. Someone was sniffing behind Laura, stifling sobs. John said he was sure it was suicide. Rumours were running around, but that was because every chef sweating in the steamy heat of the kitchen listened to his heart and wondered if he could survive to middle age. No, it was out of the question that André Bouchon, powerhouse of a man, should have suffered a cardiac arrest at what? Fifty-four.

The organist thundered out a funeral version of 'La Marseillaise' and the congregation rose to its feet. The vicar shook hands with those whom the village of Long Paxton would never see again but whose unfamiliar names would be recorded in the parish magazine for posterity. Stephen, Laura, John and Didi came forward with white roses and were about to drop them on to the coffin when a tiny woman wrapped in a black shawl elbowed them out of the way. As her kith and kin gathered round to restrain her, she let out a howl which rose above the steady moan of the wind. Struggling wildly, the woman tore off her black woollen shawl, ripped it in half and threw it on to the coffin. Tears of grief, aggravated by the wind, streamed down her cheeks. André Bouchon's widow, Odette, had understood little of the service, but had sat stony-faced and dignified, knowing only from the intense expressions of the speakers that the appropriate heartfelt homage was being made to her husband. Now she threw her arms round her sister-in-law for the first time in her life, and they sobbed in unison.

'Not fair on the kids, seeing women crying like that.' Dylan led them away. Caliope followed him.

'How very Irish. I do dislike funerals. Never mind. The church was pretty.'

She walked determinedly towards a side gate where she had parked her motorbike and tried to coax it into action.

A cough, a splutter and a roar and she was away, muffled and goggled, eating up the road to London where Lady Knowles was expecting her for dinner.

Stephen gathered up the roses, placed them on the bright green plastic turf surrounding the coffin and returned to where Laura, John and Didi had retreated, standing beside a humped memorial strewn with a few faded plastic flowers, the remains of a long-dead villager.

'Are you going back to his cottage? Personally, I've had enough death for one day.' Turning away from the now silent group bunched together by the grave, Stephen blew on his cold fingers.

'Unfortunately, I can't stay,' said Laura. 'Have to get back for a meeting. The service was beautiful, I thought. I hope his relatives appreciated it, but then we probably knew him better than his family. They could hardly have seen him for the past twenty years. Dreadful for his sister. Apparently André wanted to be buried here and she wanted him back in France. One can understand her being so upset.'

'I'm going to find the others,' said John.

'Aren't you coming back with me?' Didi said. 'I thought we'd stop off for lunch. I know a lovely little place.'

'No. You go, love. I'll stay with the lads.'

'Aren't you cooking tonight?'

'We're closed for today. Mark of respect.'

The vicar gently steered the family away from the newly dug grave, and as they walked away, the group grew into a small procession down the high street of Long Paxton and wound its way through a copse to where André's cottage chimney could be seen through the bare branches. John, Elwyn and Tad stopped as the mourners left the road.

'You want to go on, lads?' asked Elwyn. They looked at one another awkwardly.

'You think we're expected to? It'll be a crowd in that cottage.'

'We better had.'

'Had we?'

'We don't know them.'

'Makes no difference. Mark of respect.'

Tad interrupted them. 'I couldn't half fancy a beer. Bloody prat, that vicar.'

'We know religion's not your scene, Tad. Hell. Monsieur Bouchon wouldn't mind. Why don't we toast him in the pub?'

'Now you're talking, John. Right. Which one'll it be? The one for the nobs or the one for the workers?'

They retraced their steps. Tadeus paused outside the Horse and Hounds and put his head round the door. Dylan Tusk, surrounded by Coke bottles and packets of crisps, one child on each side, was attacking a large pork pie.

'How do, Tad. Can I get you a drink?' he called across the empty lounge bar.

'Awfully decent of you but I'm looking for someone. Actually.' Tadeus slammed the door shut.

'Now we know. This is the one we don't go in, lads. Fucking journalist wanker in there. Come on.'

The Greyhound was a modern box-like building of red brick, built solely to keep the sun, the rain and wind at bay and hold in the nicotine encrustations from pipes and strong cigarettes. When the three men entered, a few weather-beaten faces representing most of the agricultural labour force of Long Paxton looked up for a moment with open curiosity, registered strangers and went back to sipping their pints of beer.

'You got some champagne?' John asked the publican.

'Oh. Don't know if I have any. Not much call for it. You could 'ave Babycham. Very popular that is.'

'Champagne if you can find it.'

The publican retired to the back and John could hear him shuffling boxes around. After a few minutes he came back with a dusty bottle in his hand.

'This do you?'

John looked at the label. Méthode Champenoise. It would do. Just.

'Got any ice?'

'Ice? No. No call for it.'

'Here. Something fizzy for Monsieur Bouchon.' John uncorked the bottle and the cork flew up to the ceiling with a bang. The inhabitants with their faces to the fire glanced round.

'Wedding, is it?' said one. 'We don't get many of those.'

John smiled at them as he poured out the indeterminate fizz into some all-purpose tumblers. 'Neither do we. Here's to Monsieur Bouchon and long life to us.'

Their glasses met and there was silence. Tadeus loosened his tie.

'He did kill himself, poor bugger. One of my sous told me before I left this morning. You know what? He was given notice. No handshake. Nothing. Pum. Sacked. Twenty-five years of graft up the chimney.'

'Don't say he was blamed for the fire?'

'Who knows? Anyway, the old lizard who owns it has sold. Guess who?'

'Don't say it, Tad. Laura.'

'Even worse, Little John. Your old friend Mr Leone.'

'Jesus wept!'

'Who decided to give Big-Ears the elbow. He'll probably put in some aspiring oik from a Pizza Palace.'

'I wish Leone would drop dead. He gets fucking everywhere.'

'How about *soupe de poison*?' suggested Elwyn.

'Too good for him, El.'

'Know something?' said Tadeus, when they could see the reassuring orange glow of London. 'We're all fucking owned. The lot of us. However good we are some other cunt gets to spoon off the cream.'

Stephen wanted sky and emptiness. He walked away from the church and waved as Didi stepped petulantly into the Intertel limousine, dreading the thought of at least two hours conversation with her garrulous chauffeur when

Stephen could have been beside her, and irked that John, too, had declined her invitation.

The East Anglian blasts of cold were attacking his leather jacket, his suit, the thick sweater and thermal Christmas vest but he was glad to escape the constant shroud of comfort with which he surrounded himself. This was the world outside which Stephen sensed through his reddening nose and watering eyes. A kind of penance without which indulgence would lose its savour. He walked along the edge of a vast field, stumbling over summer's ruts encrusted with stalks of dried-up corn which had hardened into a rock-like assault course. Then he changed direction to have the wind behind him and set off at a jog, hopping across the furrows of the plough. His chest heaved with the exertion, and he changed direction again, slowed to a walk, occasionally stumbling at the edge of a ditch which skirted a field. Then he stopped. A few feet below him was a mass of grey wool and blood-soaked flesh. The face of a sheep leaned upwards against the ditch, its body savaged by a desperate predator. He wanted to look away but was drawn to the raw carnage. Disgusted at his fascination, he walked back the way he had come.

Stephen sat in the bare waiting room of the deserted station and looked at the platform encrusted with bird droppings. In two hours, a train was due. A stark black stove was rusting in the corner with ancient ashes left untouched to remind occupants of the time when the station master used to light a fire. He still had some peppermints left. A late arrival in London would mean late dinner and a tired chef, but dinner nevertheless. A warming thought.

The walls were the colour of ancient, yellowing candle wax, their surface scribbled with initials, names, hearts and obscenities. They might have borne witness to family reunions, wartime departures, vomiting drunks, angry punch-ups, bestial rape or the first fumblings of love. He opened the door and looked down the single empty track at whose side lay discarded bags of farming chemicals, tins of beer and builders' rubble which were the only indications that there had been life in the crumbling grey brick house at the end of the platform, once, presumably, the home of the station master.

He closed the door, preferring the airless waiting room to the swingeing wind.

What had led André Bouchon to take this desolation to his heart, to escape London for stretches of flat fields and downtrodden villages, the vicar with thin lips and the church of an unrelenting God? Did he discover some secret beauty which only flowered in the spring or early summer when poppies dotted the yellow cornfields with unaccustomed colour and skylarks soared singing into the sky? Or did he see reflected around him some brooding blackness of spirit which echoed his own?

Stephen did not see the train until the light from the cobweb-strewn window was blocked out by a carriage and there was a squeal of brakes. He lunged for his bag. Must have fallen asleep. There were only two carriages containing hard seats nailed down in rows, some facing one another in case of an outbreak of conversation. He grasped the handle of the door nearest him, hoping that whatever destination the train was bound for it would be a long way away from his slough of despond. He sat opposite a turbaned Asian who stared out of the window.

'Excuse me, is this the London train?'

'Eventually,' the man replied, unwilling to elaborate.

Every few minutes the train came to a halt and immediately left, for it took little time for the few passengers at each station to climb aboard. Stephen stretched out his stiff legs and opened his bag. Stephen Boyce, observer, columnist and winner of the Illustra/MacCrae award, was coming into town with a searing report from the hinterland.

He flicked through the pages and smiled at his familiar

scrawl, instantly recalling happier, warmer times and luscious fruitfulness. 'Ode to a Strawberry'. He lingered over the phrases Miss Cutbutton would never see, turned to a virgin page and programmed his mind to *Daily Reporter*. Boyce Five hundred words.

Well, my dear André Bouchon. You were pompous, arrogant and a bore. You drove us mad but you cooked like a dream. And for some inexplicable reason you chose your resting place in the windswept badlands of our glorious country.

Suppose I were to deny you the status of artist? Then I would write of you as a worker, or at best a craftsman. The death of a craftsman? Do you really think that would be of any interest except to the obituary column of your local newspaper? But if I elevate you, and describe the colours, tastes, flavours and textures of food with the high vocabulary reserved for the sanctity of art, of genius, you will take your place amongst our national heroes.

At Intertel a row was in progress. This was not unusual, for the conflicts between the technical, the financial and the creative erupted every day, but it was unusual for it to happen quite so publicly. It was an accident that the microphones were left switched on in the studio break so that Didi's altercation with her producer halted the crunching of Meanie Wheenie Bars and Whammo crisps, and the sipping of instant tea. The crew was all ears. Good value, Didi.

'Look, darling, I'm not being paid to fuck up programmes. I'm being paid to make programmes. Are you listening, Didi?'

'I told you I was going. If you paid less attention to the football results and checked with my schedule now and again.'

'Did you hear her say she was going, Deidre?'

'It was down in the diary.'

'Whose diary?'

'Mine, darling.'

'Well, darling, I was expecting you in. Four hours of studio time. Do you know what a no-show costs? Just because you can't resist stuffing your gut or lying in bed with some hunk . . . And who said you could take the Intertel car?'

'Actually, it was a funeral. If you'd have listened, you'd have remembered. I hate to say this, but you're slipping, Roger. Male menopause already. Dear. Dear.'

'You think I'd waste half a day of studio time for a fucking funeral? Whose was it anyway?'

After the recording, Roger was pleased. Didi was happy. Great team. All that momentum and energy and concentration and things going wrong, things put right. Great interview. They'd been worried about another 'boring heavy' on pesticide control, had to react to the recent potato scare, but it was good stuff. You didn't expect men from government departments to have a sense of humour, wear fancy ties, tell a joke and do five takes to the same length, but this one managed the lot. He'd be invited back. And they'd floored the expert on 'Taste for a Test'. Great programme, and what's more it ran to length. Only a top and tail in the edit suite.

'Fantastic. Well done, Didi, love. Well done, studio. Smashing show. It's a wrap. We'll be back for the next series in six weeks. Thank you everyone for being absolutely terrific. I mean that. And as it's the end of the current series, we've had a special dispensation. Drinks all round in the hospitality suite.'

The bank of screens went blank. Didi tripped into the gallery which had miraculously cleared within seconds at the mention of the waiving of the no-alcohol rule.

'Was it all right, Roger? Honestly?'

'Absolutely super. Super.'

'You didn't mind me putting that bit in about my new diet?'

'No, that was brilliant. Then we can pick up on your progress in the next series.'

'I was thinking, maybe we could put out a Didi Kowalski Personal Diet Sheet. Viewers can write in and tell me their weight problems and then—'

'Super idea. You know, love, the way things are going I think we'll be up to nine million viewers next time around.'

'Honestly?'

'That's what the AR department are saying.'

Didi threw her arms around Roger and imprinted the shape of a perfect red bow on his right cheek.

Nothing approached the euphoria of putting the last programme to bed. It felt like winning an Olympic Gold. The sense of achievement was intense, ecstatic, dizzying. And sexy. Long Paxton was a puff of smoke on the horizon of experience. That was what Stephen had said once. Something was a puff of smoke on the horizon of experience. She couldn't remember what the something was. Some trip, must have been. John, bless him, would not have understood. You didn't feel like shouting on the rooftops when you'd cooked a hundred and twenty covers, not the same at all.

'Congratulations, Miss Kowalski. I was invited to drop in for the recording. Marvellous. And I hear the ratings are approaching ten million.'

'Well, nine, actually. It's sweet of you to come, Sir Howard.'

'We've been discussing American sales.' Sir Howard beckoned Didi over to a corner of the hospitality suite. 'I don't know what you might think about the idea, but how would you react to gearing *Table For One* to an American network? The fact is, we've had some encouraging noises.'

'Are we talking about another version? I mean, I wouldn't want to have my programme full of awful American . . .'

'Of course not. No, we wouldn't consider that. But I suppose we would need a slightly different approach. Don't worry, though, we'll be consulting you if it comes to anything.'

'You'd better!'

When he spoke, he forced you to look at him. Didi opened her eyes wide and stared at him for a few seconds. It was as though he wanted her to wait while he said something else. Something intimate. He paused and scrutinized her as though he was drawing out a secret, with a hint of anguish, of obsession. Then he suddenly strode away as though the intensity of the meeting was too much to bear. Once you had fallen, it would be hard to become disenchanted. Dangerous.

What could he have done, what would he have said to Laura as he left to be with his wife? How on earth had she agreed to share him? No man was worth that, Didi decided on later reflection, as she pulled the silver lamé Gautier dress from her wardrobe.

There was a sea of bodies crammed into Le Style, and as Didi wriggled her way to the bar she felt as though everyone there was there to greet her. Smiles and waves and 'love the dress' from all sides. Oh, wasn't that Laura over there with her new escort? Yes. What was his name? All right but a little dull.

'Laura, darling.'

'What a day.'

'I've had a wonderful, wonderful day.'

Laura smiled. 'Don't tell me you enjoy funerals?'

'Oh, that was this morning. Eons ago. I've been recording the last programme of the series and you'll never guess who was there.'

Didi whispered in her ear. Laura turned her back on Peter for a moment.

'Was he with anyone?'

'No.'

'I decided not to see him any more.'

'You're so strong minded, Laura. I don't know how you do it.'

'He's a rat.'

'You look great, Laura.'

385

'You, too.'

Success made it easier to be friends, and even though Laura was wearing a stunningly simple shift (probably Ralph Lauren, Didi decided) which skimmed her elegant, slim contours, tonight Didi did not mind. They moved in the same world and sat on different thrones. The champagne was making her feel light, kilos lighter, and she couldn't quite remember where she had met the beautiful young man who said he wrote poetry as he flung his arms round her and kissed her neck. It didn't matter. She was riding on the crest of a rolling wave which would throw her on to a hot expanse of sand where she would bask under the tropical palms of paradise. The room blurred and Didi came to rest on a bar stool, her dress riding high up her thighs, admirers congregating to her side. When she said something silly they laughed, they told her stories, she laughed . . . And then Stephen, darling Stephen, he came over like a bright-coloured fish emerging from the dingy depths and she was happy.

'Sweetest,' murmured Stephen, noticing Didi's mascara which was smudged after tears of laughter.

'Touch-up time.'

She slid from the stool, steadied herself and fixed her eyes on the ladies' cloakroom. No more champagne. Stephen must take her home.

'Stephen—'

'Yes. I'll take you home.'

Stars were allowed to get drunk. Amongst friends. Everyone understood the pressures, the energy, the disappointments, the successes, which had to be drenched in alcohol (or other substances which Dorothy Dean regarded with horror) to free the spirit and release the overpowering tension with which only the truly talented were cursed, and blessed. Didi wiped away the mascara and didn't bother to remake her face, but splashed cold water over her flushed cheeks, damped down her unruly black curls, then gazed at Kowalski *au naturel*. She still looked good.

The bodies were packed less densely and they had opened a window to let in some outside air and to remind everybody that the night must end. Didi glanced round for Stephen. He must be ordering a taxi. Then amidst the familiar faces, the familiar bodies, she noticed one she did not recognize. A space had cleared to reveal a bare-backed, long-legged girl in a tiny shimmering skirt which skimmed her thighs. A cascade of straight hair the colour of a dark red tiger lily hung down to her waist. As Didi stared at her, wondering if her face would match the beauty of her poplar-straight back, two long ivory arms entwined themselves round the man who must be standing opposite her. Her head fell back in abandon as he kissed her and a male hand moved slowly down her back to caress the fine divide of her buttocks.

'You bastard!' Didi pulled the man away and slapped him with all the force she could muster. 'If you like playing dirty, why don't you take your tart to the lavatory?' she screamed. John with Melissa Desgranges. The barman stopped wiping a glass and ducked under the bar.

'Didi, love. He's drunk. She was throwing herself at him. I saw.'

Stephen took her firmly by the arm and pushed her towards the door.

The next morning, she awoke bristling with anger which swiftly changed into determination as she dissolved the natural remedy for overindulgence in a glass of Happy Springs Cornish mineral water. So. John had betrayed her. And, what's more, in public. No need to dwell on the humiliation. Who was he anyway? A chef. There was only one thing to do. Ignore him. She would look right through him as though she had never set eyes on him in her life. John Crabtree. Who? Everyone would realize he was a mere footnote in the margin of her life, the life devoted to eight – no, nine – million viewers.

And now that life was going to change. Without a

doubt. She listened to her body and as she pressed her stomach she could almost feel the fertilised egg. It really did feel different. If doctors were unable to tell after a few days, she certainly could. They could laugh at her but she knew. Instinctively. Her face already possessed that ethereal, motherly glow. She had seen it in the mirror. What a miraculous thought.

Didi's first inclination would have been to rush to the telephone and relay her secret into the ever-receptive ear of Caliope, but she resisted the temptation. She needed to think things through first, to prepare the ground for the seedling to grow.

Didi Kowalski, a mother. Didi Kowalski, unmarried mother! That's what she would be. It had never entered her plans. Could she do it? Pregnancy without the ring on the finger, without being willed and planned? But why not? Particularly when her agent had negotiated her new contract. She could be living proof of how you could combine single parenthood with a blazing career *and* breast-feed in the corridors of power . . . She would have to think hard. There was always the other choice. It would be only too easy to take advantage of the break between series to enter a discreet clinic, ostensibly to lose weight.

'Are you happy about the result, Miss Kowalski?' her Harley Street doctor asked in the manicured concerned tones which kept his waiting room crowded. Didi looked up at the reproduction Watteau on the wall, the girl on the swing, and was already thinking she would like her nursery to be in the French style.

'Yes. Yes. Yes.'

How ridiculous. Her second reaction was a sigh of relief.

Of course she could cope. Marriage? Perhaps. One day. Not that she was against it, but it would have to be someone very special. I have every advantage in the world, she told the admiring doctor. A good salary, a wonderful job, lots of friends. As she talked the revelation dawned that, without knowing it, she had been preparing herself for single motherhood for years. And Stephen would be godfather.

If only the child had been his.

Didi made one telephone call when she returned home. It was rather short notice, but Antony said he was sure Laura would be able to manage something. If not in France, then somewhere super in England. They had just taken on Inglewood Hall, which was running in an interesting young Viennese chef. Didi would love him.

'All right, sweetest. How about this?'

Didi was twisting Stephen's arm and rousing his taste buds with characteristic vigour.

'I'll postpone my trip to the Fête Gastronomique and forego my comparative tasting of the cassoulets of Castelnaudry, Carcassonne and Toulouse which I have been dreaming about for weeks. If you insist.'

'I do. Absolutely. You can go there any time.'

'Hardly.'

'Please, please. Say yes.'

'Yes, if we can drive down there in a pink Cadillac with a black chauffeur. And he must be wearing a white uniform. And I want the best suite in the place, not like last time when there was barely enough space for a breakfast table.'

Antony took the second call from Didi that day.

'Laura,' he called as she passed breathlessly through into the Sanctum, threw her bag on to the floor and picked up a phone.

'I'm in a terrible rush. I've got to be in New York for dinner.'

'It'll only take a moment.' He outlined Didi's request.

'Who pays for it?'

'We do, I imagine.'

'Intertel have a perfectly adequate car and driver.'

'She won't use it, Laura. Says she won't go unless it's a pink Cadillac.'

389

'She's only presenting a TV food programme, for God's sake. I'm getting sick of the Hollywood superstar antics.'

'I know.'

'She must promise to do a location slot on Viennese cooking using Heinrich for the next series. And I mean promise.'

Stephen mastered his disappointment at finding that the black chauffeur waiting coolly in the pink, long-finned, chrome-gleaming Cadillac was wearing not a uniform but a white polo neck sweater.

'I think we should always travel like this,' he remarked to Didi as he opened a bottle of champagne from her chilled hamper and lolled back on the pink silk cushions she had brought to give the finishing touch.

'We're not having anything to eat till we get there.'

Stephen examined his watch. 'If we get the menu before we unpack, we can order and be eating in . . . two and a half hours. Can't wait that long.'

'All right. One truffle then.'

'Young Heinrich had better be good.'

'Sigmund told me he's going to be the next Mosimann.'

'He always says that about anyone who isn't French. Any idea where we're going?'

'Somewhere like Gloucestershire I think. You know. Countryside, darling.'

The house was mish-mash Georgian with Victorian additions, which Stephen quickly registered. There was no point in making a detailed examination. Brochures told you that kind of stuff if you needed it for padding an atmosphere piece. The patron and his wife were waiting at the entrance as the Cadillac pulled up with precisely enough space to enable them to emerge, take one step and enter the hallway.

'Miss Kowalski. Mr Boyce.'

They shook hands and received the special welcome reserved for a handful of influential media folk, members of the nobility, self-made billionaires, wealthy politicians and anyone else who was able to pay several hundred pounds plus an unstinting tip for an overnight stay.

'We're so glad you could make it.'

The pretence of staying in a luxury hotel as some kind of penance would be maintained until several of the best bottles from the cellar had led to a cessation of formalities.

'We've heard so much about your chef,' said Didi as their suitcases were whisked away to the Lady Florentine and the Earl of Hardwick suites. 'And we can't wait to see the menu.'

Within seconds sheet-music-sized menus with thin parchment leaves were pressed into their hands. Didi and Stephen sat examining the contents with even greater solemnity than they had shown at André Bouchon's funeral. The owners directly withdrew to the other side of the room to leave them alone. The reading of the menu took half an hour. Stephen looked up.

'Well? Have you managed to reach a decision, sweetest?'

'Yes,' Didi replied. 'I think I have. But we can always change our minds later.'

It was galling that the girls always managed to end up in the better rooms, as though they possessed some kind of superior aesthetic sense. Stephen didn't like his gold on brown fleur-de-lys-wallpapered attempt at the Surroundings for the Stylish World Traveller seeking Peace and Tranquillity (Photograph of Stylish World Traveller in the brochure, leaning urbanely against a draped window, wearing a Burberry raincoat and carrying a portable communication centre, reclining golf clubs at his feet). The Jacuzzi rumbled like a waste disposal unit and Stephen felt singularly clean as he threw in a bottle of Old Apothecary gentleman's bath lotion and plunged beneath the heaving surface of the water. He heard a trilling beep and leaned over to grasp the bathroom phone.

'My room. It's enormous! I've just seen the price. Four hundred a night excluding breakfast. Isn't it outrageous? I'm just down the corridor.'

Dear Didi. She never gave up, but he always enjoyed sharing the ritual pre-dinner diversion of draping himself in the towelling bathrobe ('Guests wishing to purchase this item should contact reception'), totting up luxury at someone else's expense, working out what could be nicked without penalty and laughing at the ludicrousness of it all. At least it was better than the Bon Arôme bread-trip hotel at Tours.

Sitting under the moulded pillars and swathed canopy of Didi's vast bed, ideally suited size-wise either for a ménage à trois or a couple who loathed physical contact, they decided to make an inventory of the two-floored Lady Florentine suite before the descent to dinner.

No-one-could-object-to decor. Dark green (masculine) striped wallpaper. Pink (feminine) flowers. Patterned dark green and pink carpet, fitted. Drapes and drapes over drapes, and fringes and ties and bows in pink and borage green wild silk (luxury touches). Gold framed pictures of: 1, primulas 2, daisies – no, marguerites. Do you mind? Daisies – 3, roses. Old varieties of. 4, the Hunt in Full Cry (hand-coloured engraving). Three TVs (for the ménage à trois?), a safe in the wall (for her valuables and his credit cards), cream furniture in cane, repro bergère, four four-seater traditional settees (useful for penthouse cocktail parties). Sheik-sized bed. Cream acres of fitted wardrobes. Terrace downstairs. Plastic garden furniture. (Plastic? Heavens!) Own lawn with own pine tree. China cabinets with china. Floral. Two low tables, mahogany, repro. His and hers bathrooms. His grey marble, hers pink, Jacuzzis in both. Cut-glass decanter of whisky with two glasses by bed (his side). One pear, one kiwi fruit, one apple, one banana, six strawberries, one orange and fifteen grapes in china bowl (floral), accompanied by handwritten personalized greetings from the hotel manager.

For the physically immobile, there was a touch-control humidifier; there was also air conditioning and central heating, and bath-running room service.

For the perusal of the Stylish World Traveller, deliberately arranged on the mahogany bookcase were: *Field, Country Life, Vogue, Prestige, Metropolitan* (international property guide). *Essays of Elia* by Charles Lamb, *Poems* by Victor Hugo (in English), *A Christmas Carol* by Charles Dickens, *Studies of the Spiritual History of the Gael* by Fiona Macleod.

And for the perusal of more unconventional guests who read music: *Vogelweid the Minnesinger*. A poem by Longfellow set to music for children's voices by George Rathbone. Hiller's 'Song of Victory', a sacred cantata for choir and soloists. 'Souvenir' by Franz Drdla. 'Island and Highland Tunes' set to Anglo-Scottish words and arranged by Hugh S. Robertson. Handel's 'Passion of Christ' edited by Ebenezer Prout.

Didi went and sat next to Stephen on the chintz settee. 'What on earth can you say about all this? What am I going to do? Laura wants me to shoot here. Oh dear.'

'The usual how the rich live crap, sweetest. Barbed criticism masquerading as praise. Shouldn't you be starting to change for dinner?'

A little later, or much later according to Stephen, Didi descended the internal staircase in a floating tent of pale yellow silk which billowed forth from under her full breasts.

'Do you like it, darling?'

'It's . . . well. I like the colour. But, sweetest, it does look as though you're about to produce twins.'

Didi laughed and was sure her secret was growing minute by minute beneath the yellow tent like a stop-framed flower unfurling its petals on screen. It might be only two and a bit weeks, but henceforth she would be proudly wearing the insignia of approaching motherhood.

Stephen remembered every course, every sauce, every garnish, every *mise en place*, but Didi did not. She would remember the chef.

'Sweet boy, Heinrich. He'll look good even if his English is a little wonky at times.'

'Best *rosti* I've had. Good. Good. Yes, he's good.'

'So we can concentrate on the chef. Forget the rest and I'll just shoot in the kitchen.'

'Why don't you do that?'

'I could wrap it up in half a day.'

Didi smiled with relief and summoned the waiter to ply Stephen with another huge glass of that wonderful 1954 Armagnac. For herself, she held back and surreptitiously poured most of her glass into Stephen's when he was looking round the room to see what everyone was eating. Pregnancy. She was going to take it extremely seriously.

'Sweetest, I'm getting . . . awfully . . . drunk.'

'Nonsense. I've had far more than you.'

Not long afterwards they left the debris on the table and Didi steered Stephen towards the Earl of Hardwick suite.

'Are you sure this . . . this is my room?'

'Of course. Look. There are the antlers on the door.'

She took his key, opened the door and then he vaguely remembered that he had seen the gold fleur-de-lys on the walls before somewhere.

'I'm not going to allow you to sleep in your clothes again.'

Didi slipped off his jacket, released his tie and unfastened his shirt buttons one by one, running her hand across his chest. Then she pulled back the linen sheets and pushed him gently on to the bed. He lay across it, abandoning himself like a child. Once she had dimmed the lights to blackness, Didi took off the yellow tent and climbed in beside him.

'What are you doing here?' Stephen murmured as his hands felt the rounded line of her hips. Then she kissed his body, down, down, and rested her face on the hairy line of his belly, her black curls spreading across his torso.

'I dream about you every night,' she said, as she lightly caressed him and waited for him to rise to her touch.

'Didi, it's . . .'

'I don't care about anyone else but you. I love you.'

'It's . . .'

'Don't you like my body?'

'Beautiful.'

'Do you like me doing this?'

'Bliss, but I'm . . .'

'So am I. Gloriously. It doesn't matter.'

'I'm hopeless failed . . . boring. No good for you.'

'You're everything I want.'

Didi wriggled up his body and kissed him deeply. Then Stephen put his hands round her face and held her on the pillow.

'Is anything the matter? Would you rather come to my room? Do you want me to go?'

'No. Stay.'

Stephen had a strong desire to sink into sleep, but he resisted and sat up, leaning against the padded silk bedhead. Didi lay on his chest and for a while they were both still, like exhausted lovers.

'It's no good, sweetest.'

'Let me try.'

She searched in vain for the stiffening signs of desire.

'Nothing's happening. Don't be upset. I'm too drunk. Let's go to sleep.'

Tears trickled down her face. 'I'd much rather you told me. I understand. I don't mind if you're gay, honestly I don't. It doesn't make any difference.'

'Sweetest, I don't go for men. You know that.'

'Then you don't find me sexy. I suppose some people didn't find Marilyn Monroe sexy. I'm sorry I'm not thin and blonde and—'

'Sh, Sh, sweetest. You're gorgeous and irresistible. More than anyone I know. Haven't you guessed by now?'

'Guessed what?' Didi opened her eyes wide in the darkness.

'I can't.'

'Can't what?'

'I'm . . . Christ, Didi, don't you think I'd have leaped into bed months ago if I could have done anything about it? I can't do it. Not for anybody. Why do you think I stood by knowing John was fucking you like crazy every night? Because I couldn't punch him on the nose and drag you off to bed, that's why.'

'Oh, Stephen, I've finished with him. How dreadful. I didn't think you were jealous. Oh dear. I've gone and screwed up everything. I've only ever wanted you. Do let's try.'

'Didi, listen. We can eat together, drink together, laugh together. Sex for me is like homework I could never do. Not worth the effort.'

'But don't you ever do it?'

'Myself? Occasionally . . . if dinner's been really bad.'

Next morning, they had breakfast and Didi's tears splashed into the deep yellow yolk of the boiled egg which Stephen had cracked open for her. She could not pretend that it was he who had made her pregnant, she could not announce to her friends that she was having a love-child and the wild night of passion would never be.

'Stephen,' she began, trying to hold back her sobs, 'I'm going to have a baby. Shall we get married? You'd be a wonderful father.'

Stephen dipped some toast into the liquid egg and put it into her mouth.

'Are you sure you want to be a mother, sweetest? I presume it's—'

'Yes. Damn him. But that doesn't matter. It's my baby. I want it, and I'm going to have it.'

Stephen could say no more, but he was planning a trip to a very distant place for eight, nine month's time. She would tell him the date soon enough.

17

For a few days in March, no-one at the Kitchen Club paid the least attention to the crashing of governments, minor wars, epidemics, earthquakes, famine, football results or the latest Department of Health statistics for premature deaths from heart disease. Major and minor catastrophes came and went, but the day the Michelin stars were announced the world stood still. Rumours had been circulating wildly during February about who would gain and who would lose, and when the results went contrary to rumour further rumours spread of corruption and bribery amongst the inspectors. Passions were running high.

If anyone deserved his star, it was John Crabtree. Good lad, John. He opened that place from nothing. Who could possibly begrudge him the reward for hard work, imagination, technique and consistency? One thing you could say about John: you never ate half-cooked, over-cooked or stale at the Eglantine. No disputing that, and they'd all eaten there one time or another, checked him out. Had to see what the good chefs were cooking, make sure you weren't overlooking a fashion which they'd cottoned on to first, make sure you dropped lamb's lettuce if they dropped lamb's lettuce. Couldn't be cooking last year's food and you had to know which classics were in and which out. None of the chefs realized that their passionate preoccupations were entirely ignored by those who ate at their restaurants, for the intensity of their debate fired them like a peaking fever.

Elwyn was not to be seen at the bar.

'They're either fucking bent or fucking mad. Elwyn loses a star, you get one, I get two and Harry Wade gets one. Harry Wade? Just because he puts in a new kitchen and employs a few more waiters.'

'Harry's safe, Tad. He does the same dishes year after year. Maybe a little variation now and then. And he does them OK.'

'OK? Who gets a fucking star for being OK? Did you? No. You got one because you're brilliant and you deserved it, John. So if you get one for deserving it, why does another bastard get it for being an arsehole? And if an arsehole gets one star, what does that make getting two stars? Bloody hell! Who cares anyway?'

'Come off it, Tad. You're chuffed to bits. We all care.'

'You think the punters know, or even give a bugger?'

'Laura said she's going to go all out for publicity this year. Michelin awareness. Perhaps a star-chef book, if they agree.'

'Watch it. That'll up her percentage. She's not getting my recipes for nothing. I tell you.'

'But it's—'

'Wonderful publicity. I know. But we don't need it. None of us. You got empty seats at the Eglantine?'

'Not often, Tad.'

'Well. There you go. Nothing to do with Miss La-di-da inviting wanking journalists. I've decided not to speak to the press. They know what I look like by now.'

'If you stop they'll only latch on to someone else.'

'I'm going to try the Greta Garbo ploy. Alone and palely loitering. Then when I've finished doing that I'll surprise the lot of you.'

'You're going to wear a suit and tie?'

'I might join Trust House Forte and go on a management course.'

'And I might become an army caterer.'

'Melissa prefers officers, Little John. Told you that.'

'Here we go. Go on. How many times you had her, Tad?'

'Shall I be frank? I don't want to tread on your cock, Little John.'

'I'm glad to hear it.'

'She likes it in public.'

'What?'

'She's done it on a golf course, under the dinner table and up against the railings of Buckingham Palace in between promenading policemen. But she likes it best on stainless steel. Kitchen's a good place. And the loos at Lloyds of London. Did you know they were all stainless steel? If you come on stainless steel, it's a hell of a job to get it off. That really turns little Melissa on. She tells me she's done it in the bar at Covent Garden during the Ring Cycle.'

'There are plenty of long intervals.'

'Her great ambition is to do it on TV in the middle of a chat show. After a snort. Maybe you could get her invited on *Table for One*. Hah! Another first for Miss Kowalski! On second thoughts, no. Now that she's carrying the *wunderkind*, that wouldn't be on.'

'She's *what*?'

'Preggers, darling. Hasn't she told you yet? Everyone else knows.'

John leaned his head on the bar and pressed his hands to his forehead. 'I don't believe it. I haven't seen her since the night of the funeral. She won't speak to me. Saw me with Melissa. I told her nothing happened but she wouldn't listen. I mean, it's not as though we're engaged.'

'Engaged!' Tadeus gave John a pitying look and put his arm round his shoulder. 'Is it yours? The bun?'

'It bloody better be. Tad, what shall I do?'

'You've got the star. That's all that matters.'

'I want everyone to share my experience,' said Didi at the Intertel weekly programme meeting. 'I want everyone to go through what I'm going through minute by minute.' (Week by week, suggested Roger.) And so they did. They knew which exercises she performed every day, what food she ate, how much, and the exact vitamin, mineral, water, fat, protein and carbohydrate intake judged by leading dieticians to be the optimum for the baby's perfect physical and mental growth. They saw the baby growing inside the womb (Roger said he'd go for that) and heard the heartbeat. They saw Didi walking through Kensington Gardens, swimming in the pristine waters of the Park Lane Rialto Hotel pool, stretching voluptuously as she performed her ante-natal regime, with her voice-over in a lovely echo effect as she intoned: don't forget, don't forget, diet goes hand in hand with exercise.

Then there were the special meals for pregnant mums cooked by a galaxy of this year's Michelin winners. Tadeus Freeman. Harry Wade. Sebastian North . . . but not, of course, John Crabtree.

Didi couldn't understand how any woman could wait to have the first taste of motherhood. 'Pregnancy is bliss,' she sighed. Photo sessions were now rationed. Personal interviews were limited to publications with a readership of three million and over, although unfortunately Intertel had no control over the headlines.

'TV Star refuses to name father of Love-Child', 'TV Star says No to Marriage', 'Has Didi Done the Right Thing?'. But then, to compensate for the nasty probings of the press, there was 'Didi's Diary' (now a regular column, mostly written by Intertel's Publicity Department), 'Didi's Diet' and 'Didi's Nursery'. But there came a time when the nation really needed to know the answer to the burning question she would not discuss. Who was the father?

OK. Leave it to me. Don Delaney was the man. If anyone could do it without the help of divine intervention, he could. Top undercover lensman. 'I'm the worm that crawls into private lives,' he was quoted as saying in a rare interview.

Piece of cake, this one. Don Delaney pressed a button and the door of his capacious garage swung up. It contained ready-to-go vehicles suited for blending in with various terrains and social strata. A mountain bicycle (good over fields), an old bicycle (sort that people have who can't afford any other transport), a small Ford runabout (wife's shopping car), a van (Delaney & Sons Quality Meats), a Lamborghini (good for the Costa Smeralda, South of France, Monaco, that type of place), an old Land Rover (good for royals in the country), two motorbikes (a Honda and a Harley Davidson, for fun and for pulling). Further vital equipment included a British Telecom yellow tent complete with stand-up sign apologizing for the obstruction ('essential rewiring in progress'), a thermal sleeping bag and a light storm tent. Well. He had just the job for this one. Didn't she do some cooking show on the tele?

Delaney & Sons Quality Meats were doing good business in Kensington and were apparently supplying the canteen at Intertel, to judge from their regular appearance in the studio car park, as well as doing lunch trade for gynaecologists and dentists in Harley Street.

'I've spent more time in Harley Street than a sheik's harem has,' Don remarked as he shovelled up a few grand in expenses. But they left him to it. He'd get there in the end.

Early to bed and early to fucking rise. This bird was an A1 ball-breaker. The job was getting tedious and tedium cost money. Didn't she go anywhere for kicks? Or was it going to be a phone-bug job? Don took a breather and visited Madame Monique's. You had to relax sometimes, for Christ's sake. Then he had the lucky break. There was something about Don. He always got a lucky break and this one was called Melissa Desgranges. Screwed her on the back of the Harley Davidson and she came up with the goods, work-wise. Wassisname? He scribbled it down on the back of his tit-groping hand. Crabtree. You're kidding. A fucking chef? Excuse my language.

Didi was having breakfast alone with her calorie counter beside her when the door bell rang. Poor postman. Every day there were parcels of baby clothes, toys, even a year's supply of disposable nappies sent by happy readers and viewers who wanted to contribute to her experience. People were so generous. A mere mention of her strange yen for *marrons glacés* or pickled walnuts, and she was bombarded with gift-wrapped boxes and jars. The room set aside for the nursery was awash with presents, as though she had been the hapless victim of an earthquake. I really don't deserve it, she thought, as she prepared to greet the postman with a smile and a box of crystallized fruits ('No. Do take it. I insist.'). Oh, how sweet, a bottle in a little basket. Champagne. A note inside, written in capital letters:

'Please get in touch. I need to talk to you. John.'

Didi held the note in her hand, transfixed, and reached for the phone.

'Cal!'

'I'm in the middle of making marmalade, dear. Are you allowed to eat marmalade?'

'Listen, I've heard from John. You'll never guess. He wants to see me.'

'How exciting. Quite right and proper, too.'

'I told him I wouldn't. What shall I do? Should I see him? Should I phone my lawyer? Suppose he—'

'Calm down.'

'Anyone would think it's his baby. How dare he?'

'Well, he did have something to do with it, dear.'

'It was pure accident. We weren't making babies, we were having sex. Quite different. You didn't honestly think I wanted to have his child? Mrs Crabtree? Hardly!'

Privately, Caliope considered that marrying a chef would give one enviable advantages. Wonderful dinner parties . . . She so admired men who were good with their hands. Were she half the size and had she not inherited the heavy jowls of her late father, she would certainly have considered marrying the charming Greek who kept her Motoguzzi in trim. Lady Knowles had a niece who had run off with a gardener, and they were having a lovely time. Why did girls become prey to the *idée fixe* that choosing one's partner had something to do with reaching for a higher rung on the social ladder? One was either there or not. Why did it matter so? One is either nice or not nice, amusing or frightfully dull, thought Caliope, forgetting her pride in the Fortescue name which went back four hundred years and which made her a welcome guest at the dinner parties of Lady Knowles.

'I like John Crabtree. A very decent young man, as well as looking divine. Just because he had a little lapse. You were rather hard on him, dear. Men do those kind of things occasionally. It's quite normal.'

'Whose side are you on, Cal? What are you saying?' Didi bit her nail and for the first time since the doctor's diagnosis she felt a panic of doubt. 'Have I been dreadful?'

'Of course not.'

'Perhaps I should ring up and say sorry. As though nothing had happened. But it did. At least, I think it did. Does he believe I'm going to come running after that?'

'He was merely embracing the most available girl in London. No worse than feeling a mango in Berwick Street market. Hardly worth a slap, dear, let alone the sulks.'

'It was in public, Cal!'

'Nonsense. And how kind of him to write. A very gentlemanly thing to do.'

'Oh dear. Have I been awfully cruel? I suppose I could invite him back on *Table for One*. Yes, I could do that. A kind of magnanimous gesture.'

'Nothing wrong in being magnanimous.'

'Oh dear. If only Stephen . . .'

Caliope stirred the marmalade vigorously with her free hand. 'It's starting to set. Hurray! My recipe works. They don't always, you know. As my readers keep reminding me.'

The phone went dead and clattered to the floor as Caliope abandoned herself to the crucial boiling point of Aunt Matilda's Infallible Orange Compote.

Didi immediately dialled the Eglantine and held her breath.

*   *   *

Don Delaney, in Savile Row lookalike casuals, collected a load of 3000 ASA film and a heavy flash pack for a night shoot, piled himself into the black Lambo and swerved round the back doubles, heading for Kensington. Found a space between a BMW and a Ferrari, right opposite her pad, lucky sod. He sat looking in his angled mirror like a well-trained Alsatian awaiting a scent or sound to trigger instant movement. Crabtree drove a Porsche, apparently. Must be doing OK. Still, who'd be a chef? You didn't get a syndication on recipes.

Must be him. White job slowing down. Delaney's surge of adrenalin gave him eyes at the back of his head, ears at the tips of his grubby fingers. Tall bloke, easy to see. Here we go. This was better than coming. Two seconds to get the front page pic. Getaway chef in kiss-and-make-up dash. Wait till she comes out. Blimey. Like they're doing it for the TV. Standing there looking into each other's eyes on the doorstep. Go one, mate. Give her one. That's better. Lovely. *Flash*. Lovely. *Flash*. Gotcha. *Flash*. Phew. Not bad for starters.

'What the fuck are they doing?'

'Photographers. They follow me everywhere. Ignore them.'

Didi opened the front door and pulled John inside.

Quick. Now round the back. There was a garage next door. Don had each inch and each toehold sussed out. Did his homework. He climbed on to the garage roof and looked up. That one. Her bedroom. Worth a try. Oh, yeah, what a break! No net curtains, bless 'er. She was handing it to him on a plate. Well, she would, wouldn't she? Rude Food Queen.

John was standing awkwardly in the bedroom. (Come on mate, move, move, that's right. Nearer.) He wanted to take her in his arms, possess her again, impress himself on his baby growing inside her.

'Do you want to see?' Didi parted her flowing negligee. 'Feel it.'

John gently stroked her slightly stretched belly, kissed the rounded contours and then listened for the sound of life.

'Do you know yet? Is it a boy or a girl?'

'It's going to be a surprise, but I know it's a boy.'

Didi laughed and put her head to one side, like she always did, that smile which made a man feel proud.

'You're more beautiful than ever, Didi, but I still don't understand.'

'Maybe I'll change my mind. But not now. Anyway, I can't. Think of all those girls on their own, struggling to bring up babies. Millions of them. I'm giving them hope. I couldn't possibly let them down. Imagine how they'd feel if I got married? I couldn't do it, John. I couldn't. Now do you understand?'

'I'll try.'

'You can see me and the baby whenever you like and we can be wonderful friends.'

'Like Stephen, you mean? No, love. Where I come from, men have mates and girls have friends. And that's it.'

'Oh dear, I do wish you weren't so—'

'So what?'

'Conventional, I suppose.'

'And you're not? Is Dorothy Dean dead and buried in Bromley then?'

'She's taken early retirement, darling. Hove, I think it is.'

'Or Bridlington. You ever been to Bridlington?'

'Why on earth should one go to Bridlington?'

'Lobster. Crab. Oysters . . .'

'Oh, oh! Don't! I can't bear it. Oysters . . . I haven't had any for ages. Oh, John.'

'Is that what you'd like?'

'Yes, yes. I can eat those. I'm sure I'm allowed to.'

'Shall I get you some? There's a box in my kitchen. You want me to go?'

'Please.'

John wrapped her gown around her and kissed her. 'You'll let me in when I come back?'

'Here. Take the keys.'

Didi fell back on the bed, imagining the soft, cool succulence of oysters slipping down her throat.

'We're going to have such a wonderful life, us two,' she said, patting her belly.

The picture editor held up the black and white offering and wrinkled his nose. 'Great pic, Don. Bloody hell. I won't ask how you got it.'

'Don't bother.' Don Delaney stood back like a fisherman with a full haul waiting on the quay for the highest bid. 'And how about this?' He pointed to the photograph of a pregnant woman being kissed by a man.

'She got no clothes on?'

'She's got a kind of a nightdress thing. You can see it, there.'

'Oh, yeah. I dunno. We can't use that, Don. Not in a family paper.'

'Why not? That pic's inspirational, Pete. Inspirational.'

'Looks like porn to me. And they're not even married.'

'So you're not going to buy that one?'

'No, but I'll have this. And this.'

'Fine by me, Pete.'

It would have been good to get that one in. Never mind. The European mags would take it like a shot and they paid more. Just get the caption right. Didi Whatsername, mega TV star, close friend of Princess, Prinzessin, Princesse, Principessa Diana. Yeah! His agent could handle that. And it would pay for the vintage Bentley he fancied. He'd get a good deal. Don scrawled in his diary: 'Dylan Tusk. Bentley.' Time to take in somewhere like Sri Lanka before the next job. Time for a break. Wonder why he liked dusky birds? Preferably under sixteen. Still, who didn't? With that thought, the closest that Don Delaney approached to philosophical speculation, he zipped up his black case and swung through the doors, giving a languid wave at the micro-skirted girls who uncrossed their long legs and looked up hopefully from their desks.

For some weeks, Laura had been examining her arms and legs and viewing the fine down of mushrooming hair with distaste. Peter, of course, pretended he couldn't see it, but whilst he was a genius at predicting share movements his powers of observation were limited. Perhaps he really didn't notice.

'I like you just as you are.' He didn't even see any difference after the hairdresser had restyled her long tresses and removed at least a couple of inches. 'You always look wonderful to me, Laura.'

She mustn't take his devotion for granted.

She sat at her desk, spread out the cuttings which would be the subject of her next meeting and thought of Peter. Their weekends in the country. Teaching her to play golf. The sweet smile of pleasure, his boyish face as she brought him tea in bed. The way he carefully pulled his socks on first when he was dressing. Or the delicate way he decanted the fine wines he brought for her approval. His calm movements and the peace he brought her. Almost love would perhaps grow into love itself.

There was a notice hanging from the door of the Intertel Executive Boardroom. *Do Not Disturb*. The Programme Controller, Sir Howard Riley, and Roger, the producer of *Table For One*, were deep in conference. Sir Howard was studying a dossier of cuttings.

'All I can say is, thank God she's off air at the moment.'

'I think you should know, Roger, that Sir Howard is chairing a special committee on broadcasting standards. Having a leading presenter plastered over the gutter press doesn't inspire confidence in our ability to provide a moral lead. Frankly, it's embarrassing for all of us.'

Sir Howard turned towards Roger. The set concentration on his face was unyielding. 'Could we have your views on this matter?'

Roger flushed. 'We must lodge a complaint immediately

with the Press Ombudsman for the relevant newspapers. Intrusion of privacy. It's blatant.'

'Miss Kowalski's behaviour, on the other hand, is blameless. Naturally.'

Sir Howard gave an ironic smile, directed at the Programme Controller.

'Didi has been through a terrible time,' continued Roger, 'being hounded by the press day and night. It's a miracle she hasn't lost her baby.'

The Programme Controller looked at his watch. 'The invasion of privacy is most upsetting. And I know Sir Howard has a lot to say about that. But I'm afraid, Roger, you are not ideally placed to comprehend the wider implications.'

'The wider implications of Didi's decision to have a baby without being married? Personally, I think she has handled it superbly. Lots of positive publicity which means an increase in viewing figures for the next series. And an increase in the advertising spend.'

'Yes. Indeed. That is true.'

Perhaps Sir Howard was on his side, after all.

'However,' continued the Programme Controller, 'unlike you, Roger, we do not believe that all publicity is good publicity. There are times when we have to sacrifice short term benefit for long term positioning.'

Roger took a breath. 'It could have happened to anyone. I think Didi deserves your support.'

Sir Howard leaned forward. 'Roger. We all feel sympathy. But we are here to make a business decision. Have you seen this one?'

He tossed across a copy of the *National Enquirer*. The pages were clipped together and fell open at a double picture spread of Didi Kowalski. Naked. Large. With a man's head pressed against her belly. Roger mastered his revulsion. A pregnant woman sharing her joy. Remove the shrieking captions, and that's what it was.

'This is a snatch picture. Didi would never have agreed to this. We never discussed it and we discuss everything.'

'That is irrelevant, Roger.'

'Didi lives in public. She's been brave enough to put herself at risk. I admire her for that. Going through pregnancy on her own, and being honest about her lover.'

'Is she a friend of yours?' asked Sir Howard, casually.

The Programme Controller sipped at a glass of mineral water and cleared his throat.

'I'll be quite open with you Roger. We are in the middle of sensitive negotiations with an American network. And they take a firm stand on moral issues. Which I rather admire. I have discussed the situation with Sir Howard, and he agrees that we have only one course of action. *Table for One* will be taken off the air and Miss Kowalski's contract will not be renewed. I thought you should know.'

'And in the light of the public support her sexual antics seem to have generated,' continued Sir Howard, 'we would ask you to keep this information to yourself.'

'You mean you're not telling her?' Roger began to panic. He would have to go. The axe was poised.

'We will, of course, choose the appropriate moment.'

The Programme Controller picked up the dossier and rose to his feet.

'Are you going back to Illustra House, Sir Howard? I've booked a car for you anyway . . .'

The two men walked towards the door of the Conference Room.

'Could I have a word?'

'Yes, Roger? I'll see you downstairs in a moment, Sir Howard.'

'I wanted to know if, that is, now that there's a vacant slot, would there be any plans, would I be working on another . . .'

'We are thinking of a gardening series,' replied the Programme Controller.

'Everyone seems to be growing their own nowadays. Big craze. I think people have had enough of cookery programmes. Are you interested in gardening?'

'It's one of my passions. In fact, I was down at Wisley only recently, amazing new hybrids they're developing . . .'

'Jot down a few ideas for me, will you?'

Tonight she would wear a full-length dress, pile up her hair and sweep into the foyer of Covent Garden on the arm of the man who had tentatively asked if she would consider marriage. The thought lingered in her mind like the familiar presence of her perfume which sometimes she noticed and sometimes forgot until Peter said how much he liked it.

'I know we'd be happy together,' he said. 'But I don't want to press you. I will wait.'

They were all but married. Laura was still accustoming herself to the gentle plains of happiness, unsure if they led to the downward slope of old age. She was thirty-six.

'Will you lock up?' asked Antony as he reached for his coat. 'Don't stay too long, Laura. It can wait till morning.'

'No, I won't stay long. I'm off to Covent Garden.'

'*Don Giovanni?*'

'Yes. Peter's treat.'

'I saw it last week . . . The New York folder is on your desk.' He pecked Laura on the cheek. 'Have a good evening.'

Laura watched him as he wound his way round the desks of the Studio and made for the lift. In a few months, he had grown in years, as well as bringing in several accounts. She must think what to do about Simon. Antony disliked him and his polite antagonism was filtering down to the rest of the Team. Simon was good but rather pushy, useful for more downmarket restaurateurs who responded to his brash energy. His father was in the business and he knew it inside out. And he was useful. A budding Jack without the charm. Should she send Simon to New York or find a replacement? Well, it could ride a few more weeks. The papers were checked and Laura gave a last glance at the week's schedule for the Team. She could allow time for Mozart and for Peter. Everything was becoming easier now, there was no need to feel guilty at spending a weekday evening away.

The precision of Laura's life matched the precision of Peter's. He would have allowed forty-five carefully calculated minutes to bath, shave and change and he would have ordered a cab in time to pick him up, pick her up, allow for a small traffic delay, arrive approximately ten minutes before curtain up. Champagne. 'Shall we take our seats now?' Order. Jack always arrived late, his mind racing in several different directions at once. And he talked during performances. 'Hey, babe, wasn't that great?' She must have loathed that. What did they see together? It was hard to remember. When you put on new wallpaper you eventually forgot what lay underneath, preferring the new pattern to the old. Jack called less frequently. Lotta business in Spain. No, she couldn't take time to go.

Half an hour left. Laura fantasized about sharing a house with someone else again, losing the time to herself, hearing the sounds of another person opening and closing doors, and constant intimacy. He had a quiet presence. Perhaps she could change her life again. There was the studio downstairs or would they buy somewhere larger? He had a place in the country.

The bell rang. Laura opened the front door.

'Why on earth have you come? I can't see you. I don't want to see you. I'm going out.'

'Laura, I need to speak to you. Now.'

'Howard, please go. I'm going to the opera tonight and I'm off to New York tomorrow. There's no point.'

'Just one minute.' He pushed past her. 'I've got to be in Sydney for a couple of months. I leave on Friday. I had to see you first.'

'I told you. I'm going out, Howard.'

'Listen.' He looked distraught. 'I can't live without seeing you, without being near you. I thought I could. My life has been empty since we parted. You've no idea. So many times I wanted to pick up the phone and hear your

411

voice. And then I thought it wouldn't be fair. You have your own life to lead. I respected that. I had no right to intrude. But now I've decided. I'm going to leave my wife. I'll rent a flat in London when I get back.'

'Howard, I can't—'

'You don't have to say anything. I want to give you time. I know I've behaved badly. I'm ashamed, Laura. You see, I couldn't bring myself to hurt my wife. And now I realize it is inevitable. My life has got to change. I have to be with you. When I come back, we must go away together. No matter what happens, I'm going to take time—'

'You can't do this to me, Howard.'

'You don't believe me. I don't blame you. I've let you down so often.'

'My car will be here soon.'

'Let me see you later. Laura, do this for me. I just want to be with you before I go. Even for an hour.'

'Howard, I can't.'

'I can meet you somewhere in town if you'd prefer.'

He had kept his distance, but now he pulled her towards him and kissed her wildly. Then the door bell sounded again.

'I'll stay. I'll wait for you.'

Laura ran to the window. Peter was standing expectantly on the doorstep. She parted the voile curtains a fraction and waved to show that she was about to leave, then she turned to Howard.

'Let yourself out. I'll meet you outside the Studio at eleven thirty.'

She would make an excuse to Peter, tell him she had forgotten something, tell him she was leaving on an early plane, tell him it would be better if he stayed at his place.

'Are you feeling all right?'

In the bright foyer Peter handed her the glass of champagne and looked at her pale face with concern. When they moved down to the stalls he put his arm through hers, but she did not respond as she usually did.

'Is anything wrong?'

'No, of course not.'

'Is it your er . . . ?'

Laura smiled. 'Yes. The usual thing, I'm afraid.'

'I'm sure you could take some pills, Laura. We must get you sorted out.'

'When I'm back from New York.'

Don Giovanni had Howard's haunted eyes. His straight stance. His long, fine hands. Donna Anna, Donna Elvira, captivated still, flailing for revenge. The wounded girls, the outraged women, they could do nothing but wail and the ghost of vengeance was only a ghost. Who could believe in the earth opening up with hellfire flames beneath Don Giovanni's feet? And when he had descended into the bowels of the stage through the trap door, what then? Elvira to a convent and Donna Anna weeping for eternity on her husband's shoulder instead of knifing him through the heart.

'Questo è il fin di chi fa mal!' The end of the evil-doer.

No, she really couldn't manage dinner afterwards, but Peter understood. Was she sure she wouldn't like him to make her coffee before she left for the airport? Laura shook her head, and recited the schedule to herself. Six thirty leave. Check in. Jot down some more ideas. Meeting: lunch at the New York Rialto. Take in a couple of restaurants before the afternoon meeting, check out menu, decor, clientele. There was no reason to go to the Studio. She had everything she needed, Antony had been marvellous.

'Promise you'll see a specialist soon.'

'Yes. Promise. I'll call you as soon as I can.'

Peter hailed a cab and gave the driver her Chelsea address. She would have five hours' sleep. The music she had heard all evening echoed in her head, and then slipped away.

I can't live without seeing you, without being near you. I thought I could. My life has been empty since we parted.

It was half past eleven. Laura pushed open the glass partition.

'I've forgotten something. Could you drop me at Mortimer Street?'

A black Mercedes was outside. The interior light was on and he was reading a newspaper. As she stood encoding and releasing the complex front door locks of the glass building in the dark street, she knew he was behind her.

'Was it a good performance?' he asked as they went up in the lift together. 'What did you see?'

'*Don Giovanni*.'

'Ah yes. And I suppose the Don looked like an overweight grocer. I saw it last year at La Scala. Still, the music's marvellous.'

'He reminded me of you.'

'Not physically I hope.'

Laura took off her wrap, reached into the fridge for a bottle of champagne – she would need that – and banged the door shut. She could have been home by now, in bed. The rush of expectation, regret, desire and hope which had built up with every crescendo sweeping through her from the stage had vanished down the trap door. Howard didn't look as though seeing her was a matter of life or death and she could have been gazing into Peter's fresh, untroubled face as he slept peacefully beside her.

'I assume you want a drink.'

'Thank you, darling. You look dazzling tonight.'

He always began by commenting on her appearance.

'I saw that piece on you in *The Times*. Fantastic, Illustra Foods coming fourth in the top ten. But naturally, you are aiming to be first.'

Howard took her hand in his and stroked her fingers. His voice was hesitant. 'Have you . . . thought about me?'

'Occasionally.'

'Are you angry?'

'Not really. Not now that I realize I meant so little to you.'

'We'll talk about that another time.'

414

'Another time?'

'When I get back.' He picked up his glass and watched the tiny bubbles forcing their way to the surface. 'I'll say what I have to say, and then I'll go.'

Laura waited in silence. He was anxious, his brow furrowed, unable to look directly at her.

'I made a mistake. You see it was difficult for me to separate what I did and what you did, from . . . from us. Us being together.'

'Howard, I'm not asking you to explain anything.'

'Right from the beginning, all I wanted was for you to free yourself from, from—'

'Jack? We get on fine now.'

'I hope I helped a little.'

Laura pushed back her hair. 'Yes. A little.'

'But you don't need me now. Is that it?'

'If that is how you want to see it, Howard. No, I suppose I don't. On my own two feet at last. I really don't deserve it. Everything seems to be working better than I ever imagined. My business . . .'

'Ready for me to take over yet?'

They laughed.

'I've told my wife I'll be leaving. She took it better than I thought. It will be strange, at first. Being on my own again. I don't know when I'll have the time to find somewhere to live.'

Laura only saw the lilies, thrusting out of the narrow steel vase. The familiar room occupied by empty desks receded through the glass, its dimensions changing, elongating. Howard was a figure in a distant landscape, although seated next to her. For a few seconds she was no longer in space and time and recognized nothing, as though memory and feeling had been sucked out of her. She stood up. She did not recall getting to her feet but it was then that she felt the searing heat of anger.

'How can you say that so calmly? After all this time?'

'I knew you couldn't stand it any more, the compromise.

Christ, Laura! There was no point in telling you until I was free. It wasn't fair on you.'

'Not fair on me? Come, try another one. Now I know you're lying. You haven't told your wife that you're going and you have no intention of leaving her. She's probably keeping the dinner warm for you right now. Oh yes, there was a time when she suspected and you had to tell her that you'd had a quick, sordid affair. Over now. Isn't that what you said?'

Howard was silent.

'And when she howled, you thought twice. Who knows? Maybe you used to imagine being with me. Marry Laura? Why? Isn't one wife as good as another, as long as she dotes on you and does what she's told? You knew I wasn't the kind to do that. Why seek out a replacement when the first model is in reasonable working order? Why the visit, Howard? Have you been feeling bored lately? Have the office girls said no? Are you hard up for a fuck? Or is it more fun for you, now that I'm seeing someone else? Is that why you're here?'

'You bitch.' He smiled regretfully.

'Found out, Howard. But you needn't apologize. Just leave.'

'Who is this man? Do I know him? Is he better than me? Does he make you come all night or are you afraid of pleasure?'

He was on top of her. Stranger's hands. Her mind was elsewhere. She would punish through indifference. In a few hours she would be on the plane. It was no different from being screwed at the end of a drunken party.

'Now. Give, give, I want you to come.'

He pushed and pushed, his voice commanded. It was so easy to resist, it meant nothing.

Then he was turning her over, his fingers tracing a line down her buttocks.

'I won't do it if you don't want me to.' Deep and soft, his voice.

Laura lay still.

'Have you not done it before? Are you afraid? You needn't be. Would you like to try? You can stop me if you want to.'

She remained silent.

'You want to. I can feel you opening. I'll be gentle. It won't hurt. Nothing is forbidden in sex. Nothing is dirty. Are you afraid?'

'No.'

'Let me. I want you to have it. I want you to know everything.'

Howard entered behind her, insinuating like the agave worm, up into forbidden territory. Laura buried her face in the silk cushions. The final test. That's what it was. The agony, scything pain. She could take it. Then her body exploded into pleasure with an intensity which was driving her beyond his reach and into chaos.

He was leaning over her, stroking her hair, watching until she opened her eyes. Then she heard, from a great distance, the tap running in her bathroom behind the Sanctum.

'Laura, are you all right? Open your eyes. Did I hurt you?'

'N–No.'

'You're not sorry?'

'Sorry about what?'

Howard glanced at his watch. 'We have been at it a long time. It's nearly two o'clock. Didn't you say you were off to New York tomorrow early?' He dressed quickly and wandered around the Studio. 'I do like that picture. Is it one of yours, Laura? Did you paint it?'

'Oh, that. It's nothing.'

Howard took the painting down from the wall and carried it over to where she had been lying, and was now gathering up her clothes.

'You know, you have an extraordinary talent. I always said so. Have you thought of having an exhibition?'

'You know I haven't time, Howard. I have a company to run.'

'The colours . . .'

'I'm not happy with it. It was just an idea, really. An idea for a larger canvas. But my studio isn't large enough for the scale I want.'

'When I look at this . . .'

'Don't. It isn't very good.'

'It makes me wonder why on earth you have devoted yourself to this wretched business. At the beginning I could see you needed to make a success of something, of anything. It is a shame that you happened to choose something which I could have trained any of my secretaries to do. Never mind. It will make you rich, if that's what you want.'

'It's hard, isn't it, Howard? Now that I'm no longer a failure.'

'I never said that.'

'There's nothing left for you to do. Poor Howard. I've got what I want. You only found me interesting when you could help me achieve – well – everything I longed for.'

'Very good, Laura. You understand me so well.'

'Terrible, isn't it? Not needing you. Still, I'm sure you'll find another protégée.' She drained the flat champagne in her glass. 'Howard, the game is finished.'

He laughed. 'What makes you think it is a game?'

'Because the point of a game is that you can walk away afterwards and feel nothing.'

'Dear Laura, you must learn about love.'

'It's true, isn't it? You feel nothing.'

18

The velvety petals of plum and cherry were beginning to shower down in pink cascades, dropping like confetti on Laura's grey suit as she glanced briefly at the limpid blue sky to remind herself of the month of May. The exuberant prelude to summer passed her by. The April reckoning had left a residue of sombre thoughts, for underlying the buoyancy of her company's achievement lay a creeping spectre she was unable to ignore, as though the troops of a hostile country were massing on the border. The shadowy presence was mentioned hesitantly behind closed doors, for no-one could be certain whether it was a figment of a jittery imagination, a sabre-rattling to frighten the weak, or whether it warranted a full-scale alert.

Recession? Viscount Alloway gave a vigorous sniff as he observed the packed tables at the Eglantine and reached for his fourth brandy. True, chaps in the City were getting in a tizz. Technical recession? Growth recession? Did negative growth qualify? That's what the Yanks called it. Never knew what they meant, the Yanks. How could growth be negative? How negative was negative? Drop in employment? Lowering of productivity? Big minus in the balance of payments? Damned if he knew. Our chaps called it shrinkage. Too many people going under. He played it by hunch. Once too many people went under you pulled in your horns. That's how they saw it at MacCrae. Pull in the high risk and opt for the low risk, but go easy. Just common sense, adapting to the climate.

'Don't look so worried, m'dear. No-one in here gives a damn. No evidence of shrinkage. No evidence whatsoever. We're pleased. Jolly pleased. Not about to pull the rug from under your feet. No need for alarm.'

As she left for the Studio, instead of feeling calmer Laura's apprehension grew. Would everything come crashing down around her? She had lost several major accounts. Would more follow? She could see her name in the list of bankruptcy proceedings. Laura Douglas. Failed Laura Douglas. Poor Laura. From nothing to something to nothing.

There were no visits to New York in May. Stony-faced economy and set menu lunches was the new LDA rule. The white lights in the Study were beaming on to the work stations from early morning to late at night. It was not something she would have considered a few months ago. A trade exhibition? How could Laura Douglas be associated with trade? Would a member of the royal family endorse Whammo crisps? Of course not. She might be able to find the time to give her views. An hour. She could spare that.

The biennial Exposition Culinaire was to be held this year in Britain. Laura flicked through the brochure, reading only enough to carry her through a brief one hour's consultation. All the usual trade stands. Mediocre samples of dreary mass production. And this. How could she possibly?

The major stand at the Exposition Culinaire will celebrate the diverse activities of Illustra Foods, a visual and aural Fantasia entitled 'Our England'. A multi-screen video, *From Field to Plate*, will show an Illustra Foods organic farm, complete with an area of bio-engineered, prematurely waving corn, Olde Englishe traditional breeds represented by Tamworth and Saddleback pigs, Dorset Horn, Blueface Leicester and Swaledale sheep, Aberdeen Angus and Welsh Black cattle, New Forest ponies, a Clydesdale horse and Anglo-Nubian and Angora goats. Adding to the pageant, there will be a stone-wall builder and a thatcher, seen displaying their colourful skills in miniature at set times of the day, giving a panoramic foretaste of the wide-ranging scope of the Illustra Foods Group. Brightly coloured booths flying the Illustra Foods pennant will be staffed by members of the cast of *Call Me Madam* currently playing in London's West End. They will be handing out free samples of Whammo Bars, Cripes Crisps and Teenie Wheenie Bars as well as a selection of innovative dairy products . . .

She would give him her views. Certainly, she would do that. The appalling commercial exploitation of everything, turning quality to debasement. Brashness. Vulgarity. Making the prime produce of the land into a circus. No. She could not possibly associate herself with that.

The Illustra Foods Boardroom was precisely what she would have expected. Designed like an airport lounge. No wonder he appreciated her judgement. He needed it.

'How was Australia?' she asked.

'Fine.' She stared him straight in the face and prepared to attack, adopting a tone of casual regret.

'Howard, I'm not sure that I can fit it in. Much as I'd like to.'

'Think about it. If you manage this project, it will finance your New York office for a year. And think of all the companies queuing up to swell your portfolio. Can't you see what an opportunity this is for you? And I'll do everything I can – you'll meet the right people. Even my leading competitors! They'll all be there.'

'It's not that I can't see the benefits, Howard, but it's hardly the kind of thing—'

'I know it seems a lot to take on, but I'll give you any support you need. Who knows? You could beat me to it and buy out Leone Leisure.'

Laura took the Exposition brochure in front of her and shut it into her briefcase with a loud click.

'By the way, I've been asked to submit a few paintings to an exhibition.'

He seemed surprised at this intrusion into the conversation.

'I'm really pleased, but it does mean I'll need to spend more time doing my own work. So I'm being quite strict about what I take on. And I really don't see the LDA being associated with the kind of enterprise you have in mind.'

At the beginning of the second meeting, he remembered. 'I'm so glad you're painting again. It's what you should be doing. I always said that.'

There was something else he had meant to tell her, now that he was putting his cards on the table. No, he wouldn't discuss their past. Just to put the record straight. Would she allow him that?

Last year had been a bad year for him, and for Illustra Foods. It had, he realized later, affected their relationship.

'I thought we agreed we wouldn't mention us,' Laura said, as though disputing an item on the agenda. 'I came here to a business meeting.'

Howard ignored her and continued. He couldn't tell her at the time, and it was still classified information. However, he thought she should know. There had been an attempt to sabotage the Prima supermarket division. A routine chemical analysis had revealed that random batches of Teenie Wheenie Bars had been contaminated with cyanide. There was no way of telling if any children had died, but there were several hospitalized cases, so his contact in the Department of Health had informed him. People collapsing for no apparent reason.

The board had decided to maintain secrecy at all costs. It was an extremely difficult decision. They had, of course, removed suspect confectionery from the shelves, explaining that Illustra Foods, as a result of a minimum additive policy, were reformulating this best-selling brand. There was excellent cooperation with the police and hospital poison centres. After months of costly investigation, they had found the culprit. A former warehouseman from a Prima Foods depot. Thankfully, he had injected non-lethal doses, but enough to cause serious alarm. And fortunately, after examination by two psychiatrists, the man was committed to a mental institution. A court case would have been most unwelcome.

'I don't know how I managed to see you at all, but I went through weeks of hell. One crazy bastard could have finished us. Billions were at stake. And there I was planning to set up a Prima chain in Scandinavia. I've never been under such strain.'

'Why tell me now?'

'I wanted you to know. The point is, and I'm sure you'll understand, the Illustra Foods Group has got to be in an unassailable position. As yet, they aren't quite there. Rumours are still circulating round some stores, so the managers report. Now can you understand why I asked you to be involved? I – we – need your help.'

'It will mean pushing everything aside for a while,' Laura said. 'Normally, I would have asked for a year. What you're asking me to do is to promote a show with a cast of thousands in a matter of weeks.'

'I know it's a lot to ask, Laura.'

'It is possible, but it will mean hiring some more staff. I don't know where I'll put them.'

'I can find you some space at Illustra House.'

'Give me a day to work out the details.'

'Shall we talk money?'

'Why not?'

Laura scribbled down some figures while Howard poured the coffee.

'Here's the figure. For my exclusive time, plus extra staff, extra accommodation, office expenses, transport.'

'Yes, yes. Understood.'

'Five hundred.'

Howard looked puzzled.

'Thousand.'

'Darling, that's out of the question. It's a large proportion of the budget.'

'Then you'll have to increase the budget.'

'We don't have that kind of money. I'd like to give it to you, but it just isn't possible. Half a million? The board will never agree, I'm afraid.'

'I can't do it for less. It wouldn't be economical. In any case, it will mean delaying the opening of my New York office. I'll have to cover my losses, Howard. I'm sorry. That's my position.'

'Perhaps if you came in as consultant.'

'I wouldn't do that.'

Howard rose from his chair and stood behind Laura, his hands resting on her shoulders.

'You're asking for rather a lot. Don't you think?'

'Didn't you always find me terribly demanding?'

As he accompanied her down in the lift he tried to kiss her, but she pushed him away. Next morning an Illustra Foods messenger arrived at the Studio with a private and confidential letter for Miss Laura Douglas.

Memo: from the Chairman of Illustra Foods.
Re: British Exposition Culinaire.

Having consulted with members of my board, and having regard for the time pressures attendant on this sensitive project, I am pleased to accept your estimate for undertaking the promotion of the British Exposition Culinaire to be held in July. I would appreciate a detailed breakdown of costings at your earliest convenience.

Laura filed the memo and was content. She had staved off bankruptcy and would treat herself. A painting, a small sculpture, a suit from Chanel. Or perhaps all three.

Jack pushed open the eighteenth-century door (well, that's what Charlie said it was) retrieved from some monastery Charlie was changing into executive apartments up in the Dales, walked through reception and shouted, 'What's with the fountain? Have those bastards cut off the water again?'

424

'You don't have it on all the time. Not cost effective, Jack. But don't worry. It's working OK.'

'I want to see the full effect. Sound. Lights. Water.'

Jack flicked his fingers and Charlie hurried over to the control box. Idiot proof. It better be. 'Laura's coming at noon. All it needs now is something on the wall. I'll look around. Maybe she's got a painter friend who could do us something.'

'For the right price.'

'Yeah.'

The panelling, the red drapes, the heavy chairs, the dingy carpet, the gilded lights. Not a trace. Laura put her hand to her mouth in dismay.

'Hold on, babe. Hold on. Stay there. Wait till you see this.'

A fountain in the centre of the room gushed into life, underlit like some small volcano. The water followed along a winding channel crossed by a rustic bridge until it gathered in a small pool next to a bamboo bar overhung by thatched roofing. A jungle of tangled leaves hung down from a wrought-iron gallery. White-painted bamboo chairs and tables stood on Spanish rugs glowing with a kaleidoscope of colour. To one side, a shoal of iridescent fish, startled by the sudden light, scuttled across a huge tank set into the wall. And in the centre stood a wrought-iron cross taken from a wayside shrine, hung with dried flowers and surrounded by candles.

Jack came forward to where Laura was standing. 'Listen.'

A dawn chorus of tropical birds screeched and burbled above the sound of rushing water, then there was a piercing call which appeared to travel round the room. The sounds grew in volume, subsided, swelled again and faded into a subdued chatter.

'It's controllable, the birdsong. Someone comes early, say, they come into an environment. Charlie wanted music, but I said no. You think some kind of instrumental stuff?'

Laura shrugged.

'Anyhow. You like it? The effect?'

'It's . . . very innovative, Jack.'

'I dreamed it. Yes. I was having a siesta by the pool in Spain and when I woke up, I'd seen it. Every detail. The birds. The fish. The water. Even the cross. I saw that cross. It came to me. Things ever come to you like that? It's weird. 'Cause I couldn't think what to do with this place. Jesus, was it a wreck! Anyway, one thing I didn't dream. Pictures. I need something for that space.'

'I quite like it clear. Perhaps you need that—'

'No, no. Every corner's gotta hum. Everywhere you look, it's gotta have magic.'

'A wall hanging, perhaps?'

'A wall hanging. Brilliant, babe. Brilliant. I knew you'd come up with something. Yeah. A wall hanging. Those Spanish peasants, you know they still do lace? Yeah. Lace. Kind of a different texture. From Spain. I'll be down there next month. We're about to have lift off.'

'What kind of food are you planning on, Jack?'

'I've got a chef. He's coming up with a few ideas. You'll see. Don't forget. Here. The rough for the invite. "Jack Leone invites you personally to attend the opening of Leone's – a unique dining experience". Take a look. You like the invitation? Hey! The lace motif. Lace. I should have remembered. You know, Laura, I'm a happy man. This place, it's gonna be like my home. We can lunch in my place one day, your place one day. How about that? Everything OK with you?'

'Couldn't be better.'

'Still seeing that guy?'

'Yes.'

'Know what I thought? If we were back together, we'd never meet. You in New York, me in Spain. We want highs and you don't get highs waiting for the gas man and screwing from eleven thirty to twelve in a six-foot bed. And we're not corporation guys neither. So where does that leave us?'

'Chasing money?'

'Yeah. I guess that's about it.'

As they stood outside the restaurant, Jack hugged her close to him. 'You still give me a hard on. That excite you, babe?'

'Not a lot.'

There was something which was troubling Caliope, and it bore no relation to her dispiriting experiments with mille feuille, goat's cheese and anchoïade littering the tiny kitchen. She attributed her lack of inspiration to last night's soirée given by Lady Knowles.

She had been talking to Viscount Alloway about her culinary column, when he suggested a little item. Did she know that they'd taken off his favourite programme with that girl, Didi something, always gave him an appetite? Was he sure? Of course. Got it from Riley, chairman of Intertel, friend of his. And then, dammit, he remembered he was meant to keep his mouth shut. Cross my heart and hope to die, Caliope promised not to tell a soul.

After she had hurled yet another wretched failure into the copious rubbish bin, slipped on some butter on the tiled floor and burned her hand taking a tin out of the oven, she decided that promise or no promise, Didi ought to be told. Not directly, of course. But there was no harm in telephoning John to inform him, en passant, that she'd heard a dreadful rumour.

'You think it's my oven and not me? What a frightfully comforting thought. Have it tested? You are a darling. I would never have dreamed of doing that.' Then her voice sank to sepulchral seriousness. She'd heard someone say, but couldn't reveal her source, that *Table for One* would not be returning after the summer break. It might only be a rumour, but wouldn't it be sensible to find out? Then, if it wasn't true, Didi need never know.

John did nothing. Caliope spent too much time gossiping, and had no business telling people how to cook. How could it possibly be true? He was used to rumours which came to a rapid boil in the kitchen and evaporated as quickly. Take Tadeus, for example. No-one had seen him for a while, and the lads in the kitchen thought he was away doing some demonstration, some TV programme, guesting somewhere, visiting his sick mother, who knows? They didn't ask. He'd said he'd be gone for a bit. Chefs did that. The sous took over, but they did most of the cooking anyway. Made no difference. Then someone started talking at the Kitchen Club. Tad having a nervous breakdown? Don't be daft. No, John was told, it's true. He'd gone off his trolley. The pressure. Him going full pelt like a lunatic, bound to happen. A couple of weeks later, and Tad had suffered a major heart attack. Didn't he look the type to have a weak heart? And after a few more weeks' absence, it had come out at last. Suicide attempt. What? Tad? Well, you know what they said about André Bouchon. Slashed his wrists. Who? André Bouchon? No, Tad. Slashed his wrists. He'd not gone and topped himself? Tad? Don't be daft.

Didi was blissfully preparing for the final moment when nine, maybe ten, million viewers would share her ecstasy as she travelled in the Intertel limousine round the country, saying how she was hoping to give birth under water with the piped sound of dolphins playing to rapt audiences in church halls and shopping malls, beaming out her message of enthusiasm to local radio stations and creating a significant baby boom as thousands followed her example and flushed away their contraceptive pills.

And she even agreed to fleeting but rewarding (and much rewarded) appearances on commercials expressing her confidence in various brands of baby cream, baby powder, environmentally friendly nappies, foldaway ergonomic prams, baby bouncers, bio-rhythmic rattles and additive-free organic homemade farm-fresh natural nutritionally-balanced tinned baby food now available at all Prima supermarkets.

At Intertel, *Green Fingers* was in the pre-production phase and it was then that Didi's loyal researcher Deirdre learned the truth. *Table for One*, Roger explained, was no longer 'now'. Intertel had adopted the strategy, in common with other companies, of closing down top-rated series at their peak. A policy move, to prevent the slow slide to switch-off and vindictive reviews. Tough, but that's how it was.

Sitting at Didi's kitchen table, an untouched glass of champagne in front of her, Deirdre sobbed out the tragic news. When she saw Didi sitting there so calmly, with such dignity, radiant with pregnancy, she apologized for her emotional outburst.

'We're all going to protest,' Deirdre promised. 'Everyone's on your side.'

'They could have had the grace to inform me,' said Didi, opening the fridge. 'Still, I'm used to battles. Remember the *Quickie Cookie* idea?'

'Of course I do, Didi.'

'The Programme Controller won't forget me in a hurry. I'm going to make his life hell on earth. He'll wish he'd never set eyes on Didi Kowalski. Wait there. I've a phone-call to make.'

Two minutes later, Didi returned.

'Wouldn't you have guessed? The Programme Controller is out of town and the Head of Contracts is unavailable. I can see I'll have to go in without an appointment. Mean-mouthed ugly bastards.'

That evening, John came home early.

'What's wrong, love?'

He refused to believe it.

Didi rushed off. He heard her howling in the bathroom. She'd locked the door and wouldn't come out. In there for ages. More howling then silence. What was she doing? The baby. She couldn't, could she? John put his shoulder against the door, gave a mighty push and it swung open. Didi was standing in front of the mirror, leaning on the basin, having hiccups.

'You all right?'

'Hick. Water.'

'Don't do that again, Didi.'

'The baaa. Hick. The bastards.'

John wiped her eyes, kissed her and led her to the bedroom. 'You'd best lie down, love.'

'Do you think I'll change, not being famous?' she asked after another tear or two.

'Don't be silly. They'll be on their knees to have you back.'

'I'm past it. I'm getting old. I'm thirty-two, John. Older than you. There, I've told you. Still, I could always do radio.'

'Or write a book. I could help.'

'What a super idea! Didi Kowalski, the next Elizabeth David. My new career. Better than running a cookery school or demonstrating for the Gas Board. Mind you, I'll be poor. I'll only be able to afford Le Style once a week. Oh dear. No more trips. John, it's all too ghastly.'

'You can come to the Eglantine whenever you like. I'll ration the champagne, though.'

'They're not going to get away with it. When Stephen comes back from his trip, we'll write a declaration of independence and he can put it in his column. And I'll send the Programme Controller a box of poisoned truffles. A slow, lingering death. That's what he deserves.'

Next day, over breakfast, Didi began to reflect.

'I don't think Intertel would have been a suitable place to bring up a child, do you? Come to think of it, apart from Roger and Deirdre, there's no-one I really like there. They'd make me breastfeed in the ladies' lavatory. And I'd refuse. Then what would they do? Throw me out anyway.'

It was not until later that Didi asked herself: why? She was unaccustomed to considering anything that happened in the wider world, of which television formed a part, unless it was relevant to *Table for One*. And as for politics, the games which men played to secure their positions, she didn't have a clue, although Stephen was good like that.

Until then, she had seen her dismissal as one of those vindictive things that happened in television. Hollywood stars got pushed off movies for no reason. There were so many nasty people around. But they wouldn't get away with it.

Caliope was so surprised and shocked to hear Didi's news that she burned a cake. Scandal, dear. They don't like it. Specially the silent ones. I've heard Sir Howard Riley was most upset. Probably got something hidden away in the closet. They all have, dear. Let's have lunch at the Eglantine.

Dear Cal. She hadn't quite realized what it meant being a girl with No Income. No extravagant lunches or dinners, no pink champagne at the Ritz, no little forms to fill in, in triplicate. The death of the expense account. It was like losing a parent. Intertel had turned her into an orphan.

'I will be poor and honest. Well, I am honest. I'll be poor.'

Only two hundred thousand pounds to last the year. Didi sat down at her walnut desk to come face to face with poverty, a leather-bound Gucci pad resting in front of her, calculator to hand.

NO MORE, she wrote with her gold Mont Blanc pen, and made a list. Gianni Versace or Rifat Ozbek frocks, Maude Frizon shoes, Sonia Rykiel cashmere, Janet Reger undies, Chanel perfume, Hermes handbags. Goodbye to the accounts at Harrods, Harvey Nichols, Berry Brothers and Rudd, Jeroboams and Charbonnel and Walker truffles. No. She crossed that out. A limit of two boxes a week. Well, one perhaps. Not to forget NO MORE smoked salmon for the cat.

ONLY SOMETIMES. Laurent Perrier champagne, flowers from Heals, taxis. Taxis? Did this mean she had to travel by bus? On the tube? Did anybody? No-one she knew, but they would all know her. She crossed that out. She might be recognized and that would be embarrassing.

ALTERNATIVES. Didi sucked at her pen. This was hard. Get tinned food for cat. Make do with wardrobe for a few

months. (Oh, that wonderful leather coat in Browns . . .)
How lucky that she had received those presents for Baby.
There were bound to be things she needed, and there were
bound to be temptations. What did Hollywood film stars
do who were past their prime? They stayed indoors. Yes,
she would spend more time indoors. Take up knitting,
make cakes and preserves like Cal. Redecorate the flat.
Have dinner parties in aid of third-world charities where
one could legitimately serve cheap peasant dishes with
pasta and rice. And go to Le Style once a week (someone
would always buy the champagne) so everyone could ask
her how her book was progressing. Writing a book would
keep her indoors.

Didi tore off the sheets of resolution from her pad and
taped them on to her fridge, the best place for a constant
reminder.

'Oh, I'm working on something. Considering a few
offers,' she would say in common with most of the
stylishly dressed champagne quaffers who frequented Le
Style. It was vulgar to be employed.

At the Kitchen Club you didn't work on something, you
worked. If you didn't happen to own a restaurant you had
a boss, and if you were unemployed the buzz went round
the bar that you were looking for a job. No-one should be
out of work. Chefs went barmy mooning around at home,
they lost their touch, stagnated with the fear that they
would never cook again. That's all they could do, cook,
and they might forget those sauces, forget how to
construct a menu, lose their contacts, be overtaken by
fashions in eating they could no longer afford to sample.
Actors acted and chefs cooked. Resting was a killer.

'I've been going fucking crazy. I haven't cooked for
months. How d'you do boiled eggs, Little John? What's
soft and what's hard apart from my cock?'

John stretched out to collect the bucket of champagne.
'Hey.'

Tadeus caught hold of his arm and examined the heavy

gold watch spanning his wrist. 'Is that a divvy from Miss La-di-da? And have we got the Porsche to go with it?'

John laughed. 'You might say.'

'Don't buy a yacht, lad. Take my advice. And I shall expect a few handouts in my old age. Don't forget. I hear the Eglantine is still coining it. You changed the menu yet?'

'Come on, Tad. Let on where you've been hiding.'

'I was taking a sabbatical. Reading books. Meditating.'

'Pull the other one.'

'What did you think I was doing? Having a nervous breakdown?'

Elwyn Jones came in. Then Sebastian North, with George, Jean-Luc and Harry Wade tagging along. John could see Tadeus waiting for his audience, waiting for their table to be a crammed circle.

'I'll tell you what you've been longing to know. My blood pressure is slightly high but nothing to worry about, my cholesterol level is so low they can't find it, my intellect is unimpaired, my body is perfect, naturally, and my sexual performance . . .'

'What about your cooking, Tad?'

'. . . defies all known records.'

'Is it true you're out of Freeman's?'

'Bought out, darlings. Bought. Out. The accountant likes my food but hates my figures. I can just afford a bicycle to develop my calf muscles.' Tadeus looked up at the ceiling. The faces around were taut, as though facing a volley of hailstones. 'I'll read you something. Mister. Get that. Mister Tadeus Freeman, late of Freeman's, is pleased to announce that he will be appearing regularly at a novelty venue aimed at the discerning diner. Leone's, a concept restaurant reborn from the ashes of Aphrodite's, has been transformed into a temple of delights whose inspiration is culled from Thailand, Spain and the African jungle. Phone Laura Douglas Associates for further details and an early reservation. Boom. That's it. Just down the road from the Eglantine. Isn't that convenient?'

'You got a massage parlour in there, Tad?' asked Elwyn, after the silent reaction.

'No, but there's a fucking parrot.'

'The loot good then?' asked Sebastian.

'Why d'you think I'm going into this arsehole of a place? For a hand-out? I'm a tart. Anyone coming from the stinking bowels of Leeds is a tart. Isn't that so, Little John?'

'You worked out the menu yet?'

'What d'you think I've been doing all this time? Growing spuds in my fingernails? Oh yes. I've been getting on intimate terms with bailiffs. Did you know they're highly sensitive people? Hate their job, but they do like a drinkie. Let me share my last bottle, I said. Then I told them I'd put in diethylene glycol to up the proof. Don't worry, I said. It's killed a few Austrians but they've only got one kidney, that's why. After that they telephoned first. Will you be in, Mr Freeman? Mister. That's what I like to hear. I call Leone *signore*. *Si signore*. Or should it be *padrone*? I bet his uncle or his brother or his nephew is making three-lane highways across the fields in Sicily and burying a few friends in the flyovers . . . It was either that or doing commercials for Whammo Crisps. They sent me the script, I puked all over it and sent it back in a brown envelope.'

They left earlier than usual. Sometimes Tadeus was like that. Made you want to go home.

Life had taken a dismal turn. Conspicuous consumption was as outmoded as Lobster Thermidor and Stephen had no wish to appear conspicuous. The gimlet-eyed Miss Cutbutton had sunk to unimagined depths, querying the necessity for coffee, paper clips, even paper. With sinking heart he had turned down the option of a five-star hotel suite in Florence courtesy of the Organization for Italian Trade (too ostentatious by far) and had chosen instead to make himself at home on the vine-covered terrace of Signora Cuspoli's guest house at the edge of a modest

Tuscan hill town. He was 'going native' (always a wise move during shrinkage phases), even to the extent of abandoning his computer in favour of an ancient manual typewriter, an essential step in feeling his way, emotionally and physically, into the ancient traditions of olive oil production. The peace of this static, hazy landscape might even be conducive to finishing another chapter of his Divine Comedy.

Miss Cutbutton had failed to understand the necessity for sending over a photographer to Italy to complement his article. Everyone knows, was her faxed rejoinder retrieved with much gesticulation from the Ufficio Centrale Poste e Telecommunicazioni in Florence (an hour's bus ride away, bet she realized, the cow), (a) what Tuscany looks like and (b) what olives look like. But Stephen, being experienced, could read between the lines. He instinctively knew that the real reason could not be justified by *Daily Reporter* edicts calling for budgetary restraint.

Her page, his page, was being squeezed. Obviously she had done a deal with the editor. Less food, more social awareness. His article would be cut to ribbons, and hence no picture. She wouldn't fight for extra space, the bitch, and that meant there must be another wordy worthy in the pipleline, regurgitated bottom-drawer home-feature stuff written about a thousand times before, high-toned sensationalism wrapped up in socio-psychospeak. Here we go. Rape (new location, same story), street violence, hooliganism, toxic waste, mugging in schools, global warming – the same old facts, sometimes even the same old quotes – and who the hell really cares, Miss Cutbutton?

It was the hour of the mid-morning aperitif, to be taken with that indescribably luscious icecream. Ah! Stephen heaved his swelling belly to the upright position (Tuscan cuisine, oh, the *fritto mistos*, those honey-sodden nut-encrusted goodies in the *pasticcerias*) and prepared to negotiate the steps down to his favourite bar. The friendly priest, who liked to practise his English, was waiting for him as though he had had a wondrous vision on the way.

'Good morning!' The joyful greeting was accompanied by a wave, and the wave ended in a rolled-up newspaper. 'I find you English journal!'

'*Mol-to gen-tile*,' said Stephen, using his all-purpose Italian rejoinder selected from the back of the *Traveller's Guide to Italy*.

The *Daily Reporter*, a week out of date, never mind, *molto gentile*. What had she cut this time?

'Bad news, my friend?'

Stephen pursed his lips. He could not explain in phrase-book Italian.

'Yes. Bad news.'

'Never mind. I buy you drink, and we pray to Santo Stefano.'

Half a page, his half a page, devoted to a thousand, maybe more, words written by Penelope Long. Penelope Long? The impostor. What on earth did she know about food? How dare she write on his page? And what was this? Jack Leone, the Pizza Palace mogul, has taken over one of Britain's most famous restaurants. *What?* To everyone's astonishment he has employed top chef Tadeus Freeman, rewarded this year with two Michelin stars. Tadeus Freeman! 'I've always looked for a challenge. Everyone should change direction . . . people want something different now. If they want it, I'll give it to them. If they want Mexican tortillas stuffed with foie gras or an overdone steak they can have it. The new eclectic cuisine . . . total dining experience . . . value for money.'

'Jesus Christ!' exclaimed Stephen, forgetting that he was in the presence of His representative. The priest averted his gaze from the Godless *straniero* and shrugged, *ebbene*, the Inglese was *simpatico*, *generoso*.

That should have been his story. His. Why hadn't he been told first? Didn't he understand Tadeus Freeman better than anyone?

Hadn't they spent hours together? What lousy quotes! And she'd totally missed the significance of that creep Leone destroying a piece of history. Never mentioned

André Bouchon. Obvious she'd never eaten there. Couldn't that incompetent old bag tell when she was being fobbed off with lies? Tadeus must be laughing his head off. Total dining experience? Huh! Didn't she know that Freeman's was in dire straits financially? Of course not. She knew nothing. Nothing. Anybody could have written that, even someone on the news desk. Thrown away.

'I go for a walk. Walk.'

'*Si, si.* Work. *Lavoro.*'

'No, walk.' Stephen ran his fingers along the table.

'Ah. *Una camminata.* Waw-k. Wawk. *Bella parola.*'

Penelope Long had moved down from Purgatory to Hell, and was standing temporarily up to her neck in a vat of boiling sheeps' eyes waiting for Stephen to invent a more subtle form of punishment. He had walked to the bottom of the hill, until the winding road straightened out in the valley, and was leaning against a gnarled tree looking up at the slim leaves tracing a pattern of sage green against the blue-washed sky. Change was in the air, and the smooth surface of events had become subject to a kind of turbulence in which Penelope Long was the first tiny eddy, the hair-thin ring disturbing the glassy surface of a pond made by an alighting gnat, the tiny harbinger of an imminent storm. He had sensed it, but refused to recognize it.

Table for One was no more, Didi locked into mummy-hood. Aphrodite's no more. The chefs had nothing to say, all passion spent, accountants were dictating the menus and Illustra Foods were taking over the country. What was Laura doing? Organizing the Exposition Culinaire whose function was to promote everything she was meant to despise. Even Miss Cutbutton said she did want him to write something about this, we have to keep abreast of new technology, a multi-billion-pound industry, you may not like it personally, Stephen, and neither do I, you're quite free to be as critical as you like, but we can't ignore it.

Had the olive had its day? Was he blindly stumbling along an overbeaten track? Would Stephen Boyce slowly fade out in a tailpiece devoted to 'Life on the Farm', recording in archaic phrases the birth of the first lamb, the churning of butter (some could recall having tasted it), the slaughter of the beloved pig? Stephen Boyce? Is he still around? Was the human palate about to become a useless organ like the appendix? Would it go the way of the human tail, now a memory embedded in the coccyx? Was the momentous revival of British food, which he had encouraged week by week, to which his mind and body were dedicated, was it a mere flash in the pan of history? Would he one day look back on his yellowed cuttings with disbelief, remembering the bounteous Good Life with sour regret as he took his mini-snack from the microwave?

A drop of rain plopped into Stephen's eye and put an end to apocalyptic thoughts. Besides, it was time for lunch which, at least in this sleepy timeless zone, was a sacred event. That night he managed to ignore the sound of baying dogs and Clint Eastwood dubbed with the accent of an Italian provincial mayor booming out from Signora Cuspoli's palatial television set, and he wrote in his diary: 'Penelope Long. Stinking rotgut cow.' Then he crossed it out, adding only a sentence, for dinner had dulled his brain (no wonder Mussolini banned pasta) and wrote: 'Fine Good Story'. A story which would take up the whole page. With a startling picture. He would graciously accept the editor's praises for his brave initiative (an award?), and then he could retire into some monastery where working in the kitchen was crucial to the service of the Lord and finish his novel.

For the dining classes of London, little had changed. Viscount Alloway would have preferred to meet somewhere in the City; a liquid lunch would have suited, preferably within staggering distance of the office, but the American chap insisted he went to some restaurant he'd just opened. With a lump of his money. (He felt proprietorial about the MacCrae Bank.) Still. Big customer. Had to tell him to pull in the reins though. Interest rates geeing up again. Decent of him to send a car, they were good like that, Yanks, even though they insisted on calling the servants 'sir' and couldn't hit a grouse if it stared them in the face.

Was this what one called a restaurant nowadays? Good Lord! Thank heaven for Rules. He pulled back a trailing creeper which had entangled itself in the carefully guarded hairs straggling across his balding head. No, er, he didn't go in for cocktails.

'Interesting chairs,' he remarked, as he lowered himself gingerly on what appeared to be a farmyard substance.

'Bamboo. Specially designed. Can you hear those birds? Customers go wild over those birds. Mind you, had a few complaints about the fountain. Then I expected that.'

'Did you really?'

Viscount Alloway found their thought processes jolly difficult to follow. Understood Indians, though. But then they'd been trained by Brits.

'Makes ladies go to the bathroom.'

'How extraordinary. And, er, do you have bathrooms here?'

'Oh, yeah, sure.'

Jack laughed in astonishment. These old guys lived in another world. 'Let me get Charlene to explain the menu.'

'But it's in English.'

'Yeah, but first time around we like to familiarize the customers, make them feel like they've always eaten this kind of food. Research has shown that people have a negative response to unfamiliar ingredients. And we got a couple of unfamiliar ingredients, Viscount.'

A lanky girl who appeared to be constructed in a straight line back and front with no discernible breasts, hips or bottom, and attired in the Leone uniform, a multicoloured sarong, swung over to the table and revealed a set of dazzling teeth.

'Hi. May I explain the menu, sir?'

'Have you by any chance got any meat?'

There was an apprehensive note in Viscount Alloway's

voice, but Charlene had been trained to expect that.

'Oh yes, sir. Even though we major on fish, we have the most wonderful mesquite-grilled Aberdeen Angus steaks.'

'Jolly good.'

'Would you like to select your steak in the kitchen, sir?'

No he certainly wouldn't, and neither did he require a fulsome description of the bluecorn fritters, guacamole or fried goat's cheese.

'I tell you, Viscount, I've had it up to here with guys telling me restaurants don't make money. One reason I did it. Get the percentage ratios right, you can't go wrong. No-one here understands percentage ratios. Do you know something? My raw material percentage ratio is ten per cent. Show me one decent restaurant with a raw material percentage ratio under twenty. They don't exist, that's why.'

You let Americans do the talking until they ran out of steam. Not that they always did, but by the third coffee they usually expected an answer. Jack was lighting a cigar and had adopted a querying expression.

'Mr Leone—'

'Jack. Please.'

'Jack, um.' The Viscount's Adam's apple was stirring in discomfort. 'I think we should discuss, perhaps, er, the more immediate financial aspects of your, er, your Spanish development.'

'Sure, sure.'

Jack started to extract a folder from his briefcase.

'We can, um, go into details later. Tell me, in your own words, what it is exactly you require.'

'I always use my own words, they come out better. OK, I'll start with a summary of how I arrived at the top-up figure . . .'

It wasn't the way they did things at the MacCrae Bank, not at all. Discussing cash flow in some damned jungle with a parrot was a rum way to conduct business. However, it sounded plausible. But the investment chaps were unhappy, they knew about these kinds of things. He didn't play golf himself and to be perfectly honest he'd never been to Spain. Certainly, in a more buoyant economic climate, the MacCrae Bank would have been only too pleased . . . er . . . but in the circumstances, they would be unable, unfortunately, to accede to his request for an ancillary loan. The Chancellor was asking for loans to be called in wherever possible. Making life jolly difficult, but there it was. Could try elsewhere, perhaps. Might have a chum who could oblige . . .

'Are you saying you don't have confidence in Leone Leisure? You know what kind of a track record we have?'

'I really am awfully sorry, er, Jack. Out of my hands, I'm afraid to say. In the meantime, as I suggested, couldn't you, er, slow down a bit? Until things improve? Only a thought. We'd be pleased to help at any time in the future and do make us your first port of call.'

Jack was halfway up the M1 before Charlie got to the phone, and by then he was feeling like smashing a steel bar.

'Hey, Charlie, I'm coming your way. OK, OK, I'll see the monastery development. Isn't that thing finished yet? Yeah, I know you get trouble with pillars. I need some action from you. We got to move.'

And it was only many miles later when he whined the Ferrari round the bend and saw the dark firs edging the motorway which marked the end of civilization as he knew it, Notting-ham-shire, Leicester-shire – didn't remember which came first, they looked much the same, one flatter and rainier than the other – that he picked up the phone again. Miss Friday Lunchdate was still in the diary. Laura was going steady with some jerk.

'Hi, babe, you'll never guess. I'm not gonna make it. I'm heading North. Got to sort a few things out. You in Tuesday? OK, I'll call you.'

This one was great, never gave him trouble, apart from the name. He called her Rosie. Not like western girls, or black girls. If they were all like that in Hong Kong, he'd be out there like a shot. And tall. She said they'd gotten tall. Better diet. Loved steak. The way she massaged his feet, it drove him crazy.

The boardroom of Leone Leisure (Northern) Development had been redecorated in the same margarine yellow favoured by Braithwaite Holdings PLC, but the picture of workers leaving the mill now hung in Charlie's new conservatory at home. In its place was a series of highly coloured architect's drawings framed in mahogany. Along one wall, the Monastery, Luxury Apartments in a Woodland Setting, and along the other La Felicidad, the Sportman's Paradise. Jack had convinced Charlie that a small private marina would extend their catchment. Golfers, fine, but there was sailing down there, he'd seen the boats. Sailors were big drinkers, good for the club bar take. When they've got to Phase Four then they'd build something better than the dirt track which led to the small inlet they had annexed as part of Phase Two. And Phase Two was giving Jack sleepless nights.

Charlie spooned in the sugar and stirred his coffee.

'So what the fuck's happening? You only sold ten leases? For Christ's sake, tell the agent to get off his ass.'

'I told you, Jack. There's been that many scared off. They don't want to buy into a wasteland. Nowadays, they have to see the lot in position. They want to see the green grass and the pool and the fully equipped bar and the fitted kitchens and God knows what else. They want ready-made, Jack.'

'I can't raise the money.' Jack got up and paced round the Braithwaite table whilst Charlie examined his fingernails. 'MacCrae have chickened out. Call themselves a fucking bank? And if they won't hand over, who the hell will? Because they'll be bad-mouthing Leone right through the City. But I know this for sure, there's guys waiting to off-load cash up here for sure-fire investment, high return.'

'They don't like foreign. Or they want to keep it in the bank. Interest rates . . .'

'Short-term thinking, Charlie. Pisses me off.'

442

'I don't like to suggest it, but if the worst comes to the worst—'

'Yeah?'

'Sell something off, maybe.'

'Would you sell Charlie's Brasserie?'

'Never.'

'Why we talking of selling anyhow? Like some kind of cheapskate entrepreneurs. We're big time, Charlie.'

Charlie contemplated Jack's strong, confident face. He'd been rattled a moment ago and it didn't suit him.

'Tell you what. Leave me be a couple of weeks. I'm sure I can come up with something.'

'One week, Charlie.'

Even the *Northern Gazette* was going through a bad patch, and Gerry looked ten years older. The sharks are queuing up, Charlie, but I'll not see the *Gazette* sold to the Japanese. Over my dead body. They might still be ordering the same at Charlie's Brasserie (why change the menu? Folk liked it that way) but the tables were empty by two thirty. Worry, that's what it was. Down South they called it stress, but there was no cure for worry but cash. Charlie explored every avenue, every narrow snicket, starting with the bank manager, who did enjoy his lunch but was under a directive from head office, and ending with the elusive Mr Aziz whose small shop supplied the office sandwiches at Braithwaite House, but who, Charlie learned, owned a chain of hotels with his brother. He might have been interested in investing if it was a hotel and not a leisure development, and as he did not play golf, sail or swim his flicker of interest quickly turned to polite refusal. They all said the same. Six months ago, Mr Braithwaite, we could have helped. Now, everything's tight.

At the end of his allotted week, Charlie turned up at the London hotel suite which Jack used as office-stroke-bedroom. (Low overheads, Charlie.)

'I had a meeting with Peregrine Investments. The only people interested, and I saw plenty.'

'What they say?'

'Forty per cent interest.'

Jack didn't change his expression and Charlie swallowed. He'd stretched a point, for Peregrine Investments had never called back.

'That's our first term profit gone.' He cleared his throat. 'Whatever the financial climate, I'd not go along with that. Not forty per cent. Might as well give away the whole bloody lot.'

Charlie leaned back in his chair and drew up his bottom lip as though delivering sentence. 'The way I see it, though I wouldn't put this forward in every case, mind, flotation could be a positive move.'

Jack sprang to his feet and Charlie stopped. If he had a gun in his pocket, Charlie thought, I'd be dead.

'I think we should air the possibility, Jack. With the Leone name . . .'

'Exactly. You said it.'

'So have you been thinking along these lines?'

'What do you take me for, Charlie?'

'The best in business. What more should I say?'

'No. Do you see me handing over to some load of schmucks sitting in a boardroom and saying, "Point of order, Mr Chairman?" You see me saying yes sir, I say, what a good idea? You see me wearing one of those loose-assed British suits and going along with stupid decisions because I'm the only one to go against?'

There was a click and a door opened which Charlie hadn't noticed. Clever that. Looked like part of the wallpaper. A woman with close-cropped grey hair, polka dot tie blouse and a below-the-knee pleated skirt took one step into the room.

'I wondered if you and Mr Braithwaite would care for some tea?'

'Charlie will. Hey, Marjorie, bring the sugar bowl. You driving back, Charlie?'

For a moment Charlie thought this was the way Jack ended a business relationship.

'Train.'

'You should drive. Costs less. I'm going to the Health Club. Give me a call around six.'

Jack made for the door, taking his jacket off as he went, and Charlie's frown grew deeper. Time cost money. The thought of five hours' wasted travelling made him aware of his newly acquired blood pressure. Never had it before Leone. Still, mustn't brood. Got you nowhere.

'I haven't seen you before, have I?'

A tea-tray was set down in front of him. Jack was always changing his secretaries. This one was soft on him, he could see from the moment she came into the room. Anyone who looked like that, as though she served old ladies in a Harrogate tea room, was bound to be devoted. Jack wasn't stupid.

'I've been here a month, Mr Braithwaite. It's so different. I'm really enjoying it.'

'Oh? Where were you before?'

'Nothing very interesting, I'm afraid. I was in a bank. Clerical.'

'I didn't catch the name.'

'Marjorie.'

'Marjorie. I can see Mr Leone values you highly. He's a very particular man. Only likes the best. If you play your cards right, you might get a trip to Spain.'

'I'm sure that isn't necessary, Mr Braithwaite.'

'Do you speak Spanish?'

'I do. Well, a little. And I can manage some correspondence. Business Spanish, that is.'

'A talent for languages is a wonderful thing. Tell you what, next time I'm going to Spain, shall I ask Mr Leone if he can spare you? I could do with knowing what they say behind my back.'

Now she was taking away the tea tray, a smile on her face as though she was about to go on holiday, but Marjorie was thinking of the benefits accruing from a bump upwards in her static, and modest, bank account. When she returned to the MacCrae Bank she would be on

ior grade. It was working out extremely nicely.
unt Alloway had explained that she had been selected
n extremely important task. Well, she did know
something about fraud. That it happened nowadays, even
in Britain, for example. And fancy Mr Roper remembering that she was studying commercial Spanish in her
evening class! All she had to do was to telephone him once
a week with a log of phone calls and letters but, honestly,
was it right that she should be paid twice – once by Mr
Leone and again by the bank?

It had not taken very long. Sir Howard Riley opened the
safe he kept for matters confidential, and pulled out
the box labelled 'B'. He extracted a neatly clipped docu-
ment of several pages with short headings, succinct
paragraphs and certain key sentences underlined in red.

Data Summary: LEONE, Jack: family origin, career,
psychological profile, business interests, audited accounts,
private property and charges thereon, medical history,
bank history, personal history, membership of golf clubs,
sailing clubs, health club, his London club, favourite
restaurants, thirty-eight years neatly summarized in a
form which could be assimilated in ten minutes. Sir
Howard Riley was a fast reader. He scanned down the
sitings of the Pizza Palace chain, tenure, leases, realizable
assets of Leone Leisure (Northern) Developments. Five-
year accounts. Turnover. Projected downturn.

Even more interesting than he had suspected. The
patient was decidedly sick and in need of a miracle cure,
but there was no hurry. Illustra Foods would hover until
the prey was keeling over with exhaustion to make the
quick, efficient kill.

He paused at a section which was not underlined.

DOUGLAS, Laura. Formerly Laura Leone. Ex-wife. Five
lines, all correct. Miscarriage at twenty-seven? She had
never referred to that.

The folder had a pocket. Appended visual documen-
tation. Different girls photographed through the windows

of a car. Ferrari, red. Some identified. Melissa Desgranges, that name rang a bell. Hadn't Alloway . . . ? Quite a string. Oversexed. Ex-wife. He recognized the picture and smiled. The Illustra MacCrae Awards dinner. His red dress. She did look good in photographs. And out of them. Ah, excellent! Ground plans, architect's drawings and an up-to-date progress record of La Felicidad Development. He took a magnifying glass from his desk drawer and examined the site pictures one by one.

'Where was I? Guess.'

Charlie was gloomily ogling the line-up of girls queuing on the diving board to leap into the sky and down into the pine-scented waters of the Marbella Rialto landscaped pool. He covered the concertina folds of his stomach with a towel. All that well-formed nakedness made him uncomfortable. They'd noticed Jack. He'd seen them looking his way with quick glances, giggles, slight adjustments of bra straps to accentuate cleavage, bikini bottoms hitched a little higher up the sun-baked thighs. But they stared straight past Charlie as they stared straight past the dark-suited Spaniards bearing trays of cocktails overspilling with fruit and flowers.

One of the waiters stopped by a couple – must be British, you could tell. Bet she nags and he's bulging more than me and uglier, Charlie observed with pleasure – and two glasses of hot water were set beside them, each containing a floating tea-bag and a thin slice of lemon.

'Waiter, I said tea. Not water. In a pot. With a jug of milk. Milk. You hear me?'

Charlie glared at him. He didn't have to shout like that. The waiters at the Rialto spoke English and there was no need to shout when they spoke your language.

Jack leaped to his feet and plopped into the water with barely a splash, swimming underneath the surface, assessing the bodies of the diving girls heading downwards and curving gracefully up towards the surface.

* * *

ox marked 'B' had been replaced in the safe. The
us offer made by Illustra Foods to Leone Leisure
en gracelessly refused. The board was unperturbed.
It would take more than a stop-gap cash injection to keep
Leone on his feet.

19

'Stephen, dear. Where have you been?'

Caliope homed in on a passing tray and displayed a skill perfected over the years, the ability to pick up a full glass of champagne without looking.

'Tuscany again.'

'Really? Laura didn't tell me there was a Tuscan trip. Why wasn't I invited? Of course I have been awfully busy. Talking of Tuscany, I simply must have a serious talk with you about *gnocchi*. Are you a flour man, a semolina man, a potato man, a polenta man, a rice man or a pumpkin man? I was having the most terrible argument with Magnus. He would insist that the only worthwhile *gnocchi* are made with—'

'Choux dough.'

Penelope Long gave her opinion and passed by. Neither she nor Stephen acknowledged each other's presence.

'A later French variant,' said Stephen contemptuously. 'She obviously hasn't read Marcella. Or Paula. Or Claudia, for that matter.'

'They taste like kiddies' plasticine,' continued Caliope. 'At least mine do. But they're probably marvellous sources of fibre if you happen to suffer from constipation. Everything one detests is a marvellous source of fibre. Have you noticed, dear, how the British have always been preoccupied with the frequency and consistency of their stool? I've often wondered why. I heard some health doctor say one's meant to do it squatting under a bush like black men do. Where does one find a bush in Mayfair? And another thing, dear. Do you observe your motion daily?'

'All the time.'

onally I never look at mine, but I could tell you
he who does.'
n't you think we should look at the Picture?'

Caliope swept her gaze round the packed art gallery,
pleased to observe only Category A guests and even a few,
like the Maclintocks, *Hors de Catégorie*, most impressive,
and, good heavens, Lady Knowles, and she never came to
anything like this. Cal extracted a monocle from a back
pocket of her waterproof trousers.

'I'm ready. Whoopee! Charge of the Light Brigade. De
dum, de dum, de dum dum dum. Follow me.'

Caliope pushed her way through the throng with the
determination of a dawn riser stalking a Limoges dinner
service in Harrods' sale. She ignored the small crowd of
spectators, stood in front of them and positioned herself
six inches away from the Picture.

'Oil,' she announced· to Stephen, withdrawing her
monocle from the surface of the canvas. 'Not acrylic. How
surprising. Has Madam seen it?'

'Not yet. She hasn't arrived.'

Caliope took a step back. 'Not what one would put over
the mantel, but it is what they call powerful. What do you
think?'

'Very striking. If I had a talent like that . . .'

'You'd be starving in a garret, although no-one does that
nowadays, dear. Garrets are too expensive. It would have
to be a caravan. What a ghastly thought. Oh, there's
Magnus. Pretending he hasn't seen me. Hah! I must go, I
must go, for I hear the call of the *gnocchi*.'

Sigmund Halberstadt inched his way slowly forward,
ignoring the bodies jostled against his, as though the
crowded gallery space was void. He was closely followed
by the Contemporary Acquisitions Man from the Tate
Gallery, who had cancelled an appointment with an up-
and-coming artist, lured by the promise of dinner at the
Eglantine. An appreciation of the culinary arts, Sigmund
would explain later over the foie gras and the Gewürztra-
miner Vendange Tardive, courtesy of Laura Douglas *bien*

entendu, was intrinsically paralleled by an appreciation of the visual arts. Merely a question of complementary aesthetics. Later, he would mention his idea for presenting a twelve-part television series, accompanied by a lavishly illustrated book, based on culinary iconography from the Great Masters to the Present Day, once his academic credentials had been established beyond reasonable doubt. He had good reason to believe that Illustra Foods were interested in providing the bottom line in return for a discreet credit.

'I might do something but art's not my thing really.'

Virginia Desgranges turned towards her sister Melissa, barely parting her bright pink languorous lips. One was the mirror image of the other and it was such fun wearing the same things. Tonight both were sporting a *bustier* of iridescent sequins and semi-transparent black organza pantaloons hanging from the hips, swathed in silver chains. It was not quite clear whether either was wearing underwear.

'Oh, God, guess who's come.' Melissa gave a slight, unassisted snort through her aquiline nostrils. 'Alloway. Such a crashing bore. Oh well, drooling dins at the Eglantine.'

'See you there then.'

'Who with?'

'Sir Howard Thingy.'

'Oh, him.' Melissa smiled.

'I'm meant to be writing about his wardrobe. Apparently he's tycoon of the month. Doing lots of amazingly boring things. Yawn. Do you know him?'

'Sort of.'

'See you at Le Style later. We'll compare geriatric notes.'

'What do you think?'

'About what?'

Virginia swivelled slightly to look behind her. 'Oh, that. I don't think that sort of thing should be painted, actually.'

'Is is rather ghastly.'

Melissa couldn't decide whether it was super or ghastly, but Virginia, being older and cleverer, actually did know about these things (she had completed a short course on art history at the Courtauld) even though she said she didn't.

'I hate to admit it, but if I didn't know Miss La-di-da I'd say that was fucking good.'

Tadeus Freeman sucked at a sliver of raw marinated fish and wagged his finger at the Picture to emphasize his judgement.

'Colours are a bit dark,' suggested George, attempting to stand back to obtain the proper perspective.

'Just because there isn't a green palm tree and a pink bum.'

'I don't like it.' John looked uncomfortable. 'I don't see why she had to do it like that.'

'Of course you don't like it. Never mind, Little John. Love the canapés.'

It did give one a certain advantage at parties being eight and a half months pregnant. Didi was not compelled like the others to thrust her way forward. The sea of bodies parted before her belly curved like a wind-filled spinnaker and she sailed smoothly towards Laura.

'Where is it?'

Laura pointed across the room.

'Don't come with me. I want to experience it on my own.'

Didi's eyes glazed over (don't recognize me yet, I'm not ready) as she gathered the voluminous folds of the ice-blue satin maternity cocktail dress. She hoped the subtle significance of the colour would be noted. (Blue for the boy she was sure it would be.)

Didi stuck one finger in her mouth, a signal of aesthetic contemplation, and frowned. She hadn't painted the face properly. How silly. Why hadn't she painted the face? It

452

could be anybody, any old pregnant woman. What on earth was the point of posing for hours on end when she hadn't even painted her face properly? Oh. There was a title. She peered forward and read the typed label. 'Number Thirty-two. Didi at Seven Months.' What was that hand doing? It was putting something towards . . . Didi smiled indulgently. Of course. She was putting a chocolate truffle into her mouth. That's what it was. And it did look like her. Vaguely. If you looked long enough, you could see it was Didi Kowalski. Didi Kowalski with Baby. That would be a better title.

She went up to Laura who was standing in a corner with Stephen and kissed her cheek.

'It's absolutely wonderful. You're so clever. I never knew it would turn out like that. Everyone's been looking at it. Aren't you pleased?'

'I suppose so, but it's rather frightening. Like having a medical examination. Do you like it, really? I didn't think you would.'

'Didi likes it because you've put in the chocolate truffle,' said Stephen. 'You should have called it "Gourmet Birth".'

'The truffle is symbolic,' retorted Didi. 'You know what I'd like to do? I'd like to buy your painting and present it to Intertel. As a memento. With a plaque underneath: "Donated by Didi Kowalski, presenter of *Table for One*". Don't you think that's a wonderful idea? They could hang it in the foyer.'

Then Didi's face fell. She had been desperately trying to maintain her dignity and ebullience, but it was so hard being in public. At home she could forget that her nine million viewers were no more, merely a statistical mention in the Intertel annual report, but here she was being reminded with every step she took that she was just an ordinary girl.

Magnus and Sigmund had been beastly. They had spotted her and moved pointedly away. She must have given them an hour's air time, if she added it up. And hadn't she allowed them to mention their books once or twice? Wasn't that worth at the very least a 'Hello, Didi, how are you?' Sir Howard Riley had smiled and said how sad he was that *Table for One* was as yet unscheduled for a return series but he was sure she would be back very soon. That was kind of him.

It was all very well for John, standing there greeting the regular habitués of the Eglantine and everyone saying it was the best party food they'd ever had, could he possibly do something for them? And Melissa Desgranges being a little too familiar. She wasn't having that.

'John,' she said faintly in his ear, 'I want to go home.'

He stopped in mid-sentence and abandoned for a second the professional face he had learned to adopt, the bland expression, the face which pleased and which was pleasing, unruffled by doubts or passions or controversy.

'Excuse me a moment,' he said to Melissa and Tadeus and Antony and Caliope, taking Didi by the hand. 'I'll find a chair, love. Come over here. What do you think then?'

'It's a lovely party.'

'The Picture?'

'Good.'

'It's not like I see you. The photograph you gave me's much better. If someone's beautiful, why not paint them beautiful?'

'I'm not any more.'

A tear escaped down Didi's cheek.

'You're more beautiful than anyone here, and you've got more beautiful—'

'Now I'm not famous any more, you mean.'

'You're more real. Not having to come out with smart things all the time.'

'You make me sound like a vicar's wife,' said Didi, pouting. 'Am I more beautiful than Melissa, for example?'

'Dorothy Dean's jealous. Well I never!' John laughed and wiped away the tear with a silk handkerchief, a present from George. 'Come on. Sit down.'

454

Didi obeyed. She rarely saw John in a room full of people. No-one would know he was a chef now. He could be a successful businessman, international sportsman, even a television presenter. Anyone could go for him. Handsome, relaxed face, well-built but still slim, right shoes, right suit, right shirt and tie, right haircut. At her suggestion a health-club tan to counteract the pallor of the kitchen, and almost no trace of the Yorkshire giveaway.

'The picture,' he said, 'it's Laura. Her idea of being pregnant. It's not you. Don't take it to heart.'

'I don't.' Didi sniffed. 'It's not that. It's you going off with someone else. Well, you will now I'm unsexy and unfamous, won't you?'

'I might stay for a week or two. I'll be back in five minutes then we'll go.'

In the few minutes that Didi was alone she decided that either her wonky hormonal balance or some importunate star sign was conspiring against her. Why had she been so upset? There must be an obvious explanation. Perhaps everyone was embarrassed. Perhaps they didn't know what to say. That was a reason for the silence. They, the people packed like rare fish in this white-walled tank, the wealthy, the share-owning, second home-owning, the unmortgaged, the successful, the well-born, the powerful, the well-cared-for, well-medicated, well-groomed and well-travelled brigade, upholstered with expense accounts, the ones who never looked at bank statements (except Caliope who only carried coins) must feel sorry for her, she supposed.

Didi slowly raised herself from the flimsy chair and stood on the outside of Laura's group, listening to the exchange of information batting backwards and forwards. She wondered if Peter always talked about money. There was nothing she could contribute nor did she wish to. Men's talk. Laura's eyes were shining, she loved it. Couldn't they change the subject? What did they talk about in bed, he and Laura? She couldn't imagine why he was at her side more and more frequently. Decent chap,

455

but she had the whole of London, and now New York, to choose from. I have much more fun, Didi decided, even if I'm poor and unfamous and twice as big as Laura Douglas.

'Why don't you join us later at the Eglantine? Are you coming?'

Of course Laura knew she was meant to be coming. No need to make it so transparently clear. How quickly everything had changed! They were polite to her, merely polite. They were more interested in Didi at Seven Months hanging on the other side of the room.

'How are you? And when's the happy D-Day?' asked Peter. He was being pleasant because she was standing next to him.

'Two weeks. Everything's fine, thank you.'

'Very tiring, the last few weeks, so I understand.'

Didi smiled weakly and set off in search of John. What was the point in sitting at the Eglantine, bulging at table, with him down there supervising in the kitchen? She would take a taxi, go home and have some of those delectable filo parcels John had made.

'Sweetest, you're not going?' Stephen was thrusting his way towards the canapés.

'Baby's bored,' replied Didi flatly.

'But having an artistic experience. Culture in the womb and all that. I think it's time for the gastronomic experience. Share a cab?'

'I'm off home.'

'I'll have no-one to talk to. Come on. You can sleep late tomorrow.'

'Do you think we'll ever go away again?'

'Of course we will. Once you find a nanny. Italy. That's where we'll go. Bambini land. As long as I don't have to talk bambini, sweetest. That's all I ask.'

Didi leaned back her head and sighed. 'I'm tired.'

'The Picture's great. Laura's going to organize prints.'

'She didn't ask me if I wanted one.'

Dear Stephen. He didn't understand, he thought nothing had changed.

'Viscount Alloway has just been saying how delighted everyone is with what you've done with the Eglantine,' Sir Howard Riley said to John. 'The turnover is exceeding the projections by a healthy margin. That is really excellent. And only too rare.'

'I've got a wonderful team in the kitchen. It does help. And Laura's fantastic at bringing in the customers.'

'And I suppose you'll be thinking in the long term, quite naturally, of acquiring a majority share, perhaps taking over.'

'It's Laura who'd be thinking of that, Sir Howard, not me.'

'But you'd like the idea, I imagine.'

'Hadn't really thought, to tell you the truth.'

'Well, when you get round to it, I'd be delighted to help. After all, you've put in the work, built it up, given the Eglantine its outstanding reputation. We'd be very happy, and I know Cecil agrees, to help you engineer a buy-out. The shareholders will have made a handsome profit, thanks to you. We like to put something back when we can.'

'Quite so,' said Viscount Alloway. 'Banking has a human side. I often tell my chaps that. Makes the world of difference.'

'What I was going to say,' continued Sir Howard, 'was that the MacCrae Bank would look very favourably on a request for assistance.'

'What he means, in plain speech, young man,' said Viscount Alloway, noticing John's puzzled expression, 'is that we would be only too pleased to give you loan facilities.'

'It may seem strange to you, but I don't believe in credit, never have. Us Yorkshire lads are brought up that way, at least I was. Perhaps one day, when I've saved enough, after the television series and the book, then I'll get a place of my own. Although I do appreciate your offer. It's very flattering.'

'Why don't you pop into my office for a chat one of these days? Think about it.'

The two men shook hands with John, man to man, the firm handshake with financial implications, and then they slipped unobtrusively out of the gallery *en route* for the Doric Club.

'Have you seen Didi?' John asked Stephen.

'She's gone. In a gloom. Can't blame her. If I had to carry the equivalent of the weekly shop in my belly, I'd feel depressed. When the baby's born, she'll feel differently.'

'I hope so. At the moment, she just feels rejected.'

It was worse than that. Didi would point out some harassed woman with downturned mouth queuing at a bus-stop and say, 'That's me. I'll be like that soon.' And she insisted on shopping at Prima supermarkets for economy's sake, reusing plastic bags and itemizing her receipts. Letters would be sent second class in reusable envelopes. She would even take herself off to second-hand dress shops in search of a designer bargain. The cleaning lady had been tearfully dismissed and Didi did all the washing and ironing, even John's shirts. He couldn't stop her. He had never known her to be so concerned about banishing dirt. What should he do?

Later that night, when the queue of taxis and limousines had carried off the surfeited diners from the Eglantine, when the tired-eyed brigade from the kitchen and the weary waiters had gone their separate ways, John sat in the empty dining room alone. The only person he could have talked to was lying in the bleak graveyard in Long Paxton. Everything seemed simple when you were heading in a straight line, going for what you wanted, but it never was.

Back in Yorkshire they didn't ask questions, and John didn't expect them to. When he went home in the Porsche, Mum and Dad never asked how he got it. Dad said nothing, knew it would have cost too much, and Mum wouldn't go in it, thought it would go too fast and she didn't like that. In the Working Men's Club, they slapped him on the back and fell about laughing when he showed them a menu. Just the same as the Moorland Haven. Remember how it was? It never entered their heads that success meant anything more than having a lucky break and working hard.

The London vowels slipped away the moment he got to his first pint. At the Packhorse they looked up calmly and said, 'Oh, look, it's our John. How you doing, lad? Still cooking?' As though he'd only been away a week. Pete, Bob, Martin, Steve and Duncan were no different, different car maybe, new baby. When was he coming back? There was a nice place going in Elland, why didn't he have a look? Or was there some girl in London? Mebbe several, knowing our John . . .

John picked up the phone. His head was aching. Tadeus was on his own, shagged out. Yes, he'd bring something.

'It's not right.'

'Right? You stopped bothering about that when you moved into the Eglantine.'

'I'm thinking of going back, Tad.'

'You're tired. Like me. Nordic gloom hanging over the empty plates.'

'It's . . . what I do doesn't matter. They don't give a bugger. I've been bought for the Laura Douglas collection. If I make enough, I might even have my picture painted. There's no difference between me and the Grey Men. Doing what she wants. Filling up stomachs. Sometimes, I wipe off my face, come into the restaurant and I say, "I do hope you've enjoyed it," and I think, I'd like to throw the lot of you out. If I did that, I'd be in the papers and they'd come back for more. Go to the Eglantine. John Crabtree's throwing them out now. What kind of a game is this?'

'What did you expect? Choirs of fucking angels?'

'I didn't realize. I didn't realize Stephen and Didi and

all the rest. And Riley has offered to finance a buy-out.'

'Do it. Take the fucker for all he's worth and then if he's got some left over he can buy out Jaws Leone.'

'Laura's got me where she wants me. They come for my food and she rakes it in. I don't think she gives a bugger. In the end, I'm just the chap in the kitchen.'

'At last. You mean you didn't think it was always that way? You didn't think she called the tune from day one?'

'I didn't think. Everything was happening so I didn't think.'

'You got where you wanted. Nothing wrong in that. You've got your star and now you've the chance to own the Eglantine. You're made. What more do you want, you stupid bastard?'

The rumble of early morning lorries had begun when John let himself in. Didi stirred slightly in her sleep and he removed Minou who was lying on the vacant pillow next to her. Perhaps George would look after the cat when the baby was born. Couldn't have it around then. He stroked Didi's belly and sank into the warmth of mother and baby. No-one could paint that.

The morning after the Picture had been exposed to bleary gaze, the Team did little else except log the messages of congratulation which, unfortunately, Miss Douglas was unable to receive personally as she was tied up in meetings all day.

At the House of Beauty, the tiny wrinkles of fatigue were deftly massaged until Laura was convinced that they had melted away from her eggshell complexion.

'Not a trace, Miss Douglas,' said the beautician in honeyed tones.

'I don't know how you keep so slim, Miss Douglas.'

The masseuse added her tribute, having removed the superfluous cellulite which she was unable to see. By the time Laura left she felt she had defeated the puckering folds threatening her taut stomach and smooth thighs, and had been made clean again.

Laura had received notes overflowing with praise from Sigmund and Magnus and Lucy Maclintock. And a message at home from Stephen. The congratulations sank in and disappeared like light rain into parched earth.

When he looked back on it, Charlie could remember the odd occasion when he had passed the construction workers teeming round the bare timber frames, laying down the concrete, building up the breeze blocks, making spaces for windows as they slotted together fast-track villas for those in search of La Felicidad. The Spanish supervisors gave him a furtive half smile while they were talking which he didn't quite trust. They were very obliging, no doubt about that, even if they did carry out his instructions a week after he had given them. They told him, every time he visited, how happy everybody was, much work, very good for the region, much better than empty space. Now they could educate their children, even go on holiday.

Charlie had found a small beach where the young girls went after work, took off their blouses and neat skirts and raced down to the water's edge in the bikinis they had worn to the office. At the end of the day he would sit in a café overlooking the sea, park his large hired Mercedes close by and smoke a cigar. The bolder of the laughing black-eyed girls would allow him to buy them Coca Cola and ice cream. It didn't matter here that he was fat and short and had a rasping voice, for here he was a man of consequence.

You had to be careful, though, and one evening Charlie was so entranced by one of the girls that he failed to observe the entrance of her *novio*. He stared at Charlie, standing stiffly like a dog who has scented a rival in the far distance, and then leaned his large, strong hands on the table. The girl said something, which Charlie could follow. This man was very important, *muy importante*, he was building La Felicidad. Charlie smiled and waved at the barman to bring his *amigo* a drink.

'We talk,' he said, pointing to the girl and speaking loud. '*Conversaçion.*' Then he pointed to the tall young man in the white open-necked shirt and freshly laundered jeans. 'You talk.'

'La Felicidad? You?'

'*Si,*' said Charlie, puffing at his cigar.

Peals of laughter rang round the bar, and Charlie's face froze.

'La Felicidad!' the young man kept repeating, then he threw his head back and laughed. The kids in the bar abandoned the computer games and looked towards Charlie with the insolent curiosity they reserved for foreigners.

'*Por-che* you laugh?' asked Charlie.

'I no can esplain.'

'Tell me. In Español.'

Charlie listened. A wave of words swept past his ears. 'Sorry, *amigo. No comprendo.*'

Charlie scratched his head and the young man shrugged his shoulders, held the hand of his fiancée and whispered in her ear so that she blushed and giggled.

'Hey.' Charlie regained their attention, gestured to them to stay, cornered the barman and returned with a tattered envelope and a biro. 'Write, *por favor,*' said Charlie, waving the biro over the envelope.

The young man made a face, took the biro, leaned down over the envelope and wrote a few sentences in laboured loops. He left it on the table, drank the last drop of whisky from the glass Charlie had bought him and walked out of the bar with his arm round the girl's neck. Charlie carefully placed the envelope in his briefcase and went back to his hotel. Marjorie had given him her home number in case of emergencies. He could make out the writing and most of the letters, and Marjorie would tell him why they were laughing about La Felicidad.

It was almost dark when Laura arrived. The house was a sombre mass, except for the light over the porch, and the small windows were inky black as if no-one was expected. Jack usually liked to announce his presence with a barrage of floodlights. She was only half an hour late. When he failed to run out of the front door she began to regret having cancelled her early evening meeting. Did he assume she had time to waste? She had agreed to see him for a couple of hours – that was all she could spare – and couldn't understand why they couldn't have met at the Eglantine, or at Leone's for that matter. Something important, he had said. I'm not in town this week. Didn't anything sink in, after all this time? Did he think she was still at his beck and call? He knew she was never coming back to this creaking, gloomy Jacobean house. She never liked it. Jack Leone's delusions of grandeur. He had fallen for the summer roses sprawling round the porch and the sun falling on the stone and the fireplace, someone else's family portraits and the rolling sweep of grazing land. He couldn't have liked it, not really. Jack was a city man. Men rarely chose houses they liked, but they expected their wives to live in them.

If you aren't here, thought Laura as she pulled the black knob and heard the bell clanging round the hall, I'm driving straight back.

A light came on and Jack opened the door.

'Hi, Laura. I was in the kitchen. Come on in.' He pecked her on the cheek and then turned quickly away, calling out as he went back to the kitchen: 'Help yourself to a drink in the living room. I won't be long.'

She had seen his face only for a few seconds. It must have been the centre hall light, casting strange shadows. He never looked tired, but now he had the ashen pallor of exhaustion. Perhaps he was no longer up to the night-long demands of Miss Friday Lunchdate. It was comforting to know that even Jack was occasionally subject to fatigue.

'You think I'm looking older, Laura?' It was the first thing he said as he poured Thousand Island Dressing over the salad.

'Of course not.'

'Haven't seen you for a while.'

'You don't get old in a few months.'

She noticed the grey hairs caught at the side of his head.

'Could you still go for me, babe?'

Laura smiled, but he did not smile back. 'You'll always be a good looking man, Jack.' She felt herself grow cold with apprehension. Jack leaned on his elbow, as though he was alone in the room, staring at the empty fireplace.

'I've decided to sell,' he said. 'Sell the house. I'm hardly ever here. You said I should get rid of it, remember? It's OK. I'll give you half. And you can take . . . I know there are some things you like.'

'You don't have to give me anything, Jack. I don't have to worry any more, not about money, anyway. I thought recession would send me under, but I've had accounts dropping into my lap one after the other. It's almost embarrassing. Do you know, I've been nominated for Businesswoman of the Year? I couldn't believe it.'

'Fantastic. I knew you could do it.'

'But you never encouraged me to do anything.'

'Hey, don't pull that one, Laura. You never asked. A guy sees his wife happy, what's he meant to do? And you were always busy, in the garden, with the plants and the animals. I thought you liked that kind of thing.'

'You never knew what I really wanted, did you?'

'If you say so. Want to buy me out?'

'Jack, it's good to see you, but I have to finish a presentation tonight. I must leave in an hour or so.'

'Laura, hey! Listen to me. This is Jack, remember? By the end of the year, Leone Leisure and the Pizza Palace chain won't be mine any longer. I'm telling you in case it makes a difference.'

'Is it a good deal?'

'You think I'd be looking like this if it was a good deal?'

'You don't have to shout.'

'What should I do? Say excuse me, do you mind if I raise my voice?'

'Talk to me like a normal human being.'

'You think you're a normal human being? I bet when you walked out you went straight to the hairdresser.'

'Well, at least I didn't jump straight into the bed of some suburban tart.'

'This guy you're with, does he go to sleep at night? Is that all he does?'

'Do we have to go through this all over again?'

'I want to know. Jesus Christ! I lived with you for ten years. I'm entitled. Did you leave me for this creep?'

'No, I didn't. People grow up, change, want different things.'

'You haven't changed for me. Tell me, who was it? I'm not gonna give you a hard time, I just wanna know the competition.'

Laura stretched out her legs and smiled at Jack, Jack the child wanting answers. 'I don't know why you think there had to be another man. You should know me better than that. You shouldn't need to ask.'

'Of course I need. I love you. I want to know what I did wrong. You never said.'

'I was something you wanted and couldn't have. That's all.'

'Bullshit. You hated me loving you. You still do. You wanted some chinless wimp with a rolled umbrella who came home to a glass of sherry and separate beds and asked permission once a week.'

'I admired you.'

'Give me the real reason.'

Laura turned away, but could still feel Jack's eyes fixed on her face. 'You were everything—'

'Yeah?'

'—my mother loathed. Rich, handsome and American. Everything she distrusted. She referred to you as the carpet trader. When I'd left, that is.'

Jack roared with laughter. 'I love it. But hey, you're not serious? You marry me to spite your mother? No-one does that, babe. You're kidding.'

'I hated her most of the time.'

465

'But you loved me. We were in love. First time we met. What changed?' Jack rose to his feet. 'Tell me something. Why did you stay so long?'

Laura frowned and twisted Stephen's ring round her finger. 'Partly to prove that my mother was wrong in believing it would end in disaster. And partly. Who knows? When things were good with us, they were better than with anyone else. Before or since. I didn't come all this way to talk about our marriage.'

'You've got it figured out. Like some kind of a phoney presentation. I don't believe a word, Laura, but I know one thing: you want everything perfect, but life's crazy. Even for you in your tailor-pressed suit and your pale grey office like the English sky. Even though you have the string of polite young men and the guy who goes to sleep . . . You married him yet?'

'Not yet.'

'I'm not going to be around, but I don't want you making mistakes, babe. Not that kind of mistake, anyhow.'

'You know nothing about him.'

'You think I need to?'

In this quiet still room Laura wondered for the first time in years what would have happened if Mrs Leone had stayed.

'Why are you leaving?'

'So I don't murder Charlie Braithwaite.

'Seriously, Jack.'

'Seriously, he screwed up Spain. Charlie, meant to know every rule in and out of the book, fails to notice that they're gonna build a toxic waste incineration plant two kilometres down the road. The kids were protesting, but Charlie couldn't read the banners. Anyhow, the officials down there give the go-ahead, they need the employment. But who do I hear it from? My secretary, Marjorie. Charlie didn't have the guts to tell me, went back up North without a word, just a memo. Some memo. "Everything going great guns." And you know what? I get a call from

Alloway. "I say old chap, heard there are some problems with your Spanish venture." How the fuck did he know? It makes British people happy. Boom. Down he goes. Crash. Watch it all break up.'

'Alloway may be short-sighted, but I'm sure he'll try and help you out. Failure's as bad for MacCrae as it is for you.'

'Oh, he was very concerned was the Viscount. Knew everyone I was dealing with. Called me over. He'd calculated everything. The only possibility is to sell La Felicidad for a few pesetas. As a factory site. Heavy industry is what they need down there.'

'It's hard to believe. Why didn't your builders or architects say anything?'

'Work, babe. I employed around two hundred people. Let alone buying local raw materials. And then I get a handwritten letter from Charlie. He's in trouble with the two mill cash injection he put in.'

'Things like this don't happen to you, Jack. It can't be so terrible.'

'Alloway's given me two options. Liquidate or sell out. I'm not the kind of guy gets rescued by pals in the City, you should know that. That place could've been a jewel. The ultimate vacation village with three-star restaurant, pool, terraced shopping precinct, nightclub, sports facilities, even a movie house. You do one thing and you get ideas for another. Charlie cut a piece out of my brain.'

Jack sat down and put his hands over his face for a moment. 'I'd go now if I could. Alloway can have the whole damn lot.'

'Where?'

'New York, maybe. I'll hang out there for a bit.'

'If you want to use my office . . .'

'You can buy me lunch.'

They were still sitting there. Why wouldn't they go? George was surreptitiously opening the windows in the dining room to let in a little cold night air.

'Oh, Laura. How nice.' He shut the window again and wished she hadn't chosen this moment on a quiet Monday.

'We've been terribly busy,' he said. 'And two customers still here.'

John was just going home. 'Good to see you, Laura.'

'How many covers tonight?'

'About forty.'

'Any problems?'

'Why don't you come in for lunch? We could talk then. I want to get back, see if Didi's all right.'

'It's so hard finding the time. Perhaps at the end of the month.'

'When I'm a father, you'll not see much of me for a while.'

'Does that mean you'll stop cooking?'

There was a hard edge to Laura's voice which caught John by surprise.

'I'll be in charge, if that's what you mean. Laura, we do need to talk about bringing in a few changes once I've finished my television series.'

'You didn't tell me.' John waited for her to say something more, but she was looking through her diary. 'Shall we fix a date then?'

'A date?'

'To talk.'

'I'm no good with dates. Come in when you like. By the way, would you do something for me, Laura? The picture of Didi. I'd like to give it to her as a present. She keeps going on about it. I mean, I'd buy it.'

Laura smiled and shook her head. 'I'm afraid it's not for sale.'

'It means a lot to her. Perhaps you could do another one, when the baby's born.'

'I don't work like that. Painting is a sort of private notebook for me. I didn't even want to show it, but the gallery was so insistent, I gave in. Sorry, John.'

'But if no-one sees what you do . . . ? It's like me cooking for myself.'

'I'm not good enough yet. Maybe one day.'

'Does it hurt you to give? Not even a note or a phone call. Didi put herself out for you, many times, and all she gets in return is the big freeze. She's no use any more, I suppose. Crossed off the list. Do you care for anyone, I wonder?'

For a moment Laura flushed imperceptibly, and then she shrugged. 'What do you expect me to do? Beg Intertel to take her back?'

'You've got influence. Talk to a few people.'

'I'll do what I can. When did you say the baby's expected?'

'A week's time.'

'I'll be in New York, I'm afraid. Do let me know, won't you?'

It was a Sunday place, this haven far from boardrooms and airports. Peter was sitting on his favourite window seat holding a crystal wine glass and staring through the mullioned panes at the woodsmoke drifting past the late-blooming roses and the quivering movements of leaves. The muffled silence of the Wiltshire morning was broken only by the clanging of erratic bells from the local church and the occasional popping spit as the rib of beef sizzled in the oven.

'Laura, there's a date you must put in your diary.'

'Oh?'

She did not move from the fireside as she sat on the floor losing herself in the patterns of the flames reaching up the chimney breast.

'We're getting married.'

'When?'

'At the end of next month.'

'But it's—' She stopped herself. 'Yes. Yes, why not, darling? I'll cancel everything for a week. But I won't have much time to prepare. I have to go to New York again soon.'

'Leave it to me.'

After lunch they walked arm in arm through the damp, still air and stopped to look at the rain-swollen stream rushing past below the neatly rulered lines of a ploughed field.

'I thought we could have a quiet celebration afterwards. Just us. Paris or Rome. What would you like?'

'Perfect. That's just what I would like. Florence, perhaps?'

Reassured by the unpopulated landscape, Peter leaned over and kissed the cool lips of his future wife.

The idea for the celebration started modestly. No, she and Peter had planned on a quiet wedding. The Team, who moments before had greeted her news with beaming faces, looked downcast.

'A small party?' suggested Antony. 'At the Eglantine. For you, Peter, us and a few friends?'

She hadn't really thought about it, but this year, the fifth anniversary of the company's birth, she had, she remembered, promised a special occasion. The Grey Men put forward ideas. It would be a good publicity move at this point. Laura smiled. Something special, which Antony would organize. She agreed. A small celebration.

Laura gave little thought to marriage, little thought to anything except plans for the future of her company. She had accustomed herself to constant movement. Constant movement meant there was no need to look back as she pursued the restless, invigorating journey from the present to the future. Every second filled with the promise of financial reward. Each day had a purpose, each day she chipped more out of the shape which would become the Laura Douglas colossus.

She was running behind schedule, not enough accomplished, wondering what would happen in her absence. Today, New York. Tickets, yes. Wardrobe out. Everything grey and cream. On the bed. No, not that woollen dress. Vulnerable wool. Tweed better. Perfume. Which? Not that one, Peter's favourite. Too floral. The cream

470

dress. Where was it? Damn. At the cleaner's. Must wash hair.

The bell sounded through the whine of the hair drier. Antony. Good. Just the urgent stuff. All this urgent? All right. Quick read. No, only a little tired. Must go through it. Now. Champagne promotion at Chancellor's. Japanese chef at Zi-Zi's. Yes. Fine. Reads fine. John to do lunch at House of Lords? No. Make it a Monday. Sir Howard Riley rang? In New York when? Tell him I'll call him as soon as I can. Yes, I'll lunch him. And him. And her. Fix a date.

As Laura passed through customs and into the departure lounge at Heathrow airport, she was elated. Her edgy tiredness had been succeeded by a new surge of energy. She could stroll serenely into meetings as though she had been confident all her life. At last she was going forward without looking back. Why had it taken so long? Five years to rid herself of Jack's presence. Five years it had taken for her to smile back in the mirror at herself knowing that her decisions depended on neither man who had attempted to rule her life.

If she occasionally thought beyond weeks to imagine years, she saw a future of untroubled marriage and quiet weekends with Peter, and she was already rehearsing the acceptable phrases of the successful woman of business.

'Of course, without the constant and loyal support of my husband . . .'

20

Behind the bullet-proof glass of the reception booth at Intertel, the security man smiled broadly and slid back the panel.

'Good morning, Miss Kowalski. Take it easy!'

He refused to believe she had left. Didi Kowalski, whose face was known to the nation, belonged to the employees of Intertel and always would.

Didi signed the book, sprawling her signature across the ruled columns, and propelled herself and imminent Baby majestically through the marble hall. The awards for *Table for One* were still there, framed in gold but where was her photograph? Didi stood in front of the star-framed beaming faces contracted to Intertel. By concentrating her attention, she could detect the fuzzy outline of one which had been removed. How dare they!

'Waiting for someone, Miss Kowalski? Shall I ring up?'

'No, thank you.'

Didi was pondering the best place for Laura's picture. It would not be the original but Stephen had promised to give her a print, and who would notice the difference? People crisscrossed around her, hurrying in or hurrying out of Intertel. Several greeted her as they always did, with quick, minimal waves of the hand or friendly grins breaking through the strained faces. 'Hi Didi!' from cameramen, floor managers, messengers – as though she was still part of the family.

She touched the lift button and whirred upwards to her home on the seventeenth floor. The door was shut which she had always kept open. Didi approached and read the newly printed label. 'Green Fingers'. Huh! She pushed the door open. No-one in. Yes, it was the right room. There was her desk, covered in papers. But the walls! That lovely mulberry pink gone, turned into a horrid shade of green. And those beautiful dried African vegetables gone. The puppets, the paper birds, the framed menus and viewers' letters, the engraving of apples and plums gone. And the Kowalski Memo! All gone. Who had taken her treasures? Where were they now? Even the fridge had gone. Heaped up bags of compost in a corner. Forks, spades, hoes higgledy-piggledy against the wall and a wheelbarrow full of box files. Who could possibly work in here?

'Didi! How wonderful! How are you? When's it due?'

'Any day.'

'Gosh, you must be so excited!'

Deirdre was wearing dungarees and, yes, green wellies.

'I've been out on location all day. They've put me on this stupid *Green Fingers* programme. I told them I can't stand gardening . . .' Deirdre gazed down at her feet and braced herself to say what was on her mind. 'Didi. Um. You know, the rotten publicity, well, we all knew it wasn't true. Thought I'd tell you.'

The coffee maker had also disappeared.

'Awfully sorry. It's horrible instant.'

Before Deirdre came to *Table for One* she never even knew that coffee came from a bean. Didi smiled to herself. It was wonderful. You only had to show people the real thing and you could change their lives for ever.

'And since you've been away,' Deirdre burbled on, 'I have to tell you, the food in the canteen has been absolutely ghastly.'

Didi left her surrounded by camera sheets, head down, logging the day's work, and set off down the corridor to the lift.

The Programme Controller's secretary had gone home. Didi walked into her small office. Through the closed door which divided the steely-voiced decision maker from the steely-voiced tea maker, she could hear every word of an impassioned conversation.

473

'Believe me, Roger, I understand it makes sense from your point of view.'

'I'm thinking of the programme. I just can't see it. I mean, yes, *Table for One* was absolutely made for the studio, but *Green Fingers*, stylistically speaking, isn't the same. It won't come across if it's studio-bound. It'll be dead, dead, dead. Bill Dunstable won't be able to carry it. *Green Fingers* is about life. Nature's rhythms. Things growing.' Roger sounded grimly disturbed. 'And I'm terribly unhappy about the video inserts. For this programme, I really do think one has to aim for a totally uninterrupted open-air feel. The viewer should almost smell that wet earth.'

'Roger, you're a creative director. This is a challenge. I know it's hard. Believe me, if I could give you a light entertainment budget for a gardening programme, I would.'

Didi pushed open the door. The Programme Controller was sitting in the familiar, tall-backed black leather swivel chair behind his desk. Roger, seated in front of the desk, one leg across the other, was leaning forward anxiously from an inferior position.

'Good evening.'

The Programme Controller stood up and went towards her. 'Didi, how nice to see you. I'm awfully sorry. I didn't realize you had an appointment. Could we possibly make it—'

'No, I'm awfully sorry we couldn't. Don't worry. It won't take long.'

The Programme Controller masked his irritation and put his arm round her shoulder. 'Didi, it isn't a very convenient moment. We are in the middle of a programme discussion. Why don't you drop in tomorrow? I'm sure my secretary could find you a space.'

'I'd like to sit down, if you don't mind.'

The Programme Controller gestured towards his secretary's chair. 'Why don't you wait there? I'll call a cab.'

'Are you all right, Didi love?' said Roger.

Didi walked over and sat herself behind the desk. 'I think I deserve an apology.'

'Didi, why not wait until we can talk in private? I really do have to sort out some things with Roger.'

'Roger can listen in. I don't mind.'

The Programme Controller looked at Roger, then at Didi, and sat on the edge of his desk, pursing his lips. She was heavily pregnant, after all. He had to be a bit careful.

'Roger, give us ten minutes or so. Do you mind?'

The door clicked shut and Didi found herself staring at the square jaw of the Programme Controller, wondering if anyone had ever hit it.

'I have given five years of my life to Intertel,' she began. 'When I first came here, *Table for One* was only an idea on a piece of paper. An idea for an afternoon cookery programme. It could have been golf or fishing as far as you were concerned. No-one cared. But I did. What could be more important than what you put into your mouth every day? We are what we eat. Food is life. I've always believed that, and I wanted to show that the quality of life depends on the quality of food.'

'Indeed you did show it.' The Programme Controller gave a conciliatory nod.

'I wanted people to wake up and discover all that they had been missing, to bite into an apple and have an experience, to smell the aroma of coffee, the earthiness of fresh-baked real bread, to gasp at the skills of the fantastic chefs who opened everyone's eyes to the—'

'Yes, yes. Of course. And we acknowledged your extraordinary contribution. On many occasions.'

'*Table for One* changed people's lives. Do you realize that?'

'In a sense. Yes. I suppose you could look at it that way.'

'And they responded. Hundreds of letters every week. How do you think they are going to feel when you decide to tell them *Table for One* has gone for ever? They are

475

going to feel betrayed. I think you have acted in a callous, unfeeling, brutal way. I am ashamed for Intertel.'

The Programme Controller drew in his breath and paced round the room. 'I hear what you're saying, Didi. But you have rather got the wrong end of the stick. There is no question of axing *Table for One*.'

'Oh?' Didi looked startled.

'I don't know who told you we were. All we're doing is putting the series on hold while we have a slight rethink. This happens every now and again. We don't want the format to become stale.'

'We had already planned the next series. You know that.'

'Plans change, Didi.'

'And my contract? No-one will discuss it.'

'I understand. Believe me, you're quite free to go elsewhere for a time. You know we'll be only too happy to have you back. But at the moment my hands are tied. It was a management decision to make a twenty-five per cent cutback. Not mine, I hasten to add, but it does mean stringent budgeting to put our house in order.'

Didi stared straight between the watery blue, inexpressive eyes of the Programme Controller and forgot the rest of the speech she had rehearsed in the mirror.

'You rotten lying bastard. You think I believe that? You wanted to get rid of me but you didn't have the guts to tell me. You're pathetic.'

Her voice rose and she was Dorothy Dean in the playground shouting down the school bully. Then she clutched her belly and let out a scream, and then another which could be heard right down the corridor of the twenty-fifth floor. The Programme Controller was transfixed.

'It's not . . . you're not . . . shouldn't you lie down?'

'Do something. It's coming. Quick.'

Roger heard the piercing screams as he was coming back, fired with determination to reach a compromise solution with *Green Fingers*, and changed from a purposeful walk into a run. There was Didi, lying on the floor.

'Roger, oh, Roger.' She lay back, breathless. 'Could you cancel my room at . . . at . . .'

'Don't worry, love. Just relax.'

'I've dialled nine nine nine. They're sending an ambulance,' said the ashen-faced Programme Controller. Roger ran through in his mind the sequences of a film he had shot two years ago. The women on fertility drugs had given birth on camera. Those interviews with scientists and gynaecologists and midwives. The animated diagram of each stage of the birth process. He remembered every single shot of the rushes. He had run them backwards and forwards a hundred times, spent days writing the voice-over commentary.

Could these be final stage contractions? Roger timed them with his stopwatch. Didi was pushing and bellowing and gulping air.

'Super, love. Easy does it. You're doing fine.'

He looked at the panic in her eyes and willed the baby to be alive, to be healthy, as he willed the studio to produce perfection in every shot, as if his whole career was at stake.

The ambulance men came running in and witnessed Didi progressing through the last stages of labour, with Roger at her side holding her hand and mopping her brow while the Programme Controller sat in a daze, worried mainly about the state of his carpet.

What happened next passed into the transient history of British television, and then into folklore memory. Didi Kowalski, star of *Table for One*, gave birth to a perfectly formed baby boy not underwater, not with the sound of playing dolphins but in the Programme Controller's office at Intertel.

'I didn't mean to.'

These were the first words which Didi uttered when she awoke from a deep smiling sleep, glancing first at Baby cradled in the Italian crib and then at John sitting on her bed wondering if she would ever open her eyes.

'Isn't he divine?'

'No. Just bloody marvellous.'

'You know what we're going to call him?'

'What?'

'Stephen. Don't you think he's like a Stephen?'

'No, Didi. He's not a Stephen. He's an André. I think he's an André. He's got that determined expression, you can't mistake it.'

'He's upset because I didn't have him underwater. John?'

'Yes?'

'The photographer. I didn't have a picture, and I did so want you to be there.'

'You didn't give me much warning.'

'But I needed the pictures for my column.'

'Bugger your column.'

Didi laughed. 'You mean I can be a Mum for a while and push the pram down the street like everyone else?'

'Why not?'

'All right then.' Didi stroked John's hand with a limp finger. 'But not for long.'

'Do you fancy some champagne?'

'Yes. We'd both like some.'

The sleeping baby stirred as John dabbed his tiny lips with the first taste of the drink of chefs. He did not shrink away. André. That would be his name.

It was going to be a fairy-tale party, the party to end all parties. Antony was learning to delegate in Laura's absence, supported by the Team. The phone calls to New York were becoming less frequent. Leave it to us, he told Laura with new-found firmness.

George had also found a new role. The maestro of the dining room had become the master of ceremonies, the guiding spirit behind the Great Celebration, and he had taken to wearing a cloak as befitting his status. Only he had the experience which counted. (The Team were merely responsible for paperwork. Anyone could do that.)

He was disappointed that Laura had not invited him to the register office ceremony, but some like it quiet second time around. Heavenly food and the best champagne. It would be pure theatre and he planned a grand finale that would take everyone's breath away, even these southerners who thought they'd seen everything.

John called them together in a private room at the Kitchen Club. George, Tadeus, Sebastian, Elwyn, Jean-Luc and, oh all right then, Harry Wade.

'Over a thousand people at the Doric Club. Laura's hired the whole building and she wants a feast. Everything we ever dreamed of cooking, the things you say to yourself you couldn't do. The things André Bouchon used to tell us about when he cooked in palaces. The secrets of Escoffier. The things we used to dream about when we were chopping up the veg. How one day we'd cook for a Texan millionaire or a sheik or the most fabulous party in Hollywood. Money no object. That's what she said. She said she wants us to create something that'll be written in the history books.'

John looked at the bewildered faces sitting round the table.

'A function, a buffet or a banquet?'

'A feast, El.'

'The Chinese do them superbly,' began Sebastian. 'When I was in Beijing last year—'

'We're not copying the fucking Chinese.'

'Can I do the patisserie? I've something special in mind, as a matter of fact.'

'OK, Harry, you're on patisserie.'

'So what is it? An offloading operation to kid the taxman?'

'She's getting married, Tad.'

'How about that? Who's she marrying? A bank?'

'Peter Henderson. He is in the City, I believe.'

'Told you. She's marrying a fucking bank. Well, if he's financing the do . . .'

'No, she is. That's not the point. We can do anything

we like. Anything. It's our big chance to stop thinking about getting the mark-up right and to do away with nicking bits off portion sizes.'

'Who's it for exactly? Her or us or a gang of ignorant punters?'

'It's for us, Tad. Our chance.'

'Tell you what, though,' began Sebastian in his slow drawl, sensing the withdrawn mood of the chefs, 'how about paying homage to the man who taught us more than anyone? André Bouchon.'

The chefs raised their glasses.

'Monsieur Bouchon.'

There were several scrawled messages waiting at the reception desk of the Rialto. Laura Douglas from John Crabtree. Laura Douglas from Antony at the Studio. Laura Douglas, urgent. Ring Howard. What a time to choose. Probably wanted her advice on where to take a client. Something trivial. He only contacted her about trivial matters. If it had been important he would have notified her earlier that he was in New York. She did not return his call and then he rang her as she was packing her case preparing to catch the Wednesday afternoon flight.

'Allow me some time with you. It's been so long.'

'I can't, Howard. I can't possibly.'

'Are you angry with me?'

'Not at all. I'm rushed off my feet and Peter and I are getting married on Friday in London.'

'Really? Why didn't you tell me?'

'Why should I?'

'Because I care about you.'

It was impossible. Impossible? He was asking for so little. One last chance to say farewell. Or had he meant nothing to her? Suppose she caught the early morning plane on Thursday? He was leaving the following day, and they could spend one last night together. As friends. That was all he wanted. To part as friends. There were things he wished to say, certain things which could not be left unsaid. Then he would go. A promise. Laura put the phone down and dialled the London code.

'Peter, I'm awfully sorry but I've been delayed. A crucial meeting tonight. I'll catch an early flight tomorrow . . . Of course, I'll be there.'

That night, in the isolated splendour of her Rialto suite, they made love, but it did not touch her. She was thinking of the day ahead.

'Are you coming to my party?'

'What party?'

'Didn't you receive an invitation? Antony should have sent you one.'

'No. My secretary would have told me. In any case, I couldn't have accepted. Not feeling as I do. But I'm sure you're making the right decision.'

'It's not a wedding party, Howard. I'm having it for the company. It seemed as good a time as any. You'll enjoy yourself. All my top chefs are cooking.'

'It's tempting, but as it happens I have to entertain some German food manufacturers tomorrow night.'

There was no need for Laura to explain, and she was relieved. Howard, she could tell by the tone of his voice, realized that he would not be seeing her any more.

During the flight to London, he asked for details of her plans, asked about each member of the Team, how she saw the future direction of her company. And he told her that Illustra were completing the takeover of Leone Leisure.

'Does that upset you, Laura? I thought you ought to know.'

'Why should I be upset?'

'You might be.'

'Jack made a mistake. That doesn't mean he's a failure. He'll find something else.'

'I did think at one moment he might have guessed about us.'

'Because he saw us having lunch? Really, Howard!'

481

'I was sorry I had to get rid of him. I couldn't see him fitting into the Illustra philosophy. Jack's a likeable chap. I admire his energy and bravado. He wasn't right for you, but he's not a monster. Are you still friends?'

'I guess so.'

'One shouldn't cut people off.'

He was looking at her, intently.

'I wanted to give you something. A present.'

Laura smiled. 'You didn't have to.'

Reaching into his briefcase, Howard took out a large envelope and withdrew a sheaf of papers.

'Illustra shares. In your name, my love. Hardly romantic, but they'll be worth ten per cent more next week. A better investment than silk knickers.' He handed her the papers.

'Ten thousand pounds? Howard!'

'It's the least I could do. A small reminder.'

Laura pressed her lips to his. He placed his hands on her face and kept them there for a while, as though to preserve an imprint of her features.

'You know where I'll be if you ever need me.'

Then he stared out of the window as the plane passed through indigo skies, and tentatively reached for her hand. His long fingers rested on hers, and she felt guilt, guilt because she was the one who was walking away.

In memory of André Bouchon, five of the best restaurants in London closed their doors the day before 24 October, the allotted day for the Grand Celebration. Over one hundred cooks and chefs in five kitchens rushed to greet the early morning suppliers as they queued up with their boxes and trays. Crayfish of the pearliest salmon pink from Turkey, langoustines from the clear deep waters off northern Scotland, lobsters from Cornwall, glistening sides of beef from the Highlands, well-hung venison and arrays of neatly tied quails from Norfolk, foie gras from Alsace, salt-smelling spiky black sea urchins from Brittany, vast reclining shiny-eyed turbot fished in the depths of the

Channel, chalky gnarled oysters from the Irish coast, caviar from Astrakhan, wild strawberries from New Zealand, asparagus from California, perfectly formed roots and brassicas and delicate leaves and herbs releasing their scent from far-away fields. And, finally, the truffle cabinets were unlocked, the massed black diamonds from Périgord, the final *collier* to set off the magnificence of fish, flesh and fowl.

On the silvery surfaces of the Eglantine's kitchen tray after tray of crayfish were inspected. They were then plunged into saucepans of finely diced carrots, onion, thyme, parsley and bay leaves. The *Mirepoix à la Bordelaise* was gently steeped in butter then splashed with bottles of the finest champagne. When the crayfish was cooked enough to retain the fresh succulence, the shells were removed and pounded to release yet more flavour, swimming in fish stock and velvety sauce. The crushed ice was rushed from the freezer, the bowls placed on top ready to receive the finely strained steaming liquid until it cooled ready for the butter-coloured cream and the transformation into a mousse.

The lads from the brigade sat in the kitchen waiting for the moment when John would announce that the next stage could begin. He opened the capacious fridge and brought out the silver timbales. The mousse was firm enough for the embroidery to begin. Without speaking, they laid the tails of the crayfish this way and that across the creamy surface, interspersed with black slivers of truffle and aromatic herbs in traditional symmetry.

John looked and saw that it was good. He brought over a pan of darkly golden fish aspic and poured it slowly over the timbales in a thin stream.

'You've done well, lads. It's exactly how it should be.'

Each kitchen reflected the character of the chef who ran it and in each the atmosphere was as different as the restaurants which they served. In some a steady calm reigned, in others there were clatters and shouts, swearing and praise in equal volume.

Tadeus stood arranging forest mounds of inky *trompettes de mort* around the blackened and glazed head of a wild boar.

'Look, lads. What a bastard. Bet he had a few in his time.'

A young sous-chef was eyeing the long tentacles of a squid.

'Come on you lot,' yelled Tadeus. 'Cut the foreplay and get on with the action.'

'Quails, see. They used to be wild,' explained Elwyn, holding up the small carcass of a parcelled bird. 'You could see them flying around Africa and India. Like my design? Patterns inspired by India and Africa, see. The black bits are truffle. Carrots, red. And we have to cut the parsley so it looks like a jungle tree. Where's the forcemeat stuffing?'

Elwyn scraped a shaving with a slim spoon and they waited as he moved his tongue round the smooth mixture.

'Good. The truffle and foie gras make all the difference. A marriage made in heaven. A hint of brandy. This is going to be marvellous, boys. In it goes. What a joy. Eat these and you'll be singing all night. We'll have some, don't worry. Just a couple. Don't cook them too long, mind.'

Sebastian watched intently as the elaborate shiny brioches slid slowly out of the hot oven, topped by a wide petalled rose. Next day he would cut through the carefully moulded shapes with a silver knife, slide through the jelly steeped in champagne to reach the earthy richness of the truffle-studded goose liver, reminding him of textures and flavours he had long since abandoned and would never serve again.

It was four in the morning, but the only time that mattered was the time of the oven. Harry Wade was by himself in the kitchen, gazing in wonder at the towering *Croquembouche,* adding the finishing touches of crystallized violets. The racks of his cold room were weighed down with *Pithiviers, gâteaux aux marrons, millefeuilles,* yeast cakes and petal-shaped chocolate cakes, *pâte frolle*, *pâte feuilletée*, *pâte à choux*, custards and *crème pâtissière*, pralines, sponges and meringues, spicy breads and biscuits. All would be manipulated into extravagant shapes arising from the untroubled waters of Harry's imagination. With only the hum of the coolers for company, his thick-fingered virtuoso hands caressed and shaped and twisted and moulded and sprinkled giving the final elaboration to the flower shapes, the crescent shapes, the horn shapes, the rings and circles and squares ranged round the kitchen, covering every surface so that the profusion of form and colour resembled a wild cottage garden with every flower in perfect bloom.

At three in the afternoon the gloomy back entrance doors of the Doric slowly opened and the trail of worker ants entered bearing the fruits of their labour.

'If we'd had a crash in the van,' remarked John, 'British cooking would have been put back twenty years. Think of that.'

'And if we put a bomb under this place,' added Tadeus, 'we could have a revolution and take over the country.'

They walked through to the rows of tall fridges occupying the rooms once used as basement store-rooms, each neatly labelled by John. Jean-Luc stood first by one, then by another, and the elaborate cargo was slipped on to the shelves . . . *Homard Gramont, Suprème d'écrevisses, chaud froid de cailles, foie gras à la strasbourgeoise, faisan à la Croix-de-Berny, turbot à la purée d'oursins.*

'Isn't it fucking obscene? You could buy a restaurant with this lot.'

'It's art, Tad. If it isn't, what is? And if art costs, so it should.'

'*C'est triste.* Tomorrow, there will be nothing, chef. All this time, we work . . .'

'That's what it's about,' said John. 'Think of the pleasure of doing it. Then we make something else. And the something else is even better. You're always beginning again. That's not sad.'

'*Oh, mon Dieu. Je suis foutu.*'

Far from prying eyes and tape-recorders, three sombre men were helping themselves to slivers of toast from a breakfast tray. They would not be staying long in this rooftop suite at the Connaught Hotel, an hour at the most.

'What's the latest?' asked one, a flight bag at his side.

'Fifty fifty chance.'

'When they say that, they're confident. In my experience.'

'The surgeon said he'll have to operate. Blood clot in the brain.'

'I want the top man.'

'Of course.'

'How's the girl?'

'Smashed up but nothing serious.'

The eldest of the three, who had declined refreshment, sucked wearily at his cigar and watched the smoke curling towards the window.

'Anyone with her? Family?'

'Fiancé. She was supposed to be getting married this afternoon.'

'Tragic.'

'I had a word with him. Decent chap. Stockbroker. Henderson, Peter. Terribly upset but understands. Luckily he's in the City.'

'Are you absolutely sure we can embargo this till the end of next week? The lawyers won't like it!'

'We've taken care of the police. And the hospital are used to this kind of thing. Lady Riley is being marvellous.'

'One of you must be there. All the time.'

'Of course.'

'If this leaks, Illustra will . . .'

'It won't.'

They left the hotel at staggered intervals, anonymously merging with those hurrying to work.

*   *   *

486

Earlier that morning, when dawn was breaking, Antony had been awakened from fitful sleep. He had told John that he would be on call.

'Sorry to wake you. Peter Henderson here.'

It was unthinkable. An accident? On the way from the airport? But Laura never had accidents. Ah, so she wasn't driving. Howard Riley? When? Last night? But she told him she was coming back from New York the day before. Delayed. Yes. Must have been. Business meeting. Another project with Illustra. She didn't tell him everything. Laura in intensive care. She would pull through? Of course she would. No, he couldn't visit yet. Soon, when she was well enough. And Howard Riley? A brain operation? Terrible. No, it wouldn't have been his fault. One has to be thankful. At least they're both alive.

'I'll cancel everything, naturally,' said Antony, blenching at the thought of contacting a thousand guests, cancelling the staff, disposing of the food, all that effort and expense, everything ruined because of one oaf in a lorry.

'I want the party to go ahead.' Peter sounded strained.

'But that's out of the question.'

'Listen, Antony. This isn't just a private matter. I wish it were.' He paused. 'Thinking of myself, I am only concerned for Laura. Selfishly, perhaps. But it isn't that simple. Sometimes one has to . . . Can I say something in the strictest confidence?'

'Of course, Peter.'

'Next Monday, Illustra will announce their new share prices. They are riding high. Because of new acquisitions, the value will have risen by ten per cent. Everyone in the City will know that the upsurge is entirely due to the outstanding chairmanship of Howard Riley. He has taken Illustra to the top. A brilliant achievement, I have to admit.'

'But that has nothing to do with Laura! Or you.'

'Antony, be reasonable. If anyone suspects that Riley's life is in danger, the shares will plummet. Without him,

Illustra would sink into the second division. We have to keep this quiet. No-one must suspect. The party must go ahead. If it gets out that Laura was with Howard Riley in a possibly fatal accident . . .'

'I can't agree, Peter. And I'm sure Laura wouldn't want it hushed up.'

'I've discussed it with the Illustra Board. They were most understanding. Sometimes one has to make an unpleasant decision.'

'So what am I supposed to do? What do I say to everyone?'

'The honeymoon. In Florence. We had planned to go to Florence.' There was silence.

'Yes?'

'I'll speak to you later. Lady Riley is here. Giving me fantastic support. So concerned about Laura. A remarkable woman.'

Antony put down the phone. He wanted to be there, to make sure they kept her alive. She would live, she had to live. He could manage it, he could run the company. Until she was well enough to come back.

George was lost for words, but the doorman at the Doric Club did not seem inclined to speak. It was only after he had watched the careful unloading of a giant carving, a sparsely draped feminine figure with outstretched hand, whose full-formed breasts were barely covered by a grey banner emblazoned in pink with the Laura Douglas motif, that he allowed himself a modest comment.

'Very good.'

'And carved out of ice. Must have taken absolutely hours.'

'Ice? Real ice? I trust there will be no mess on the floor.'

'Didn't you know? It's the kind of ice that doesn't melt,' said George tartly, shivering in the unheated marble hall.

The grey-suited trumpeters arrived and unpacked their instruments.

'I was told there would be three, not four,' remarked the doorman.

'There's always four of us,' answered a high-pitched Scots voice.

The doorman walked forward, and thrust back his chin. 'I will need proof of identity, gentlemen.'

George opened the heavy studded door and peered down Carlton House Terrace. Lucky Laura. It had stopped raining. Then he thought he saw what he had been expecting, or was it a trick of the light creating shapes in the distance where there were none? Yes. There it was. On time. Walking calmly down the street amongst the cars, and the passers-by hardly turning their heads. Not like that in Bradford. They'd want to know where it had come from, where it was going and what it was doing. George, at any rate, was going to touch it because he'd never done that and he always liked a new tactile experience.

Those wrinkles, hard, like ridges on dry earth. You didn't expect that, and those little spiky hairs like bits of teasel. Then he jumped back as something groped at his pocket.

'Oh!'

'She always does that. Quite friendly.'

It was a she. Saucy bitch. Might have guessed.

'Can I take a picture?'

The doorman emerged to ascertain whether the forecast rain had held off and noted the presence of one tail-swinging baby elephant accompanied by two keepers. An elephant-sized parking space would be allotted on the pavement to the right of the Doric Club entrance.

As the first limousine disgorged its long-skirted occupants, Don Delaney crossed the road and took up his position next to the elephant. 'Hello, Grace,' he said, handing her a mint. They liked mints. Mind out for the trunk, though. It was going to be a long night. Ah. Here we come. Happy couple time.

A white Rolls Royce drew up, must be them. Wrong.

This was Mary-Lou Harvey, eternal starlet, always in white, trying to upstage everyone and he wouldn't waste a shot on those over-exposed tits. He wasn't that desperate.

Emerging from behind a flapping grey ear, he produced his crumpled press pass, and moved inside.

The crowd of guests was crushed together, waiting expectantly. George gave a signal and the four trumpeters raised their instruments and gave a welcoming salute. As soon as the echoes of the martial sound had died away, he took up his microphone and stood in front of the massed white lilies, looking past the ice-hewn heroine pointing purposefully towards the sweeping marble staircase. Beckoning the couple nearest to him, George cleared his throat and proclaimed their names in ringing tones which had once reached to the back of the Alhambra in Bradford.

Following those in front of them who were obviously familiar with the geography, Stephen and Didi found themselves a space in the gallery encircling the rooms of the Doric Club bordered by busts of Greek and Roman philosophers. Spaced around them were small clusters of guests, each cluster ignoring the other.

'I hate the beginning of parties.'

Didi was wondering if baby André would have woken up by now and if Nanny Ward had given him the milk she had expressed into the perspex milk machine standing like a space goblin in a corner of the kitchen. It was her first night out since the Birth, and she felt uneasy.

'Do you think they'll be happy?'

'Laura and Peter? I don't think that's what she's after. Happiness is paying the mortgage and going on package holidays. Hardly part of the Laura Douglas portfolio.'

'Well, anyway, I think I'm . . . yes, I am.'

'What, sweetest?'

'Happy.'

Stephen looked at her downcast face. 'I'd never have guessed.'

'It's my breasts. They're enormous.'

'The dress is a teeny bit tight. Come on. Let's have a look around.'

He took her by the hand and opened one of the doors leading off the gallery, which was hung with a swathe of beribboned roses. In the centre rested a hand-painted card on which was written: 'The Pink Room – John Crabtree.'

The room was lit by a thicket of tall candles standing upright in a crystal chandelier. A long table was covered in watered dusky pink silk and in the centre a silver cherub was holding aloft a bunch of multi-coloured quails' eggs.

They barely noticed the pink camellias, the trellis of fine leaves spraying down the walls, the silver chairs, the trompe l'oeil picture of receding Corinthian columns.

Stephen sighed and buried his head in Didi's dark curls. 'Do you think we will have to wait all night to eat John's food?' He slipped his hands on to her full breasts. 'If only these were foie gras.'

'You know I disapprove, really.'

Didi stiffened her neck, recalling her impassioned plea to put an end to the torture of geese.

'They're so beautiful. Will you allow me to see them?'

'Someone might come in. You've seen them before. They're larger, that's all.'

'Wait.'

Stephen shut the door firmly.

'What are you doing?'

'Come here. This is the last time we'll be together for a while, sweetest. I shall miss you most awfully . . .'

'You can't go away. There's the christening.'

'I'm going to sojourn amongst the natives of Africa.'

Didi shuddered. 'What on earth for? What's wrong with the palm trees at Kew? At least you can park there. Why go to Africa of all places? Nobody's interested in African cuisine, not that there is such a thing. They put everything in stews and you hate stews. Oh, Stephen, you keep going to places and coming back and going to more places. I don't understand. When John and I get a bigger house, you can have a lovely room at the top and live with us.

We're going to have a huge fridge you can walk inside. André is such a good baby and he wouldn't disturb you, honestly. And then there'd be dinner parties, and going to the country for my famous champagne picnics. It would be so perfect.'

'Dearest Didi, it's your dream, not mine.'

'But it's not a dream! Oh dear, have I missed something out? Is there something I haven't thought of? Stephen, tell me, you're so difficult sometimes. What on earth do you want?'

'Your breasts.'

'No, really. Be serious.'

'I am.'

He moved close to Didi who was glowing like a wax madonna in a pink shrine lit by the steadily burning candles. He scooped out one laden breast from between the folds of her dress, bent and placed his lips over her nipple. She felt the sweet milk streaming into his mouth and stroked the back of his neck as he eagerly gulped the liquid. Oh, such joy! A new experience. Stephen slowly relinquished the nipple, gave a prolonged 'ah' of satisfaction and hugged her to him.

'I think I can wait for the rest now.'

'At least this doesn't remind one of a Bangkok brothel.'

Penelope put her large handbag on the floor and arranged herself on a brown velvet chair. ('The Brown Room – Elwyn Jones.') She had made an effort, in so far as she ever made an effort with outward appearances. A fine-looking woman, thought Miss Cutbutton, observing her long black taffeta skirt and the high-necked silk blouse caught at the throat with a cameo brooch, and just a hint of colour on the lips.

'I've never been to Bangkok.' She was a little in awe of Penelope and responded over-emphatically, although Penelope suspected this was a mask for shyness, or her way of fending off importunate journalists. They had both come alone. 'But I can see the reason for your remark.'

492

'All this excess. Why? Should one celebrate when there is nothing to celebrate? If we were witnessing the birth of a nation, I would understand. Or the light of freedom after the darkness of oppression. This is mere clothing for the corpse. And what, one should ask, lies in the coffin? No-one asks questions any more. It isn't done. People don't. They shrug their shoulders at corruption and describe it with delight.'

'We have learned to live with it, I suppose.'

'What's in here?'

Virginia and Melissa Desgranges opened the door to find two elderly women deep in conversation.

'Must find the loo.'

'So must I.'

The two girls turned on their heels and headed back to the dance floor.

Miss Cutbutton took Penelope's hand. 'I think you should do something serious for us, Penelope. A proper investigation. We need people like you on the *Daily Reporter*. People with commitment.'

In the Great Hall of the Doric Club, the music was gathering momentum. The band upped the tempo as well as the amplifiers, and the arms of the barmen were aching as bottle after bottle of Laura Douglas Classic Champagne was uncorked to fuel the celebration. The Grey Men, all with sculpted short hair and fresh pink rosebuds in their lapels, wound their way around the guests with solicitude, and longed for midnight when the feast would begin and Laura, their Laura, would make her triumphal entrance.

Didi could hear the music thumping through the wooden floors. The sound excited her. She wanted to dance with every man, to throw herself into the arms of anyone who would drive her into wild-limbed abandon before she settled into the warm maternal nest. Just one night of promiscuous physical sensation, one night of pressing herself against strange bodies, feeling herself grasped by unknown hands, one night of unbridled sensuality before the retreat into motherhood and penury.

'I wish Laura and Peter would hurry up. I want some grub,' complained Lord Maclintock as he retired from the dance floor, having managed to execute a bumpy quick-step with Lucinda despite the conflicting rhythms of a disco number.

'It's a midnight buffet. You know they're never on time.'

'They should stop the staff getting at the bottles. I want my food.'

At this rate baby André would be drunk. Oh dear. All that champagne. Didi promised herself she would never do this again. Stephen came to her side with another full glass and handed it to her.

'Stephen, honestly! I mustn't. Well, not all of it. I'll just have a sip. Has John arrived yet?'

'No sign.'

'I'm so hungry.'

'So am I. Do you fancy hamburger and chips?'

'Stephen, how could you!'

'There's stacks in my freezer.'

'Stephen. It's dreadful.'

'Puts everything in perspective, sweetest.'

'I think it's disgusting.'

Didi's expression changed from indignation to surprise. There was Magnus with Mrs Magnus. Oh dear. Poor thing. Stephen put on his serious face and walked over to him.

'I've been trying to decide whether cold food is making a comeback. The Rothschilds used to go in for it years ago, and I told them then that the distance of the kitchen from the dining room should not influence *l'art culinaire*. I dislike cold food intensely. What is your opinion?'

'I will have to think about it.'

Magnus Shaw gave Stephen such an anguished look that he almost felt sorry for him.

Dylan Tusk had managed to get himself invited at the last

494

minute. Someone else must have nicked his invitation, he explained to Antony. Always doing that at *Freewheel*. His wife Tina kept worrying about the poor baby elephant who must be getting cold out there. He was hungry, she was hungry. Why wasn't there anything to nibble? Laura and her new husband were going to make a brief appearance, the doorman had told him. Not everyone knew she'd nipped down to the register office. Could get a para out of that.

'Go on, take your shoes off, no-one'd notice. Don't be daft. Who looks at feet?'

He'd never been to a do with so much bubbly. Made him feel queer if he drank too much. Not a glass of beer to be had.

'Oh, look, Tina. There's a room we haven't seen. Locked? Can't be. It's got a label. "The White Room – Sebastian North." Oh yeah. Know him. You're meant to go in, course you are.'

He leaned his shoulder against the door and gave a hearty shove so that it flung open. Tina squealed. Neither of them noticed the decor.

A young man was lying on the floor face downwards with his trousers pulled to his knees. Melissa Desgranges was seated on top of him in the sidesaddle position, tickling his squirming white buttocks with a white lily.

'And that wasn't all. You had to look. In the corner was a magnolia tree, all lit up from underneath, in a white pot. There was this bloke. Know what he was doing? Trying to aim a stream of piss into the pot. And you know what the bloke lying on the floor said? Do join in. Do join in. In an upper crusty accent. It's the honest truth. Tina, that's my wife, Tina nearly threw up, said we ought to tell someone but I said forget it, if that's their idea of a good time, they can have it.'

Caliope was in seventh heaven, her glass permanently awash with champagne.

There were so many people she knew, she could flow

wherever fancy took her, backwards and forwards, churning her way through the cream of society. Such was the headiness provoked by this grand occasion that she had forgotten the hard prongs of her iron corset forcing out folds of flesh and pictured herself floating vertiginously to the ceiling, flipped upwards in a benign air current.

'Where is the heavenly bride and the handsome groom?' she asked, seizing Antony by the arm before he could escape.

'Didn't you see them? They came in for a moment. Then had to rush to the airport. Off to their honeymoon in Florence.'

'Then I shall have to do the honours in their absence.'

Caliope opened her beaded bag and threw out a small shower of pink paper petals which fluttered down unnoticed amongst the throng.

Once again the trumpets sounded, and the band of white-hatted chefs walked slowly up the marble staircase bearing great silver trays with awkward solemnity. They paraded round the gallery and broke ranks, filing off to their allotted rooms.

It was as though the last train to freedom was pulling from the platform. The light-headed guests crowded into the rooms, jostling, pushing past one another, squirming round corpulent stomachs, elbowing, thrusting out arms, leaning over one another, grabbing spoons, forks, knives, intent on thrusting whatever was in reach into their mouths. Elwyn was backed against a corner of the Brown Room watching helplessly as they seized upon his quails, tearing away the flesh, sucking out the stuffing, bones falling to the floor, their faces contorted as they gnawed and chewed and grunted.

Magnus and Sigmund were impervious to the crush of bodies pressing and pushing around them as they fingered and prodded and sucked, straining to identify the black banquet in front of them attributed to Tadeus Freeman: black *oursins*, black *trompettes de la mort*, black pudding, black truffle-glazed foie gras, and the princes of blackness, the charred, shining head of a boar, its mouth half open, smiling, and a suckling pig glistening with black crackling, a dark toffee apple in its mouth.

'My dear man,' shouted Sigmund to Tadeus, who had given up trying to hand out plates. 'Only you have understood the theatre of food. You can serve this at my funeral. Perfect. Perfect.'

'I haven't tasted a thing,' shouted Didi to John, reaching out in vain as plate after plate was wiped clean by the carrion crowd. 'Move out of the way,' she screamed, groped for John's hand and pulled him away out of the Pink Room, round the packed gallery and down the stairs past the figure of ice which was slowly dripping into formlessness, a stumped hand still pointing upwards.

Horrified by the seething spectacle, Penelope picked up her handbag and wormed her way downstairs as guests continued to arrive. Holding her handbag as a shield, she pushed past a group of girls in metallic dresses with glittering faces and spiked cloches, resembling frenzied stag bettles whose biological clock had been rephased to night-time activity. She was jabbed by gesticulating arms as though she was invisible.

Their escorts were shouting at the doorman, 'We're friends of Laura Douglas. Oh, go on. Let us in. Tell her we're here, there's a good chap.'

Penelope took a deep breath and started walking, thankful that the whole of London was not celebrating. The Special Enquiry section. Investigation by Penelope Long. Her name there. At last, at last, something worthy of her name. A chance to dig and probe and stretch her every faculty. Those contemptuous young men in news, thinking they knew everything, relegating her powers of investigation to battery hens, bovine spongiform encephalopathy, salmonella, listeria or E numbers on food packets, not knowing and not wishing to acknowledge her distinguished past. Penelope Long, who used to be pointed out in awe as she walked down Fleet Street. She would show them. She would write the quintessential report of the decade, the writhings of a *fin de siècle* society in confusion and decay. The facts.

The stag beetles joined forces with the drunken friends of Melissa and Virginia. One of them lunged at a lobster and charged through the crowds waving it aloft while another took a mousseline and squashed it into a startled face. Then they formed a shrieking band, going from room to room, scattering the gobblers and munchers, stuffing food into each others' mouths and hurling whatever they could find into the air, on to the floor.

'Super party!'

'The more sober guests retired to the library. The young people were having a good time. Not our kind of party, but does them good to let off steam.

'Isn't it time they turned up?'

'Who?'

'Laura and Peter.'

'Got better things to do, Lucy! And so have we. Come on. We're leaving.'

George was grappling with a young man who was attempting to aim a stream of vomit down the stairs.

'Get the police, I would,' called out Harry Wade as he beat a retreat.

'No point,' replied Elwyn, steering him towards the exit.

'Have you seen Laura and Peter?'

The chefs were standing gloomily on the pavement outside the Doric Club.

'No. But no-one seems bothered.'

'Fucking disaster,' said Tadeus.

As their plane touched down at Heathrow Airport, New York already a distant memory, it was as though they had already parted. When they walked through the glass doors into the familiar autumn drizzle, Laura forgot for a moment that Howard was at her side.

'I'll drop you off.'

His voice sounded matter of fact.

'I'd prefer to go back on my own. It would be better, Howard.'

Laura spoke quietly, with sadness. A prolonged leave-taking would hurt them both. His eyes belied the tone of his voice, for they were full of anguish. Such dignity. She still admired him.

'I won't come in.'

She wavered. 'You know I wouldn't let you.'

The quiet hum of the engine was soothing. The heavy heat of the car surrounded her like a fur blanket. Howard was quiet, his gloved hands resting on the wheel, his eyes fixed on the road ahead. It was as though he was commanding the traffic, as though a way would be cleared for his passage. The New York days had been long, exhausting, but she was used to exhaustion. She leaned against the window and felt her eyelids close.

Usually Laura could tell how long she had been asleep, as she had perfected the art of the cat-nap, quick refreshing bouts of unconsciousness to clear the mind before the next meeting. She must have been tired. This time it felt as though she had been sleeping half the night, and it was a struggle to become fully awake. The note of the engine sounded different, higher pitched. She opened her eyes and saw only blackness outside punctuated by the dazzling headlights on the motorway. Howard's hands were still in the same position.

'Howard, where are we? I should be home by now.'

Howard did not answer. He was looking far into the distance, to the end of the light beams showing miles of rain-drenched tarmac.

'Where are we?'

Poor Howard. He hated driving in the rain. It irked him and he preferred to keep quiet when he was irritable but she wished he would say something, even snap at her. As the minutes passed in silence, Laura's drowsiness gave way to a prickle of apprehension.

'What are you doing, Howard? You don't have to go so fast. Slow down. Slow down.'

His foot continued to inch down on the accelerator. Why did he say nothing? His expression was relaxed, as though he was driving alone, deep in thought, as though she were not sitting beside him. Laura took a deep breath. And then, as she glanced at his face again, she noticed a different expression, one she had not observed before. It could be fatigue, which could cloak the familiar with strangeness, like failing to recognize the street in which you lived, but it was as though someone else had inhabited his powerful frame, a stranger with a chilling mission, planned well in advance to the last detail.

Then her voice welled up and she screamed.

'Howard! Slow down for Christ's sake.'

'Surely you're not frightened?'

This time he responded, turned towards her, smiled quizzically, and took his foot off the accelerator but it was too late. The high mass of a heavy lorry pulled out in front of them.

21

From time to time, as he sat in his eyrie in Illustra House looking down on the minute signs of movement below, Sir Howard Riley speculated about humanity. The surgeon, anticipating a full recovery, had advised him to curtail his demanding schedule and delegate more to others, but he had strongly recommended mental activity of a non-stressful nature.

He had been reading about the behaviour of rats. Rats provided a striking parallel in some ways, and he liked rats. Intelligent creatures.

The dominant characteristics of the male rat were pleasingly unambiguous, for they demonstrated aggression, drive and curiosity, whilst the females were habitually docile and more timid. Sex differences appeared to be clear-cut, but, interestingly enough, they could be altered. If one injected female hormones into male rats, they would abandon their habitual behaviour patterns and show the typical female characteristics, proving that the differentiation between male and female was hormonally activated rather than environmentally conditioned. If one gave the appropriate stimulus, however, it should be theoretically possible, he reasoned, to affect this sex-differentiated behaviour without a hormone exchange. It was a question of finding the appropriate stimulus. Humans, unfortunately, were a difficult model with which to work. Unlike rats, they showed a certain capriciousness in accepting the role of the experimenter. They might even, in certain circumstances, question the methods employed. However, there was not necessarily a correlation between the intelligence of the subject and the tendency to question.

Surprising, but that was what he had observed.

Studying behaviour, female behaviour in particular, was not listed as one of his hobbies in *Who's Who*. It was a solitary activity, in common with many other hobbies, and he had no desire to compare notes with fellow enthusiasts, but it kept him amused. (He was intolerable when bored, as his wife could testify.) His hobby was far more productive than a game of chess, which it frequently resembled, for pitting one's wits against a female adversary and winning had wider implications and was indirectly beneficial to the activities of Illustra Foods. The more one understood the female response, the easier it became to work out the tactics of manipulation and control. And maintain market supremacy.

How strange that so little was known, but then one could hardly study humans in the clear-cut conditions of a laboratory. (Not in the foreseeable future, but this could always change. Medical ethics were becoming more flexible.) Freud and his followers had attempted to expose some features of the female psyche, but their method was scientifically suspect and incapable of proof. Others homed in on specific, and therefore only specifically relevant, aspects such as sexual behaviour, environmental factors or historically conditioned aspirations towards an unattainable equality. There were those who took refuge in the eternal mystery of femininity but for the scientifically inclined, or even for a scientist manqué as he regarded himself, a mystery was merely a problem which had yet to be solved.

The next stage would need careful consideration. He was not yet sure how to proceed. There comes a certain point in a series of experiments when the hypothesis appears to be justifying itself, when all the results appear to concur with the hypothesis, but, at the same time, the amount of predictable and replicated data is not conclusive enough to allow for incontrovertible proof. He might have to alter his approach, to take a leap in the dark in order to give his hypothesis – that women were biologically patterned to accept male dominance – the status of fact. A lifetime's work, but hobbies could last a lifetime.

Laura Douglas had been a difficult subject, far more difficult than his wife whom she resembled physically to a striking degree, but that was why he had chosen her. Her suppressed male characteristics of drive, determination, even ruthlessness, which he sensed even when she was immersed in her wifely role, made her an interesting variant.

The techniques he had adopted for his experiment were so crude he wondered why she had failed to detect the underlying principle. It might be that intelligence, in this case, was the obstacle. It was the same at Illustra Foods. Even the brightest junior managers well versed in the application of marketing techniques failed to identify his strategy, but they were not trained to make connections. (Fortunately.) It was said that no-one understood how his mind worked. How strange. He thought it was so obvious. Were he to be found at the head of some laboratory of animal behaviour, someone might have targeted the set of his mind. But humans were addicted to the predictable, even the most sophisticated.

He did have certain regrets in not pursuing an academic career, but as chairman of Illustra Foods he had the advantage of raw material at his fingertips. The particular field he had chosen provided the right kind of soil for his specimens to grow, far better than nineteenth-century Vienna or the dispiriting environs of an under-funded university research department. The feeding of appetite. What better way could be found for the study of female behaviour?

The act of purchasing food and drink gave rise to apparently random patterns of desire and satisfaction, but he was beginning to determine the far boundaries of predictability. If one gave every encouragement, by way of psychological merchandising and efficiently directed advertising, to the obsessional driving force of greed – the overriding desire for instant satisfaction, the object of desire mattered little, for it could be projected at will – this would override the mechanism of restraint (either economic or moral) and it mattered little whether this mechanism derived from Church or State.

It was always useful to take an individual case, to relate the general to the particular. Laura had been surprising, in several respects. She had, he noted, curiously for someone catering for appetite, small enthusiasm for eating. Or food. The alternative, closely allied appetite, that of sex (in her case surprisingly dormant) had served as a trigger mechanism to determine her characteristic behaviour, although it had taken a while for him to work out the pattern of arousal. This avenue needed further exploration. The desire for punishment appeared to be a potent motivating force and could have wider application. For someone demonstrating such outward confidence, she possessed remarkably little self-esteem. If this was a characteristic of the majority of women, and was not a determinant of her particular personal history, it could be further exploited.

Punishment and reward. Lies and truth. Promises and unkept promises. The random alternation of opposites, these simple tactics to create confusion, familiar to specialists in the practice of indoctrination, had been more successful than he had hoped. Laura, whilst appearing to make lucid decisions herself, failed to observe him with the same lucidity. He was surprised by this ability to switch behaviour from rational to irrational, but the phenomenon of instinctively adapting to contradictory patterns might be described as a secondary female characteristic. Perhaps that was why she had failed to observe his tactics, perhaps that was why she had responded so readily.

He wondered why it had taken so long to persuade her to leave Jack Leone, to eradicate his influence. The length of time, the conditioning period during the marriage, he concluded, had been a significant factor.

There were still things which puzzled him about Laura.

It had been so much easier than he had expected. He had, for the sake of his experiment, assumed that the primary stimulus for altering adult female behaviour was a collection of responses which would be termed bonding in animals, but which in humans was imprecisely described as love. She had received his selected verbal and physical cues as though they related to an emotion when in fact they were the product of observation, a sophisticated form of acting. How had it taken so little to make her imagine that he loved her? Despite her intelligence? Despite his erratic and unpredictable behaviour? Once she had accepted the illusion he had created, she had taken whichever path he had chosen for her at the time, and there came a point at which constant reinforcement, even his presence, was no longer necessary. (Could this throw light on the human need to invent a deity, another illusion without substance? An intriguing thought.)

He always found the idea of love, interminable female topic of conversation, difficult to comprehend. No-one had ever given him a satisfactory explanation. As far as he could see, it appeared that interest in the other, plus the occasional reward, was the trigger mechanism for such an emotion. That was all it needed, and this simple trans-action had provided the key which made Laura accept his dominance, to change direction according to his whim.

Another interesting idea. Had he employed the outward form of the emotion described as love as a tool? Or had he, the detached experimenter in the art of control, become unwittingly subject to its influence? Difficult to deter-mine, for he was unaware of being affected by this mask for irrational behaviour. Even though it was commonly assumed to distinguish human from animal, as far as he was concerned the distinguishing factor lay in the appli-cation of reason and logic. Sadly, few people gave these faculties their proper value. Most lived in confusion.

Suppose, for the sake of argument, he accepted that love existed as a definable state? Yes, he could say, perhaps he had loved Laura when he was with her, in the sense that she gave him pleasure. Intelligence was always pleasing. And he found her visually satisfying. But he hardly thought of her at other times. (Extraordinary how women seemed to rely on men to fill out their landscape. Certain women, that is. Most, in his experience.)

The next choice of subject needed careful consideration. He felt inclined to give himself an even greater challenge, to select a young girl with little ambition and low motivation, a typical representative of the coming generation. One should always think ahead and, besides, Sir Howard Riley, who had just turned forty-five, was beginning to feel old.

Did she return to London? With Howard? Alone? Laura could not remember.

She did go to Chelsea. She must have done because she had spoken to Antony in her house. Had he gone with her? He could have done, he was at her bedside. An accident. It was an accident. She had been in a crash, a car crash. Coming from the airport. Antony would not allow her to return to the Studio.

Was it when she was with Jack or Peter (it would not have been with Howard) that she had run out into the fields and heard the rumble of thunder echoing round the skies? Where exactly was this field whose every contour seemed so familiar? There were several canvases stacked round the white room and on each she had painted the same field, curving upwards towards the horizon marked by a solitary oak tree and a tall distant figure, always a distant figure standing upright, unfeatured, to the right, to the left, in front of the tree. She knew every blade of grass, as though she had spent hours watching the changing light describe first a meadow soft as boa feathers and then a wilderness of spiky pampas. At one time she had felt the savage wind-driven rain pelting her face, dripping down her hair which whipped against her burning cheeks like wet rope. The tumultuous cracks of thunder had come in quick succession, and she had sat under that tree looking up into the frantic leaves (sometimes green, sometimes autumn red), waiting for the burning forks above to pierce her shivering body until the zig-zags left the cloud-strewn sky and turned into distant sheets of silent light.

For weeks she sat alone in the house. It was hers, but it was as though it had been reclaimed by previous generations. Jack's presence had been stripped away, the furniture sold except for the odd remnant which nobody wanted. Leaves filled the cracked swimming pool, the tennis court was fissured with weeds, the pots in the atrium were full of blackened dead plants. When her energy returned, she removed the decaying foliage and painted out the flowered panels supporting the glass. She went round the house taking down the heavy chintz curtains, blasting away at the walls, ripping up carpets, rejoicing in bare plaster and boarded floors.

She felt like a hostage freed after years in a besieged city, who, in order to blank out the face of the torturer, sees nothing. There were no mirrors in the house to remind her of the scar across her forehead, although she ran her finger along it several times a day. Sometimes she awoke with the thoughts of violent revenge for a life in pieces, and then the blackness returned. She would be nothing, do nothing except make marks on canvas.

In Le Style, they continued to mention Laura Douglas for a few months. Remember her party, that party, did you go? She didn't even turn up. Horribly injured in a car crash the day before. Wasn't she supposed to be getting married, to some stockbroker? Never happened. She ditched him. Hasn't been the same since, so they say. In New York? Really? Making big money. It's all she cares about. You know Antony? Laura's stooge in London? Good for a hot dinner. Tell him you're a friend of hers.

And in the Kitchen Club, the chefs raged as they always raged, all those French and Italians and Scandinavians and Greeks and Spaniards moving in on their patch, what's happening to this fucking country? No-one wants to know about British chefs or decent restaurants, fuck the EEC, and remember the good old days when you could get on television if you were good and were born talking English? Tadeus Freeman was still pouring out champagne and anger in equal measure. John Crabtree? Never saw him. He'd had a postcard or two from Little John. Silly cunt buggering off like that. What a waste. Bet he'd got peacocks on the lawn by now.

Sir Charles Braithwaite puffed at his cigar and sank back on the feather cushions as Lady Elaine Braithwaite reached across his well-padded knees for another chocolate truffle.

'I shouldn't but I will.'

It was a long journey but worth every minute. Mr and Mrs Crabtree were running a grand place. He always knew John would come back. A bit far out was Stamford Bridge, but you could eat and drink your fill and go up to a room with a four-poster bed and en suite bathroom. Good thinking, that.

At first, Didi had objected to taking off for somewhere north of the Rosslyn Delicatessen in Hampstead, the most northerly place she knew apart from Maclintock Castle, but John had persuaded her to abandon city life for a while so that baby André could grow up imbibing the knowledge of the seasons, surrounded by free-roaming animals in the country of cheese-makers and pie-makers, as his namesake had done in the depths of Brittany. And the moment she laid eyes on the small run-down Georgian hotel with the rambling grounds and the remains of a kitchen garden, orchard and fish pond, she told Charlie (recently knighted for his major contribution to the preservation of Yorkshire's industrial heritage) that he had found them absolutely the perfect place, the place she had always wanted. If only she had realized earlier that it wasn't much use running her mission from the seventeenth floor of Intertel. It was here, here amongst the people of the earth who instinctively understood about real food, and who lived close to the mysteries of nature, that her heart really lay.

Why, she exclaimed to John, had she never seen the light? How could she have been ignorant for so long? Why had no-one told her of ham cake and mushy peas, goose pie, stringy pie, ling pie, Denby Dale pie, bacon roll pudding and dock pudding, havercake, pikelets and muffins, teacakes and barley bread, fritters and parkin, Nidderdale yule cake and ginger bread, Wharfedale tart and Swaledale cakes?

'Who could possibly want to live in London? What a thought!'

Didi said this many times, as her figure grew rounder, her skirts became fuller and her cheeks were tinted with the colour of cherries. Eventually she even stopped ordering the *Daily Reporter*. Dear Stephen. He had no idea.

Two years had passed since the Eglantine had closed its doors. John saw no reason to make the journey South, even though George, pulling in the customers at Chancellor's, kept urging him to come. Now John Crabtree, chef-patron, was doing what he had always wanted to. Cooking the best he could. Wife and kid. Second on the way. Nice clientele, friendly atmosphere. And the Didi's Table range of pies, puddings, jams, chutneys and chocolate truffles was doing a treat.

He'd been open a while, must be three years, when he recognized a familiar figure in the dining room. The grey suit. No-one local would wear that kind of grey.

'Well done, John. First class. I hear they're all talking about you up here.'

'Be with you in a minute, Antony.' He looked much the same. John smiled.

He was running the company for Laura Douglas. How was Laura? He never saw her, she spent most of her time abroad. But quite frankly it made no difference. People still said they had seen her around, when they hadn't. Bit of a mystery was Laura.

'What kind of customers do you have here?'

'From everywhere. York, Harrogate, Manchester, Leeds. We've a good crowd of regulars.'

'Do you mind if I tell you what I thought?'

'Go ahead, Antony.'

'Well, everything was beautifully cooked, excellent sauces, but it's a little – how shall I say? – old-fashioned. Rather the way André Bouchon used to cook. Don't you feel rather cut off here? I mean, every chef needs to be in touch, to change, to develop . . . In fact, only the other day Stephen Boyce was asking me whatever had happened to you.'

'I've to get back to the kitchen. Thanks for coming.'

'Here. My card. In case you think of coming back to civilization. Do call me if you feel like it. Any time. I'm sure I'll be able to help you.'

John took the card, went through the swing doors into the kitchen and threw it into the bin.

THE END

IN SUNSHINE OR IN SHADOW

BY CHARLOTTE BINGHAM

In Sunshine or in Shadow is a novel of memories – of childhood darkened by cruelty and rejection, of a house in Ireland filled with laughter and warmth, and of a glorious sun-lit summer before the war.

In Sunshine or in Shadow is a story of love – of a triangle of emotion and feelings destined to remain in turmoil.

In Sunshine or in Shadow is, above all, a story of the friendship between two girls – unlikely, but strong enough to endure through all that fate throws at it.

In Sunshine or in Shadow will capture the hearts of Charlotte Bingham's many fans. Written with all her characteristic charm and wit, it will make them laugh and cry all over again.

Available in Bantam Paperback
0553 40296 X

A SELECTION OF FINE NOVELS
AVAILABLE FROM BANTAM BOOKS

☐	17632 3	**Dark Angel**	*Sally Beauman*	£4.99
☐	17352 9	**Destiny**	*Sally Beauman*	£4.99
☐	40427 X	**Belgravia**	*Charlotte Bingham*	£3.99
☐	40163 7	**The Business**	*Charlotte Bingham*	£4.99
☐	40428 8	**Country Life**	*Charlotte Bingham*	£3.99
☐	40296 X	**In Sunshine or in Shadow**	*Charlotte Bingham*	£4.99
☐	17635 8	**To Hear a Nightingale**	*Charlotte Bingham*	£4.99
☐	40072 X	**Maggie Jordan**	*Emma Blair*	£4.99
☐	40298 6	**Scarlet Ribbons**	*Emma Blair*	£4.99
☐	40321 4	**An Inconvenient Woman**	*Dominic Dunne*	£4.99
☐	17676 5	**People Like Us**	*Dominic Dunne*	£3.99
☐	17189 5	**The Two Mrs Grenvilles**	*Dominic Dunne*	£3.50
☐	40364 8	**A Sparrow Doesn't Fall**	*June Francis*	£3.99
☐	40407 5	**The Green of the Spring**	*Jane Gurney*	£4.99
☐	40479 2	**Keepsakes**	*Barbara Harrison*	£4.99
☐	17207 7	**Faces**	*Johanna Kingsley*	£4.99
☐	17539 4	**Treasures**	*Johanna Kingsley*	£4.99
☐	17504 1	**Dazzle**	*Judith Krantz*	£4.99
☐	17242 5	**I'll Take Manhattan**	*Judith Krantz*	£4.99
☐	17174 7	**Mistral's Daughter**	*Judith Krantz*	£2.95
☐	17389 8	**Princess Daisy**	*Judith Krantz*	£4.99
☐	17503 3	**Till We Meet Again**	*Judith Krantz*	£4.99
☐	40206 4	**Fast Friends**	*Gill Mansell*	£3.99
☐	40360 5	**Solo**	*Gill Mansell*	£3.99
☐	40363 X	**Rich Man's Flowers**	*Madeleine Polland*	£4.99
☐	17209 3	**The Class**	*Erich Segal*	£2.95
☐	17630 7	**Doctors**	*Erich Segal*	£3.99
☐	40262 5	**Family Fortunes**	*Sarah Shears*	£3.99
☐	40261 7	**The Village**	*Sarah Shears*	£3.99
☐	40263 3	**The Young Generation**	*Sarah Shears*	£3.99